J.G. W

DO OR DIE, ROYAL

ANOTHER MARINE DACRE ADVENTURE STORY
AND THE SEQUEL TO *NEVER SURRENDER*

ABOUT THE AUTHOR

JG White is a former Royal Marines Commando. As a young man he saw service and action in the Far East, particularly in Singapore, Malaya, Brunei and Sarawak during the 1960s. On leaving the marines he went to college, and then to the University of London where he gained a Certificate and then a Degree in Geography and Education. Later he received a Master's degree from the University of Loughborough. He is also a Fellow of the Royal Geographical Society.

He had a very successful career teaching Geography and Geology in secondary schools. He became a Head of Department, a Head of Faculty, then a Deputy Head Teacher and finally a Head Teacher in an 11-18 Catholic Comprehensive School.

He is happily married (54yrs), has four wonderful grown-up children and five amazing grandchildren.

On retirement, he took up writing on a part-time basis. His two previous books are: *Operation Saint George (2013)* and *Never Surrender (2016)*, both published by Austin Macauley.

JG White now lives in Nottingham.

Books by J.G. White

Stories Featuring Marine Dacre

OPERATION SAINT GEORGE
ISBN: 978-1-84963-33900

NEVER SURRENDER
ISBN: 978-1-78612-677-1

Copyright © J.G. White
ISBN 978 0 86071 841 3

The right of J.G. White to be identified as the author of this work has been asserted by him in accordance with section 77 and 78 of the Copyright, Designs and Patents Act, 1988.

All rights reserved. This book is sold subject to the condition that it shall not, by way of trade or otherwise, be lent, resold, hired out, or circulated without the author's prior consent in any form of binding or cover other than that in which it is published and without similar condition, including this condition being imposed on the subsequent purchaser.

Any person who commits any unauthorised act in relation to this publication may be liable to prosecution and civil claims for damages.

This book is a work of fiction, except in the case of historical fact or persons. Names and characters are the product of the author's imagination and any resemblance to actual persons living or dead is entirely coincidental.

A CIP catalogue for this title is available from the British Library.

Please note that this book contains an excerpt from JG White's forthcoming adventure story *First Ashore Royal!* This has been set for this edition only and may not reflect the final content of the new book when published.

For my children:
Alan, James, Richard and Philippa

One for all and all for one.

PART ONE

....

INCEPTION

*Beginning, birth, commencement,
initiation, origin, outset, rise, start.*

Form R138

WAR DEPARTMENT

Royal Navy and Royal Marines Service and Employment History

Surname	Christian Name(s)
DACRE	_Alan John_

Official No.	**Ch/X 06821**	Description of Person				
Rank:	**Marine 1st Class**					
Date of Birth:	**1st August 1922**	Stature	Feet	**6**	In.	**2**
Town/Village	**Ruislip**	Colour of	Hair	**Brown**	Eyes	**Hazel**
County:	**Middlesex**		Complexion			**Fresh**
Trade/profession:	**Scholar**	Marks, scars or wounds	**Knife wound & scar on L. hand**			
Religious denomination:	**C of E**					

Unit or Ship	Rank	Trade/Tech Qual of SQ	Capacity in which employed	Dates (from-to)	Remarks as to professional/instructional ability/special qualifications, awards, characteristics, etc.	Signature of Head of Dept., etc
RM Depot	Mne 2nd	-	Recruit	Feb 39 to Sept 39	Best all-round recruit in his squad. Awarded King's Badge. Marksman.	J Bateson Capt. RM
Chatham Division	Mne 2nd	-	Trained Soldier	Sept 39 to May 40	Further training in Royal Marines Company. Excellent potential.	V Taylor Capt. RM
RM Company	Mne 1st	-	Trained Soldier	May 40 to Feb 42	Underage; unable to go to France with Company. Volunteered for small boats: to Dunkirk on Gypsy Rose. Awarded Légion d'Honneur. Detached duties London.	H Derry Major RM OC Coy
Training School	Mne 1st	-	Commando Training	Feb 42 to Aug 42	Trained at RM Depot Deal, Achnacarry and Isle of White. An outstanding marine.	J Graham Capt. RM

Next of Kin	Relationship:	None
	Name	
	Address	

ENGLAND
1942

PROLOGUE

In 1939 Admiral Donitz had been appointed by Adolf Hitler as Commander-in-Chief of all German submarines, or U-boats as they were better known. Even before war was declared, Donitz had had the foresight to send his U-boats into the Atlantic, fully armed and ready for action.

These trade routes were vital for Britain. As an island nation, the country depended on its imports for survival and on its sea trade for economic success. However, neither the country in general, nor the government in particular, were fully aware of the threat posed by these U-boats. Sadly, nor were they prepared.

British Merchant ships began to sail in convoys. It was considered safer than being at sea on one's own. Many of these ships were old and in a poor state of repair. They were slow and, of course, heavily laden. Weather conditions in the North Atlantic were often poor; dense fog, icebergs and easterly gales made the crossing hazardous. Then there were the German submarines to contend with. The Royal Canadian Navy provided escort vessels but were outclassed and outnumbered. They fought valiantly, as did, of course, the merchant ships.

With the success of *Operation Dynamo* in 1940, Britain had managed to rescue over three hundred thousand men of the British Expeditionary Force (BEF) from Dunkirk. At that time Britain had a population of over forty-five million people to feed, as well as a shattered army to re-build, re-arm and re-equip.

As the country moved onto a massive war footing, it required huge amounts of supplies to be brought in from overseas. A minimum of three point five million tons of food and raw materials was needed every month if the country was to survive. Much of this had to cross the North Atlantic.

Admiral Donitz ordered his U-boats to concentrate on cutting off these vital supply lines. The effect on Britain was instant and disastrous. By April 1940, one hundred and seventy-two merchant ships had been sunk by enemy action. With the surrender of France in 1941, the tonnage loss rapidly increased to about ninety ships per month. The French ports gave the German submarines unlimited access to the North Atlantic. Britain could not survive another year unless some of the convoys managed to get through.

The Admiral, in an effort to maximise the advantage that they held, instructed his captains to operate in groups. These became known as the 'Wolf Packs' and were greatly feared. They were incredibly successful. One convoy of twenty-two ships had no fewer than eleven sunk.

The greatest advantage the Kriegsmarine (German Navy) had was its unbreakable communications system. The Germans had already broken the British Admiralty codes just after the outbreak of the war. However, they possessed a more sophisticated system of encryption using Enigma machines which were invented by the German engineer Arthur Scherbius at the end of World War I. These machines were capable of producing up to twenty-two billion different code combinations. The ability to break these codes had defeated Allied Intelligence and, in particular, the 'boffins' at Bletchley Park, the school of cypher breaking. To make matters even worse, the U-boats operated a completely different system to that of their comrades on surface vessels.

However, in May 1941 an unforeseen incident occurred just off the Hebrides. A U-boat was forced to the surface. On board was an Enigma machine with all the relevant code books. Thankfully these were rescued before the submarine sank. Within hours the machine was on its way to Bletchley Park. Shortly afterwards all signals between the U-boats and German Naval Headquarters were being read by the British. As a result, convoys were able to take avoiding action and so the much-needed supplies were able to cross the Atlantic relatively unscathed. Britain could breathe again.

By early 1942, Admiral Donitz was beginning to suspect that his coded messages were being read. On the 1st February, he ordered each of his submarines to have an updated version of the Kriegsmarine Enigma installed. From that point onwards a fourth rotor wheel was added. This resulted in an immediate code blackout at Bletchley Park which meant that the messages that the codebreakers received could no longer be decrypted. Once again, the Germans had the upper hand. It was now vitally important that the British Admiralty should obtain one of these new machines and the accompanying codebooks. Britain's very survival depended on it.

CHAPTER 1

'Good morning, sir. You wanted to see me?'

Anthony Eden, newly appointed to the post of Minister of War, stood facing his Prime Minister. The old man looked exhausted. Churchill sat hunched in his chair behind the long conference table in the Cabinet Room of number 10 Downing Street, the official residence of the Prime Minister of Great Britain. Winston Churchill was staring morosely at some official papers that were spread out before him. One of his favourite cigars, a Corona Corona, was clamped firmly between his teeth. A cloud of pungent smoke hovered in the air above his head. He removed the cigar before speaking. Eden noticed that his hand was shaking very slightly. Churchill pointed to the papers in front of him.

'These are the final numbers for *Operation Dynamo*,' he said. 'We didn't do too badly all things considered. The Navy and that armada of small boats managed to rescue more of the BEF than we ever hoped for. It was a miracle, Anthony, a bloody miracle.'

Churchill paused, re-living his own visit to the Port of Dover in 1940. He and Vice Admiral Ramsey had, at the height of the evacuation, interviewed two men from one of the small boats that had already completed five trips across the channel. What a salutary lesson that had been for both him and the Admiral; official reports and messages could not, they had learned, compare to the actual experience of being there in person. The two men, one of whom had been a serving Royal Marine under the age of eighteen, had shocked and sickened everyone with their frankness regarding the horrific conditions on the beaches at Dunkirk.

Anthony Eden nodded his head in agreement, 'There was also BEF2. That went quite well.'

Winston Churchill looked up sharply. 'Yes,' he growled in response, 'but at what cost? We had to sacrifice the whole Scottish Brigade in order to save the remainder of the force. What a damn waste of good men.'

Both men sat silently reflecting on what might have been.

'You know, Anthony, I may have misjudged the situation in France. I should have known that our French allies were going to collapse under the German onslaught.'

The Minister of War looked at the Prime Minister. This was the closest he had ever known Churchill admit that he may have been wrong.

'Well, that's all behind us now, sir. We must move on and face the future. The re-arming and re-equipping of the army is going well. The 'hostilities only' call-up is proceeding as planned. Aircraft production is exceeding our initial predictions and the Royal Navy still controls the Channel and the North Sea. The Royal Air Force is well prepared to defend our skies, should Herr Hitler decide to invade our shores.'

'Not 'should', Anthony, not 'should' but when! We are the only country standing in the Fuhrer's way to his complete domination and occupation of all Europe. He will come. I feel it in my water. But to do that he first has to control the skies with his Luftwaffe. Mark my words, Anthony, like my distinguished ancestor Wellington said at Waterloo, this will be a close-run thing.'

'I agree with you, sir, but only time will tell.'

'Quite so, Anthony, quite so! Anyway, that is not why I have asked you to come and see me. I do not intend that we should sit on our backsides and wait for the invasion. I have given this a lot of thought and have decided that we must take the fight to the Germans. Somehow or other we must attack and harry the enemy as much as we can, albeit on a small-scale of course. What do you think of the idea?'

Eden sat quietly for several moments with his eyes closed trying to imagine in his mind the picture that Churchill had of these attacks.

'You mean rather like a fly or a mosquito that can be really annoying?'

'Yes! Yes, you have it! Just like a mosquito. I must say that I like that idea. Small stinging attacks that annoy the hell out of the Germans and, like that damned insect, you don't know where it is going to attack next.'

'I think it is a rather good idea, sir. We shall need a special force of men, volunteers perhaps, who are highly trained and can deliver these raids, perhaps like a storm from the sea. You will, of course, have to convince the Chiefs of Staff, but that shouldn't be too difficult.'

'I hope you are right, Anthony. Anyway, I have arranged to see them all tomorrow afternoon at two thirty in the underground war rooms. You will be there of course?'

'Yes gladly, Winston. I wouldn't miss this meeting for all the tea in China.'

CHAPTER 2

(i)

Royal Marine Dacre was standing perfectly still. He was on guard duty outside the main door to the conference room that was located deep beneath Whitehall in London. It was 0715 hours. His tour of duty had begun at 0600. He and his fellow marines took it in hourly turns to guard the door or to man the small cubbyhole that served as the guardroom. It was here that they kept the ledger for visitors to sign in and where they managed the keyboard. The Prime Minister had already been at work for over an hour.

Standing on your feet for a long time was not an easy thing to do. However, there were little tricks of the trade that a sentry could do to help pass the time and perhaps, more importantly, prevent his leg muscles from developing cramp. Dacre had just finished counting the bricks on the wall opposite him, there were two thousand and nineteen, and was part way through a discreet and invisible set of exercises when the conference room door opened. Winston Churchill stuck his head out. He checked the corridor in both directions, then addressing the marine said, 'Come inside will you please?'

Although it was phrased as a request, it was, in reality, an order. Dacre followed the Prime Minister into the conference room and quietly closed the door behind him.

'Sit down and take the weight of your feet. Remove your cap. Make yourself as comfortable as you can.'

This was not the first time that Winston Churchill and the young marine had sat and talked. This strange alliance had begun shortly after Dacre had been transferred to the Royal Marine Detachment that guarded the Prime Minister. They had first met, albeit briefly, back in 1939 when

Churchill, then the First Sea Lord, had been guest of honour at the Depot RM in Deal when the King's Squad had had their passing out parade. Mr Churchill had presented Dacre with the much coveted King's Badge, instigated by King George V in 1918 for the best all-round recruit. They had met again in 1940 during *Operation Dynamo*. The marine, although fully trained, was underage and unable to serve with his company. He had volunteered to crew one of the small boats. Together, with the boat's owner, Lesley Thomas, they had taken the thirty-five foot motor cruiser *Gypsy Rose* to Dunkirk to help evacuate the troops from the beaches. Impressed by the young man's initiative and zeal, Churchill had personally asked for the youngster to join his detail of 'Royals'. Their first conversation had taken place late one evening when the Prime Minister had enquired as to how the marine was settling in.

Other conversations had followed, often in the early hours of the morning when no-one else was around. Gradually, this very unusual relationship between the young marine and the old man had developed, borne out of mutual respect and understanding. Churchill had soon realised that this youngster was no ordinary bull-necked marine. He was bright, intelligent and well educated. He had been to a good public school in the outskirts of North London at Mill Hill. He was a gifted linguist in Italian, French and German, and was an outstanding sportsman who excelled in canoeing and mountain climbing. Churchill often wondered what this young man was doing in the ranks. Clearly, he should have been an officer. However, the Prime Minister supposed that that was the marine's business and he must have his reasons.

Dacre had found it difficult at times to comprehend how this clandestine association had developed. Whilst he would be the first to admit that he enjoyed their regular meetings, he was intrigued that the Prime Minister of Great Britain should actually seek his opinion on a whole range of military and other matters. After all, he had absolutely no experience or wisdom of years that would give any substance to what he might say. He found the whole thing totally perplexing.

In one of their earlier conversations, Winston Churchill had let it slip that as the Prime Minister he was surrounded by people who either told him what they thought he wanted to hear or were too afraid to tell him what he really needed to know. Once, perhaps after too much brandy, Churchill had casually mentioned that there were, perhaps, only five people that he could really count on to tell him things as they really were. One of those was this young marine!

(ii)

The Prime Minister looked directly at the marine. Dacre held Churchill's gaze. He was not in the slightest bit intimidated by the great man.

'Well, my young friend,' growled Churchill, 'what do you know about the Boer War?'

The marine thought for a moment or two, martialling his thoughts.

'Not too much, sir. I know that it took place in South Africa between 1897 and 1902. I understand that you served there in the army and then later as a war correspondent. I believe you were captured but then escaped. I also know that the British Army learnt some hard lessons at the hands of the Dutch Boers, particularly with regard to their irregular forces. I seem to recall that most of these men were farmers who were mounted on horses and were excellent shots with the rifle. They could live off the land almost indefinitely. They would attack and harry the British at will and then disappear, only to re-appear later somewhere else. Some of our generals considered them to be an ill-disciplined rabble because they would not stand and fight in the traditional manner. But having said that, they were very effective and nearly cost us the war.'

Churchill stared at the young marine intently.

'You seem to be remarkably well informed. How does that come about?' he asked.

'My history teacher at school happened to be a Welshman. He was particularly interested in the African Wars. I think he had an uncle who had been at Rorke's Drift.'

'Ah I understand. What a battle that must have been! However, in the early days of the Boer War things were going so badly for us that England was soon drained of men to cope with the increasing demand. Fortunately, there was no shortage of volunteers. However, their training left a lot to be desired. It became so bad that in some instances these volunteers became more of a hindrance than a help. On more than one occasion the Boers sent derisive notes to the British Commanders asking them not to clutter up the field of battle with such men because they were getting in the way of both sides. There were even several instances when the Boers sent whole detachments of these captured raw recruits back across the lines. Talk about adding insult to injury!'

'I didn't know about that, sir.'

'No, well not everything gets into the history books. But I was there, and I saw it all for myself. Anyway, enough of that, I digress. Do you recall what General Botha of the Boers called his irregular troops?'

'No, sir, I'm afraid I do not.'

'He called them 'commandos'.

Dacre wondered where this conversation might be going.

Churchill continued. 'Even though we may be facing the fight of our lives, if and when Herr Hitler and his Nazis decide to invade our island, I think we must take the fight to the enemy, much like the Boers did to us. It has been suggested to me by a senior officer that what we really need is a special force of highly trained soldiers. Lieutenant Colonel Clarke, who is on the CIGS staff and has lived in South Africa for a number of years, thinks that this might be a good idea. He thinks that they should deliver a series of lightning attacks on the enemy coastline. I have it in mind that we should call this force the 'Commandos'.

Dacre sat quietly for a few minutes thinking through what the Prime Minister was proposing. It had occurred to him almost immediately that the Royal Marines would be perfect for this role. Their long history of being the Royal Navy's sea soldiers would make them ideal. After all, they were used to carrying out small-scale operations on land from the Navy's ships, which was reflected in their Corps motto, *Per Mare Per Terram*, which meant by sea by land. However, at the last minute he decided not to say anything, particularly since Mr Churchill had, on this occasion, not asked for his opinion.

The Prime Minister sat staring at a spot on the wall behind the marine. He was deep in thought. With a slight start Churchill realised that the marine was still sitting quietly in front of him.

Curtly he said, 'That is all, young man. You can return to your duties.'

Dacre stood up, put his cap back on and snapped up his smartest salute, longest way up and shortest way down. He did a sharp about-turn and marched to the door in order to return to his duty in the corridor beyond. As he opened the door, Churchill looked up from the papers that covered his desk, his spectacles were perched on the top of his head, the overhead light reflected off the lenses.

'Thank you very much for listening to an old man rambling on,' he growled.

The marine just nodded and quietly closed the door behind him. There was just a hint of a smile on Dacre's face.

CHAPTER 3

(i)

Marine Dacre stifled a yawn. He was bored, deadly bored. Since his adventures during the evacuation of the British Expeditionary Force from Dunkirk in June 1940, where he had helped crew one of the small rescue boats, he had been stationed here in London.

At first the move from the Royal Marine Barracks at Chatham to join the small but elite detachment of 'Royals' who were responsible for guarding the Prime Minister, had been very exciting, particularly since he had it on good authority that Mr Churchill had asked for him personally. Deep beneath the offices of Whitehall, the security and safety of the War Rooms had been an interesting challenge. Certainly, it was better than being stuck in a cold, draughty barracks. However, this much-prized posting had sadly not turned out to be what he had expected.

Basically, he and his fellow marines were 'watch keeping' which, as anyone in the Navy or Marines knows, that whilst this was essential work it was also extremely monotonous. The marine detachment consisted of a sergeant who was also the detachment commander, a corporal and eight marines. Several of the older men had been recalled to the colours. All of them, with the exception of Dacre, had seen some sea service and carried long service stripes as evidence of their time in the Corps. It was true that their accommodation was good. A marine barracks had been set up for them on the first floor of the nearby buildings used by the Household Cavalry. Originally both the Foot Guards and the Household Cavalry had occupied the building. Now it was only the Horse Guards although, of course, the horses had been sent away for the duration of the war. The food was plentiful, despite the rationing experienced by the civilian population. Everyone realised how fortunate they were. Indeed, their duties were anything but arduous.

The marines worked in two teams of four men, twenty-four hours on and twenty-four hours off. Each tour of duty was divided into six-hour watches. Dress of the day was 'Best Blues' Number One uniform with white blancoed belt and peaked cap. Attached to their belts was a white canvas holster which contained a Mk1 Webley .38 calibre revolver. Attached to the pistol butt ring was a white lanyard which, in turn, was secured to the right-hand side shoulder. When on guard duty, as opposed to manning the very small guardroom - more of a cubby hole really - the marines were required to wear clean white cotton gloves. In addition to this, the Prime Minister had insisted that all sentries should wear their white 'tropical' cap covers. This was not really according to Navy Dress Regulations, but then who was going to deny the great man his request? Certainly not 'their Lordships' at the Admiralty. Uniforms, belts, buttons and badges were all 'marine clean' and sparkled brightly even in the dimness of the underground lighting, deep beneath Whitehall.

These marines were, without doubt, extremely smart and well turned out. They always drew admiring glances from all the visiting members of the armed forces, as well as from the regular members of the war-time cabinet. The very presence of these 'Royals' gave the War Rooms complex a real sense of safety and security. 'Look at me' they seemed to say, 'the Royal Marines are here, and you are quite safe with us on guard.' Winston Churchill loved having them around. He had always had a soft spot for the Corps, ever since his very first days of being the First Lord of the Admiralty back in 1915.

Their main duties were to guard the front door and the conference room. They also manned the keyboard and checked on everyone's identity on entering the complex. They also kept the visitors' book up to date. Each of these duties were, of course, important. Security and safety were essential to the smooth running of the War Rooms. Dacre knew that. However, it was not long before he found the work very undemanding.

(ii)

Dacre constantly tried to keep himself busy and motivated. Boredom, as everyone knew, was the worst enemy for watch-keepers. On his days off he kept himself fit by running in nearby St James's Park, or by using the gymnasium of the Guards Regiment over at Wellington Barracks, much to the initial surprise and amusement of some of the soldiers. However, he persevered. Anything the Army PTIs could do in the gym, he could, and would, do better. Competition always brought out the best in him. He thrived on it. Over a period of time, Dacre won the Guards' grudging respect, and even their admiration, and had to confess that their 'very best' often had difficulty in matching his performance. More than one soldier had found himself urging the young marine on to even further feats of strength and endurance.

On the downside, London had little to offer Dacre, particularly anything that he could afford. It was true that he and the other Marines all had a London Allowance but in truth this didn't amount to much. The restaurants and night clubs that had survived the Blitz were way beyond his pocket. Even the art galleries and museums had little to offer because most of the exhibits had been spirited away to places of safety, somewhere deep inside the Welsh Mountains, so it was rumoured. There had been the occasional concert or lunch-time recital that he had quite enjoyed, although he would have been the first to admit that he knew very little about classical music. Nevertheless, he knew what he liked, and that was good enough for him.

Usually, he just went for long walks, often as far as the East End of London, which had sustained terrible damage during the bombing. He had heard how badly the people had suffered, and now he could see with his own eyes the devastation that had resulted from these raids. Night after night, the German planes had dropped high explosive bombs, capable of boring through fifty feet of earth. In addition, incendiary bombs had fallen which had started fires that raged throughout the city. Each night Londoners had taken cover in the underground tube stations, in brick and concrete community shelters or in Anderson shelters which they had built in their back gardens. Failing that, they hid under the stairs which, of course, gave them very little protection. Each night hundreds of men, women and children had been killed and thousands injured. It had been relentless and bloody.

Sometimes Dacre would take himself off to one of the news theatres that seemed to be on every street corner. They were always packed with people eager to see how the war was progressing. However, with nearly everyone smoking, it was sometimes difficult to see the small screen. For many this was the only way to keep up to date with what was happening in Europe, North Africa and other theatres of war.

Dacre would treat himself to a proper high tea at the Lyons Corner House opposite Charing Cross Railway Station after a couple of hours spent in the cinema. Here, the waitresses, or 'Nippies' as they had been nicknamed, in their neat black and white uniforms, would fuss around him, each one trying to out-do the other in order to spoil the dashing marine with the most beautiful hazel eyes. He loved all the attention. One, in particular, had caught his eye. She was a tall, pretty brunette with long hair that was usually tied up in a ponytail. The tag on her blouse revealed that she was called Marian. She had taken an instant liking to Dacre, who would always sit at the same table by the window. Eventually she would chivvy the other girls away so that she alone could serve him. He would have liked to have asked her out, and no doubt she would have loved to have been been asked. Sadly, though, he knew that he could not because his duties did not give him that sort of freedom, and for him duty always came first. So, he had to content himself with just being fussed over.

Generally, he found London a dark, dusty and dirty place. The electric trams rumbled and creaked around the capital as far as their tramlines would let them go. Often, even during the daytime, they had to have their headlights on in order to see through the murky gloom. Most of the buildings had sandbags protecting their doorways, whilst the windows were taped in a criss-crossed pattern, in an effort to prevent bomb damage.

By day the pavements were crowded with men and women going about their everyday business, trying to carry on with life as best they could. Uniforms of all shades and colours were to be seen everywhere - Navy, Army, Air Force and Merchant Marine. From the continent there were the Free French, Poles, Belgians, Dutch, Danes, Norwegians and many others. From further afield there were the Australians, New Zealanders, Canadians and a host of other representatives from other British Commonwealth countries. Since Pearl Harbour in 1941, the

Americans had joined the melee. It seemed, he thought, as if the whole world and his neighbour had descended onto this little island called Britain. For the first time, Dacre began to realise just how widespread this war had become. It really was a 'world war' in every sense.

In the parks and open spaces, anti-aircraft guns and searchlights had been set up, crewed by men and women of the armed services. Here and there could be seen the winding machines that controlled the enormous barrage balloons, of which there were about four thousand over London. These balloons formed a fairly successful defence against low flying enemy aircraft and dive bombers, thereby helping to protect the skies from enemy raids. These massive dirigibles were to be seen straining on their cables like guard dogs eager to be off the leash.

Despite everything, Dacre was fit, in fact very fit. He stood at just over six feet two inches tall in his stockinged feet. He had put on some healthy weight, all of it muscle, and weighed in at an impressive thirteen and a half stone. He had become broad at the shoulders and narrow at the hips, and his uniform fitted him like a glove. He looked and felt like a real bull-necked marine. On his days off he would wear his Number Three walking out uniform with all the necessary red badges in place. On his left shoulder, he proudly wore his unique King's Badge cypher. Lower on his right arm was the crossed rifles badge of a fully qualified marksman for which he was paid the princely sum of an extra three pence per day. On his chest, just above his left pocket, was the medal ribbon of the Légion d'Honneur presented to him by Charles De Gaulle, the self-appointed leader of the Free French Forces in Britain, for rescuing a French General at Dunkirk in 1940.

(iii)

It was an unusually bright, but rather cool day. The sky was electric blue with numerous puff balls of white clouds that seemed to be competing with the scores of barrage balloons. Dacre's favourite walk took him across Horse Guards Parade, through to the courtyard and into Whitehall. The pre-war ceremonial sentries in their Life Guards uniforms, so beloved by visitors and Londoners alike, had long gone. In their place were dark, brooding, khaki uniformed soldiers who manned the machine guns from behind sandbag emplacements. One or two nodded at the marine as he strode past. He was a familiar figure. From there he turned left and walked up to Trafalgar Square where all the fountains and statutes had been boarded up to prevent bomb damage. Further on he passed the Church of Saint Martin's in the Field, and then the National Gallery which was on the opposite side beyond the statue of Edith Cavell, the First World War heroine executed by the Germans for allegedly spying on them. On he walked, cutting through Leicester Square, up to Wardour Street and into Soho. Dacre liked this part of the city, particularly because it had a real cosmopolitan feel to it. Here, there was a sense of normality that he could enjoy. He felt comfortable and welcome, perhaps because of his Italian background. He wasn't in the slightest put off by the neighbourhood's somewhat seedy reputation, in fact rather the opposite.

On this particular day he hesitated at the crossroads. Should he turn right into Old Compton Street or left into Brewer Street? Routine took the better of him as he chose his normal route and walked smartly down Old Compton Street. Over the last few months his walks had become so regular that some of the shopkeepers and bar and restaurant owners had begun to remember him. Often, he was greeted by a cheery and friendly, 'Hello Royal'. This afternoon's walk took him down Greek Street, where he suddenly came across two drunken American soldiers who had picked a fight with one of the bar owners. The hapless man was pinned up against a wall whilst the two soldiers laid into him, none too gently. The bar owner's face was cut and bleeding, and he was clearly in a bad way. Dacre recognised the little man at once as one of those who always greeted him. Without any hesitation, he went into action. Grabbing the two soldiers by the collars of their jackets, he pulled them off the defenceless little man. Then using his superior strength, he cracked their heads together in one swift and efficient move. The two Americans, taken by surprise, found themselves suddenly lying in the gutter, their heads pounding from the impact. They both looked up at the huge marine towering over them. Neither of them liked what he saw. Suddenly they were very sober. Staggering to their feet, they decided to beat a hasty retreat and disappeared down the road as quickly as they could. Meanwhile, a number of passers-by and shopkeepers who had witnessed the whole rather unpleasant incident, broke into a spontaneous round of applause. Many of them, also, went up to the marine to shake his hand and offered him their congratulations. Dacre, more than a little surprised by this accolade, blushed to the roots of his hair with embarrassment. It was, he considered, unseemly for one of His Majesty's Royal Marines to be seen brawling in the streets. However, in this instance he thought it was more than justified.

Wiping some of the blood from his face with a silk handkerchief, the grateful bar owner ushered his 'guardian angel' into his dimly lit establishment where he offered Dacre a delicious cup of real coffee and, to his surprise, a large tot of Navy rum. Both were very welcome. He drank them slowly, enjoying to the full the exceptional taste. He decided not to ask any questions about their origins, since both were virtually impossible to get in war-torn London at that time. He sat for quite some time just enjoying the aftertaste and the stillness of the closed bar.

Realising that he should make a move, he got up to leave. The proprietor introduced himself as Sammy Gould and mentioned that he was originally from Malta. He had a small round face with twinkly but shrewd eyes. Sammy liked what he saw. He asked the marine if he had ever thought of doing any part-time security work. He would be more than happy to employ the youngster on his days off. He even offered to find him some 'civvies' to wear if that would help. The pay would be very good he added. Dacre gave this some serious thought. It was a tempting offer and the extra money would be very useful. He might even be able to afford to take Marian out. However, in the end he reasoned that he just couldn't give that sort of a commitment for a prolonged period of time, so regretfully he refused the offer. Sammy Gould was obviously disappointed but said that he understood the marine's dilemma. They shook hands in friendship.

'Anytime you find yourself passing by you are always welcome to drop in for a drink. If you ever change your mind about the job, my offer will always stand.'

CHAPTER 4

(i)

The Government Code & Cypher School (GCCS), affectionately known as the 'Golf Club & Chess Society', was established in 1919 to decipher all foreign encrypted messages. It was moved from London to the mansion at Bletchley Park in 1938, where it was designated as Station X. This was an elegant building which dated back to the late 1870s. It had been purchased by a wealthy stockbroker in 1883. The GCCS had needed more space, largely due to the increase in the number of young men and women who were required for intelligence work. Initially, the codebreaking sections worked in the mansion, mostly on the ground floor, including the use of the library. The billiard room and the very fine ballroom were used as the communications centre.

The staff's basic task was to try to break the secret military codes that the Germans were using. However, the main difficulty was that the Luftwaffe (the German air force), the Wehrmacht (their army) and the Kriegsmarine (their navy) all had their own variations of a very clever encrypting machine known as the 'Enigma'. The Enigma machine had been designed by Arthur Scherbius, who had unfortunately been killed in 1929 by a runaway horse. Nevertheless, it was a masterpiece of ingenuity, one that could create both order and chaos.

The early machines had actually been developed during the 1920s for industrial companies to combat commercial espionage. The invention had been registered and marketed in the usual way. Despite modifications in its cryptographical systems, portability and suitability to commercial requirements, it never really succeeded in convincing industrialists. The German military, however, soon saw its potential and by the mid-1920s were modifying Enigmas to suit their need for more strengthened ciphers.

The encrypted system of communications the Enigmas made available, which transmitted random letters in groups of four or five by radio, were considered to be unbreakable. The Kriegsmarine began using them as early as 1926. The British War office had looked at the machine as a possible means of secure communications but had considered the prototype to be too big and bulky.

As soon as the Fascists came to power in Germany, the Enigma machine was taken off the market. Fortunately, someone in Britain had had the foresight to purchase an early version, so all was not completely lost. In due course the staff at Bletchley managed to break the codes of the Luftwaffe and the Wehrmacht. However, those of the Kriegsmarine had proved to be extremely stubborn. There had also been an additional problem: the German surface vessels had a completely different set of codes from that of their U-boats. Therein lay the real problem.

During the dark days of 1940 and early 1941, Britain stood alone against the might of the German Empire. This stubborn little island had to depend on aid, such as food and military hardware from across the North Atlantic Ocean. Large convoys of merchant ships would assemble in the eastern ports of the USA and Canada before trying to make the hazardous crossing. As if the bad weather wasn't enough of a problem, they had to contend with their Wolf Packs, which would patrol the seas ready to attack and sink the ships of the convoys, virtually at will. The coded messages sent by the Enigma machines, up until then unbroken by Bletchley Park, meant that the Germans always knew where and when to strike.

The situation had become intolerable. In Britain, strict rationing had been introduced. The population were urged to tighten their belts and encouraged to grow their own food. In London even the Lord's Cricket Ground had been dug up and turned into allotments. But still the merchant ships of the convoys were being sunk; thousands of tons of shipping and much needed supplies were going to the bottom of the sea. Then there was the huge loss of lives as the sailors of the Merchant Marine died in their hundreds. The Admiralty were continually on the phone to Bletchley Park wanting to find out how things were progressing and were constantly badgering the codebreakers to find a solution as quickly as possible. Both the Prime Minister and Rear Admiral Lord Mountbatten RN (recently appointed as Chief of Combined Operations) made it perfectly clear that failure to crack the U-boat codes was not an option that either of them would entertain. To this end, the Admiral appointed one of his junior officers from the Naval Intelligence Division to liaise and co-ordinate the work being done at the Bletchley Park.

(ii)

The 8.52 am train from Euston to Bletchley steamed slowly out of the station. Recently promoted Commander Ian Fleming RNVR from Naval Intelligence had settled himself comfortably in his first-class compartment. He looked out of the window at the passing buildings, and he automatically fitted yet another cigarette into an elegant holder that he favoured. He knew he smoked too much. The holder was a little conceit, and he was often ridiculed by his friends and colleagues for its use. However, he was never one to be put off by other people's opinions, which was why he was so valued in Naval Intelligence. He lit the cigarette with a gun-metal grey lighter and drew the smoke heavily into his lungs. The journey would take just over an hour. It was a dull and wet overcast day. War-torn London was not at its best. How he longed for the good old pre-war days when he had worked for Reuters as a fledgling journalist, and life had been easy going and carefree. There had been the wonderful parties, either in town or down in the country, and the fun. What glorious times they had really had. And the women - Ann, Loelia and Maud to name but a few, as well as his ever-forgiving girlfriend Muriel. He had loved them all, yet at the same time disliked being tied down. Writers, musicians, artists and politicians - everyone had been welcomed. Mostly gone now, he thought. What little was left of the socialising was only a pale shadow of what had gone before. He sighed, then mentally shook himself out of his maudlin thoughts. He had a job of work to do and this was not the time to be daydreaming of better times.

Bletchley was a railway town. The great mainline from London to Scotland split the town down the middle. A smaller branch line from Oxford to Cambridge swept in like a giant s-shape, which divided the town neatly into quarters. Wherever you stood, you heard and saw evidence of trains – the noise, the soot, the grey-brown smoke rising up above the roofs of the railway houses, built in the same drab red brick that matched the station buildings and engine sheds.

As the train pulled into the station, Fleming already had the carriage door open before it had stopped. There was a real sense of urgency to this visit, and he was anxious to get on. As he alighted, he noticed that it had stopped raining. Dressed in his naval uniform and dark blue greatcoat, he had his gas mask and steel helmet slung over his right shoulder. Walking quickly, he made his way the short distance to Witton Avenue and the main gates of Bletchley Park which bordered the railway line. An armed RAF guard emerged from his concrete sentry box to check Fleming's identity card and security clearance, then passed him through with something resembling a salute. Fleming walked briskly along the road from the entrance. Ahead and to his left he could clearly see the old mansion. Scattered around the grounds were a number of large wooden huts, their dark windows staring blankly at him, whilst sturdy brick walls protected each building from possible bomb blasts. On his right was an ornamental lake and beyond that he could just make out a recently built two storey block building adjacent to which there was another under construction. At the road junction up ahead, he could clearly see a sandbagged gun emplacement, manned by the Home Guard, their Lewis gun pointing menacingly down the road towards him. The first wooden building that he came to was Hut 1. Fleming turned right, then left at the bicycle stand. He could see Alan Turing waiting for him at the main door to Hut 8, halfway along the building.

Turing was a tall, gangly man who looked like everyone's image of an absent-minded professor. He had been recruited in 1938 and had taken up his post in 1939. He was a quiet, rather shy man who dressed in a scruffy manner and was known for being somewhat eccentric. Like many of the others at the Park who had been dons at either Oxford or Cambridge University, Turing had been a Fellow at King's College in the Mathematics Department. He had also been one of the leading brains behind cracking some of the early Enigma codes. Turing had, however, come to dislike these meetings with Fleming. They were, in his opinion, a distraction from the vitally important work of trying to decipher the codes, particularly those used by the German Navy. What annoyed him most was Fleming's constant insistence that they must work harder and longer hours, as if he and his team didn't already know that.

When the two men entered Alan Turing's office, they found his assistant, Joan Clarke, deep in conversation with Hugh O'Donel Alexander, Turing's second in command. They both looked briefly at the

Commander before they discreetly left. No words of greeting were exchanged. Fleming had seen the look of hostility and anger in their eyes. For them, and perhaps the rest of the occupants of Hut 8, he was obviously *persona non grata*. Not that it bothered him. He had a very thick skin. Besides, he had a job to do, and do it he would, regardless of being liked or not. He had not come to Bletchley Park to make friends.

By now both men were seated, Turing behind his small desk and Fleming in the one available chair for visitors. As the Head of Hut 8, Turing rated only a fairly primitive office of about ten-foot square. The floor had bare boards and the walls were just flimsy partitions. The room was just big enough for two desks, a couple of filing cabinets and a hat stand. There were several noticeboards on the walls as well as a blackboard. Joan Clarke had been in the middle of typing up a document which had been left in the typewriter. Fleming craned his neck and tried to read what it said but Turing blocked his view. The office had two doors: one that led into the corridor and to the main entrance, and a second door that led directly into the codebreaking room. Fleming noticed a cardigan on the back of Joan Clarke's chair and on the floor, her handbag. She returned a few minutes later with two cups of something that passed for coffee, by colour if not by taste. Placing each cup in front of the two men, she then retrieved her cardigan and handbag, and removed the document from the typewriter with a little flourish. She then turned and left, quietly closing the door behind her.

By now cigarettes had been lit. Turing took time to study the Commander carefully through the haze of smoke, and thought, not for the first time, how pretentious Fleming was using a cigarette holder. It was just typical of the man. Turing had decided that he would try out a new strategy for this meeting. He would initiate the conversation just for a change, in order to have his say and to try to get his demands across.

'Now look here Fleming old chap, this sort of pressure can't go on you know. You are constantly coming up here bothering and distracting us from our real work. The more you harass us, the less we seem to be able to do.'

The Commander looked directly at the Head of Hut 8, his cold grey eyes unblinking, a penetrating stare. In the brief moment that followed, Turing suddenly thought that some women might find that an attraction in a man. Personally, he did not. He found Fleming to be somewhat boorish and a bit of bully.

'And why is that Alan, may I ask?' Fleming always made a point of calling Turing by his first name which he knew irritated him. He felt that it gave him a slight advantage.

'Because you are creating extra stress which we could do without. We are trying our level best to break these wretched codes, and you and your masters constantly nagging at us to do better does not help in the slightest. In fact, I believe it has the opposite effect. We will manage eventually to crack these codes, but it will be in our own time and in our own way.'

Fleming sat quietly, smoke from his cigarette slowly escaping from his nose.

'May I remind you that my 'masters', as you put it, are also your masters.'

'Yes, yes I know all that. But you know what I mean. You need to leave us alone. There is enough pressure on us as it is without you constantly breathing down our necks, and besides...'

'Besides what?' said Fleming rather too sharply.

'Besides, we are so desperately short of everything: pencils, typewriters, personnel and space. Even the manufacturers at Letchworth who make our bombe machines are short of parts and manpower. The situation has become so desperate that some of us have written to the Prime Minister to ask for his help.'

'Have you now,' said Fleming sarcastically. 'That's very interesting.'

Turing chose to ignore the sarcasm. He continued. 'Are you aware that many of my people are working around the clock, some of them are reaching exhaustion point, and will go under if they don't get any rest.'

The commander nodded his head sympathetically.

'I'll see what I can do to speed things up. No promises, mind you, but a word or two in the right quarter might help, you never know.'

'Thank you, Fleming. That would be very kind of you.'

'Oh, it has nothing to do with kindness. It is all about getting the job done. We are, after all, on the same side, are we not?'

'Yes, yes, of course, I do realise that,' replied Turing hesitatingly.

Suddenly he felt cornered, his dominance of the meeting slipping away. There was a momentary lapse in the conversation. Turing seized the moment. He leant forward, picked up his telephone and dialled the number ten.

A female voice answered. 'Yes, Mr Turing?'

'Will you ask Susan Graham to come and see me right away?'

The Commander lit another cigarette and raised his eyebrows in something akin to a question. Turing saw this and smiled inwardly to himself. For some time, he had been planning this little surprise, one that he hoped might allow him to score a point or two off the Commander. It was petty, he knew, but nevertheless very satisfying.

He continued. 'Susan Graham is one of our best codebreakers. We pinched her from the University of London where she used to lecture in mathematics and logic. You may be interested to know that she can do the Times crossword in under ten minutes.'

Fleming was impressed, very impressed. It took him well over an hour and that was on a good day.

(iii)

There was a knock at the door. A very small woman in her late forties entered. She looked frail, almost bird-like in her thinness. She had a kind face and short grey hair cut in an old-fashioned bob. But it was her eyes that caught Fleming's attention. They were the most amazing pale blue that he'd ever seen, and they seemed to sparkle like gemstones.

'Ah, Sue. Would you be kind enough to show Commander Fleming our bombe machine and explain to him the difficulties we have in trying to break the codes.'

'Of course, Mr Turing, it will be a pleasure. If you will follow me, Commander?'

Fleming stood up and stubbed out his cigarette. He towered over the diminutive figure of his guide, and he was barely five eight himself. This was the first time that he had been allowed behind the scenes to see for himself how this whole business of codebreaking was undertaken. It was a revelation. The tour would last for well over an hour.

'If I may, Commander, perhaps I could set the scene, so to speak?'

'Please do,' replied Fleming.

'Well, prior to 1939, and then during the early part of the so-called 'phoney war', much of our work in cryptography was based on the help given to us by our Polish allies who, in turn, had received help from their French counterparts, in particular Gustave Bertrand. It was only after a joint conference in Warsaw that we, here at Bletchley Park, really began to move forward. It was also at that time that Mr Turing was busy developing his idea for a bombe machine based initially on the Polish 'Bombas'.'

Fleming interrupted. 'I've heard a lot about these machines, but I don't really know anything of the details.'

Sue Graham's face lit up with enthusiasm. 'Well, we'll just pop along to Hut 11 which is the Bombe Hut and you can see for yourself.'

They stepped outside into a day that was still wet and windy. They passed between Hut 1 and Hut 6, and then walked the short distance along a side road to the Bombe Hut. Fleming shivered involuntarily. Sue Graham seemed not to notice the chill despite her frail frame.

'Do you have an understanding of the hut system?' she asked.

'No, not really,' replied Fleming. 'I know that Hut 8 is Naval, but as for the rest...?'

'If I may correct you Commander?' He smiled a 'please do'. 'Hut 8 is actually Naval Enigma where we are focusing particularly on *Shark*. Hut 4 is the Naval section where they translate and analyse whatever we have deciphered in 8. They are located up by the big house. Hut 5 is the Military section, and Hut 3 translates the German that Hut 6 (which is run by Mr Welchman) manages to intercept from the German air force and army. There is a small chute that links the two buildings. The information is put in a basket and pushed through with a broom handle. Not very technical, I know, but it works. Hut 1 is the Transport office; originally it was the sick bay and, before that, a wireless transmitting station. In Hut 7 we have some Hollerith machines which are used for scanning cipher text for decryption. Of course, the card indexing system for retrieval is still all done by hand. Hut 9 is Administration and Hut 12 is an annex to 3.

By now the two of them had arrived at Hut 11.

'Shall I go first?' she asked.

'Before you do - what about Hut 2?' he asked.

Sue Graham was already standing on the top of the two steps that led into the hut. She turned and looked directly at him, a slight smile played at the corners of her mouth and her eyes sparkled mischievously.

'Oh, very good, Commander, very good. Hut 2 is for recreation. That is where we serve tea and sticky buns, and it also has a lending library.'

With that, she threw open the door of Hut 11. The noise was unbelievable. There was a cacophony from the half a dozen machines that clattered away like enormous printing machines. Fleming could barely hear himself think. Sue Graham was waving her arms at the machines and talking. Fleming had to lean down to try and hear what she was saying.

'The first bombe machine that Mr Turing developed was called 'Victory'. Now we have about fifteen machines, some of which are here whilst others are scattered around the country. You see, Mr Turing has an amazing gift of building things from scratch. When it comes to electrical experiments, what he calls 'lash-ups', he is unequalled. His idea for a universal machine was so much more than just an extension of the Polish bombas. His was quite different, and brilliant. Initially the whole thing worked electro-mechanically. Then along came Mr Welchman who added a circuit board, and what you see is the result. What took us days to achieve, we can now do in hours, thanks to his inspired improvisation. Each machine weighs about half a ton and, as you can see, is mounted on castors.'

Fleming was utterly amazed and dumbfounded. He was looking at a number of black metal cabinets, about eight-foot high and six-foot wide, with dozens of small steel drums set into the front. He suddenly realised that he needed to revise his opinion of Alan Turing. He had grossly underestimated the man. This was pure genius. He pointed towards some of the uniformed WRNS who were busy operating and feeding the machines. All of them had cotton wool sticking out from their ears.

'What about them?' he shouted.

Sue Graham moved towards the door.

'Shall we go outside now?' she replied.

He didn't catch her words, although her meaning was obvious.

'There, that's much better,' she said closing the door. 'Sorry, what did you say?'

'I was trying to ask you about the WRNS.'

'Oh, like everyone else, they work eight-hour shifts around the clock. But in their case they are allowed regular breaks from the noise. Not to do so would be inhuman. They refer to Hut 11 as the 'hell hole'. That's appropriate don't you think?'

'Yes, I suppose so,' he replied hesitatingly, his ears still buzzing.

'Shall we go back to Hut 8?'

She led the way, silent for a moment or two. Then she turned and looked up at him. 'Do you really have any idea how hard people are working here?'

'Well I think so,' he managed to reply.

'May I be so bold as to suggest to you, Commander, that you do not.'

Fleming was taken aback. He wasn't used to being spoken to like this. He felt like a naughty schoolboy who was about to be chastised. It brought back some unpleasant memories of his childhood and he didn't like it, not one little bit.

'I suggest, Commander, that you and others in the military see us here as a bunch of eccentrics, tucked away in this countryside retreat, pottering around in our casual dress, with little apparent discipline and calling each other by our Christian names. I think you must find this all rather disturbing and are, perhaps, alarmed by our informality. Well, we are not like that. You see, whilst informality is a rigid rule here, we civilian amateurs will eventually defeat the might of the so-called disciplined Nazis. This has become our mantra. When we started this whole business, we were reading just a few messages a week and we thought we were good. Now it's over fifty.'

She paused.

Fleming was nonplussed. 'Why that's amazing,' he said.

'Yes,' she replied quietly, 'It is, especially when you consider how much time and energy is spent on each decryption; and the number of messages is increasing all the time.'

By now they were back in the quietness of Hut 8.

'So how does it all work?' he asked.

'Put simply, coded German messages are sent and received by Enigma. These are picked up by our listening stations. That information is brought to us by a team of forty armed motorcycle dispatch riders who have colour-coded arm bands, here, to Bletchley Park from our 'Y' stations, or listening posts, which are located all over the country. The encrypted message is then decoded using the bombe machines. These are then sent for translation into English. Once that is completed, the Duty Officer has to decide what is important and gives it a priority rating. This intelligence is sent to the Secret Intelligence Service (SIS), the appropriate Military, Navy, Army, Air Force headquarters and then to the relevant commander in the field. Remember, that at Bletchley Park we have been reading all the German messages for quite some time, all, that is, with the exception of *Shark*. The whole thing is rather like a production line in a factory. At the end of the day, every bit of paper is filed in the German Book Room. The girls doing the filing have seen more operational details about German forces than most, and, I suspect, know more than Mr Hitler does.'

'These code names you've been talking about - how does that work?' asked Fleming.

'Here, at the Park, we have allocated a series of names for each code. So, for the German Navy we use sea creatures such as *Limpet*, *Oyster*, *Porpoise*, *Winkle*, *Dolphin* and *Shark*. For the Luftwaffe we use either insects or flowers such as *Locust* or *Foxglove*, whereas for the Army we use birds, so *Vulture* for example is the Russian front. There are dozens of call signs all originating from the Enigma keys. And, also, please don't forget that the Germans have a number of different cipher systems of which Enigma is only one.'

Fleming was stunned into silence as the facts began to sink in. He had never fully understood or appreciated the codebreaking system. Now he had seen first-hand the systems and processes involved, he was determined to do what he could to help speed up the procedure.

That's, that's absolutely amazing,' he managed to stammer out. 'Thank you very much for such a gainful insight,' he said, and he really meant it. 'Just one last thing. If my arithmetic is correct, you haven't mentioned Hut 10.'

Sue Graham paused before answering.

'Haven't I, Commander? I do apologise. You see Hut 10 is the only hut not working on Enigma. Their main task is to process all the weather reports that come in. Equally vital and no less important, so please do not read anything into my failure to mention it. If there are no further questions, then there is just one other thing. Well, actually two really and I don't know if you can do anything about them. Firstly, our huts leak like sieves when it rains. They are cold and draughty in the winter, whereas in summer they are stiflingly hot. Secondly, like the rest of the country, we do not have enough of life's little luxuries such as toilet paper, soap, matches, baths and clean clothes. We civilians smell, Commander. We smell so badly that some of my colleagues no longer notice.'

Fleming nodded his head in agreement. 'I completely understand what you are saying, and I will do my very best to see what I can do to help resolve some of your problems.'

However, as fascinating as the whole visit had been, Fleming was even more intrigued by his guide Susan Graham. Her knowledge and expertise belied her frail demeanour. She clearly had a razor sharp, analytical mind.

He had tried unsuccessfully to engage her in more general conversation about how the Park operated as they toured the facilities, but much to his annoyance she remained totally focused on her task. Fleming was very impressed, and it took a lot to impress him. It was only at the end of their time together that she began to relax a little.

'You know, Commander, we do not need any urging to work harder. Many of us have family and friends serving overseas in one way or another. Why only last month my sister and I lost our only nephew in one of the Atlantic convoys that was attacked by U-boats. Both of his parents were killed in the Blitz.'

Fleming didn't know what to say. This was probably the first time in his life that he was lost for words. The realities of war suddenly struck home. He felt embarrassed and, for some reason, ashamed. He decided to change the subject.

'Have you worked here long?' he asked.

'About three months,' she replied. 'They poached me from London University where I used to lecture. I quite liked being there because I could travel up to town each day from my home. Here, I can only go home once a month. It's not the same,' she sighed.

'If you don't mind me asking, where do you live?' asked Fleming.

'Oh, a little place you will never have heard of called Tankerton which is on the North Kent coast. My sister, Lillian, and I have a small house there that overlooks the sea. It is very beautiful and unspoilt. Unfortunately, they have had to take down all the lovely beach huts – a great pity. It's the war, you know.'

The Commander was amazed by the coincidence. 'Why, we are neighbours then,' he exclaimed.

'Neighbours? What do you mean?' she replied.

'I have a cottage in Whitstable, up on Island Wall. Do you know it?'

'Well yes, I know Island Wall, but not your cottage of course.'

They both laughed.

'You said you have a sister. Is she at home?'

'Oh no, she works in London, something at the War Department I believe, secretarial or something like that, I think. We never talk about our work to each other. As the poster says, *Walls may have ears.*'

(iv)

Later, on his way back to London, Commander Ian Fleming was thinking through the events of his visit. It had all been very informative and more than a little intriguing. Of course, he realised that Turing had set the whole tour business up for his own reasons. He accepted that. The situation at Bletchley Park was actually quite straightforward and he probably could do something to help.

However, the two sisters intrigued him. He was racking his brains for something that was tucked away in the dark recesses of his mind. But what? Suddenly the penny dropped. Susan Graham's younger sister, Lillian, or Lil as she liked to be called. Of course, he thought, how stupid of him not to realise. He just hadn't made the connection. Lil was the Head of Operations at the SIS. He had met her once at some joint intelligence meeting. Although he worked for Naval Intelligence, his particular brief was to support and advise the Chief of Combined Operations, thus Admiral Mountbatten was his superior officer. What a formidable lady she was. Her sharp, incisive mind and her ability to plan and organise the most complex of operations was legendary. She frightened the hell out of just about everybody. The Director of Intelligence, General Sir Stewart Menzies, held her in the highest esteem. Mountbatten had crossed swords with her on several occasions. Each of these meetings had been a bruising experience for him and he had not escaped entirely unscathed. Her ability to identify the pitfalls and problems of his schemes through pure logic had been most frustrating. Out of earshot he referred to her as 'that damn woman'. Yet deep down Mountbatten knew that she was always right.

Thanks to Lillian Graham, he thought, he had become wiser and better at planning, something he decided to keep himself.

The intercom light on Turing's desk started to blink. He reached forward and flicked the switch to 'talk'. His secretary spoke.

'There has been a call for you from London. Commander Fleming would like you to call him back on the secure line as soon as possible.'

'Thank you, Rachel, I'll do it right away.'

He picked up the green phone and dialled the appropriate number. His call was put through immediately.

'Fleming!' The tone was abrupt.

'Alan Turing here, you wanted to talk to me.'

The Commander's voice softened and became almost friendly. Turing was immediately wary.

'I am sending you a little surprise. Make good use of them.'

With that he hung up.

Fleming sat quietly reflecting on the report that was sitting on his desk. The clock on the mantelpiece ticked quietly in the background. The first few months of 1941 had proved to be a disaster in the Atlantic. German spies in both American and Canadian ports reported to the German High Command. Consequently, attacks by their U-boats on the convoys had greatly increased which, in turn, had caused massive problems for Britain. There wasn't enough food to feed the population, let alone military supplies and fuel oil. By chance, ships of the Royal Navy in the Arctic had attacked a German trawler. On board was an Enigma machine with current codebooks and papers. The captain had managed to ditch the machine over the side into the sea but the documents, which were of greater importance, had been captured.

Shortly afterwards, a submarine, the U-110, which earlier in the war had sunk the *Athena,* was itself depth-charged and captured. Amongst the documentation was a set of bigram tables.

Within several days, Alan Turing's Hut No. 8 at Bletchley Park had, with the aid of the bombe machines, broken both the codes for the German surface vessels and for the U-boats. The decoding became so fast and accurate that British Naval Intelligence and the Admiralty knew exactly what messages the Germans were sending, even before their own superiors did. As a result, nearly all the Atlantic convoys managed to avoid the wolf-packs and a watery grave. Britain had been given a reprieve as supplies and essential foods began to arrive at the ports of London, Southampton, Bristol and Liverpool.

CHAPTER 5

(i)

Rear Admiral Mountbatten RN sat quietly twiddling his fingers. He disliked being kept waiting. However, in this instance he had to put up with it. The Prime Minister, Winston Churchill, had requested his presence for a one-to-one meeting. Churchill wanted to be brought up to date with the situation with regard to Combined Operations for which he, Mountbatten, was now responsible. The door to the anteroom opened and an under-secretary ushered Mountbatten into the cabinet room of Number 10 Downing Street. Churchill was alone, sitting at his usual place at the centre of the long table with his back to the fireplace. He looked up and waved Mountbatten to the seat opposite him. Churchill's coat was on the back of his chair and the sleeves of his crisp white shirt had been hastily rolled up. A notepad and pencil were set out in front of him. The Rear Admiral was well prepared for this encounter. His personal knowledge of the current situation was good. Where he felt he lacked any information, he had made sure that he had been well briefed by his subordinates. Many people were more than a little afraid, or even intimidated, by the 'great man', but he was not. He respected Churchill as a war-time leader and enjoyed his confidence; after all he was a cousin to King George VI and he had seen action in the North Sea and the Mediterranean. He knew that Churchill valued experience. Yet he still felt slightly nervous. Why he wondered?

'Good morning, Dickie. Thank you for coming to see me,' said Churchill in his deep gravelly voice. 'I should like you to bring me up to date with what has been happening in Combined Operations, if you would be so kind?'

'Certainly, sir. If I may, I should like to set this briefly into a historical context.'

Churchill nodded assent.

'Following your directive in June of 1940, and with the agreement of the Chiefs of Staff, we began the task of setting up and organising the first of these special units which, at your suggestion, we called 'Commandos'. You will recall that John Durnford-Slater received his authorisation on the 28th June and that the unit paraded for the first time in Plymouth on the 5th July. They were called the No. 3 Commando.'

Churchill smiled to himself. He had been impressed by the speed at which the War Department had reacted by cutting through much of the red tape, something almost un-heard of.

Mountbatten continued. 'This Commando was composed of trained soldiers of the highest quality, all volunteers to the man, who had had real fighting experience. On the 11th July a small party raided the occupied island of Guernsey. It actually achieved little strategically but they learnt much from the experience.'

Churchill held up his hand to stop the Admiral.

'I do recall that raid. It all seemed a bit of a fiasco to me. You say that all the volunteers were from the army?'

'Yes, sir.'

'Did no-one think that the Royal Marines, with their long-standing tradition of amphibious activities, might be well suited to this role of commando?'

Mountbatten felt himself go cold. A small blush begun to creep up his neck, he began to sweat, the drops running down inside his uniform from under his armpits. Damn it! Churchill was renowned for asking awkward questions and he, the Head of Combined Operations, had just walked straight into a blind alley. Mountbatten did not have a suitable answer.

'I'm afraid that I cannot comment on that, sir. It was before my appointment. I am given to understand that the directive only went to the Army.'

Churchill raised his eyebrows in a question that he decided not to ask. Besides he already knew the answer.

'Please continue,' he growled.

'Initially, you appointed General Alan Bourne of the Royal Marines to take command of all raiding operations. Later, you asked Admiral of the Fleet, Sir Roger Keyes, a veteran of the Zeebrugge Raid back in 1918, to become the first Director, with Bourne becoming his second-in-command. Meanwhile, more army commandos were being trained.

Initially, they formed one Special Service Brigade. By the end March 1941, there were over four thousand trained men in eleven commando units. All were busy training and exercising along the South coast. To my knowledge, none of these were Royal Marine units although, I believe, a few marines did join No. 8 Army Commando.'

Mountbatten paused and checked his notes, then continued. 'The first serious operations by the commandos took place on the Norwegian Lofoten Islands. This was very successful. Later, other raids took place at Spitsbergen and then along the French coast. On Boxing day 1941, the oil installations at the port of Vaagso were destroyed.'

Churchill interrupted again. 'This is all very good news, Dickie, but much of it, you will appreciate, I already know. However, it's good to have one's memory refreshed, so thank you. However, as I have already indicated, I have heard nothing about the Royal Marines Division. What plans are being made for its deployment? I have personally written to General Gort our CIGS, but I haven't received a satisfactory reply to date. So, what progress has been made?'

Double-damn, thought Mountbatten. He's done it again, caught me out. Blast the man.

(ii)

'Well, sir, you may recall that back in May 1940 the Admiralty received orders to raise the Royal Marines Brigade to a full division which would consist of three brigades, each with two battalions. However, with Dunkirk and the evacuation of the British Expeditionary Force, the expansion of the Marines was put on hold.'

Churchill was becoming more than a little exasperated with Mountbatten and his constant stating of the known.

'Yes, yes, I know all this! Tell me something I don't know. What in blazes are the Marines doing now?'

'Yes, sir, of course.' Mountbatten was somewhat rattled; not something he was used to. 'As always, the Corp's first priority has been to man the ships of the fleet: *Chatham, Portsmouth* and *Plymouth* being the three main providers. The MNBDO have been increased and other units, such as the Royal Marines Siege Regiment, have been raised.'

37

Churchill interrupted again. 'Just remind me what MNBDO means and what they are supposed to do?'

'It stands for Mobile Naval Base Defence Organisation. It was set up in the 1920s, and allows the Navy and Marines to seize, hold and defend bases and anchorages in any part of the world. At that time the Madden Committee suggested that it might point the way for an amphibious role for the Royal Marines. However, the government of the time declined to provide the necessary funding for amphibious infantry which, of course, was then a new idea.'

The Prime Minister nodded. He sat very still staring at a distant spot on the wall just over the Admiral's shoulder.

'I seem to recall that,' he replied. 'Hindsight is a wonderful thing is it not? How amazingly short-sighted everyone was at that time, including me.' He paused for a second or two. 'Carry on please, Admiral.'

'Thank you, sir. When the first 'Hostilities Only' men joined the Corps, they generally went to the MNBDOs for the defence of temporary naval bases and to provide 'striking forces' for amphibious operations. This allowed the full-time marines and the reservists to be sent for sea service with the fleet. If I may suggest, this would seem to indicate where the real priority should be for the Marines, at least at their senior officer level. Indeed, only recently I overheard several officers discussing the fact that they hadn't joined the Corps to run around playing soldiers.'

Churchill pondered this idea for a second or two. 'I believe I heard that story, or something similar, when I was First Lord of the Admiralty.' He indicated for Mountbatten to continue.

'There was a plan for a joint force of Royal Marines, together with a Special Service Commando Brigade, to invade the Canary Islands should Spain have entered the war on the side of Germany. But, as you are aware, that came to nothing. More recently, there have been plans once again to bring the 'Royals' up to a full division in strength. To this end, two new battalions have been formed, the Ninth and the Tenth. The division will have two brigades rather than the three, as originally planned in 1940. However, they still lack operational employment. Indeed, they are short of artillery, transport and logistical support. That, sir, is the current situation, to the best of my knowledge.'

Mountbatten held his breath, wondering how the old man was going to react. Churchill just sat quietly doodling on his notepad, mulling over what he had just been told. He looked up and held the Admiral's gaze with a steely glare.

'It seems to me, Dickie, that we may have difficulty in persuading some of our beloved marine colonels, whose principal interest appears to be naval gunnery, that their marines can do just as good a job ashore. Perhaps they needed to be reminded of their own Corps motto, *Per Mare per Terram*, By Sea, By Land. So, I suggest that if we come up against any objections, we simply work around them.'

'I completely agree, sir,' replied Mountbatten.

'Good! So, here is what we will do. Let us send a priority signal to all parts of the Marine Corps asking for volunteers to join a new Royal Marines Commando. Will you speak immediately to their Adjutant General and, between you, get things going. I know he will be delighted because we have already had several discussions along these lines.'

The Admiral got up to go. He paused, then said, 'You know, sir, the Army won't be very pleased about the Marines trying to usurp their role. They have been given the task of being commandos and they think it's theirs by right. They will not thank us at all.'

Churchill spent the next minute or so reflecting on what Mountbatten had just said, then replied, 'That can't be helped, Dickie. I cannot abide petty squabbling. Anyway, I am not suggesting that we turn over a Marine battalion to be commandos just like that. As good as the Marines are, they must do their best to weed out anyone unwilling or unsuited for commando operations. They must go through the training like everyone else. There will be more than enough war for everyone.' Churchill paused and then said, '*Out of this nettle, danger, may we pluck this flower, safety.*'

'Sir?'

'It's from Shakespeare's *Henry IV, Part One*, I believe. Chamberlain quoted it before flying to Munich to see Herr Hitler.'

'I don't follow you, sir,' said a confused Mountbatten.

'Oh, never mind, Dickie, never mind.'

With that, the Prime Minister lapsed into silence, his mind already moving onto a thousand and one other things that required his personal attention. Mountbatten, realising the meeting was over, got up from his chair and quietly left the room.

In February a priority signal was sent by the Admiralty to all His Majesty's Ships and Royal Marine Barracks calling for trained marines as volunteers for 'special duties of a hazardous nature'. This new unit assembled at Deal in Kent. Some of the volunteers came from a battalion that was part of 102 RM Brigade of the RM Division.

CHAPTER 6

(i)

Marine Dacre stood to attention in front of the Detachment Commander's desk. Sergeant 'Tug' Wilson looked the young marine up and down. He liked what he saw. This was a young, smart, diligent and dependable 'Royal'. Truth be told, he was one of his most reliable marines; not that the others weren't good. But this lad, he just knew, could be relied on to deliver the goods. From his long years in the Service, the sergeant knew that no one man was irreplaceable, but this youngster came close. He was going to miss him. He spoke slowly and carefully; his Scouse accent as clear as a bell.

'Your application to volunteer for this new commando malarkey has been approved. You are to return to Chatham immediately. Get your bags packed and onto the first available train. Dress of the day will be battledress serge, with webbing equipment and marching order. Here is a list of essentials that you are to take. Use only your small kit bag. Your best blues, which won't be needed where you are going, and the rest of your gear are to be stowed in your naval kit bag. This will be forwarded to Chatham and put into storage, so make sure it's well labelled. Draw your rifle and bayonet from the armoury, and don't forget your tin hat and gas mask. And if I were you, I would take your greatcoat as well. Here are your transfer orders and a railway warrant. Any questions?

The youngster was speechless. It was all happening so quickly. He hesitated for a moment or two.

'Come on, come on, spit it out,' the Sergeant said sharply.

Dacre took a deep breath. 'I was just wondering about the 'old man'.

'Old man, old man! Are you referring to our beloved Prime Minister?'

The youngster blushed. 'Yes, Sergeant. I was.'

The older man's voice softened and became almost avuncular.

'Don't you worry about him, lad, he'll be fine. Anyway, who do you think countersigned your application? He asked to do it personally. Now then, if there are no more concerns, go on, hop it and good luck to you, I think you're going to need it.'

(ii)

The trip, by an old Southern steam train from London Victoria Station down to Chatham, was uneventful. The day was grey and overcast. The view from the railway carriage window showed a country at war. The sky seemed to be full of more large white barrage balloons doing their best to protect London and its citizens from the lethal attention of the Luftwaffe. The windows of the houses were all taped up in an effort to restrict injury from bomb blasts. Many of the gardens had been given over to the growing of vegetables, whilst Anderson shelters could be seen dug in, tucked away in convenient corners. Here and there, he could see bombed-out and burned houses, shops and factories, all evidence of how successful the German raids had been.

Dacre got off the train at Chatham, hoisted his kit bag onto his left shoulder and his rifle on the other, and marched the short distance down the steep hill from the railway station to the Royal Marines Barracks. Having reported to the Headquarters Company Sergeant Major, he was told not to unpack because he would be shipping out within the hour. The advance party, made up of two corporals and thirty-four marines, was to travel down to Deal in order to open up the North Barracks. The main force, Dacre was told, was due to arrive in two weeks' time on the 14th February.

Dacre made his way across to the NAAFI for a mug of tea and a sandwich. Because he wasn't 'on roll' he couldn't make use of the dining hall. It was pretty crowded when he entered the smoke-filled room, mostly marines judging from the variety of their uniforms. He waited patiently at the counter for his turn, placed his order with the pretty girl behind the counter, then struggled with a mug and a plate, as well as his rifle and kit bag. Turning around he spotted a seat at a small table in the corner. Another marine was already sitting there. He saw Dacre approaching and casually pushed out the other chair with his foot. Gratefully, Dacre dumped his gear and collapsed into the offered seat and nodded a thank you. He immediately tucked into his roll which was Spam, and rather dry. He hadn't realised how hungry he was. Meanwhile his companion, a small nondescript sort of a chap aged about thirty years old, gave Dacre the once over.

'Shipping out to Deal, are you?'

The young marine nodded, his mouth full of food.

'Me, too,' the other marine replied. 'I go by the name of Peter Wills, but I answer to Pete.' He held out his hand and they shook hands. Dacre introduced himself.

'So where was your last billet, Pete?' he asked.

Pete Wills smiled. 'Late of HM Prison, Wormwood Scrubs. I got caught breaking into a safe. I was pretty good, had something of a reputation in the underworld. I've been breaking into safes since I left school, aged twelve. Anyway, I got a bit careless. This was the only time I've ever been caught. The judge handed me a sentence of three years, first offence you see. Normally it would have been much longer. Anyway, the Prison Governor knew someone who knew somebody else, and here I am out on parole just as long as I volunteered for this new commando training, whatever that may be. What about you?' Dacre was just going to reply when the NAAFI room door was thrown open and in marched a very tall, lanky corporal.

'Anyone going to Deal fall-in outside at the double now!' With that, he was gone.

Later, in the back of an old but serviceable three-ton truck, Dacre gave a brief account of his own exploits to his new-found friend. When he had finished, Pete Wills looked at him with a look of respect and admiration.

'Bloody hell, Dacre, and I thought I'd had an interesting life.'

Dacre just grinned. 'I think life is going to get a lot more interesting over the next few weeks, just you wait and see.'

CHAPTER 7

(i)

Deep within the bowels of Whitehall were the Cabinet War Rooms. The entrance was to the right of Clive Steps, between the Foreign Office and the Treasury. Entry was beneath a sand-bagged lintel where you had to pause to allow your eyes to adjust to the dimness of the low wattage lighting. It was a warren of small interconnected offices. On the walls and tables, maps were spread out with round headed coloured pins denoting some action or disaster. Other walls had wooden pigeon-holes that contained dockets and files. A large wooden sign told everyone what the day was like outside. No matter where you went there was the sound of typewriters clacking away. The typists were all in uniforms of the three services. The primitive air conditioning system consisted of a few ancient wall fans and a solitary unit from America which failed miserably to keep people cool.

Here, safe in the underground headquarters of the British High Command which had become the nerve centre of the war effort, the Prime Minister sat waiting quietly. His War Cabinet was gathering for their regular morning meeting. It was 9.30am. The Deputy Prime Minister, Clement Atlee, and John Anderson, the Lord President of the Council, were already seated, as was the Foreign Secretary, Anthony Eden. Churchill took from his waistcoat a Hunter pocket watch which had belonged to his father. It was 9.31 precisely. How he disliked tardiness. Suddenly the door to the room was opened by the marine sentry and Sir Stafford Cripps, Oliver Lyttelton and Ernest Bevin were ushered in. They quickly found their places at the conference table, not wanting to catch Churchill's eye. The Prime Minister looked around at his colleagues, cleared his throat and began.

'Good morning, gentlemen. To business, if you please. Firstly, you will have noticed that we have some visitors today. I have invited a number of the military to join us. So, on your behalf, I welcome them to our meeting. Firstly, we have General Alan Brooke who, as you know, is the Commander in Chief of the General Staff. Also with us is the Head of MI6, Sir Stewart Menzies. Next to him we have Admiral John Godfrey, Director of Naval Intelligence, and Admiral Percy Noble who is the Commander in Chief of the Royal Navy's Western Approach. His particular responsibilities, by the way, are the North Atlantic and the safety of our convoys. I have also taken the liberty of inviting Admiral Mountbatten who, as many of you know, was recently appointed as Chief of Combined Operations.

'To begin with I think it is proper that we have a brief overview of the current situation. I know this will not be very pleasant, but we cannot, and must not, stick our heads in the sand like some damn ostrich. So, to this end, I have asked the Deputy PM to prepare a summary. Clement, the floor is yours.'

Winston Churchill sat back in his chair and relaxed. Whilst he recognised that he and Atlee were poles apart politically and rarely seemed to agree on anything, he knew that his Deputy could be relied upon to do a thorough job.

'Thank you, Prime Minister. I will keep it brief. My review takes in all of 1941 and up to and including January of this year. As Mr Churchill has already indicated this is generally not good news. However, we must face up to the situation and our deficiencies. I will begin, if I may, with some good news. By the end of March 1941, the Army had raised and trained some four thousand commandos. Raids have taken place in Norway and along the French coast. However, in May the battleship *HMS Hood* was sunk by the *Bismark* with a huge loss of life. Three days later the *Bismark* was sunk by ships of our Navy in a tremendous action. That same month the Houses of Parliament were bombed by the Luftwaffe for the first time. Shortly afterwards, Rudolph Hess, Hitler's Deputy, parachuted into Scotland.'

Churchill interrupted. 'Remind me where exactly Hess is being kept?'

'Perhaps I can answer your question, sir,' replied the Head of MI6. 'He is at present safely locked away in the Tower of London. There are, I believe, plans to move him to Mytchett Place which is down in Surrey.'

Churchill nodded a thank you.

Clement Atlee continued. 'Crete was invaded on the 20th May. In June, Herr Hitler was pursuing his Eastern Front ambitions by invading Russia, despite their non-aggression pact. By August the Germans were at the gates of Leningrad.'

Mountbatten put up his hand, like a small boy in a school room.

'If I may say so, sir, I believe the Germans may have bitten off more than they can chew.'

Churchill gave the Rear Admiral a withering look. He wanted to say that there was always one who would state the bloody obvious. Instead, he gave a slight smile and replied, 'I believe you may be right. Carry on please, Mr Atlee.'

'Thank you, Prime Minister. At the end of October, the Germans sunk an American warship the *USS Reuben James* by mistake, killing seventy men. In November, *HMS Ark Royal* and *HMS Barham* were also sunk. On the 7th December the Japanese attacked Pearl Harbour and, despite our warning the previous month, they were caught completely unawares. We declared war on Japan the following day, and two days later the United States of America declared war both on Germany and Japan. On the 9th and 10th of that same month we had the unmitigated disaster of Force Z, which was under the command of Admiral Tom Phillips, being attacked by the Japanese. As you all know, the battleship *HMS Prince of Wales* and the battle cruiser *HMS Repulse* were torpedoed and sunk with a huge loss of life, both sailors and marines. The *Prince of Wales* lost three hundred and twenty-seven crew members, whilst the *Repulse* lost a staggering five hundred and ten. Then, to make matters worse, on Christmas Day, after a valiant resistance, Hong Kong was forced to surrender to the Japanese who, by this time, were quickly gaining the upper hand in the entire Far East. In January there were two further setbacks: firstly, the Japanese took Manila, and secondly, they invaded the Dutch East Indies. This means that the whole of that region and much of the Pacific would now seem to be at their mercy. As a result, they are now within striking distance of Australia.'

Atlee paused to get his breath. A deafening silence had descended on the room. Much of this information the members of the Cabinet already knew. However, when it was read out to them in such a dispassionate manner, it made the situation seem even more desperate, which was bad enough.

He continued. 'There is also a crisis in North Africa where General Rommel has seized the initiative, forcing our troops to retreat. That is the end of my report, Prime Minister.'

Churchill looked round the table. Nearly everyone avoided eye contact with him. Mountbatten was the exception. He held Churchill's gaze without wavering.

'Thank you, Mr Atlee. That was most helpful. Does anyone have anything else to add?'

Ernest Bevin raised his hand. He spoke quickly and without any notes.

'As Minister for Labour, I should like to state for the record that last August we introduced rationing for clothing and coal. We also began the 'Women into War Work' scheme in order to release more men for active service. We have also moved the department for rationing up to Colwyn Bay in North Wales for security and safety reasons. The department is being accommodated in a number of schools and large houses. Next month, I am afraid, we shall have to ration soap. Our food and supplies, that are held centrally, are getting dangerously low. Because very few of the convoys are getting across the Atlantic unscathed, I have to tell you that the country, as a whole, is close to verging on starvation. In addition, sir, I have received a report from Geoffrey Lloyd, our Secretary for Petroleum. He informs me that we only have fuel stocks for about two months. We shall shortly be rationing petrol, with priority going to military and essential civilian vehicles. On a more positive note, and rather surprisingly, he tells me that we are actually drilling for oil in one of our coal mining areas.'

Churchill looked up sharply, a look of curiosity on his face. 'Really? We are drilling for oil here in England?' he asked.

'Yes, Prime Minister. Somewhere in Nottinghamshire, I believe. I think it may even be in Sherwood Forest. I understand the Americans are helping us out with their knowledge of drilling.'

'Absolutely amazing, bloody amazing. Whatever next? Keep me informed about how things are progressing.'

Churchill then let out a long and heart felt sigh. He knew that Bevin was a good man. He also knew that he worked long hours at his Ministry and always had the welfare of the British people at heart.

'There is one further thing, Prime Minister – the Black Market.'

Everyone in the room sat up. Suddenly, he had their full attention.

'Despite the good work being done by Scotland Yard, this epidemic is getting out of hand. The quantity of goods being stolen from the docks and the railways is enormous. For example, the Great Western Railway had over two hundred thousand pounds worth of goods stolen last year. The other railway companies are in a similar situation. Despite the increase in prosecutions, fines and even imprisonment, the Black Market continues to flourish. Food, clothes, petrol and whisky are all readily available if you have the money and are prepared to pay.'

At that precise moment there was a certain amount of paper shuffling from around the table and even one or two red faces.

'Prime Minister, there is a serious danger of the country being split into two halves: the haves and the have nots. We must act quickly and tackle this vile, destructive activity.'

'What do you suggest?' asked Clement Atlee, who had a very real look of concern on his face.

'I suggest we set up new regulations which will apply both to those stealing the goods and those who receive them. Let us implement heavier penalties. We can increase the fines, perhaps, by three or four times, and we should set the prison sentences to perhaps fourteen or fifteen years instead of the short time served currently. We need to get really tough with the organisers, the big bosses. Let us call upon the general public to help us by urging them to be patriotic and not buy from these crooks.'

Winston Churchill was more sanguine about this whole issue. Being a realist, he didn't think that these proposed alterations to the law would change the situation very much. Nevertheless, something had to be done and, perhaps more importantly, be seen to be done.

'Very well,' he growled. 'Implement the changes and let us review the matter in one month's time. Thank you, Mr Bevin, you have clearly given this matter a lot of thought. It is good for us to be reminded of the seriousness of the situation.'

Ernest Bevin looked at the PM carefully. He could not decide whether Churchill was being sarcastic or not.

'If no-one objects, I think it would be best if we paused now for a comfort break and some refreshments, and then continue afterwards.'

Since no-one raised an objection the meeting broke up.

(ii)

'Right gentleman, we come now to the second part of our meeting and why the Military are here.' Churchill scanned the table to make sure that he had everyone's full attention. 'Admiral Godfrey, perhaps you would be good enough to start us off.'

'Yes, sir, certainly. The main problem we have had with deciphering the Kriegsmarine communications is that Admiral Donitz decided that all surface vessels, codenamed *Dolphins*, should have a different Enigma signature from that of their U-boats, codenamed *Shark*. This meant that we in Naval Intelligence and our co-workers at Bletchley Park had double the problem in trying to decipher their codes. Thankfully, the capture of the German submarine U-110 gave us access to vital papers and codebooks which allowed the boffins at the Park to crack what had been believed to be unbreakable German naval codes. The speed at which our chaps deciphered these messages was extremely impressive, so much so that those of us at the Admiralty were receiving the information faster than the Germans at their headquarters. Consequently, our convoys were able to avoid the wolf packs, so that huge losses were avoided. I am sure that Admiral Percy can confirm all of this.'

Churchill looked at Percy Noble. 'Well, Admiral?' he growled.

The C-in-C of the Atlantic disliked being the centre of attention. He usually tried to remain in the background, out of sight and invisible. Today, this morning and at this meeting all eyes were on him and he felt distinctly uncomfortable.

'I can confirm everything that Admiral Godfrey has said, sir. We were in a dreadful state. Virtually every convoy was at the mercy of those wretched submarines. Thousands of tons of shipping and vital supplies, armaments and ammunition, were lost, as were hundreds of good men from the Merchant Marine. All this changed when the German codes were broken. This meant that our convoys could evade the enemy submarines and cross the North Atlantic safely. However, a week ago, this suddenly stopped. Once again our ships are being chased and sunk at will.'

Churchill peered questioningly over the rim of his glasses at Admiral Godfrey. At that moment Clement Atlee raised his hand to speak. The Prime Minister, more than a little exasperated, gave him a nod.

'Sir, before we get into the details of this vital issue, do you think that the Admiral might explain to us lesser mortals how the German Enigma machines actually work. I feel sure that it would help those of us that are civilians to understand the gravity of the situation a little better.'

Winston Churchill glared at his deputy. The man had no sense of urgency, he thought.

'Of course, Mr Atlee, why ever not,' Churchill replied, unsuccessfully trying to keep the annoyance at the delay from his voice. 'Admiral, if you please.' Time was of the essence, if only everyone could understand that.

The Admiral looked round the table at each of the individuals gathered there but chose to direct his attention to the Deputy Prime Minister.

'In principle, the Enigma machine enciphers at one end, for example the German Naval Headquarters, whilst at the other, let us say a U-boat, the message is deciphered. The operator types in the message on a normal looking keyboard into the machine which holds the current settings of the day, according to the codebook. In this way, a couple of seconds after the original letters have been typed in, via an electronic current sent through the rotating code-letter wheels, a different set of letters are selected by the machine. The substitute letters would then be noted. When completed, the whole message would be sent by Morse code to its intended destination. Here, with his machine set up in exactly the same way as the sender's equipment, the reverse happens. The U-boat operator taps in the encoded message, which would then reveal the real message.

'Just to make things more complicated, the machine's settings are changed at least every twenty-four hours, sometimes twice a day. This means that they have access to millions of possible letter combinations. The German High Command considers the Enigma to be a perfectly secure form of communication.

'These machines are ingenious pieces of equipment and very portable. They are made of Bakelite and brass, with an interior of complicated wheels, studs, pins and rings, plus a complexity of electrical wiring. The Germans have made thousands of them.

'Thank you, Admiral, that has been very helpful,' said a thoughtful Atlee. 'Just one further thing, if I may?'

The Deputy Prime Minister looked questioningly at Churchill.

'If you must, Mr Atlee,' sighed the Prime Minister. This was becoming unbearable he thought. He could feel one of his dark depressions descending on him like an oppressive cloud, his 'black dog' as he called it.

Churchill felt as if he wanted to scream out loud. Of course, he could not, which made him feel even worse.

Clement Atlee continued completely unaware of the Prime Minister's demeanour.

'Admiral, could you just remind us of how successful we have been in breaking these codes?'

The Head of Naval Intelligence looked towards his leader for permission to proceed. Churchill nodded an affirmative.

'Yes, sir. The German Army code was broken in January 1940. In May of that year Bletchley Park broke the code for the Luftwaffe, and in December the code used by the German Intelligence Service was also broken.'

Clement Atlee looked pensive. Other members of the War Cabinet were beginning to get restless. Atlee chose to ignore this.

'Thank you, Admiral, that will be all for now,' he said.

He looked towards Churchill and allowed himself a rare half smile. The DPM knew that the Prime Minister was both an admirer and a great supporter of the work being carried out at Bletchley Park. He also knew that the PM had intercepts sent to him on a daily basis, sometimes delivered by Stewart Menzies himself, the Head of SIS. Atlee also knew that everyone else, ministers and military alike, believed that Churchill's information came from a number of spies abroad. Much to everyone's annoyance, the PM was always better informed than they were. Atlee also knew that Churchill sometimes referred to his bundles of intercepts as 'eggs from the Bletchley geese who never cackled'.

At last, and with much relief, Winston Churchill was able to regain control of the meeting. Addressing all the Admirals present he spoke.

'Well, what a bloody mess! Perhaps with your collective wisdom you might care to tell us exactly what is going on in the Atlantic and, more importantly, what precisely you are doing about resolving the situation.'

The PM's sarcasm was not lost on anyone in the room, least of all the Admirals. The Head of SIS was the first to reply.

'Our security services, in an operation known as *Double X* in which we have made use of double agents, have informed us that Admiral Donitz suspected that his codes had been broken and were being read by us. Consequently, on the first of this month he ordered all his submarines to have an updated version of the Kriegsmarine Enigma installed. From that point onwards a fourth rotor wheel was added and, as a result, there's been a complete blackout at Bletchley Park. Suddenly, and without warning, all messages received could no longer be decrypted. As the Admiral has already stated, this means that all Atlantic convoys are once again extremely vulnerable to attack.'

The confirmation of this news was greeted in complete silence, as the information and the consequences began to sink in. The Prime Minister was the one who spoke first.

'What is to be done about this appalling turn of events?' he asked quietly.

Menzies replied. 'Naturally we are doing everything we can. The boffins at the Park are working round the clock to try and break the new code, but so far without any success. To be brutally honest, we can do very little about this until we manage to obtain a new version of the codes or an actual Enigma machine.'

Churchill sat back in his chair and let out a long, low breath.

'So, what are we to do now?' he asked with an almost desperate edge to his voice. The room remained very quiet. Finally, Admiral Mountbatten spoke.

'Back in 1940 when we were still trying to break Enigma, one of my officers came up with a scheme for capturing a machine. His plan was to use a captured German aeroplane with a crew in German uniforms, and at least a couple of men who were fluent in the language, then crash the plane deliberately into the Channel and wait to be rescued. They would then kill their rescuers and return to England with the boat and the machine. We provisionally codenamed it *Operation Ruthless*. However, for a number of reasons the project never got off the ground.'

'And your point is?' the Head of MI6 asked.

Mountbatten thought for a moment or two.

'Perhaps we could adapt the idea, maybe turn the plan into a sort of 'Trojan Horse,' he replied.

'I cannot see it working,' said Menzies dismissively.

'I don't see why not,' replied Mountbatten stubbornly. 'Do you have a better idea?'

Churchill decided to interrupt the argument before it got out of hand. 'Nevertheless, it is an idea. Get your people to work the plan up further, then perhaps we can make an informed decision. In the meantime, let us hope and pray that something else turns up, although goodness knows what.'

It was clearly time to end the meeting. 'Thank you all for your attendance and contribution to this morning's discussions. We will meet again tomorrow at the same time. I bid you all a good day.'

With that, the meeting finished.

PART TWO

TRAINING

discipline, coaching,
education, grounding,
guidance, tuition,
proficiency, practice.

CHAPTER 8

(i)

The journey from Chatham to Deal was largely uneventful. The four vehicles, packed to the gunnels with horsehair mattresses, pillows and blankets, proceeded in a convoy along the main A2 road. Dacre knew this as Watling Street, the old Roman road that once linked Dover to London, via Rochester. Past the small towns of Gillingham and Rainham, little more than large villages really, then on through Sittingbourne and Faversham, both built along tidal creeks, many of which could be found in this part of Kent. This was the heart of the 'Garden of England' with its hundreds of apple and cherry orchards, and field upon field of hops. Apart from the odd vapour trail in the sky, there was little evidence of war in this corner of England.

At Brenley Corner, where the Thanet Way headed eastwards towards Whitstable, Herne Bay and the coastal towns of the Isle of Thanet, stood an elderly man dressed in an old AA uniform, a row of medal ribbons on his chest. He was there to render assistance to motor users and to direct traffic. Behind him was his black and yellow box surrounded by a colourful and well-attended garden. His ancient motorcycle was propped up on its stand. As the convoy passed, he gave them a smart salute and a wave; the marines shouted back a reply. The vehicles continued on, up and over the North Downs, through the village of Dunkirk and down towards the city of Canterbury. Having passed through the outlying district, they continued over a level crossing and entered the historic city through the mighty 14th century Westgate Towers. The marines were able to see quite clearly that the city had so far been spared any of the ravages of war.

'It's only a question of time,' said Pete Wills. 'If Hitler has his way, he'll smash this place up good and proper because it's a garrison town.'

Dacre nodded his head in agreement. 'I'm sure your right. I wonder how well it's defended? We haven't seen any anti-aircraft guns anywhere.'

They lapsed into an uneasy silence. The convoy moved slowly up the narrow High Street, past the Weavers Cottages on the left and the medieval Pilgrim's Hospice on the right, then over the River Stour. The town was quite busy, people going about their normal daily business. There were also a number of soldiers in evidence which reminded everyone that this was an important town in the grand scheme of things. One or two gave the troops a wave or a victory 'V' sign. At the top of the town the convoy passed Saint George's Church and then passed through the city walls once more. A little further on the vehicles turned left towards the local prison. They ground their way slowly up St Martin's Hill, past the old windmill, and at last out into the open countryside. At Wingham the convoy turned off the main road and took the back road to Deal and Walmer.

Forty- five minutes later the vehicles rumbled onto the small parade ground by the guardroom of North Barracks. This was the home of the Royal Marines. Climbing down from the trucks, the marines took the opportunity to stretch their legs, whilst one or two lit up a crafty cigarette. For many of them this was the first time they had returned to their *alma mater* since they had been here as recruits.

Dacre and his new friend, Pete Wills, were walking around the edge of the parade ground inspecting the tall brick built Napoleonic buildings.

'Do you know anything about this place,' he asked Wills.

'Not a bloody thing. This is all new to me,' he replied.

'I'll give you a brief history if you like. They have been training Marines here since 1861. Back in those days there were 'red' marines and 'blue' marines. The 'reds' were the Royal Marine Light Infantry, or RMLI, so called because of their red jackets, whilst the 'blues' were the Royal Marine Artillery, or RMA. They amalgamated in 1923. Deal, or to be more precise Walmer, became the Depot. This whole place is actually made from four different barracks. The North barracks, where we are now, was originally built as a hospital but has always been used for training. This is really the main place where all the recruit training takes place and, of course, still does. It has one of the biggest parade grounds that you've ever seen. Take my word for it. I have marched over just about every square inch of it. There is also a dining hall, a NAAFI and a wet canteen. Behind us we have the guardroom, and down at the far end are the detention quarters. Then, there are the South Barracks just across the road, sometimes referred to as the Cavalry Barracks for obvious reasons. The officers and the sergeants have their messes there. It also has a gymnasium, some playing fields, a twenty-five-yard range and an assault course. Most of the buildings are old, built nearly two hundred years ago. Then, there are the East Barracks. Again, they are Napoleonic. They're said to be haunted by a drummer boy who appears at the stroke of midnight, but I never saw him when I did guard duty. It's a spooky place, though, particularly if you are on your own. The Band Service have their quarters there as well as the tailor, the cobbler and the clothing store. Lastly, there are the Infirmary Barracks which house a fully equipped sick bay and also a school.'

'You seem to be remarkably well informed,' said Pete Wills.

'Yes, well, I was here quite recently. I did my basic training in 1939 and I had two very good squad instructors,' replied Dacre.

At that moment the two corporals arrived back and ordered everyone to gather round for a briefing.

(ii)

The advance party was divided up into pairs. Rooms had been allocated in the two blocks nearest to the stables. They had to accommodate the three hundred and fifty other ranks as well as the eighteen officers that were all expected to arrive in two weeks' time. Each room had to be cleaned from top to bottom, beds set up and made. Apparently, it had been decided by the new Commanding Officer, Lieutenant Colonel Picton-Phillipps, that the eighteen officers and SNCOs should all be accommodated in the same buildings as the other ranks. All meals were to be taken together in the main dining hall although an area was to be screened off for the officers and sergeants. Clearly, the new CO had a very definite view about how he wanted his Commandos to operate.

The first week flew by as each barrack room became 'marine' clean. Then, there were the showers and the heads, as well as the corridors and the staircases to be scrubbed. It was a thankless job. The two corporals kept everyone on their toes, constantly checking and pointing out something that had been missed.

'Goodness knows when this lot was last cleaned,' said Pete Wills one day. 'I have never seen so much dirt and muck.'

Dacre allowed himself a smile before replying. 'Save your energy. I think you're going to need it. Have you seen the state of the urinals? I wouldn't let my dog piss in there.'

'You have a dog?'

'No, I don't have a dog. I was just saying that if I did have....... Oh, never mind, just keep on cleaning.'

A friendly silence followed as both men put in plenty of elbow grease.

Apart from his cleaning duties, Dacre felt that his main responsibility was to keep himself fighting fit. This he did at least twice a day by pounding up and down the nearby shingle beach. Naturally, he took Pete with him who, because he was so unfit, did nothing but complain all the time.

In the evenings most of the marines visited the wet bar for a couple of pints of the local brew, Shepherd Neame. It had been made very clear to everyone that they must keep well away from the main parade in Walmer, the 'Holy of Holies'. Failure to do so would result in the Barrack's RSM giving them a short but brutal course in close order drill with full equipment as a punishment.

On the third night, the marines were allowed shore leave. Dacre took his friend the short distance down to Walmer, to the Admiral Nelson public house on The Strand. The beer was just as good as he remembered. Memories of his recruit training days came flooding back, of Jock, Scouse and Jacko. He wondered where they were now. He looked around at all the recruits with their girls. He half expected to see his old girlfriend Dorothy and her friend Joan but they were long gone, since both of their fathers had been serving 'Royals'. They had clearly moved on, which was the way in the marines - another posting, another place to call home. Dacre was not too disappointed. It would have been a complication and a distraction that he realised he could well do without.

It was during the beginning of the second week that news of the disaster in Singapore was made public. Throughout the country, people were shocked. The seemingly impregnable island fortress had surrendered to the Japanese. How had this happened? Why had General Percival given up with over sixty-two thousand troops on the island? It was widely known by those in the know that the 18th Division based in Singapore, which comprised three times more soldiers than the Japanese had in Malaya, were expected to fight to the very end, and that included senior officers and the Commander in Chief. The honour of the British Empire was at stake. There were, of course, dozens of questions, but sadly no answers.

In the pub that night a group of older marines were telling the 'Hostility Only' men about some of the pleasures of a run ashore in Singapore or 'Singers' as it was known. Like Gibraltar and Malta, ships of the Royal Navy with their Marine detachments would call at the island to refuel and refurbish supplies. The naval dockyard was the largest in the Far East and included some of the biggest dry docks in the world. *HMS Terror*, the shore base was always welcoming, as were the unbelievable trips down into the city by naval bus to the Britannia Club, better known as the 'Brit Club'. Other delights could be found in China Town or Bugis Street, or at the dance halls of Geylang. They had to be seen to be believed. All this had gone now. A whole way of life, disappeared, destroyed. Singapore was now part of the expanding Japanese Empire. Everyone wondered what was going to happen to all the prisoners, British and Empire military and civilians alike. The locals, too, the Chinese, the Malays and the Tamils. It was rumoured that the Prime Minister, Winston Churchill, had aged ten years over night and had suffered with chest pains on receiving the news. The future looked extremely bleak.

CHAPTER 9

(i)

Dacre stood and looked out of the barrack room window. He had a fine view from the top floor. It had been a bleak, cold, grey day, typical of February. He could clearly see clouds, heavy with rain, that had begun to gather out over the sea. They were moving rapidly towards the land and the town of Deal. He looked round the room at his fellow 'Royals' who, like him, were getting ready for their first parade as a unit. His friend Pete Wills, the ex-safe breaker, was desperately trying to sort out his webbing. The air was blue with his frustration. The other marines in the room had all arrived the night before from Stonehouse Barracks in Plymouth. Burt Kelley and Stephen Whitnell were both full-time members of the Corps, whereas Paul McNight, or 'Mac' as he was known, David Taylor, Ken Shakespeare and Baz Phelps were all HO marines. Over the last couple of days, over three hundred and fifty marines and officers from the Royal Marine Division had gathered here at the Depot. All were volunteers, destined to become the first commando unit in the Corps.

On the main parade they formed up ready for inspection. It had started to rain. The Commanding Officer, Lt Col Picton-Phillipps sat majestically on a large white horse. At that moment, he felt immensely proud of being a Royal Marine, not just because this was his first command as a colonel. The Adjutant, Captain Alain Comyn, reported to the second-in-command, Major 'Titch' Houghton, that the unit was all present and correct. He, in turn, informed the CO that all was ready for his inspection.

Dacre watched spellbound as the Colonel brought his horse closer to their front rank. He sensed rather than saw some unease amongst the marines. Horses and men on the ground do not generally mix well. He recalled an incident during his recruit training days when the inspecting officer's horse had relieved itself, splattering many of those in the front rank with dung and urine. It had not been a pleasant experience. The whole parade stood ramrod straight with not even a flicker of an eyelid as the rain poured down. That was everyone except the corporal standing next to Dacre who, for some unaccountable reason, chose that very moment to adjust part of his webbing equipment. As quick as a flash the CO spotted the movement and in an extremely loud voice bellowed, 'Sergeant Major that man is moving. Take his name.'

QMS Chris Brennan looked along the line of his men. Then, in an equally loud voice replied, 'Sir, that man is a corporal.'

Without any hesitation Colonel Picton-Phillipps replied, 'Well take the name of the man next to him.'

So Dacre's name went into the punishment book. However, the Sergeant-Major conveniently forgot to follow it up, perhaps as a way of an apology.

The first couple of days were spent in sorting out the men into something resembling a fighting unit. The Colonel and the Adjutant had decided that this Commando would be organised into a headquarters and three rifle companies, namely 'A', 'B' and 'X', and that each of these companies of about thirty men would be divided into three smaller groups called platoons. The HQ Company being the smallest, and therefore having only one platoon, would be Number One Platoon. The other three companies would then number their platoons sequentially two, three, four and so on. Dacre and his roommates all found themselves allocated to Number Ten Platoon of 'X' Company. Once this had been organised, each man and officer was interviewed either by the CO or by the second-in-command. While this was going on, stringent medical and physical tests were carried out which were designed to weed out the faint hearted or those considered to be unsuitable.

(ii)

Dacre arrived at the company office at 0855 hours, ready for his interview with the Major. He knew that a good marine was always five minutes early. He knocked at the office door and entered. In front of the officer's desk he halted and snapped up a smart salute. He stood to attention waiting, his thumbs in line with the seams of his trousers. Dacre knew what was required.

The Major looked up from the papers in front of him and immediately liked what he saw. With his twenty years of service in the Corps, he prided himself on being a good judge of character. He checked the file on the desk to refresh his memory. This young man, whilst still under the age of eighteen years, had been awarded the King's Badge for being the best all-round recruit in his squad, a rare and unusual honour. Later, as a volunteer, he had helped crew one of the small boats that had rescued the BEF from Dunkirk in 1940. He had also been awarded the Légion d'Honneur by no less than General de Gaulle, the leader of the Free French Forces in Great Britain. The medal ribbon on the marine's blouse confirmed this. Yes, thought the Major, this was an impressive marine, without a doubt, who had tremendous potential and, by rights, should certainly have been promoted to the rank of corporal, maybe even sergeant. He wondered why not.

'Stand at ease. Stand easy, Dacre, and sit down please,' said the second-in-command.

The young marine did as he was ordered. He looked at the Major directly, making eye contact for the first time.

'It says in your file that you speak fluent Italian, French and German, is that correct?'

'Yes, sir.'

The Major held up his hand and beckoned. A small, elderly civilian who had been sitting behind the door came forward. He limped on his right leg. He had shoulder length, fly-away white hair and an unkempt beard to match. His once elegant dark grey overcoat with a black velvet colour was crumpled and stained, and his shoulders were covered in white dandruff. Beneath his coat, the collar of his shirt was frayed and grubby, and his blue and red spotted bow tie had been tied hastily.

In a crisp and somewhat deep voice, he asked the marine, 'Sprechen sie Deutsch? Parlez-vous Francais?'

Dacre, although surprised, replied the affirmative in both languages. Then, for the next twenty minutes or so, the two men spoke rapidly and effortlessly in both German and French, changing from one to the other completely at random. The visitor was constantly trying to catch the marine out but failed to do so. Major Houghton decided to stop this verbal dual.

'Enough, please. Well, Professor, will he do?'

The elderly man thought for a second or two.

'Yes, Major. He will do nicely. His French is superb; his German a little less so, but only an expert like me would be able to spot the difference.'

He smiled at his own little conceit.

'Good,' said the Major. 'Thank you very much for your time, it is much appreciated. If you would see yourself out?'

'Yes of course,' replied the Professor. 'It has been a pleasure.'

Then turning towards the marine, he added, 'Your language skills are quite exceptional. In fact, I would go as far as to say that you are one of the best that I've encountered in a long time. In my humble opinion you are wasted here running around playing soldiers.'

The Major interrupted somewhat briskly. 'Thank you, Professor, that will be all.'

As he reluctantly left the room, he could quite clearly be heard muttering under his breath, 'What a waste, what a waste.'

The Major studied the marine carefully then said, 'Well done. Praise from Caesar indeed.'

'Sir?'

'That was Professor Paul Ellwood from the University of London. He's one of the country's leading linguists and, also, I understand, an adviser to the War Cabinet. So, as I said, praise from Caesar.'

Dacre remained silent but blushed slightly with embarrassment from the compliment.

The Major continued, 'When our training is over and the unit becomes operational, I am sure we will be able to put your language skills to good use.' For the first time he gave the young marine an encouraging smile.

'That will be all for now. Carry on.'

Dacre stood up, saluted and left the room.

The Major sat ruminating for a moment or two. Dacre really was a most unusual marine but why was he still only a marine? He shook himself out of his reverie. Time to move on. He had a job to do. He reached for another file just as there was another knock at the door.

CHAPTER 10

Lieutenant General Bernard Montgomery, Chief of South Eastern Command, sat facing the Prime Minister. Churchill was flanked on either side by the CIGS, General Alan Brooke, and the Director of Naval Intelligence, Admiral John Godfrey, as well as the Head of Combined Operations, Rear Admiral Mountbatten. Beside Mountbatten sat the Air Chief Marshall, Charles Portal, and next to him the Commander-in-Chief of the Home Fleet, Admiral 'Jock' Tovey, and the First Sea Lord, Sir Dudley Pound. If Montgomery felt intimidated by this high-powered meeting, he certainly didn't show it. He was here this morning to put forward a plan that had already been allocated the codename of *Operation Rutter*. Montgomery was anxious to create the right impression. These were powerful men, perhaps the most powerful in the country. They could help lift a man's career or set it aside in some backwater of the Army, if they so wished. It was important that he should make a good impression.

Montgomery had been chosen to oversee an operation that had been originated by Mountbatten and his Combined Operations Headquarters. The idea for a raid on occupied France had been in response to the Prime Minister's need for something to happen this summer. When Mountbatten had taken his idea to the Chiefs of Staff Committee, General Brooke felt that whilst the raid was worthwhile it should come under the command and control of Home Forces. Mountbatten was furious at this slight, but the Committee refused to give approval unless he gave way. He was left with no choice but to agree.

The plan was bold and ambitious. Montgomery knew that it was just the sort of thing that the Prime Minister would support. The idea of taking the fight to the Germans had always been a high priority for Churchill, ever since Dunkirk.

Montgomery had a rather high-pitched voice that in anyone else would possibly have sounded unauthoritative. Equally, his stature was not particularly imposing. Despite this, all eyes in the room were fixed on him because of his reputation as a brilliant commander in the field. Everyone present knew that he could be relied upon. If Monty had a plan, they, the Admirals and Generals, wanted to hear about it. Speaking in his crisp, staccato voice Montgomery began.

'Gentlemen, I put forward for your consideration and approval the idea of a raid on the French coast. I have identified the key points in my report, which you have in front of you. With your agreement, I shall be pleased talk you through it.'

Montgomery proceeded by reading the report verbatim.

'Firstly, the type of action: Commando raid
Code name: *Operation Rutter*.
Proposed date: to be announced.
Target: the port and town of Dieppe.

'Secondly, the Mission:
1. To seize and hold the port and the town during daylight hours.
2. To capture enemy officers and soldiers, particularly of a senior rank.
3. To obtain secret documents from German Divisional Headquarters at Arques-la-Bataille.
4. To seize and remove any enemy boats, such as landing craft and invasion barges.
5. To destroy enemy gun emplacements, oil and petrol storage tanks and other supplies.
6. To disrupt and destroy enemy communications including Radar defence facilities.
7. To destroy the airfield at St Aubin.

'Thirdly, the Execution:
1. The town and port are to be heavily bombarded by capital ships of the Royal Navy and bombed from the air by the RAF.
2. Parachute troops will seize the high ground on either side of the town and will destroy the enemy guns.
3. Two army units will be put ashore from landing craft to storm the town in a frontal assault, whilst smaller groups, perhaps marines,

will enter the harbour on small gunboats to carry out their allotted task.
4. The RAF will provide fighter aircraft cover for the ground assault.
5. All troops will re-embark in good order when the raid is completed.

'Finally: Considerations
1. With the 'softening up' by the navy and air force, it is anticipated that the   enemy will be unable to put up much resistance.
2. Putting ashore a small raiding party on the enemy-occupied coast is a relatively simple thing to do. All you need is a dark night, a handful of men and a fast boat or two. If we increase the size of the force and the diversity of the troops taking part, then the whole thing becomes far more complex and difficult.
3. Recent intelligence suggests that Dieppe is defended only by low category German troops. In our planning we need to take into consideration such things as food, ammunition, reinforcements, transport, evacuation of the wounded and, of course, the removal of prisoners.

'To conclude, this extended raid should also give us some much-needed experience in landing troops from the sea, something we are terribly short of. When the time comes to invade Europe, as it must, what we will have learned at Dieppe will most certainly help.
I submit this plan for your consideration and approval.

Silence descended on the room. One or two of the Chiefs of Staff began to shuffle their papers. The Prime Minister was the first to speak.
'Thank you, General, for your detailed and thoughtful report. As ever, you have been most thorough. I must say that I really like the idea of a large-scale raid. It would also be good for morale. The people need something to give them heart, and so do we, gentlemen, so do we. Are there any questions for the General?' Nobody looked up. 'In that case, General, I will ask you to retire whilst we consider your plan.'
Montgomery got up from his chair and left the room.
Churchill paused before speaking. 'Well you are all very quiet. Do I detect a problem or two?'
Mountbatten raised his hand.

'I am very keen to hear what Admiral Tovey has to say about using capital ships on this raid.'

'Thank you, Dickie, so would I. Admiral?'

'I am not too happy about it, sir. Montgomery's plan has many good points and I applaud his initiative. However, I don't want to put any more of my big ships at risk, possibly to be blown out of the water by the Luftwaffe.'

Churchill turned to the First Sea Lord.

'I presume, Dudley, that you agree with Jack?'

'Yes, sir. For once we are in complete agreement.'

'As it happens, I agree with both of you,' replied Churchill. 'It would be a waste of precious resources. We've had enough with the loss of the *Prince of Wales* and the *Repulse*. However, I would like to hear what Air Chief Marshall Portal has to say. Charles?'

'Well, sir, we can provide air cover but only for a limited time. Our planes - let us say they take off from Biggin Hill - will have some distance to fly. There is a fuel limitation. So, the cover we can provide for the Navy would be limited. The Luftwaffe, on the other hand, have a number of airfields close to Dieppe, so they would be able to carry out a greater number of sorties with considerable ease.'

Churchill pondered this thoughtful reply before speaking.

'So, gentlemen, how do we proceed from here?'

Brooke spoke first.

'I suggest, sir, that with everyone's agreement we allow Monty's plan to proceed. We might also suggest to him that he considers using some of the Canadian troops who are at present under his command. I believe they are currently in Sussex, undergoing yet more training. General Paget, the officer commanding Home Forces, tells me he is constantly being pestered by senior Canadian officers to be given a chance to prove themselves. They have been kicking their heels for nearly two years.'

Churchill's face broke into a broad grin as he smacked the table with the palm of his hand.

'What a splendid idea, just capital! As you may know, I've also been under some pressure from the Canadian Government to find something for their troops to do. We can kill two birds with one stone. Make it clear to Paget and Montgomery that this is what we want.'

Mountbatten indicated that he had something else to say.

Reluctantly Churchill asked, 'Yes, Dickie?'

'There is just one thing, sir. These Canadians are, as yet, unseasoned. Indeed, some of their officers have never actually commanded in the field. I am just not convinced that using them is a good idea.'

The Prime Minister looked at Brooke. 'Well, General, what do you say to that?'

Without any hesitation the CIGS replied, 'I think, sir, that we must leave it up to Monty. The ball is now firmly in his court.'

Mounbatten raised his hand again.

'Yes, Dickie, what now?' Churchill was beginning to get cross. Why wouldn't the man leave well alone?

'I don't believe that a frontal assault is the best method of attack. In my original plan I favoured the idea of taking the two headlands, then overrun the town and port with troops landed at Quiberville and Puys. I also intended to use commandos and marines who are, in my opinion, better trained for this type of work.'

General Brooke interrupted him sharply, a very real look of distaste on his face.

'I believe, Admiral, that as I have said before, we must now leave the choice of tactics and troops up to the Home Forces.'

Reluctantly, Mountbatten realised, perhaps too late, that he had backed himself into a corner. He looked at Churchill. It was clear that there would be no support from that quarter. The Prime Minister was quite obviously prepared to let Monty have his way in order that the raid got off the starting blocks.

CHAPTER 11

(i)

Over the next few weeks, the unit's training became tougher and rougher. Officers, NCOs and marines all sweated and groaned alongside each other. There was no distinction or allowance made for rank. As the tests increased in difficulty, so more and more men were returned to their parent units, classified as either unfit or unsuitable. Meanwhile, more volunteers were arriving to take their places. By the end of February, nearly one hundred marines had been sent home and replaced.

The training continued to a level unknown by most of those taking part. Dacre was thankful that he had maintained his own level of fitness. Nevertheless, even he struggled at times. The runs on the shingle beach with full packs, equipment, platoon weapons, rifles and steel helmets proved to be extremely challenging. Up and down the steep berms they went, never stopping. It was far worse than anything he, or anyone else, had experienced in recruit training. Many collapsed with exhaustion. Some were pulled to their feet by their mates. Others lay where they fell, totally shattered with nothing left to give. It was punishing and relentless. Every day began with this torture, so much so, that some men began to fear it. But it was working. Gradually, the unit was getting fitter and stronger.

Then came the speed marches - three, six then nine miles. They were expected to be able to do a mile every ten minutes, and then to accurately fire their rifles at the end of each march. More often than not, this was followed by physical training, where the PT instructors exercised muscles that they never knew they had, to screaming point. Pulled muscles and torn ligaments were part and parcel of the training regime. If anyone needed to report to the sick bay, they were expected to do this in their own time. For those who were foolish or brave enough to want more, there was the assault course over in South Barracks, as well as shooting practice on the twenty-five yard range. However, what really sorted the sheep from the goats was the march in double time down to the old musketry range on the beach at Kingsdown, near Saint Margaret's Bay. Naturally, once you had finished there and had achieved the required level of accuracy, you were expected to double all the way back to barracks without stopping. This became a regular activity for all officers, NCOs and men at least two or three times a week. No-one was exempt, not even the Colonel. More often than not, he was out front leading the way.

One morning, Dacre was returning to his barrack room, when he met his roommate Ken Shakespeare on the stairs.

'You look pleased with yourself,' he said.

'I am,' replied Shakespeare, 'In fact I am very pleased with myself. I've just been promoted to Lance Corporal. I'm on my way to the tailor's shop to get my stripes sewn on.'

Dacre did a double take. 'You've been promoted? How did that happen?' His curiosity suddenly aroused.

'Well, I was on stag last night. I had the dawn watch. It was very dark when this chap leapt out of the shadows and tried to grab my rifle. So, I just lamped him one, straight on his chin. Down he went, onto his backside. I called out the guard, then went to see if he was alright. To my horror it turned out to be the CO that I'd hit. So, I pulled him to his feet and helped to brush him down. He just looked at me, then told me to report to the Orderly Room at 0900 hours. All night long I've been worrying that I would be charged with striking an officer or, at the very least, returned to my unit. Anyway, to cut a long story short, this morning he told me that he was pleased that I had been an alert and aggressive sentry, and that I was to be promoted to Lance Corporal, immediately. I was so surprised you could have knocked me over with a feather.'

Dacre didn't know what to say. He'd never heard of anything like this in the Corps before. He knew, of course, that it was widely known that the Colonel used to roam around the barracks in the early hours of the morning, trying to catch out sentries who might be asleep at their posts. But this? He'd never heard the like of it before.

'All I can say is congratulations, Ken. I'm very glad it worked out for you.'

'Thanks, AJ. That's much appreciated. The only downside to all this is that I now have to change platoons because there isn't a vacancy for a corporal in Number Ten. Oh well, I suppose you can't have everything. I shall really miss you and the lads. Give them all my best.'

With that, Lance Corporal Ken Shakespeare skipped down the stairs whistling *A Life on the Ocean Wave*.

(ii)

In a further effort to promote fitness, the Colonel stopped all shore leave. Each member of the unit, including the officers and NCOs, was now only allowed two pints of beer at the wet canteen in the evenings. Dacre, always a sucker for punishment, continued his early morning runs on the beach, despite everything else that was being thrown at them. Somehow or other, he had managed to convince his roommates to join him. Many in the platoon thought that they were just plain daft. Others admired their tenacity and dedication. Even the CO got to hear about it; Major Houghton made sure of that. In truth, both officers were intrigued.

'It will never last you know,' said the Colonel, one evening in his office.

'Oh, I don't know,' replied the second-in-command, 'they appear to be a pretty determined bunch of chaps, particularly with Marine Dacre leading them.'

'Yes, well, we shall see. Time will tell, but to be honest I wouldn't put money on them staying the course. They have too much else to do. What about the rest of the unit? How are they shaping up?'

'Pretty well, sir, all things considered.'

'How about those Irish lads from Dublin?'

'No problem there. They've fitted right in with the others. To be honest, you can't tell them apart.'

'I must say that is good news. Just between you and me, I wasn't sure how it would work out. I did think that one or two of them might even be Fenians. Anyway, for whatever reason, they are on our side at present. After all, their enemy's enemy is not always their friend.'

There was a long pause.

'Quite so, sir,' replied the Major. 'You can rest assured they will turn out to be good marines.'

'I hope you are right, Titch. I really hope you are right.'

The unit's time at the Depot RM was fast approaching the end. Colonel Picton-Phillipps was pleased with the way the training had progressed. He felt certain that his marines would give a good account of themselves when they got to Scotland and took on the infamous commando course at Achnacarry. However, before they left Deal, the Colonel thought that he might put the unit to some sort of a test, perhaps something that would be suitable for aspiring commandos. He had just the idea. He reached across the desk for his telephone.

CHAPTER 12

(i)

It was 0910 hours. The unit's senior officers were gathered in the small room that the CO used as an office. There was insufficient room for everyone to sit down. There were only two spare chairs, so most of them made themselves comfortable leaning against the walls.

'Good morning, chaps. Sit or stand easy. Smoke if you wish,' said Picton-Phillipps as he entered the room. Clearly, the Colonel was in a good mood because he generally frowned on smoking, being a non-smoker himself.

'I've called this meeting because I want to put to you an idea I have regarding the unit.' The Colonel had everyone's attention. 'Before we leave for Scotland, I want to test the unit's ability to undertake a typical commando raid.'

There was a collective sharp intake of breath from those present. Just what had the old man got in mind?

'Now I know what you are all thinking – we haven't done any training for this sort of thing. In fact, apart from the odd night-shoot down on the ranges, nearly all our training has been done during daylight hours.'

Major 'Titch' Houghton, the second-in-command put up his hand.

'Is this wise, sir? We know the men are fit, but surely they lack the skills necessary for such a venture.'

'You might well be right, Major, but I firmly believe in nothing ventured, nothing gained.'

Captain Comyn, the Adjutant, spoke next. 'What do you have in mind, sir, and when?'

'I want the unit to carry out a raid on Walmer Castle in two days' time.'

There was stunned silence in the room. Captain Simon Standwell, the OC of 'X' Company, broke the silence.

'But surely, sir, that's not a castle or fort in the traditional sense. It's more of a country residence used by the Lord Warden of the Cinque Ports.'

'Yes, I know all of that,' replied the Colonel somewhat testily, 'but it still looks like a castle from the outside and will, I think, serve the purpose. Anyway, I have already spoken to the present incumbent, and he is more than happy for us to use the castle as long as we don't do too much damage.'

'Who is the present Lord Warden, sir?' asked the Adjutant.

'Well, actually, it's the Prime Minister.'

'You mean Winston Churchill?'

'Yes, that's exactly who I mean. He was appointed some time last year, I believe. Anyway, he's always been a great supporter of us 'Royals', so it wasn't too difficult to convince him.'

'Are you suggesting that we actually break and enter?' queried Major Houghton.

'I don't think that will be necessary, although the building is actually empty. All the contents have been moved to somewhere in the Welsh mountains for safety.

'A bit like all the galleries and museums in London then,' said Simon Standwell.

'So, I believe,' replied the Colonel. 'Now, what I have in mind is that we aim to put some men up on the central tower and get them to hoist up a flag of some sort, just to show that they have been there. At the same time, we could put a small section of men up on the gun platforms. I had a walk down there yesterday afternoon to have a look around. The central tower has four semi-circular lobes. It's surrounded by a moat that has been turned into a garden, and there's a curtain wall that has perhaps a ten or twelve-foot drop. On the upper levels, the original gun embrasures appear to have been replaced by windows quite some time ago. The battlements are still in place, but whether or not they are the original is difficult to tell, not that that should bother us.'

Captain Peter Hellings, the OC of 'A' Company, indicated that he wanted to ask a question.

'Is this going to take the whole unit or just a single company, sir?'

The Colonel paused before replying. 'I want the whole unit to be involved. I thought, perhaps, some sort of a defensive screen around the castle and grounds would be ideal. Then three small sections of hand-picked men, one from each platoon - let's say no more than four in each group - who will carry out the actual raid.'

'Do we have any marines who can actually climb?' asked Captain Richard Whyte the OC of 'B' Company. 'Only we haven't done any training for this sort of thing - well, not yet.'

'I appreciate that,' replied the Colonel. 'I think we just need two or three chaps who can free climb. They can then let down ropes for the others. I'll leave the choice of men to you Company Commanders. You know your marines better than anyone else.'

'Are we going to attack from the sea, which is how I understand most commando raids begin? It's just that the fortifications along the beach are pretty substantial, what with the sand-bagged emplacements, the minefields and all the barbed wire,' asked the Major.

'No, I think not,' replied the Colonel. 'I've had a look and it's clearly not on. Besides, we don't have any landing craft available and the requisitioning of fishing boats would be out of the question.'

'We could go on foot,' said the Adjutant. 'The castle isn't too far, and the men are fit enough, surely.'

'Yes, I agree about their fitness. I had initially thought it would be the best plan. However, the thought of trying to get two hundred and fifty marines to move silently through the streets in the early hours of the morning is just too much to contemplate. So, on this occasion, I have decided that we will have to use lorries to move the unit. I have already had a word with the Depot's Motor Transport Officer, and he has assured me that by begging and borrowing from the Army he can provide enough vehicles for our needs. The downside is that they can take us there but not bring us back. We will have to make our own way home, not that I see that being a problem. Anyway, I propose we stagger our departure times by half an hour. That way we should make a little less noise and perhaps attract less attention.'

The Colonel paused and looked round the room. He had everyone's attention.

'So, Dick, you and your 'B' Company will leave the barracks via the East Gate on North Barracks Road at precisely 0130 hours. You will be dropped off at the junction of Granville Road and Kingsdown Road. Your men will dig in and form a defensive screen along the beach to the east of the castle.

'Peter, your 'A' Company will leave the main guardroom on Canada Road. You will be dropped off at the junction of Liverpool Road and Saint Claire Road, then take up position to the west and north of the castle. It's mostly open grassland, so you shouldn't have too much of a problem. Your transport will leave at 0200 hours.'

Then, turning to the OC of 'X' Company, 'Simon, you and your marines will leave from the Cavalry Gates over in South Barracks at 0230 hours. You will be dropped off at the crossroads of Liverpool Road and Grams Road. Yours is a heavily wooded area, plus there are gardens and allotments, so take extra care. I want your men to form a screen to the south of the castle. I shall bring up the rear with HQ Company and, of course, the climbers.

'Now, to make this raid slightly more realistic, I have asked the Army to provide a number of sentries, to which they have agreed. So, remind your men that we are all on the same side because I don't want any serious injuries reported to me. Having said that, tying and gagging is perfectly acceptable.

'HQ Company will split into two groups. The Adjutant will take one group and secure the access to the main door. When this is done, Major Houghton's group will enter the moat and ensure that any wandering sentries are silenced. As soon as this is accomplished, the climbers will be able to drop into the moat. One team will go for the main tower whilst the other two will head for the gun platforms. Remind everyone that there may well be sentries on these platforms, and that they will need to be dealt with. Those climbing the main tower, once on top, will head for the small square tower and the flagpole, where they will hoist up the flag that I am having made up at the tailor's shop. It's nothing too pretentious, Corps colours diagonal on a blue background, with a large letter 'A' in the top right-hand corner.'

There was an immediate murmur of approval from everyone in the room.

'Send your climbers to me at 1400 hours this afternoon so that I can give them a detailed briefing.

'Company Commanders, there are motorcycles or bicycles available to you should you wish to carry out your own reconnaissance this afternoon. I leave that up to you. One last thing, I want all ranks issued with woollen cap comforters. If we are going to be commandos then we may as well look the part. Are there any questions?'

Silence descended on the room, each officer trying to come to terms with the CO's demands. They all knew that he was asking a lot at such short notice. Those who didn't know the Colonel might have said that he was more than a little mad to have even come up with such a scheme, let alone expect it to work. Now, it was up to each of them to do his very best to ensure that not only did the plan work, but that it exceeded even the Colonel's expectations.

Major Houghton raised his hand. 'How will we know when the raid is finished, sir?'

'Good point, thank you. I'd overlooked that.' He paused for a moment thinking quickly on his feet. 'I will fire a green flare. That will be your signal to withdraw in good order. Now, as I have already said, there will no transport, so I want everyone to march back to barracks in double time.'

Someone let out a quiet groan which the Colonel chose to ignore.

(ii)

At precisely 1355 hours on the day of the raid, Dacre and eleven other marines assembled for the CO's briefing. Only two marines had any free-climbing experience and he was one of them. The Colonel explained what was required of them and did his best to describe the condition of the walls.

Number Ten's Platoon Officer, Lieutenant Huntington Whiteley, knew immediately who to select for the task, and so Dacre was chosen to lead the assault on the North Bastion. He was allowed to choose his three climbing companions, so he picked Baz Phelps, Paul McNight and Dave Taylor from his platoon. He would have taken his mate Pete Wills, but he knew that Wills hated climbing and would probably be a liability. Meanwhile, the other two teams, led by the second climber Bob Ward from 'A' Company, would scale the smaller gun platforms. It all sounded so simple really, what could possibly go wrong?

By 0245 hours, all groups were in position and ready. The HQ group ran the short distance in almost complete silence. Making use of the cover available, they approached the main entrance. The night was dark and cold; large clouds were scudding across the sky, blocking out the full moon. It had rained earlier in the day, so the ground was damp, which helped deaden the sound of the marines' boots. A light wind was blowing in off the sea, and the smell and taste the salt was in the air.

There were two guards standing on the pathway which led to the main entrance. One of them had lit a cigarette which he had craftily cupped in his hand. The Adjutant's group took them completely by surprise, silenced them, tied and gagged them within seconds. The Major's men dropped quietly into the moat unobserved. Within minutes the wandering guards had been expertly disposed.

Now it was time for the climbers to play their part. Dropping into the moat, Dacre led his group to the foot of the North Bastion Tower, while Bob Ward led his group round to the gun platforms. Dacre attached a rope to his waist belt and slung his rifle sling across his shoulder. Then, reaching up with both hands, he began to climb. He quickly realised that this was not going to be easy because the stonework was set very closely together and had been well mortared. There were very few handholds and almost nothing to support his feet, except the occasional edge. Reminding himself that a climber generally prefers three points of contact at any one time, he realised that this was going to be even more difficult than he had first thought. He hadn't climbed more than twelve feet, when he slipped and fell. Like a cat, he landed on all fours, rolled to one side and back onto his feet in one fluid movement. Unhurt, he brushed himself down, much to the relief of his mates. Fuck, he thought, this was going to be a bit of a bugger. He tried again. This time, he was only about eight feet from the ground when he slipped again and fell. He picked himself up. Double fuck, he thought. His mates gathered around, concerned that if he got much higher and then fell, he might well do himself some real injury. Dacre sat down on the ground. He had one last trick up his sleeve. He removed his boots and then his socks. He would climb in his bare feet.

'Is this a good idea, AJ?' one of his mates whispered.

'No, it's not, but unless you have another idea…?'

Fifteen minutes later, he reached the top of tower and the battlements. The sweat was pouring off him and his heart was pounding like hell. The knuckles of his hands, though well calloused, were raw and bleeding; the hand holds had been few and far between. His feet, especially his big toes, hurt like blazes. He thought that he might have torn off a toenail or two. He had needed all his mountaineering skills to make the climb. Cautiously, he peered over the top of the battlements. Fortunately, there were no guards that he could see. Securing the rope, Dacre gave it two definite tugs. Within minutes he was joined by the other marines, all breathing heavily, the adrenalin coursing through their veins. He replaced his socks, winced from his painful toes (thankfully the nails were still in place) then put on his boots. He was good to go. Keeping close to the cold damp walls, the little group moved off.

As they approached the flagpole, a small door in the square tower, until then unnoticed, opened and out stepped a guard. The marines stopped suddenly in mid-step, almost like some bizarre ritual. Dacre pointed to the soldier who, by chance, had his back to them. Two of the marines moved silently forward, step by step, as if in slow motion. The first and last thing the sentry remembered was a large hand clamped over his mouth. He felt himself picked up, as if by an unknown force, and dumped down heavily onto the wooden walkway beneath his feet. A knee on his chest drove out all the air from his lungs. A piece of cloth was then stuffed into his mouth as a gag. His hands and feet were quickly and expertly tied. Checking that there were no more surprises, one of the marines produced the unit flag from his pocket. He attached it to the flagpole halyard and hoisted the ensign. The pulley squeaked all the way to the top, making enough noise to wake the dead. Glancing over the battlements the marines could see the gun platforms below. At that moment the clouds parted briefly allowing the full moon to shine through. The scene below was as clear as day. Several guards were lying trussed up neatly where they had fallen. Bob Ward and his men were in the process of leaving, rappelling down to the ground on half a dozen ropes. Some comedian had written between the old cannons in large chalk letters, *RM CDO waz ere*.

Back on the ground, the Colonel, checking his wristwatch, was finally satisfied that he had counted all the men back in. He pulled out his Very pistol, pointed it skywards and fired the green flare. The time was 0330 hours.

An hour later the whole unit was back in barracks, showered, changed and ready for an early breakfast. Colonel Picton-Phillipps was delighted with the way the raid had gone. Deep down, he knew that he had taken a risk, yet he had been proved right. His men had performed so well that he knew he had been justified. However, not so pleased were many of the residents of Walmer. Their night's sleep had been disturbed in the early hours by the sound of hundreds of boots pounding through the streets.

Not surprisingly, many of the menfolk awoke and cursed. What the hell is going on? Lights were switched on as they leapt from their beds and cautiously went to the windows. Perhaps the threatened invasion had begun. Then, ignoring the blackout regulations, they peered out of their windows, only to find that the streets were completely deserted.

(iii)

After breakfast that morning, Dacre reported to the sick bay to have the injuries to his feet seen to. Thankfully, it was nothing too serious. His toenails were still in place, which was a great relief. Feet bandaged and with a few pain killers, he was put on light duties for a couple of days, which was no bad thing, except that it meant he couldn't take part in any further training for a while.

At the end of the week the Colonel sent for him in order to express his thanks for a job well done. Major Houghton had already made it clear to the Colonel that the success of raising the flag was largely down to this single marine and his ability to climb.

'You mark my words, sir, that young man has the potential to go far in the Corps, if I am any judge of character. We need to keep a close eye on him.'

Sometime later, when the Colonel had a chance to look at Dacre's file and reflect on what the second-in-command had said, he was sure the Major was correct in his assessment of this most remarkable marine. Men like this didn't come along very often, even in a Corps that prided itself on being the best of the best.

CHAPTER 13

The oak door to Room 37 in the main house at Bletchley Park was closed. A piece of paper had been pinned to the door. In handwritten letters it said, 'CONFERENCE IN PROGRESS'. The room was large, light and airy, and overlooked the driveway and the lawn to the front of the house. The lake was clearly visible, as were the numerous huts scattered around in the grounds. The room had been beautifully panelled and there was a coal fire burning in the grate. The room was thick with smoke from the numerous cigarettes that had been lit. Behind his desk sat Commander Edward Travis RN, once the Deputy Director of Bletchley Park, now the Director. He had recently replaced Commander Denniston, who had been moved to London, to run the diplomatic and commercial side of codebreaking. Denniston was an excellent codebreaker but had found leadership and the administration side of things difficult. Edward Travis was a very different kettle of fish. He had something of the 'British bulldog' about him. Yes, he liked things done his way, but he had a great feeling for the job. He got to know people, visited all the huts regularly, and showed a personal interest in the work of individuals. He had the gift of the human touch, and was good at organisation and administration, something his predecessor had not been. Also, in the room, and seated in the semi-circle in front of the desk, was the Head of MI6, General Sir Stewart Menzies. Next to him sat Alan Turing, the Head of Hut 8, then Commander Fleming from Naval Intelligence. Then, finally, Frank Birch the Head of the German Team of the Naval Section at the Park.

There was tension in the room, largely because Travis and Menzies did not see eye to eye. They were poles apart in their thinking, especially on how the Park should be managed. Menzies was an Army man, a World

War I hero and 'old school'. Service rivalries die hard. Despite his very best efforts, the Director could not get the General to see his point of view. They had already exchanged sharp words, much to the embarrassment of the others. Frank Birch had tried desperately to pour oil onto troubled waters but without much success. Menzies would have none of it. He had the bit firmly between his teeth and had gone for broke.

'I do not understand what the problems are,' he said belligerently. 'Here we are faced with the nightmare situation of our vital supplies in ships sailing from Canada and the USA without any meaningful protection from these bloody U-boats. All you can tell me is that you don't need a four-wheeled Enigma machine, but you do need these books and tables to break the codes. Have I got that right?'

Travis tried to control his growing sense of unease. Whilst he was a patient man most of the time, he did not suffer fools gladly. Was this man from MI6 being deliberately obtuse, he wondered. Taking a deep breath to try and calm his nerves, he replied as honestly as his temper would allow.

'Yes, sir, that is correct.' Then, through clenched teeth, he said, 'May I continue?' Menzies shrugged his shoulders. Travis took this as a yes.

'It's all quite simple really. The U-boats operate a system of communications that those of us at Bletchley Park know as *Shark*. There is a complete blackout on all their coded messages. The German surface vessels, however, use a different system which we call *Dolphin*. We can, and are, decoding all their messages without too much trouble. Let me give you an example. In March this year, the German pocket battleship *Tirpitz* was stalking an Arctic convoy, bound for Russia. It posed a real threat. However, thanks to our almost instantaneous decrypting of the code, we were able to immediately advise the Admiralty, with the result that the convoy was able to take successful evasive action.'

'Yes, thank you,' replied Menzies with just a hint of sarcasm in his voice. 'I believe I can understand that, but I had the impression that with your so-called bombe machines most of the decoding problems were at an end.'

Travis let out a long sigh of exasperation.

'No, sir! The bombe machines do not do the decryptions. What they do is key finding: that is to say, they look for the key to a particular network. Once that has been established, then work can start on the decryption. The key finding needs to be done every day.'

Frank Birch chose that moment to interrupt.

'Perhaps, General, you might be interested to hear what Mr Turing has to say on this matter. Remember, it has been largely down to him and his team that we have already been able to do so much.'

The Head of MI6 reluctantly nodded his head in agreement.

'Alan, over to you.'

Turing was considered by some of his colleagues to be something of an eccentric. He had been a former don at Cambridge and, as a keen cyclist, was often seen riding his ancient bicycle around the local countryside with his gas mask on, trying to resolve his hay-fever problem. He was also a very shy man, with a high-pitched laugh. His friends and colleagues referred to him as 'the Prof'. He hesitated before speaking, trying to marshal his thoughts. He was, truth be told, terrified of this man from MI6. Plucking up all his courage, he nervously began.

'I have always thought that for any mathematical problem a human could solve, a machine could do it as well, if not better. The first machine we built was a bit of, what I call, a 'lash-up'. I won't bore you with the details but, as crude as it was, it worked. You see any combination of numbers thrown up by an Enigma machine could, I believed, be decrypted by another machine. Of course our system needed a bit of a push start in the form of a crib - that is to say, a series of words or a phrase guessed at and offered up to our machine. In other words, it required someone to feed it the necessary information.'

Turing paused for effect. Travis nodded encouragingly for him to continue.

'Because the Germans had developed new ways of encrypting, we had to find new methods of breaking their codes. Essentially these cribs or guesses were nothing more than us trying to understand bits of messages, followed by testing them out on the bombe machine. Incidentally, the bombe machine is really just like a giant calculating device. It can process every possible combination of numbers used by the three-wheeled Enigma that all the German military use, with the exception of their submarines.'

'Not their U-boats?' said Menzies.

'No sir, not their U-boats.'

Turing looked directly at the Head of MI6, making eye contact for the first time. He expected another question. There was none, so he assumed he should continue.

'A later development by a colleague of mine, Gordon Welchman, greatly improved the electro-mechanical device. He did this by adding a series of circuits known as a 'diagonal board'. This electrical circuitry allowed for an almost instantaneous flow of electricity into the bombe machine. I have to say that it was a spectacular improvement of uncanny elegance. After this, more and more machines were built. Altogether, we now have about sixteen. Each one requires its own operator, most of whom are WRNS.'

Menzies looked up sharply and asked abruptly, 'Why women?'

'That's because, sir, the nature of the work requires considerable concentration and focus. Accuracy is extremely important. Women tend to have more nimble fingers and are, therefore, more dexterous.'

Menzies seemed satisfied. Turing assumed he should again continue.

'There are further things that I would like to add, if I may. I don't think you appreciate the complexity of the problems that we face here at Bletchley Park. The Germans have thousands of these Enigma machines in operation: every army headquarters has one, every Luftwaffe base, every warship and every submarine. Then, there are the railway stations plus every SS Brigade and Gestapo Headquarters. You might wonder how we know all this. Well, prior to sending an Enigma message, each call sign identifies itself in 'clear', that is, not in code. Why? We do not know. My colleague Gordon has been carefully plotting these so that we know for sure where each one is located. You see, never has one nation depended on a single device for its secret communications. Now, here at the Park, we are very good at what we do. Dozens of German Army and Luftwaffe messages are decoded every day. Each branch of their military uses a subtly different version of the Enigma system. However, the Kriegsmarine is a different proposition. Their system is more complex, with extra wheels, more disciplined, and with stricter settings. The *Dolphin* codes are difficult to break because they use bigram tables. But we did it.'

The General interrupted. 'Just what is a bigram table?'

'Bigram tables set out the substitutions for the pairs of letters used by the three-wheeled Enigma machine. They are vital to our ability to break the codes and to read the messages. However, to break *Shark* we desperately need the up-to-date short signal codebooks and tables. You must remember that *Shark* is the pride and joy of the German Navy. Also, the Germans are not fools. It doesn't matter how many machines you capture, they are useless unless we know the starting order of the rotas or the plug-in boards, and for that we need up-to-date codebooks. Its sheer genius, of course, lies in the enormous number of different permutations that an Enigma machine can offer.'

Menzies looked confused. For a second or two Turing felt some sympathy for the General, the war hero. He was clearly out of his depth, struggling to understand what the hell these boffins were on about, but he wouldn't admit that to anyone, not even himself. Whether it was pride, or vanity, or perhaps some other reason, no-one knew. Instead, he continued to bluster on, to make a nuisance of himself by questioning and challenging everything set before him. Turing looked at the General carefully. Suddenly, in the short space of time that they had been in the room, Menzies seemed to have aged. He looked tired, less fearsome and somehow less threatening.

'Let me see if I can explain, sir,' he said gently. The Germans are using a machine with five wheels. At the moment they are using only three of these wheels so that two are kept as spares. With these three wheels there are just six possible orders that they can be put in. However, if they were to increase the number of wheels to eight, for example, that would give you a possible three hundred and thirty-three combinations. The number of possibilities increases greatly with the addition of only a few extra wheels.'

Turing paused to allow Menzies to absorb what he had said. The General leant forward, staring at the Head of Hut 8 intensely.

'You see, each wheel has the letters of the alphabet fitted to it, on a free rotating tyre. When the three wheels are fully loaded into the machine and each wheel is set to a different letter, that would give you approximately seventeen thousand possible settings. Or, to put it another way, you would need to turn the wheels seventeen thousand times, or so, before they came back to their original settings. To scramble the letters even further, some Enigma machines have a Steckerbrett, or plug board, attached to them. These have ten double ended jacks or Stecker plugs. So, together with the normal wheel settings, this gives the Enigma operator possible settings of about one hundred and forty million, million combinations, give or take a few.

The room was absolutely silent, so much so that you could have heard a pin drop. Everyone was contemplating the implications of what Alan Turing had just said. Frank Birch chose that moment to speak.

'You see, sir, we believe that the Germans assumed we would use people to try and break their codes. Had we done that, it would have taken us so long that the information we gained would have been out of date and, therefore, useless. What they do not know, and could not possibly have guessed, is that we have been using the same machines, together with a small army of mathematicians, engineers and filing clerks. But, as successful as we have been, *Shark* has defied everyone's efforts. We have even tried out some pretty daft ideas to see if we can break the code. For example, we recently got the RAF to drop some mines outside a known harbour. An hour or so later, the efficient harbour master sent out a message using that day's settings to warn shipping. The signal was picked up and flashed to Hut 8 in the hope that it might give us a clue, or crib as we call it. Unfortunately, it just doesn't work for *Shark*.

'So, sir, as I hope you now appreciate, we are desperate for the appropriate codebooks. If you and Naval Intelligence could find a month's key bigram and short signal codebooks, or perhaps even steal them, then we shall be able to get on with the business of cracking the U-boats' codes.'

Commander Fleming looked up from his notebook at the mention of Naval Intelligence. Now that, he thought, is a very interesting idea. It seemed to him that the important question that should be asked was not 'Can you steal the codebooks?' but 'How, and from where, would you steal them?' He would have to give it some thought. There must be an answer somewhere, he reasoned. If he could only find it, that might be a feather in his cap.

PART THREE

COMMANDO

toughness, self-discipline,
intelligence, unorthodox,
intrepid, fighting spirit,
state of mind

CHAPTER 14

(i)

At the end of March, two hundred and fifty officers and men of the Royal Marines 'A' Commando boarded a special troop train laid on by the Southern Railway Company. They were en route for Glenborrowdale in Scotland. By rights, the unit should have gone directly to the Commando Basic Training Centre at Achnacarry. However, Colonel Picton-Phillipps was an independent sort of an officer and decided that his men needed further training before they took on the notorious commando course. Failure to pass the course was not an option that he wanted to consider for his unit.

The train took them to London Victoria Station, where the unit was moved by Army trucks to St Pancras Station in order to catch an overnight London Midland Scotland train to Glasgow Central. It was a long and slow journey north through dark countryside and blacked out towns, where not a single light could be seen. The pre-war journey time would have been only about six and half hours, particularly if the train pulling had been the *Coronation Scot*. However, what with wartime restrictions, the journey time was almost doubled. Most of the marines took the opportunity to get their heads down for some well-earned sleep; the gentle rocking of the carriages together with the soft blue ceiling lights worked their own kind if magic.

In the early hours of the following morning, the LMS train steamed slowly into Glasgow Central Station and, with much shuddering and clanking, came to a halt. Dacre glanced at his watch. Bloody hell, he thought, it's only 0445 hours. It's still the middle of the sodding night. The station was virtually deserted, and a cold wind was sweeping along the platform, creating small eddies of dust and dirt, and tossing the odd discarded newspaper along the ground. The marines stepped down stiffly onto the platform, dragging their kit and equipment with them, and began to sort themselves out. Nearby, Colonel Picton-Phillipps seemed to be in a foul mood, largely because the transport that he had arranged had not arrived. Major Houghton was trying to placate him, but without much success.

'It's not your fault, sir. Besides which, we can easily march the men up to Queen Street Station from here. They can carry their kit bags easily enough. It will only take us about fifteen minutes, if that.'

Somewhat mollified, the Colonel agreed.

The unit was quickly formed, rifles slung and kit bags hoisted onto shoulders. They marched smartly out of the station, up Union Street, right past the Stock Exchange and left into George Square, continuing uphill to the station. The sound of their studded boots striking the cobblestones in unison echoed off the walls of the nearby buildings. Dawn was just beginning to break as the marines marched directly onto platform nine.

The engine was standing quietly, smoke and steam gently escaping into the high canopy above, as if it was fortifying itself for the long effort that lay ahead. Rather surprisingly, this troop train was made up of only third-class carriages with their hard seats. Undeterred, the marines clambered aboard, stowed their kit and equipment, and began to make themselves as comfortable as they could. Shortly after, with a piercing whistle and much steam, the train jolted its way out of the station, clattering over numerous points as it headed north. As they passed through the suburbs of Clydebank and Dumbarton, and along the northern shore of the River Clyde, it was just possible to make out recent bomb damage, where Hitler's Luftwaffe had attempted to hit the Clydeside docks of Port Glasgow and Greenock.

As the engine began to haul its carriages up into the Highlands, Dacre and his mates, along with the rest of the unit, began to relax, despite the overcrowded and cramped railway carriages. They were heading for Dorlin, on the shores of Kentra Bay. They spent most of their time playing cards, smoking or sleeping. If they wanted exercise, they could walk up and down the narrow corridor. Where a corridor didn't exist and the marines wanted to join other colleagues, they simply opened a carriage door and walked along the running board, hanging onto the side of the train. Thankfully, none of the officers or SNCOs witnessed this flagrant breach of 'railway regulations'. Had they been spotted, those involved would have been for the high jump, maybe even RTU'd. However, Dacre suspected that whilst the CO would never condone such behaviour, he might secretly applaud their bravado.

Few of those on board noticed the magnificent scenery as the train steamed alongside the top part of Loch Lomond. Dacre took it in. This was his first time in Scotland. As he looked out of the train's window, all he could see through the early morning mist were mountains and moorlands. Then suddenly the sun broke through, just for a moment, to reveal the Highlands in all their glory. It took his breath away.

From the junction at Crianlarich, high up in Glen Falloch, the single-track split into two. To the west the line headed for Dalmally and Oban on the coast, but the troop train continued climbing steadily north through scenery that became wilder and more forbidding.

They passed Tyndrum and the Bridge of Orchy in a cloud of steam and smoke, as the train struggled up the steep gradient. At last they crossed the bleak Rannoch Moor, passed Loch Treig and then descended into Glen Spean. The train swept through a small station without stopping, its name indistinct in the gloomy weather. It was raining heavily, the water pouring down the carriage windows like mini waterfalls. At last they arrived at Fort William where there was a thirty-minute delay, caused by the train being shunted into a siding in order to allow the engine to move from the front of the train to the rear. Eventually a green flag was waved and the signals set, so that the troop train could slowly move forward over the Caledonian Canal, then alongside Loch Eil. They were now heading west towards the port of Mallaig.

At the small station at Glenfinnan, the train shuddered to a halt. The cry of 'Out troops. Out troops,' by the station staff could be clearly heard. Somewhat surprised, the marines grabbed their equipment and stumbled out, onto the narrow platform. The junior officers and NCOs quickly sorted them into their companies. Then they marched the short distance to the edge of Loch Shiel. To their amazement, lined up along the sandy beach were half a dozen landing craft manned by sailors of the Royal Navy. As it turned out, this was the main way to reach the peninsula which was their destination. All goods, stores, weapons, ammunition and personnel had to be transported down the loch. The trip took nearly two hours. It was painfully slow, with the wind and rain blowing into their faces. Everyone was soaked to the skin and a good number of the marines were seasick.

One of the sailors helming the boat turned to his mate, 'Just look at those poor buggers. Royal doesn't know what he's in for. I've been here four weeks and it hasn't stopped raining once.'

Lieutenant Colonel Picton-Phillipps had chosen Dorlin or, more correctly, *HMS Dorlin,* situated on the shores of Kentra Bay, quite deliberately. Originally the camp had been established by the Scottish Army Command back in 1940 for special military training. They had taken over the empty and somewhat dilapidated Jacobean House which they used as an officers' mess and lecture rooms. The camp had been set up in the grounds, using Nissen huts and tents. Recently, it had been taken over by the Admiralty as Number Three Combined Training Centre, along with numerous other out-stations in the area. This whole part of the west coast had become a 'protected area', with checkpoints on all access roads and ferry ports. *HMS Dorlin* specialised in commando training that particularly made use of small boats and landing craft, which was just what the Colonel wanted for his marines.

(ii)

The unit's stay at Dorlin was short and sweet. For the ten days they were there, it rained every day.

The marines were allocated the tented encampment and, within minutes of having arrived, every piece of equipment and clothing had been soaked right through. The HO marines, McKnight, Whitnell and Kelly, constantly complained as if it was the end of the world. Dacre began to get fed up with their continual moaning, as had the other two long-service marines, Dave Taylor and Baz Phelps.

'For goodness sake, lads, give it a rest, will you?' said Dacre one evening. 'You're wet and you're going to stay wet, so I suggest that you get bloody used to it.'

At that moment the flap of their tent opened and in stepped their platoon SNCO, Sergeant Ernest Throttles, and a young officer. Rainwater dripped off their waterproof capes onto the deck boards that made up the floor of the tent.

'Everything alright in here?' Thrattles asked jovially.

'Yes, Sergeant,' they all chorused back in reply.

'Good! I don't want to hear any grumbling about a little bit of rain. I know a marine is never happy unless he has something to 'drip' about, but I don't want to hear it. Is that understood?'

'Yes, Sergeant,' they answered in unison.

'Now then, listen up you lot of shirkers. This young gentleman with me is Second Lieutenant Graham Ellis. For the time being, he will be working with our Platoon Officer, Huntington-Whiteley, until he gets the hang of how a platoon operates. So give him your full support will you?' The sergeant looked around the tent approvingly.

'This lot, sir, are probably the best section of men in the whole of 'X' Company, maybe even the whole unit. They are tough, fit and reliable, although perhaps a little irresponsible at times, if you know what I mean, particularly when travelling on trains.'

The Lieutenant gave a shy smile to show that he understood. He really didn't have a clue what the older man was talking about, but he wasn't going to admit it.

The sergeant continued, 'Alright then, lads, get yourselves over to the mess tent for a hot meal, then parade at 1800 hours, full equipment and weapons. Tonight, the whole unit will be going on night manoeuvres, courtesy of the CO. Don't be late!'

With that, the Sergeant and the young officer were gone.

The days passed quickly and, although the weather did not improve, most of the marines enjoyed the challenges that they faced. Their levels of fitness continued to exceed even the CO's expectations. Speed marches, live firing exercises, rock climbing, map and compass work, the assault courses and, using the variety of small boats and landing craft, all blended into one mass of activity, albeit day or night. Most of the training was carried out at either platoon or company level. The competitive spirit was extremely high; each body of men trying to outdo the others.

One morning, the platoon had been practising beach landings. The cry from the helmsman of 'down ramp, out troops' had become second nature to them. Wet landings, when the water came to a person's chest, or the occasional dry landing straight onto a beach, was an everyday occurrence. On this particular day, the sun was actually out. By mistake, the helmsman had put into the wrong beach. As soon as the ramp was down, thirty Royal Marines, fully armed to the teeth and with blackened faces, stormed up the beach, screaming like wild banshees, only to find a walking party of civilians sitting quietly enjoying the scenery, having their morning break. As per their training, the marines charged up the beach scattering the civilians, their vacuum flasks and sandwiches flying everywhere. Throwing themselves down onto the soft sand, they began to dig shell scrapes. Dacre found himself lying next to a very attractive young woman with long red hair and the most amazing legs he had ever seen. In one hand she delicately held a cup of tea and, in the other, a slice of cake. He looked up at her startled face; she looked down at his sweaty, blackened face. She smiled, and without saying a word offered him the cup. At that moment it was the most magnificent cup of tea he had ever tasted. How this walking party ever got into the restricted zone, no-one ever found out.

One evening after supper, Dacre and his mates were busy cleaning their weapons and kit. Surprisingly, the need for a bit of 'spit and polish' was still required, though not to the extent that the marines were used to, as the Colonel took the view that a man who could keep his equipment clean would also be able to keep his body and mind tidy and alert.

'What do you think Achnacarry will be like?' asked Pete Wills, as he struggled with the pull-through, stuck in the barrel of his rifle.

Dacre thought for a moment or two. Because of his experiences at Dunkirk and in London, the group tended to look on the youngster as the natural leader of their little band of brothers. Truth be told, this was not something he was too keen on.

'Well, I think it will be a lot tougher and harsher than the last ten days, that's for starters. I imagine it will be a bit like our recruit training days. The instructors will know the rules and we won't. Perhaps we should look on it like a game, them versus us. In order to survive we will have to learn the rules as quickly as we can. Once we've done that, then we can try and beat them at their own game. I imagine that, like our instructors at Deal, they will want us to pass the commando course, but will not hesitate to fail us if we do not come up to scratch. For what it is worth, that's how I see it working out.'

Baz Phelps chipped in with another question. 'So, AJ, what makes you so sure that this is how it will work?'

'I'm not sure at all, but that is how I am going to approach Achnacarry. It's up to each of you to decide how you want to take on the challenges ahead. If you really want to be a commando then you need to get this sorted out in your own mind, because for me it will be a question of mind over matter. If you just remember that it is only a state of mind, you should be alright.'

He didn't feel that he had anything else to add, so he went back to cleaning his rifle. They could either accept his ideas, if they wished, or they could do their own thing. He didn't mind which. It was their choice. The other marines all looked at each other. One or two shrugged their shoulders. Deep down they all knew that the youngster was probably right.

Mac McKnight plucked up the courage to say aloud what everyone else was thinking.

'We will be there for each other, won't we AJ? You know, when things get really tough.'

Dacre looked across the tent at his friend. Although they were both the same age, nineteen, Mac looked up to the full-time marine both as mentor and guide, and, interestingly, so did the others.

'Of course, we will. We are Royal Marines, aren't we? What do they say: 'One for all and all for one'? Well, that's us and make no mistake about it. We will do this together or not at all. Just remember the old saying, *Do or die, Royal, do or die.*'

'*Do or die, Royal?* What the fucking hell does that mean?' asked Pete Wills. He had a look of horror and confusion on his face.

'Don't you worry about it,' replied Mac, 'just do what AJ says and you'll be fine.'

(iii)

The following morning Dacre was sent for by the unit second-in-command, Major 'Titch' Houghton. When he arrived at the officer's tent, he was surprised to find both his platoon sergeant and officer present, together with the young officer. The marine entered the billet and saluted.

'Ah, Dacre, come in and sit down, old chap'. The major pointed to a nearby canvas stool. 'Take off your cap comforter if you wish.'

This was all most irregular, thought the marine, just what the hell was it all about? The major continued, 'I, or rather we, have a little job for you.'

Dacre tried not to look surprised. He just gave a quick nod.

'What we want you to do is assemble a small, hand-picked team of men to carry out a night raid. Your objective will be to capture an 'enemy communications expert' without being discovered. You may choose who you want for this exercise, with the exception that Mr Ellis, here, will accompany you. To all intents and purposes, you are to treat him as another marine. Is that clear?'

Dacre was totally bewildered but managed to reply, 'Yes, sir.'

'Good. Do you have any questions?'

Of course he had questions. Why him? Why not an NCO? Why include the young officer? Why wasn't he in charge? Dacre looked the Major in the eye.

'No, sir. No questions,' he replied.

'Very good, then. The Sergeant will give you a full briefing after we have finished here.'

Dacre replaced his headgear, saluted and left the tent. He was thoroughly perplexed.

As soon as the marine was out of earshot, the Major looked at the Sergeant who was hovering nearby.

'Well, Sergeant Thrattles, will he do?'

The SNCO thought for a moment or two before answering, not that he had any doubts about the young marine's capabilities.

'He will do fine, sir. I've had my eye on him for some time, particularly after the raid on Walmer Castle. He has all the right qualities we are looking for. His King's Badge and his performance at Dunkirk would seem to make him an ideal candidate for promotion, Although, why he hasn't been promoted already is something of a mystery to me. The other men in his section already look to him as their natural leader.'

The Major began to tap his teeth with his pencil, with a thoughtful expression on his face.

'Yes, I agree, that is strange. I thought as much when I first interviewed him. There must be some reason, but I haven't worked it out yet. Anyway, better not let on how the others see him just yet. Let's keep that up our sleeves, shall we? By the way, did you know that he is fluent in several languages, including German?'

'No, sir, I can't say that I did. But to tell you the truth, I'm not surprised. He's a bit of a dark horse and that's a fact.'

'Anyway, give him a full briefing and then we'll see just what he can do.'

'Yes, sir.'

Two hours later, Dacre was sitting in his tent, surrounded by his mates. Also present was Lieutenant Ellis, who looked more than a little self-conscious. The other marines had welcomed him into their group without another thought. None of them was surprised that Dacre had been selected for this task. His natural ability to command, his experiences in France and his very physical presence ensured their loyalty. He cleared his throat.

'Right then! We've been chosen to carry out a raid on a highly 'secret' enemy radio transmitting station. It is located about six miles from here on the edge of a wood. It is well camouflaged and guarded twenty-four hours a day. Our mission is to capture the technical expert, plus his machine and cyphers, and then to destroy the building.

'We'll be dropped off by vehicle about one mile from our target. The lorry will not stop, so be prepared to bail out. We will speed march the first half-a-mile in single file. I shall lead. We will then crawl the next five hundred yards on our hands and knees, and then on our stomachs for the last leg. Everything will be done in complete silence, so no rattling of equipment, or coins, or anything else. Check each other over and remember the 'jump test'.'

Pete Wills, the former safe breaker, looked somewhat puzzled and asked, 'What the hell is that when it's at home?'

Dacre was about to reply when Lieutenant Ellis interrupted. 'May I?'

The Marine gave him an encouraging smile. 'Be my guest, sir,' he replied.

'Jump up and down in front of each other. If you have anything loose in your pockets or in your equipment it will rattle. Then you can sort it out and not endanger the mission. In real time this could mean the difference between the life and death of your mates.'

The group went really quiet. Everyone knew, of course, that this was just an exercise. Nevertheless, the young officer's words had struck a real chord with all of them. It had gently reminded them that they were training in the deadly art of death and destruction, and that was a very serious business.

Dacre gave a small chuckle. 'That was very well put, sir, I couldn't have expressed it better myself.'

Lieutenant Ellis flushed slightly with the praise from the marine. Then, for no apparent reason, he suddenly felt tears begin to well up. He hoped that no-one had noticed. No-one had, except for Dacre, and he chose to ignore it. The marine continued with his briefing.

'Look at this sketch map I have drawn.'

They all leant forward, eager to get a better view, knowing that their understanding of the details could make the difference between success and failure.

'Mac, I want you to be at position 'A'. Your task is to give covering fire should we need it. You should have a good field of fire from the woods across to the track. Steve, I have put you at position 'B'. I want you to cover the back door. If the Bren starts firing, then make sure you keep your head down. Burt, Pete, Baz and Dave, you four will deal with the sentries at point 'C'. I'll leave you to work out the best way to do that. Once you have completed your task, you are to move back to Steve's position to provide additional cover. Be ready to move out instantly. That just leaves you and me, sir, here at Position 'D'. Our job is to snatch the boffin and his equipment, then to carry out the demolitions. Any questions so far?'

No-one answered. Everyone was trying to imagine the part that they had to play in this mini scheme of things. The Lieutenant sat there, impressed that this young marine had managed to put together such a detailed plan, yet had made it all sound so simple. None of his officers' training had prepared him for this.

Dacre continued. 'There will be a full moon tonight and no cloud cover, so use plenty of 'cam' cream on your hands and faces. Only Mac and Steve will carry weapons. Make sure you both draw sufficient ammunition. If you have to engage the enemy, make bloody sure you aim high. We don't want any casualties. The same goes for the rest of you. Go in hard by all means, but remember that this is an exercise, so no broken bones please. Dress of the day, or rather the night, will be normal combat clothing and light order, so no equipment. Scrounge some pickaxe handles from the rest of the Company - that will have to do.' Someone let out a groan. Dacre smiled to himself but chose to ignore the comment. At least it showed that his mates were really up for this exercise.

'There will be a hot meal for you at 1800 hours. At 1900 there will be a final chance for you to practise your snatches and attacks. At 2100 hours the transport will take us to our drop-off point. It will drive without lights. Make sure you practise your rolling techniques. Remember, the vehicle will not be stopping. We should be at our start point ETA 2130 hours. Then, say, ten minutes to speed march the mile, another fifteen minutes to crawl the first two hundred and fifty yards, and another fifteen minutes for the last leg. An additional ten minutes to carry out the attack and the snatch. That should take us to about 2220 hours. If all goes well, we should be safely picked up at the agreed RV and back here by 2300 hours, give or take ten minutes or so. We shall leave as we went in, but in reverse order. Hot chocolate and sandwiches will be available on your return. One last thing: somewhere in the vicinity of our little operation will be Major Houghton and our Sergeant-Major. They will be acting as umpires. There may well be other interested parties present, such as the CO and our own Company Commander. Whatever you do, make sure you leave them all well alone. Any last questions?'

Burt Kelly raised his hand.

'What about communications? Are we taking radios?'

'No, we're not. They are bulky and heavy and will slow us down. Besides, let's be honest, they rarely work properly. This is supposed to be a 'lightning' raid - in, do the business and out again. No messing about.'

Baz put up a finger.

'What are you going to use for explosives, AJ?'

'Mr Ellis and I will have several thunder flashes. That should leave a lasting impression.'

Everyone went very quiet.

'Okay, that's it, let's get moving!'

The raid went as well as Dacre's planning had allowed, with the exception of two things. Firstly, on bailing out of the lorry, Steve Whitnell landed on a large stone and managed to turn his ankle. This was not a major setback but, despite his protestations, it did mean that he had to be left behind at the RV point, so that their 'back-door' would now be wide open. Dacre hoped it wouldn't be a problem. It was a risk certainly but one that he was prepared to take. The second problem, although humorous, contributed to the whole exercise being delayed for nearly half-an-hour.

The speed march had gone well and on time, as had the first crawl of five hundred yards. However, when the group entered the drainage ditch for the last part of the approach, they found it was full of weeds and sludge. Undaunted by this, they inched their way slowly forward until they came to the small footpath that led to the transmitting station. Suddenly they heard voices just in front of them. Dacre, who was bringing up the rear with Lieutenant Ellis, couldn't believe this. The two umpires were standing right above the group looking up and down the track.

'Where the bloody hell are they?' asked Major Houghton in a stage whisper.

'Damned if I know, sir,' replied the Sergeant Major. 'They should be here by now.' Then, to make matters even worse, Lieutenant Ellis, who was 'tail-end-Charlie', suddenly got a fit of the giggles. To be fair, this was largely caused by the ridiculousness of the situation together with his inexperience, although it was not unheard of. Ellis bit down hard on his battle-dress jacket to try and stifle his laughter, which he only just managed to do, despite getting a mouth full of mud and weed which made the situation even worse. All he wanted to do was to just burst out laughing. However, his whole body shook silently, causing tiny ripples of water that moved slowly towards the other marines, who were doing their best to remain silent. Dacre, realising immediately what was happening, pushed back with his boots as a warning, unknowingly to find the officer's face and, in particular, his nose, which he managed to squash with the heel of his boot. Of course, that sort of insane silliness can be highly infectious. Dacre knew that the whole mission would be in danger of becoming a farce if the situation continued unchecked. What to do was the problem. Thankfully, the two umpires decided to retreat to their allocated positions in the nearby woods, so consequently heard absolutely nothing.

The disaster averted, the group got themselves together and moved forward as planned. The sentries were disposed of, ruthlessly and efficiently. They would probably have headaches in the morning but nothing worse. Now it was Dacre's and Lieutenant Ellis' turn. Rising from the ditch like two phantoms or monsters from the deep, mud, water and weed falling from their shivering bodies, they moved silently into the woods and towards the hidden building. The door was slightly ajar. The communications expert was seated in a chair with his back to them. The room was in shadow, with the exception of a small table lamp that lit up the equipment on his table. He was listening to some intermittent and crackly dance music on what might have been the BBC's Light Programme. The whole scene seemed to be completely incongruous.

Moving silently and amazingly quickly for his size, Dacre slipped into the room. He clamped a large hand over the radio operator's mouth and lifted him bodily backwards out of his chair. Seizing the opportunity, the officer hit the man with a sudden sharp blow to his stomach. If the marine had not been holding him, the operator would certainly have collapsed on the floor. He was completely winded and hurt - oh how he hurt. Quickly, they bound and gagged him. Then, leaving the explosives on a very short fuse, they beat a hasty but tactical withdrawal. Meeting up with the others, they all doubled silently back along the track to the RV point where Mac was waiting, dragging their prisoner with them. Climbing aboard the lorry, Dacre took the opportunity to check his watch. They were exactly half-an-hour adrift. In the darkness he couldn't see the faces of his mates because of the camouflage cream they were still wearing, but he could see their white teeth in the moonlight. They were clearly all grinning at him.

'Mission accomplished,' he simply said. 'Now, let's get home.'

Together they let out a massive cheer.

The following day, the group was debriefed by Major Houghton. Thankfully, he was the first to admit that the umpires should have stayed in the woods. By not doing so, they had delayed the whole exercise by a good thirty minutes. Nothing was said about Lieutenant Ellis's corpsing, although, privately, he did apologise to the whole group.

'Think nothing of it, sir. It can happen to any one of us. It's a combination of tension and adrenalin. Just chalk it up as another experience and learn from it.'

Several hours later the second-in-command was bringing the CO up to date with the events of the previous night. The Colonel looked very pensive.

'It's all very well, Titch, making allowances for a training exercise, particularly when the umpires are at fault. However, when we get to Achnacarry things will have to be very different. Anyway, enough of that. How did that young marine perform? You seem to have taken a shine to him?'

'I have, sir. He did very well. The whole raid was methodically planned and well executed. I don't exaggerate when I say that a good many officers and SNCOs would be hard put to match his abilities. His comrades, and the young officer, were a great credit to him. I believe he has tremendous potential and I shall certainly be recommending him for promotion to corporal.'

Several days later, Colonel Picton-Phillipps mentioned to his second-in-command that he hadn't seen the young marine in his Orderly Room. Major Houghton was clearly embarrassed.

'To tell you the truth, sir, Marine Dacre has asked not to be promoted.'

The CO was naturally astounded.

'Not to be promoted!' he spluttered. 'I have never heard such nonsense. What's the matter with the man? Do you want me to see him? I will if it will help knock some sense into him. Whatever next?'

'Thank you, sir, but I don't think that will help. We know that he is more than capable, but he just insists that he would prefer to remain in the ranks. I feel that we ought not to force the issue. After all, we can't make someone take promotion, can we? So, with your agreement I propose that we leave him as he is?'

'I suppose you're right. But I tell you, Titch, I am not happy about this. In my experience it's unheard of, refusing to be promoted. What does his Company Commander say?'

'Like you, sir, he can't understand what's going on.'

'Well I'm not surprised. Damn the man for refusing. Just what the hell would happen if everybody turned down promotion? He could be setting a dangerous precedent, don't you think?'

'I think it's unlikely, sir.'

'Well let's hope not. I'll leave it up to you to sort out. Just keep me informed when he's changed his mind.'

Major Houghton had a nagging doubt. He wasn't certain that Marine Dacre would change his mind, but why was a complete mystery to him.

CHAPTER 15

(i)

The Commando Basic Training Centre at Achnacarry was located not far from Spean Bridge in the Highlands of Scotland. The camp sat on the banks of the River Arkaig in the heart of Lochaber, the historic seat of the Chief of Clan Cameron. The nearest railway station was seven miles away, and the nearest town, Fort William, was eighteen miles away. It was an ideal location for the rugged and realistic training needed to produce a commando. The Centre had become a byword for the most strenuous training anywhere, whilst the term 'commando trained' became a new military term with a clearly understood meaning. This highly intensive course lasted a full six weeks. Its single aim, and the very reason for its existence, was to produce the finest and fittest type of fighting soldier.

The Commanding Officer, Lieutenant Charles Edward Vaughan, ran a very tight camp. He was an Army man through and through. He had risen from the ranks, having been an RSM in the Guards. He knew every wrinkle and dodge that a soldier could possibly know. At first glance he seemed the most unsuitable person for this command, a real square peg in a round hole, yet he was remarkably successful in producing this new type of soldier, a highly trained commando who was required to think for himself.

As the train came to a halt, a porter could be heard calling out, 'Spe-e-e-an Bridge'. Immediately the carriage doors were thrown open as the marines, ignoring the platform nearest to them, leapt down directly onto the track. They shook themselves into some sort of order, whilst pulling on their equipment. In the background, amongst the smoke and steam, a kilted piper was marching up and down, playing a Scottish marching tune. Those who were observant would have noticed a small group of soldiers

standing at the far end of the platform. They looked extremely fit and weathered, and were wearing waterproof combat jackets. The senior officer stepped forward and introduced himself to the Royal Marines Colonel. They shook hands and exchanged a few pleasantries. Meanwhile, the
marines, having loaded their kit-bags into the waiting vehicles, formed up in three ranks with their rifles slung on their shoulders. Having made his excuses, Colonel Vaughan moved to address the unit. He had an extremely loud voice which carried to everyone without any effort.

'My name is Charles Vaughan and I am the Commanding Officer of the Training Centre, and this is my Sergeant Major, Donald James. He indicated the giant of a soldier beside him, fully six foot six and wearing a splendid kilt. I have been a commando since the Army first asked for volunteers back in 1940. Together, with my team of dedicated instructors, our task has been to produce fit, tough and disciplined men who, whilst they will obey an order instantly and unquestioningly, will also have the intelligence to be able to proceed on their own initiative. Self-discipline has been the fundamental basis of our training. Where you are concerned, we will achieve this, come hell or high water, and over your dead bodies if necessary.'

'Fuck my old boots,' muttered Pete Wills. 'The bastard really means it.'

Dacre gave him a sideways glance and whispered, 'Remember, it is just a game.' Colonel Vaughan continued. 'All officers and NCOs will be treated the same as the other ranks. There will be no exceptions. We begin your training right now by marching to the camp. It's only seven miles. You may like to know that we normally expect troops to do a mile every ten minutes. However, because you are Royal Marines, we shall require you to do the entire march in just one hour. Carry on Sergeant Major.'

'Bloody hell,' said Dave Taylor to no-one in particular, 'what a welcome!'

Everyone in the unit, including the CO, was thinking the same thing. Dacre just smiled to himself. *Let the game begin*, he thought.

With the two colonels in the lead, the marines marched down the lane from the station to the main road. The instructors began to call out the time, 'Left, left, left, right, left,' but they quickly realised that these 'Royals' knew how to march. They wheeled right at the bottom of the hill, through the village, past the Spean Bridge Hotel and over the bridge, where they automatically broke step. On they marched, perfectly in step, their studded ammunition boots pounding the road. Up and up a long steep hill they sped, those at the front taking slightly shorter steps. It had begun to rain, light at first then turning into a real downpour that lashed the marching men, instructors and marines alike. Everyone was soaked to the skin. At the top of the hill the column swung left into a narrow lane that swept up and down, rather like a scenic railway. To their left, a loch could just be seen. There were no houses or signs of cultivation, just hills, bracken, trees and more hills. Where the lane crossed the Caledonian Canal, the unit had to halt while a sailing barge passed through. It was a timely and most welcome break, as the pace set had been furious. A combination of body heat and sweat could easily be seen evaporating from each man in the column. All too soon, the bridge was back in place and the march continued, ever faster. On they went, up an even steeper, back-breaking rise that never seemed to end, sapping the stamina of even the best of them. Suddenly the lane levelled out. Deep breaths were taken, as the adrenalin coursed through their bodies. At last, the gates to the camp came in sight.

The whole unit managed the distance in just under the hour, primarily due to their intensive training at *HMS Dorlin*. Outside the gates, the marines halted. The order was given to tighten slings. Then, with rifles at the slope, they marched in as only Royal Marines can: perfectly in step and not a hair out of place, although there were one or two red faces. The Army instructors were impressed, not that they would ever tell the marines that. As they entered the gates, Pete Wills noticed a number of graves, each one marked with a white cross. Nailed to each was a small board that had name, rank and number on it. Underneath was the cause of their death: *This man was too slow,* said one; another read, *This man forgot to duck.*

'Will you look at that, AJ. They fucking kill people here.'

Dacre and the rest of the marching column of marines had, of course, noticed. They were supposed to.

'Someone has a grim sense of humour,' replied Dacre.

Burt Kelly chipped in, 'Don't you worry, little man, just remember what AJ said.'

'Yea, I know,' replied Wills, 'It's all part of a game.'

(ii)

Colonel Vaughan explained to the Marine Colonel that Achnacarry House was the Officers' Mess and that the Royal Marine officers were most welcome to use it. To his surprise, Colonel Picton-Phillipps told him that he, his officers and NCOs would use the same accommodation as the men. Somewhat surprised, but nevertheless impressed, Vaughan agreed. Unloading their kit bags from the trucks, the marines began to settle into the prefabricated Nissen huts. Inside each hut were rows of bunk beds, three high. Each bed had a thin, horse-hair mattress, one blanket and a groundsheet. At each end of the hut was a small black stove. On closer inspection it was obvious that these had not been used for months, maybe even years. After a late supper at 1900 hours most of the marines turned in for an early night, wondering just what the following day would bring.

That evening, by coincidence, two meetings were held in very different parts of the camp.

The first meeting took place in the big house. Colonel Vaughan stood in front of his instructors and stared thoughtfully at them. They, in turn, waited patiently for him to start his briefing.

'Gentlemen, the Marines who have just arrived, as you know, are the very first unit to undertake our commando course. It would seem that the Chief of Combined Operations, Admiral Mountbatten, wants them to be put through their paces.'

The room went quiet. Very few of those present had any knowledge of the Marines other than what they had witnessed that day.

'Now, I'll be the first to say that I know very little about them, other than that they are the Navy's sea soldiers and that they have a long and distinguished history. They also have something of a reputation. But how tough they really are is something that we shall have to find out. Does anyone have anything to add?'

There was some shuffling of feet and one or two whispers could be heard.

The Adjutant, Captain Johns, raised his hand. 'Yes, Andrew. As you know, sir, I was at Narvik in Norway when the Marines landed. I can tell you that they are a pretty tough bunch and they are bloody good soldiers.

Although they were ill-equipped and unprepared, they put up a damn good show. If push came to shove and I had a choice, together with the Guards, I would want them fighting alongside me.'

'Thank you, Andrew, for your opinion. As to how tough they are, as I have already said, we shall find out. Anyone else?'

RSM James raised his hand.

'Yes, Donald?'

'Sir! They pride themselves on their drill and discipline. They consider themselves to be the best of the best – even better than your old regiment.'

'Better than the Guards?'

'Yes, sir.'

'What makes them think they are so superior?'

There was a long pause before the RSM answered.

'Well, sir. How many regiments do you know can fix bayonets on the march with absolute flawless precision?'

'You've seen this yourself?'

'Yes, sir. Beating the retreat at Eastney Barracks in Portsmouth, back in '38.'

Colonel Vaughan began pacing up and down the room, pensive and deep in thought. The instructors held their breath; what was their CO thinking? At last, he turned towards them. He had a very determined look in his eye.

'Very well then, we shall put these Marines to the test. We shall increase our demands. We shall reduce the times on every challenge we set them. We shall make everything tougher and harder. We shall push them to their very limits and, if necessary, beyond. Then we shall see just how really good they are. Is that agreed by everyone?'

The nodding of heads around the room confirmed that it was, although one or two of the instructors privately wondered if their CO had, perhaps, gone too far.

The second meeting took place in Colonel Picton-Phillipps's hut. He had called an 'O' group of all officers and NCOs. His briefing was short and to the point.

'I want all training to be undertaken at platoon level. In this way we will generate a real competitive spirit among our men. I believe that this will allow us not only to take on everything that the Army can throw at us, but it will allow us to exceed everyone's expectations. Finally, on advice from Major Houghton, I also want Number Ten Platoon from 'X' Company to be the first to tackle whatever comes our way. They will be our 'stalking horse'. They will set the standards for the rest of us to follow. I am assured by the second-in-command, and by Captain Standwell their Company Commander, that they are just what we need because they are the fittest men in the unit.'

There was a collective sigh of agreement. Nobody present disagreed with the CO.

'That is all – thank you.'

(iii)

Dacre found himself strolling through a field of ripening wheat. His hands were lightly brushing the ears. He plucked a few and rubbed them in the palm of his hands. They seemed to be ripe and perhaps ready for harvest. The sun was warm on his back, and overhead the sky was a brilliant blue. Not a cloud could be seen. Somewhere nearby he heard a bird begin to sing. Then he saw them. A small patch of the barley had been trampled down. There, in a neat row, were the children lying as if asleep, their hands neatly folded across their chests. There was not a mark on them.

He awoke in a cold sweat and sat up. It was that damn dream again. Dunkirk! Would he never be able to forget? He couldn't be doing with this, he thought, enough was enough. He checked his watch. It was 0600 hours precisely.

At that very moment, the door to the hut was thrown open, and a piper playing a Highland skirl marched through and out the other end of the hut. Both doors were left open, which was no joke at that time of the year. Everyone was up, if not yet fully awake. That soon changed, as they all had to wash and shave in cold water. This was followed by an hour's physical training, stripped to the waist. As the marines later found out, this morning ritual took place in all weathers, come rain, sleet or snow. A quickly eaten breakfast followed, consisting of a thick glutinous porridge followed by fried bread with bacon. One of the instructors approached the Marine CO said that the whole unit was to undertake the assault course that morning.

The sun was only just rising over the top of the nearby mountains. In another hour or so it would ease the highland chill from the damp air, and perhaps lift some of the mist that clung to the blackness of the surrounding hills. Dacre looked across the rough grass ahead, to the upper moorland and the patches of bare rock. A vicious cold wind was blowing down the glen. He shivered involuntarily. The sun would bring little warmth today, he thought. He shrugged his shoulders. What the hell! Time to get going. Their commando training begins now.

Each of the platoons was divided into groups of six. Initially, they were allowed to walk the course in order to familiarise themselves with the obstacles. Then, with the stopwatch ticking, the groups set off, one after the other at five-minute intervals. As agreed, Dacre, Pete Wills and four of their mates were the first to go. It began to rain. Down a steep slope the group charged, their boots churning up mud and water. At the first obstacle each of the marines made a slithering dive under a low, barbed wire fence that had been laid flat, and was only about twelve inches off the ground. The group, already soaked to the skin, were now covered in a slimy, brown peat. Ahead of them lay several long tree trunks, sloping up to a small rocky outcrop. Throwing caution to the wind, the marines charged up the trees without giving any thought to the danger of a slip or a fall. Sweating and panting, they reached the top, and then ran full pelt down into a little gorge, where a number of ropes hung, suspended from the trees. Jumping and grabbing the ropes, they successfully swung themselves over to the other side in one fluid movement. Then, the little group scrambled up to a marked tree, turned and tore down a steep incline, leaping over rocks, boulders, fallen trees and little streams. Increasing their pace, with Dacre in the lead, they dashed across a small wooden bridge over a burn, then up a short hill. Chests heaving, they were confronted by several dummies suspended on wooden frames. Screaming out unbelievable war cries and obscenities, the marines bayoneted the figures with such ferocity that the wooden frames collapsed. Dashing down the hill, they crossed the finishing line.

The instructor clicked his stopwatch. The marines were breathing heavily and grinning at each other. They had actually enjoyed the challenge of the course. The instructor looked at his watch again, shook it, then looked at his wristwatch. Damn it, he thought, these marines had just knocked five minutes off the best time ever set, and this was their first time around. What if all the other marines could do this, he wondered.

Over the next few weeks, most of the training was extremely physical. They ran or doubled everywhere, even when off duty, or even if they were going down to the sick bay to have their blisters seen to, as Pete Wills found out.

'Bloody hell, AJ, is this all part of the game?' he said one evening, as he limped back to their hut, struggling to keep up with the others.

AJ burst out laughing at the sight of the pained expression on his friend's face and replied kindly, 'Just play up and play the game, and save your energy. I think you are going to need it.'

(iv)

Every aspect of the commando training at Achnacarry was tough, although some parts were tougher than others. One morning, the marines were introduced to the toggle rope. This was a curious, yet useful, piece of equipment. It was about four feet in length. At one end it had a wooden toggle and at the other, a loop. Several ropes joined together could make a chain that could be used for scaling walls or even cliffs. By using a good many, they could be interlaced to make a bridge. Thus, it was, that the marines were introduced to the Achnacarry toggle bridge that crossed the River Arkaig. Strung between two tall trees, it presented a real challenge. One slip and anyone crossing the bridge found themselves entangled upside down. The more they struggled, the worse it became until, with a yell, they plummeted down into the icy waters below. More than one marine met his match and received a ducking. Undeterred, and with good humour, they clambered out and tried again, much to the amusement of their comrades.

To make things even more interesting, and to suggest battle conditions, instructors fired live rounds as close to the marines as possible, whilst at the same time throwing hand grenades and explosives into the river, sending up huge spouts of water, rocks and pebbles. Many of the marines stepped onto dry land dazed, grazed and drenched to the skin, but undaunted.

As the days passed, so the training became more and more intensive. No matter what they were doing, the instructors were constantly firing live ammunition over their heads from Bren or Sten guns, as well as using live grenades and smoke bombs. A good number of the marines received injuries, some of which were quite severe. These men were patched up at the sick bay, and then they carried on. No-one ever considered giving up.

Speed marches became a regular feature. They started with a one-mile sprint, then five, then seven, then nine, as they worked their way up to the fourteen-miler. Calling it a march had become something of a joke. Each distance was covered by doubling or running along the flat and downhill. Actual marching was only accomplished when going uphill, however, this was done at such a pace that it was lung-tearing. The marines had to do this carrying their rifles, equipment and full packs, as well as their platoon weapons. Each march had a time factor allocated to it. So, for example, the fourteen-mile march should be completed in just two hours. From experience, the instructors knew that very few managed it in that time, most needing an extra ten minutes or so. The marines managed it in one hour and fifty minutes – another record was set. Immediately after the march, the platoons moved onto a nearby hillside where, at various distances, small metal plates had been set up as targets. All the targets had to be shot down. Taking it in turn, the marines adopted the prone position, loaded their rifles and steadied their thumping chests. Then, coolly and calmly, took aim and squeezed the trigger gently, dispatching each target in turn. Once more the instructors were impressed but, remembering what Colonel Vaughan had said, kept their comments to themselves. If these marches weren't enough, once a week the whole unit was expected to run up the nearby mountain of Ben Nevis. The great joy of this was that they didn't have to wear equipment or take their rifles with them.

At night, with their faces blackened with either 'cam' cream or burnt cork, the marines undertook field exercises, involving map reading of the highest order, as well as tactics and live firing. Great emphasis was placed on field-craft, which was the ability to conceal oneself using camouflage and the natural flora. They were also expected to be able to move across the countryside unseen and unheard in the age-old manner of a poacher. They practised this skill day and night, until they were perfect.

Next, came the notorious 'death slide'. This was a rope, drawn taut between two trees across the river. On the far side, the rope was tied high up on one of the tallest trees available. At the other end, the rope was secured at the base of a suitable tree. The distance from tree to tree was only about fifty feet, but it was about forty feet above the raging water. As instructed, each marine had to throw his toggle over the slide rope and grasp both ends tightly. He descended at an incredible speed, which was an exhilarating experience. As per usual, the instructors added the battle conditions of firing live ammunition and throwing explosives. The marines really took to this challenge and went back time and time again, just for the hell of it.

This was immediately followed by the newly constructed 'Tarzan course', which had been designed to test even the stoutest of hearts. Amongst the trees, about thirty feet from the ground, a network of ropes led from tree to tree. The marines were required to cat crawl along these by lying flat on the rope with one leg hanging down like a pendulum for balance. By pulling with their hands and pushing with the other leg, they were able to move across the rope quite quickly. On one rope, in particular, each marine was required to roll off it and hang in mid-air just by his hands. Then, by bouncing, they were encouraged to do a 'regain', back onto the rope. Because of the weight of their equipment and their rifles, this was not easy. Many of the marines struggled, but the alternative of the long drop to the ground spurred them on to be successful. Thankfully no-one failed this test. At various intervals there were small wooden platforms. Near each was a suspended climbing rope. Grasping the rope, they had to swing out into a nearby grappling net, climb to the top, roll over and down the other side. Then, they continued to climb up more ropes, and on again. The marines became so good at this that some of the instructors began to despair. Was there nothing these lads couldn't do?

The marines were also introduced to the idea of working in pairs - what the instructor referred to as 'me and my pal.' The guiding principle behind this was that two heads were better than one. Dacre teamed up with his friend Pete Wills. They made an odd couple, with Dacre standing at just over six foot two and weighing about fourteen stone of pure muscle, whilst his companion was little more than five foot six and weighed about nine stone. Their mates nicknamed them 'Lofty and Titch.' As a team they were good, in fact very good. They took on all the tests that the training staff could throw at them, and then came back for more. There was nothing they wouldn't attempt. In particular, Dacre and Wills would make use of the vile weather conditions or hostile terrain in order to achieve a surprise and successful attack. Day after day, the two of them would be soaked to the skin, yet they chose to ignore any personal discomfort in order to achieve their objective. It was, as Dacre said one evening, that you just needed a certain state of mind. Inspired by this example, the rest of the platoon and the remainder of 'X' Company, and indeed the whole unit, raised their performance to an even higher level. Colonel Picton-Phillipps's prediction seemed to be coming true.

Weapon handling and musketry skills were of the highest priority. Every marine was expected to qualify as a First Class shot with their .303 Lee-Enfield rifles. Many went on to achieve the crossed rifle badge of a marksman. In addition to their own weapons, they were also required to become proficient in the handling of both allied and enemy weapons.

It was at this time that every marine in the commando was issued with some alternative and additional weapons. Some chose to keep their reliable rifles, while others opted for the new 'Tommy' gun as their personal weapon. Regardless of this, everyone was issued with .45 calibre pistol and holster, a black fighting knife in a leather scabbard and a set of brass knuckledusters.

Dacre took some time to study the knife more carefully. It was a beautifully made weapon. Light and well balanced, with a double-edged blade that tapered to a sharp point. It had a distinctive foil grip.

The last piece of kit was, of course, their own toggle rope, which by now had become indispensable to them.

The final part of the course introduced the marines to the new idea of 'unarmed combat'. These lethal skills, devised by two former Shanghai police officers who were now instructors at Acknacarry, had, in the main, been developed from oriental methods of defence and street fighting, and taught the individual how to defend himself and how to attack without the use of a weapon. It was a brutal and often bloody experience, even though they were just training. No quarter was given, and none was asked for. The instructors constantly stressed the importance of these skills and went to some lengths to emphasise that this style of combat promoted that extra fighting spirit that the commandos were noted for. At the end of the course, one of the instructors let slip, with a nod and a wink, that as good as unarmed combat was, there was, in his opinion, no substitute for a seven-pound lump hammer.

'Nobody ever gets up from a blow to the head like that,' he said.

It was a salutary lesson for all.

(v)

At the end of the fifth week, Colonel Vaughan called a meeting of all his instructors. He wanted to review the progress that the Royal Marines had been making. He had, of course, seen for himself how well they were doing and had heard various comments about this record or that record having been broken. Not one of the instructors had anything to say but praise and admiration.

The Adjutant summed it all up rather neatly. 'We've never seen anything quite like this, sir. For a unit of men to be this fit and to learn so quickly is quite remarkable. Some of these marines are even doing the assault and Tarzan course in their own time for fun.'

Colonel Vaughan simply nodded his head. It confirmed his worst fears. 'RSM, do you have anything to add?'

'Aye, sir, I do. Their drill has been nigh on perfect. I couldna fault them at all. It was a joy to behold, I can tell ye.'

'Thank you, Mr James, that will do!' snapped the Colonel.

He was worried. The Commando Depot's honour was at stake. His idea of putting the marines to the test, with a training regime that had been nothing short of murderous, wasn't working out as he had planned. He paced up and down the room, deep in thought.

'Very well then! We must make it even harder for them, make everything more difficult. Reduce the timings for the speed marches and the assault course even further. Have them run up Ben Nevis more often. Do everything you can to make life here more difficult and more demanding. Do not, for one moment, let up, any of you. The final exercise will be coming up soon. I shall have to give some thought to how we can make even that more challenging.'

Several of the instructors looked at each other with concern on their faces. Had the CO gone too far this time, they wondered. Nobody said anything. They all knew better than to question Colonel Vaughan's leadership.

At last the final week arrived. Despite Colonel Vaughan's instructions, the Royal Marines had continued to excel. All the final tests had been taken and passed with outstanding results. Not one marine failed. All that was left was the final exercise – the night assault. This was by far the most demanding of all the training schemes. Colonel Vaughan had sworn all of his instructors to secrecy; he didn't want the Marines to get a hint of what to expect.

(vi)

The assault was to be an amphibious operation carried out at night and would be as close to battle conditions as possible. The marines had to cross Loch Lochy by boat, and then carry out a mock attack against a heavily defended position. Orders and maps were issued and studied carefully. Sand models of the area to be attacked were constructed. Boat drills had been practised, both day and night. Dress rehearsals had taken place until everyone knew exactly what they had to do. They were ready.

As darkness fell on the chosen night, it began to rain, light at first, then increasingly heavy, until it was coming down like stair rods. Final checks were made of weapons and equipment, watches synchronised. The marines were a fearsome sight: faces blackened with burnt cork or soot and grease; the brasses of their equipment dulled down. Moving off in troops, the unit made its way down to the boat station at Bunarkaig Pier. It had turned bitterly cold and everyone was soaked to the skin. Although Achnacarry had a wide range of craft such as LCAs, whalers, cutters and canoes, Colonel Vaughan had, at the last minute, decided that the Marines should only be allowed to use some flat bottomed collapsible pontoons that had once belonged to the Royal Engineers. These boats were extremely frail, offered almost no protection from the weather and would have to be paddled across the choppy waters of the Loch. This was part of his plan to, yet again, test the resolve of these damn marines. Undeterred, the marines responding to their Corps motto *Per Mare Per Terram*, picked up the paddles and moved silently out into the loch. There was no sound other than the gentle swish of blades and the hiss of rain as it struck the surface of the water. About midway across, the pontoons changed formation from line astern to line abreast, a manoeuvre of which

Admiral Nelson would have been proud. The paddlers sweated as they bent their backs to the task in hand, their blades rising and falling in unison, whilst the other marines could only sit and shiver both from the cold and the expectation of what was to come.

The faint outline of the shore ahead suddenly appeared from the darkness, a gap in the trees marking the landing spot.

'It won't be long now,' Dacre whispered to Pete Wills.

Suddenly the whole shoreline seemed to erupt. Machine guns chattered away, unleashing a rain of tracer bullets that curved and whined overhead. Bren guns sprayed the water around the incoming fleet of boats, just as dozens of mortar bombs fell from the night sky, sending up huge plumes of water. Very lights and parachute flares added to the intensity of the situation by illuminating the attacking force like targets at a fairground. The noise from the live firing and explosions was deafening. The men who were paddling re-doubled their efforts, while others lent a hand by using their rifles as paddles, sending the pontoons surging ahead until they hit the sandy beach. Voices shouting in German could just be heard as live hand grenades and thunder flashes began to explode all around them. Live ammunition fired by the instructors could be seen plucking at the water as the marines charged ashore with blood-curdling war cries. In several cases, the bullets came so close that several of the paddles had neat holes shot through them.

The marines moved quickly off the beach, charging through peat bogs and mud, whilst explosions went off all around them, sending up showers of earth and stones. Undaunted, the marines charged on, stumbling, slipping and cursing. Smoke and the smell of cordite was everywhere. As they gasped for breath, they could even taste it. Without pausing, they plunged on up the steep-sided hill. By now, the opposing gunfire had ceased, and the covering fire had begun. From behind, bullets and tracers whined overhead into the hill in front of them. Mortar bombs and other explosives thudded into the ground, adding to the mayhem, leaving craters big enough to swallow a man whole. As fit as the marines were, many of them were gasping for breath as they dived for cover. Steaming with sweat, their ears still buzzing, they lay and waited while Dacre and his mates from Number Ten Platoon, under the command of Lieutenant Ellis and Sergeant Thrattles, moved to the top of the hill to lay the demolitions. Working with practised speed, they laid the charges, lit the cord, then fled back downhill to the rest of the unit. By now, all the firing had ceased, and an uncanny silence descended over the whole area. Everyone was waiting, counting the seconds. Then, when they least expected it, there was an earth-shattering explosion that shook the ground and echoed across the loch to the Highlands beyond. Heads were buried deep in the damp bracken, as earth and flying stones pelted down on the attacking force.

'Bloody hell,' said Pete Wills, to no-one in particular, 'not much subtlety there.'

Without any commands being given, the marines began to move slowly back down the hill in a strategic withdrawal. As they did so, the covering fire opened up again. The noise was unbelievable, like the loudest thunder you could imagine crashing around their ears. By the time they had reached the beach, hand grenades and other explosives were erupting all around them. Undeterred and showing great determination, the marines quickly climbed into their boats and paddled away as fast as they could. The covering fire now turned to opposing fire again, as machine guns and mortars opened up. Several of the bombs had fallen so close to the retreating boats that some of the marines had to paddle through the spray. About half-way across the loch the firing stopped. Ahead of them lay a welcoming darkness and silence. Quietly, the unit paddled on.

By the time they reached the boat yard, the adrenaline in their bodies had calmed down and a great sense of achievement set in. Colonel Picton-Phillipps was delighted with how his marines had performed. Having arrived back first, he stood on the pier congratulating the men in each boat as it came in. Then, forming up, the unit marched back up to the camp. Despite everything that they had endured, there was a real spring in their steps. The Royal Marines had been put to the test and, despite Achnacarry's best efforts, they had not been found wanting.

At the gates, Colonel Vaughan and his instructors lined up. Standing to attention they saluted as the Marines marched past, which was their way of saying, well done.

(vii)

The final day at Achnacarry was, by tradition, more light-hearted and relaxed. In what was known as the 'Commando Games', each company competed against each other as well as against the clock. The games included a five-mile speed march and the assault course (all without weapons and equipment), a boat race on the loch, target shooting on the one hundred-yard range, tug-of-war and a 'milling' completion. The day began with an inspection of huts, followed by a parade and drill. Points were awarded for each of these. As the day progressed, so the competitive spirit increased. By mid-afternoon it was neck and neck between all the three companies. It was clear to everyone that the competition would be won or lost that evening by the last event, the 'milling'.

Dacre was walking back from the rifle range, when Lieutenant Ellis caught up with him.

'Ah, Dacre. I see from your records you are something of a boxer.'

'No, sir. Not a boxer. But I did do a bit of milling when I was a recruit,' he replied.

'Really! A bit of milling you say. Your file says that you were the Corps Novice Champion in 1939.

'I just got lucky, sir, that was all.'

'Will you represent 'X' Company this afternoon?'

'Do I have a choice, sir?'

'To be honest with you, no, not really. I, or rather we, need you to do this. At the moment there is nothing between the three companies. A win in the ring could just tip the balance in our favour. What do you say?

'Alright, sir. I'll give it a go for you, but no promises mind you. It's been a while and I'm a bit rusty.'

Colonel Vaughan had been under the impression that milling was unique to Achnacarry. He was somewhat surprised, and more than a little disconcerted, to find out that the Royal Marines had been doing this for quite some time as part of their recruit training. Although milling usually takes place in a boxing ring and the contestants do wear boxing gloves, there is little resemblance to the actual sport of boxing. Put simply, the two competitors rain or windmill punches onto each other in a flurry of powerful, yet controlled, aggression. The last man standing is the winner.

'We normally do this for just one minute,' Colonel Vaughan explained to the Marine CO.

Colonel Picton-Phillipps humphed a little.

'We actually do three, one-minute rounds. But when in Rome… Let it be as you suggest.'

The evening was fine and dry for once. The ring had been set up in the open, in front of the big house. The entire camp had gathered, talking and enjoying the occasion. The Pipe Major was playing a selection of Highland tunes. The atmosphere was relaxed; instructors and marines mingling like old friends. Each of the three companies had chosen ten men to fight, who were waiting somewhat apprehensively by the side of the ring.

Suddenly there was a loud command, and everyone sprang to attention. The two Colonels entered the space and took up their seats on a raised dais. The timekeeper blew his whistle and the first two marines entered the ring. Immediately, they tore into each other like ferocious beasts, no quarter given, none asked. The crowd roared with encouragement as one man went down under a barrage of fists. The whistle blew, and as they left the ring, the next pair entered. As the evening progressed, it became clear from the chalkboard that this was going to be a close-run thing between 'B' and 'X' Company. In all probability it would be decided by the final bout.

The marine from 'B' Company was a big lad and had something of a reputation as a real boxer. He had been watching Dacre during a previous fight and was confident that he had worked out how to beat him. The whistle went, Dacre charged across the ring like a bull, windmilling like mad. The boxer stood his ground. Light on his feet, he danced to one side and, at the same time, slammed a vicious right hand to the side of Dacre's head. Caught by surprise, he was knocked off his feet onto the canvas, onto the seat of his pants. The crowd let out a long and angonised sigh. Angry with himself for being caught out like that, Dacre immediately sprang to his feet. The crowd roared their approval. Dripping with sweat, the two marines waded into each other, throwing punches left and right, blow after blow. Neither would retreat. The marine from 'B' Company let fly a tremendous uppercut which, had it connected, would have sent his opponent flying out of the ring. Dacre cut loose with devastating punches to the head - left, right, left, right - followed by a scything haymaker that smashed into the side of his opponent's jaw. Down he went, down he stayed. It was all over. The battle of the night had finished. Dacre stood over his victim who lay on the floor, totally exhausted and dazed. Gallantly, he helped him to his feet as the whistle went. The whole of 'X' Company screamed with pure delight. They had won the competition, but only just.

The following day the Royal Marines officially received the title of 'Commando'. It was an extremely fit and proud unit that marched the seven miles back to the little railway station at Spean Bridge, where they boarded the train which would take them south. They were heading off towards their new base on the Isle of Wight.

CHAPTER 16

(i)

The planning for *Operation Rutter* moved ahead quickly. At the Combined Operations Headquarters, those who were responsible for gathering and assessing intelligence on Dieppe had a serious problem. There was almost no information to gather, let alone assess. Aerial reconnaissance had been ordered but the photographs revealed little about the two headlands, although the gun emplacements around the harbour and along the sea wall were clear enough. The beach, its nature and gradient, unfortunately could only be assessed by studying pre-war holiday snaps and postcards. These were obtained by sending an urgent message around the offices at Combined Operations Headquarters asking if anyone had been on holiday in Dieppe before the war. Intelligence on troops and troop movements was still vague, although it was confirmed that the town and port were not heavily defended.

In May, the Chiefs of Staff Committee approved the final outline plan, *Operation Rutter,* was given the go-ahead.

On the same day, the Canadian troops were moved in secret from Sussex to Freshwater on the Isle of Wight. The local residents in Sussex were pleased to see them go. Over the previous two years the troops had gained something of a reputation for being ill-disciplined and rude. They liked English beer and English women far too much. Rather surprisingly, Montgomery, well known for being teetotal and abstemious in his habits, put this down to youthful 'high spirits'.

The Isle of Wight was chosen because security on the island was already tight. In addition, the beaches and chalk cliffs were suitable for training, as they resembled those at Dieppe. In addition, the local populace was used to seeing soldiers on manoeuvres because of the numbers of troops already training there.

In early June, Montgomery held a meeting at Combined Operations Headquarters with three Force Commanders: Major General G Roberts, the Ground Force Commander; Air Vice-Marshall Leigh-Mallory, Number 11 Fighter Command; and Rear Admiral Baille-Grohman RN, Commander of the Naval Task Force. Together, they were responsible for all further planning of the operation, except for the final decision as to whether the raiding force should finally set sail. The Chiefs of Staff Committee had insisted that this was to be the responsibility of the nearest Naval Commander-in-Chief, Admiral W James RN, who happened to be in Portsmouth.

(ii)

Mountbatten missed the meeting because he was in the USA, trying to persuade the President and his military advisers not to push for the opening of a second front in the autumn. Like Churchill, he urged them to consider supporting the campaign in North Africa as a way into the soft underbelly of Nazi Europe - Italy. As soon as he returned to London, the Admiral requested an urgent one-to-one meeting with the CIGS. At first, Brooke was reluctant to see Mountbatten, but knowing that as Chief of Combined Operations he had the ear of the Prime Minister, he allowed caution to prevail, despite his increasing personal dislike for this interloper. The meeting took place the following morning in Brooke's office, in Whitehall.

'I'll come straight to the point, sir, if I may.'

Brooke was resting his elbows on the edge of his desk, the fingers of both hands forming a steeple.

'I am still not happy about the way that *Rutter* is developing. As you may know, Montgomery held a meeting recently when, in my absence, it was decided not to bomb Dieppe prior to the landings. I am given to understand that Major General Roberts actually supported the idea in the belief that bomb damage would hinder his tanks from moving through the town. I believe this to be a mistake, sir.'

Brooke looked steadily at Mountbatten from behind his 'steeple' before replying. He needed to be polite, but firm. Losing his temper would serve no purpose.

'Thank you for your thoughts on this matter, Dickie. I agree with you that it was unfortunate that you were not able to attend the meeting. Your presence there might have made a difference. However, the decision has been made by Monty and the Force Commanders, and I believe that it must stand. Of course, you are aware of the Prime Minister's view and those of the cabinet that, where possible, we must avoid destroying French towns, lest we alienate the people. Am I correct in thinking that instead of a dawn air attack against the two headlands and the beaches, they propose to bomb an airfield near Boulogne as a diversion?'

Mountbatten replied rather quietly, 'I believe that is correct, sir.'

Brooke thought for a moment or two, then decided to throw the Admiral a very thin lifeline.

'You might possibly consider approaching the First Sea Lord to see if he might change his mind about risking some of his big ships at Dieppe. I suspect I know what the answer will be, but it might be worth a chance.'

Somewhat mollified, Mountbatten said he would go and see him at once.

The Chief of Combined Operations went immediately to see Sir Dudley Pound. As an experienced sailor himself, Mountbatten knew there would be objections to exposing one of the navy's capital ships in the narrow confines of the English Channel. However, he was hopeful in so much as the Germans had just sent three of their principal warships through the Straits of Dover undetected, and then down the Channel into the North Atlantic.

Mindful of the recent loss of the *Prince of Wales* and the *Repulse* in the Far East, Pound was horrified at the very idea of losing one of his ships to an air attack by the Luftwaffe.

'My battleships by day, off the French coast? You must be mad, Dickie.'

Chastened, but not entirely surprised, Mountbatten beat a hasty retreat. It had been a gamble, he knew, but on this occasion not one that had paid off.

(iii)

Meanwhile, Major General Roberts, after consulting with the senior Canadian military officer in Britain, General Andrew McNaughton, had decided who would make up his ground force. He would take battalions from the Royal Regiment of Canada, the Royal Hamilton Light Infantry and the Essex Scottish, all from the Fourth Brigade, under the command of Brigadier Sherwood Lett. Then from the Sixth Brigade he would take the Fusiliers Mont-Royal, the Camerons of Canada and the South Saskatchewan Regiment whose Brigadier was William Southam. These formations were all from the Canadian 2nd Infantry Division. Roberts also included the 14th Canadian Tank Regiment.

Training on the Isle of Wight began at once. The officers and men were pitchforked into a most strenuous course, designed to increase their stamina, fitness and fighting ability. Route and speed marches, obstacle courses, bayonet fighting, beach landings and demolition work were all part of a fast and furious regime. The infantry were out every day, practising house-to-house street fighting and beach landings, whilst the huge Churchill tanks clanked on and off the landing craft and up and down the beaches, from morning until dusk.

CHAPTER 17

(i)

It was on the 23rd of May that the Royal Marine Commando arrived on the Isle of Wight. This was a very different kettle of fish from what they had been used to. Instead of being in barracks or a camp, the men of the Commando found themselves billeted with the civilian population in the coastal towns of Sandown, Shanklin and Ventnor. Travelling across the island from the ferry port by army trucks, it was immediately obvious that the whole island was like some large transit or training camp for troops. Everywhere you looked there seemed to be row upon row of tents or Nissen huts.

'Bloody hell,' said Pete Wills looking out from the back of one of the trucks, 'There must be thousands of troops on this island. No wonder we are going to live local.'

By and large the marines were well received by these 'civvy' digs. After Achnacarry, it seemed like luxury.

Dacre and Wills found themselves staying at Ventnor with a Mrs Lynne Peacock. She lived in a small Victorian terraced house, just off the High Street. The house had a small front room, used only for best, a kitchen and a scullery-cum-washhouse. The toilet was outside in the backyard. Upstairs, there were just the two bedrooms. The house was amazingly clean and tidy, and smelt of beeswax polish. Lynne Peacock was a large, kindly lady in her late fifties. There was no Mr Peacock as he had died of influenza in 1934. She made a great fuss of 'her two boys', as she liked to call them, in a well-meaning and motherly way. They took to her immediately.

The landladies were all paid the princely sum of six shillings and eight pence per day. For this they were expected to provide lodgings, two meals – breakfast and supper - and a packed lunch for each marine, every day. Life on the island was going to be good for these tough marine commandos. This 'living out' meant that the men had the chance to practise self-reliance, something that Colonel Picton-Phillipps was very keen on. The marines were also responsible for getting themselves onto parade, at the right time and at the right place, without being chased by their NCOs. It also meant that the Commando was spared all the administration. However, the CO was anxious that these civvy billets did not blunt the finely honed 'edge' of his beloved Commandos which he had worked so hard to create.

Consequently, the training regime was even harder than before. The hours that they worked got longer and longer. Street fighting and cliff climbing seemed to be the priority, followed by more and more speed marches, which were designed to increase both strength and stamina.

One day the marines all had to hand over their studded ammunition boots, to be replaced with rope-soled boots. The studs of their old boots made them too noisy for the stealth that a commando needed. Later, the rope soled boots were replaced with rubber soled boots.

The colonel was more than happy with the progress being made in the further training of his unit. The men were responding well to each new challenge, with an energy and enthusiasm that constantly surprised him. However, one thing that he was less happy about was that his unit had now been attached to the Army Special Service Brigade. He didn't have an issue with the Army Commandos, they were fine chaps and equally as fit and dedicated as his own men. No, it wasn't that. It was the fact that the abbreviation SS Brigade had certain connotations with Nazi Germany. Many people were uncomfortable about this, including himself and his officers. He had raised the matter several times with the Brigadier and the Admiralty. Gradually, this concern spread slowly up the chain of command, but it wasn't until November 1944 that the title of 'Special Service' was dropped.

At their billet, Dacre and Pete Wills continued to enjoy all the comforts of home. It was true that they had to share a large double bed, piled high with blankets and a thick eiderdown. Mrs Peacock always made sure that the little fire in the lads' room was lit and welcoming, although where she got her supply of coal they never found out. The large copper bowl in the washhouse would always be full to the brim with hot water, and the tin bath ready for whoever was to go first. The two marines decided to take it in turns to share the water. Their lovely landlady, quite unperturbed by their naked bodies, would fuss around them, collecting up their dirty clothing, doing her best to ensure that their uniforms were clean and dry for the morning.

After a huge evening meal, both lads would help clear away and wash up the pots and pans. Later, they would sit at the table spread with old newspapers, stripping down and cleaning their weapons. Mrs Peacock would sit quietly in her favourite chair knitting with her glasses perched on the end of her nose, her needles clicking away.

Over the days and weeks, she began to realise how much she enjoyed the company of these two tough men. She would smile to herself, much the way a mother does when watching her children.

At the end of the evening, sharing the double bed wasn't a problem. Pete Wills loved all the comfort and softness; he was like a pig in clover. On the other hand, Dacre found the bed too soft for him. Consequently, he slept on the floor. There were more than enough blankets for both of them. Each morning they would re-make the bed so that Mrs Peacock never knew, lest she be upset that the bed wasn't good enough for one of them.

Occasionally the two of them would stroll out in the evening down the High Street to a local public house for a quick half pint or two, despite the fact that the CO frowned on his men drinking. The short distance that they had to walk always proved to be challenging. Strict blackout conditions were imposed at night. People had to learn how to manage without streetlights and illuminated shop windows. Neighbourhoods were plunged into total darkness after dusk. Pedestrians had to rely on using torches, pointed to the ground, to help find their way around. Even cars and buses had half of their headlamps blacked out. White lines had been painted down the middle of the roads and many of the kerbstones had also been painted white to help avoid unnecessary accidents. Anyone caught by the Air Raid Wardens showing a light in their house could find themselves taken to court and fined as much as two pounds. Unlike the locals, the marines found that they didn't need torches to help find their way. Over the previous weeks of training, their night vision had been developed to a high ability, so that whilst each trip out was, of course, challenging, they found that it was well within their capabilities.

(ii)

Their training continued apace and, as they had learnt previously, not without risk. Accidents were frequent and sometimes even fatal. One early morning Dacre and Wills, as part of Number Ten Platoon, found themselves on the pier at Ventnor. Part of the pier had been breached in 1940 to stop the Germans, should they decide to invade. The marines had put together a toggle rope, which they had strung between the two parts of the pier. Several marines had already managed to get across, whilst two others were midway on the rope. It was Pete Wills's turn next. Just as he climbed onto it, one of the toggles snapped sending the two other marines crashing down onto the rocks, some thirty feet below. As luck would have it, Dacre was the next in line. Somehow or other, he swung out and managed to catch hold of his mate's webbing equipment. For a brief moment, Wills hung dangling in mid-air, his arms flailing around like a demented spider. To make matters worse, his rifle and sling had slipped from his shoulder to around his throat and was doing its best to strangle him. Exerting all his strength, and with the help of another couple of lads, Dacre managed to haul Wills back onto the promenade deck to safety where they all collapsed in an undignified tangle of bodies. Sergeant Thrattles had been watching all of this with considerable concern. As soon as he could see that everyone was safe, he bellowed out, 'Come on, come on you idle buggers. Pick yourselves up and get moving. You still have that gap to cross.'

'No rest for the wicked. What a bloody slave driver that man is. Still it's good to know that he cares about us,' said Dacre somewhat sarcastically.

The two marines that fell onto the rocks below both survived but needed hospital treatment. They did not return to the Commando.

CHAPTER 18

(i)

Commander Fleming was beside himself with excitement. He could hardly contain himself. These were feelings that he was not used to having, and he felt more than a little strange. His colleagues knew him as a man not given to public demonstrations of his feelings. He preferred to remain somewhat cold and aloof from his peers, something he had perfected over the years. But today was different, very different. He felt that he wanted to run and shout out his good news. It was only with a great deal of effort that he managed to control himself.

Naval Intelligence had just received reliable information from the French Resistance that a four-wheeled Enigma machine and encrypting codes were to be found at the German Naval Headquarters in Dieppe. This was a gift. Bletchley Park staff desperately needed these codes to help them break the Kriegsmarine's complex communication system with their U-boats. At this very moment, the Allies were planning a full-scale raid on that self-same port. The coincidence was too good to be true. Fleming quickly realised that this was a heaven-sent opportunity. It was, he felt, up to him to seize the initiative and to somehow or other use the raid to capture the codebooks. He had decided that he would create a special unit, dedicated to the task of obtaining enemy documents and equipment from under the noses of the Germans. Of course, this unit would naturally be under the overall command of Naval Intelligence, but it was, he felt, just the sort of thing that the Royal Marine Commandos had been trained for. Without waiting to clear his idea with his immediate superior the Director of Naval Intelligence, Rear Admiral Godfrey, he knew that, ultimately, Mountbatten, as Chief of Combined Operations, would approve. Fleming decided to act immediately. He quickly sent a signal to the CO of the unit, requesting an urgent meeting. Then he booked himself onto the next available train from London to Portsmouth. He also took the time to pull a few strings in order to arrange for a staff car and driver to meet him at Portsmouth station and to take him across to the Isle of Wight to meet the Commanding Officer of the Royal Marines.

Lieutenant Colonel Picton-Phillipps's office was in the dining room of a rather nice Victorian house in which he and his senior officers were billeted. The Naval staff car swept up the gravel driveway and came to a halt in a cloud of dust, in front of a neo classical portico. Fleming got out of the car quickly, and was met by the unit's Adjutant, Captain Alain Comyn, who escorted him inside.

(ii)

Truth be told, Fleming was somewhat taken aback by the number of people assembled in the room. He shook hands with the CO briefly, who then introduced him to the others. Everyone sat down around a very elegant table, complete with a matching pair of Georgian candelabra. The Colonel spoke first in his rather sharp, incisive way.

'Well, Commander. Perhaps you would be kind enough to explain to us just what all this is about.'

Fleming looked around the table at these rugged, tough men. He saw that no-one was smoking and, although he was dying for a cigarette, thought better of lighting up. Briefly, he explained that he wanted to put together a special unit of marines, capable of acting independently, who would be tasked with stealing codebooks from the Germans. What he really wanted was a platoon-sized group, who would go on detached duties for special training to Portsmouth Harbour. He explained that at present he could neither tell them the place nor the date of the special operation because it was still classified as 'Top Secret'.

The assembled company sat in stony silence. Nobody liked the sound of this madcap plan. Major Houghton spoke first. Although he was extremely angry, he managed to control his voice.

'Let me get this clear, Commander. You want to take one of our best platoons of highly trained and fit marines off on some wild goose chase, God knows where.'

Fleming was somewhat taken aback by the outburst. He was used to being in the driver's seat, in control. He felt his plan slipping through his fingers.

'Yes, I do, Major. Firstly, if it will help all of you to focus on the urgency of my request, then the Chief of Combined Operations would be pleased to send a direct order.' This was not actually true, he knew, but he reasoned that fortune favoured the brave, or was it the fool hardy, he couldn't remember. 'Secondly, this is not some wild goose chase, as you put it. The stealing of these documents will undoubtedly save lives and shorten the war. In the short term, it will certainly help Britain in its current hour of need. I can say no more than that at present.'

The CO held up his hand to quell the discussion, lest it turn into a full-blown argument which would do nobody any good.

'An order from Mountbatten will not be necessary,' he said. 'We shall be pleased to co-operate as fully as we can.'

An uneasy silence descended on the room. So that was that, thought Fleming. It had not been as difficult as he had imagined. The Adjutant took the opportunity to ask a question that all those present were thinking.

'May I ask…, Commander, what about the rest of the Commando?'

Uncharacteristically, Fleming felt a wave of sympathy for the Marines. Here he was descending on them from on high, so to speak, and absconding with one of their prized platoons without as much as a by-your-leave.

'Well, obviously I cannot give you any details yet.' Then looking directly at the CO, he added, 'If I were you, sir, I would put my men on a 'ready to move' order in the next couple of weeks or so.'

There was a collective sigh from around the table. Fleming gave a small smile.

'Now, sir, what about this platoon?' Picton-Phillipps looked across the table to the
'X' Company Commander.

'Well, Simon, what do you suggest?'

'To be honest, sir, it is extremely difficult to pick out any one platoon. In terms of fitness and commitment, there is nothing to choose between any of them. If, however, we look at individual marines to see if they have any particular strengths that might suit Mr Fleming's purpose….' He paused for effect.

'Well, go on, man, go on,' said the Colonel, in a rather strangled voice.

'In Number Ten Platoon we have a marine who is fluent in German and French, and another who was a safe-breaker in civilian life.'

'Titch' Houghton interrupted. 'I can speak for the linguist, Marine Dacre. I interviewed him when we were at Deal. He really impressed our visiting professor at the time. You will recall, sir, that this was the marine who persuaded his roommates to go running on the beach every day. He also led that very successful night raid exercise to capture an enemy communications expert.'

Everyone looked expectantly at the Commander.

'That sounds ideal, Colonel,' replied Fleming. 'How do you suggest we proceed?'

'I don't wish to be awkward, Commander, but this is your show. You tell us what you want, and we will do our best to comply. You will understand, I am sure, when I say that I want an officer and a SNCO to be part of this group. It's all about the chain of command. I think both Lieutenant Ellis and Sergeant Thrattles will fit the bill nicely.'

Fleming looked at the two men sitting quietly in the corner of the room. He hadn't noticed them before. He suddenly realised that he had been outmanoeuvred by that wily old bugger of a colonel. He looked at the two men again. The officer was young and inexperienced, so he wouldn't be much of a problem. But the sergeant, he was another matter. He looked to be very experienced and sharp with it. There would be no pulling the wool over his eyes, that was for sure.

CHAPTER 19

(i)

Two days later, the whole of Number Ten Platoon moved into temporary accommodation at the Royal Marines Barracks at Eastney, which was on the sea front of Southsea, a suburb of Portsmouth. The barracks overlooked the Solent and the Eastern part of the Isle of Wight. For Dacre it was a return to the scene of his so-called boxing triumph, when three years earlier he and his squad mate 'Jacko' had taken part in the Corps Championships. However, for many of the marines, particularly those who were HO, this was their first visit to what had been the renowned home of the Royal Marines Artillery or RMA as they were known, that was until they amalgamated with the Royal Marines Light Infantry in 1923. Now it was the *alma mater* of the 'sea going' marines. Of course, for many in the Corps, this is what they believed being a 'Royal' was all about. Together with the Divisions at Plymouth and Chatham, the Portsmouth Division at Eastney Barracks provided detachments for the ships of the Royal Navy's Grand Fleets around the world.

The platoon's trucks were halted by a red and white striped barrier at the imposing red brick entrance gates to the barracks. Two large Royal Marines Policemen, with their red caps and MP armbands, checked the vehicles over, while Sergeant Throttles reported to the guardroom. He could be seen laughing and joking with someone he obviously knew. The Corps was like that, you were always meeting up with former mess mates, often in the most unlikely places. Lieutenant Ellis remained in the cab of the vehicle, feeling more than a little out of his depth. The sergeant returned and, hanging onto the running board, directed the driver the short distance to the drill shed and their accommodation. As luck would have it, the platoon had been allocated two rooms on the ground floor over-looking the main parade ground.

Whilst they were sorting out their kit and their beds, several of the lads took the opportunity to look out of the large windows. They could clearly see that the parade ground was a hive of activity. Company upon company of marines were being put through their paces in close order drill by eagle-eyed drill instructors. Their commands, given in that distinctive staccato voice that only Drill Instructors can have, could be heard drifting across on the wind.

'Will you look at that,' said Pete Wills in wonderment. 'I've never seen anything like it before, so many marines all drilling at once.' Then he asked, 'What's that big white building over there?' He pointed to the far end of the parade ground.

Dacre looked up. 'That's the Officers' Mess,' he replied. 'It's very grand looking, especially with those two sweeping staircases at the entrance. However, I've been told that it's so cold that the officers have to wear their greatcoats when they have their meals.'

'Poor buggers,' said Baz Phelps. 'They should be so lucky.'

At that moment, the barrack room door opened and in walked Sergeant Thrattles, followed by Lieutenant Ellis who seemed somewhat reluctant to enter. Both the Sergeant and the Young Officer had chosen not to live in their respective messes. Instead, they had agreed to share one of the small rooms, normally put aside for corporals.

'Anyone been here before?' asked the Sergeant.

One or two put up their hands including Dacre.

'Okay, your job is to make sure that everyone knows where the NAAFI and the dining hall are to be found, and also where the sick bay is located. The rest of the afternoon is yours. Supper starts at 1800 hours. That's the good news. The bad news is that tomorrow morning at 0800 hours you will be on the main parade for inspection, along with the rest of the barracks.'

This news was met by a huge groan of dismay from everyone.

'There was nothing I, or Mr Ellis, could do about it. The RSM has told me that his Colonel insists. So, make sure you are clean and smart, and that your equipment and weapons are immaculate. I am given to understand that the Colonel will be inspecting you himself. You are the first commandos that he's come across, so don't let yourselves, or us, down.' Turning to his officer he asked, 'Is there anything you would like to add, sir?'

'Only this. The CO, here, is of the old school. For him Royal Marines should be on ships, not running around pretending to be like the Army. You will have noticed how everyone in barracks is dressed in blues, and march about as if they are still on the parade ground. That's how the Colonel likes it. To achieve this, the RSM and the Adjutant run this place like a tight ship, and with a fist of iron. Nothing is out of place, and everything is shipshape. The last thing they really want is a load of 'khaki marines' mucking up their sense of order. Because we dress differently, and are trained differently, they will try to and catch us out. So, do not give them the slightest reason to. Remember, you are also Royal Marines.'

Sergeant Thrattles glared at everyone. 'Alright, you 'orrible lot. You heard this officer of marines. Just remember you have been warned.'

(ii)

It was a very cold and blustery morning. The wind blowing in from the sea, swept across the main parade ground unabated. Dark, heavy storm clouds gathered over the Solent, and were moving slowly towards land and the barracks. There were about five hundred marines, formed up in companies and detachments, all of them in their best dark blue uniforms ready for inspection. They all stood formally at ease, waiting for the arrival of the Commanding Officer. Whether it was the anticipation of what was to come or just the cold wind, quite a few men began to shiver. Occasionally, the voice of one of the
drill instructors could be heard shouting out, 'Stand still in the ranks, damn you!'

At the very far end of the parade ground Number Ten Platoon stood ready. Despite being dressed for combat, they all looked very smart. They had clearly taken their officer's words to heart. At last, the Commanding Officer arrived accompanied by his Adjutant. The RSM called the whole parade to attention, his deep voice echoing off the walls of the nearby buildings carried effortlessly to the four corners of the parade ground. A bugle sounded for the officers to take post. The RSM then made his report to the Colonel that all were present and correct.

It began to rain. Just a few drops at first. Then, within seconds, it turned into a deluge, which made even the hardiest of Marines flinch. The order to 'stand fast' could be heard up and down the ranks. Unlike the rest of the parade, the platoon were not the slightest bit bothered by the change in weather. After Acknacarry, this was a walk in the park. They stood their ground, heads held high with an air of confidence and just a little sense of arrogance, that said, we are proud to be Commandos. The platoon stood at open order and the rain continued its torrential downpour. The Colonel arrived accompanied by Ellis. The CO was drenched to the skin: his cap and uniform completely sodden. Rainwater dripped down his face and off his large white moustache. He was cold and wet, and he felt bloody miserable. But as wet as he was, he was a professional. His thirty years in the Corps had taught him that an officer must never ever show his true feelings in front of the men. He was the Barrack's Commanding Officer, therefore he must always behave and act like one. At that moment the RSM could be heard giving the order to 'break ranks'. This was followed by a mass exodus from the parade, as officers and men dashed to the shelter of the nearby buildings. Number Ten Platoon stood fast, facing an empty parade ground. To give him his due, the Colonel took his time to walk slowly up and down each rank, stopping here and there to question a man about a piece of kit or a particular weapon. At the end of the inspection he congratulated Lieutenant Ellis on the turnout of his men, particularly in such horrendous conditions. He added that there would be no further need for the unit to parade again.

(iii)

Later that morning, the Platoon was driven down to Portsmouth Harbour where Commander Fleming had been waiting for them for nearly an hour. He was not best pleased by the delay. Nevertheless, under his watchful eye, they began their training for the forthcoming pinch raid. The first part of the day was spent speeding around the harbour in very fast motor gun boats, which would race up to a wharf and disembark the marines. Well, that was the theory. Time and time again, the boats missed their mark and, when they did manage to stop in the right place, the disembarkation was chaos. Men fell or tripped over each other. Some couldn't get up onto the wharf-side, whilst at least three marines missed their footing and fell into the water. Fleming was not happy. He stomped up and down the quayside smoking cigarette after cigarette, cursing the marines for all his worth. Lieutenant Ellis tried to placate him, but he was having none of it.

Sergeant Thrattles took a more pragmatic approach, as he explained to the young officer when there was a lull in the training. 'I see it like this, sir. This Navy gentleman wants us to be his little army. He clearly has a taste for action and adventure. To him, I suspect, it's a bit like playing cowboys and indians. This whole business is clearly his idea and he doesn't want it to be seen to fail. He knows bugger all about training and expects everything to be done perfect first time out. Well, life and soldiering ain't like that. We will get it right, of course we will, but in the meantime, he's going to have to be patient and lump it.'

Ellis looked at his Sergeant in a new light. He realised how right the NCO was. Better to concentrate on the men and their training than wasting time trying to keep the Commander sweet and happy.

Gradually, over the next few hours, things began to improve. They could now at least get off the boats and onto the dockside quickly and efficiently. Fleming, with his stopwatch and clipboard in hand, seemed to be a little happier. The next part of their training required the platoon to break into specific teams of four men. Each team was allocated a particular task. Some were to secure the buildings, others the dockside, and others to capture prisoners.

Dacre and Wills were in the same team. Their task was to head for the communications office on the first floor of the German Naval Headquarters. They would be accompanied by a four-man protection team whose job it was to make sure that these two got there safely. Once there, they were to seize the codebooks. When this task was completed, Wills was then to open any safes that they came across. Dacre was to check the contents and remove any documents he considered to be of value. Fleming had briefed him as to what to look for. Finally, they would be escorted back out of the building to a waiting boat and away as quickly as possible to the ships lying offshore. The platoon rehearsed this part of the plan, time and time again. Fleming would stand close by urging them on, constantly checking his stopwatch. Of course, they got better and faster, to the extent that after three or four days they could have done the raid in their sleep. In the meantime, Wills found himself sharpening up his civvy skills when he was presented with a room full of different sized safes.

'It's rather like learning to ride a bicycle,' he said to Dacre one evening. 'It's something you never forget.'

By the end of his part of the training, he could open each one of the safes put in front of him. Fleming was most impressed.

At the end of the fifth day, the Commander declared that he was finally satisfied with the progress that the platoon had made. He just knew that this raid was going to be a great success, he felt it in his bones. The platoon was dismissed, for the time being, and allowed to return to their commando unit on the Isle of Wight.

(iv)

Fleming returned to the Admiralty and reported both to his boss and to Rear Admiral Mountbatten. As he had anticipated, the Chief of Combined Operations was delighted that Fleming had seized the initiative. He knew that Churchill would give this pinch raid his blessing. This was right up his street. The only down-side to all of this was that Fleming would not be allowed to lead the raid himself. He was bitterly disappointed, mainly because he had already imagined himself leading 'his' men in a glorious and successful raid. However, it was not to be. Mountbatten pointed out to him that his work at Naval Intelligence made him too important. The Germans would love to capture him, particularly because he was privy to the planning for an eventual D-Day landing. As much as Fleming protested, it was no good. Mountbatten would not be moved. However, in the end he relented slightly and agreed that the Commander could be on one of the ships several miles offshore, there to wait and receive the much-prized Enigma codebooks and bigram tables.

CHAPTER 20

(i)

Colonel Picton-Phillipps stood staring out of the window of the dining room that served as his office. The view across Ventnor Bay, from the elegant Victorian house that had been allocated to him and his staff, was magnificent. It was a warm, sunny day, with the odd puffball of cloud in the sky. Overhead, dozens of seagulls wheeled and dived towards a small group of fishing boats that had just entered the tiny harbour alongside the pier. But the Colonel did not register any of this. He was in deep thought. Truth be told, he was a worried man. He rubbed the back of his head with his left hand, then automatically stroked his chin with his right. Those who knew him well, particularly his Headquarters staff, would have recognised the signs. This was someone struggling to resolve a dilemma.

The main cause of this concern was that his beloved Commando had come to the peak of their fighting condition. Like a finely-honed sword, (or should that have been a fighting knife?), their training both at Achnacarry and here on the Isle of Wight had brought them to a high state of readiness. Now that Number Ten Platoon had re-joined the unit, he didn't want the unit to lose the sharp edge that he and his fellow officers had worked so hard to achieve. In his view, and those of his training team, his marines were as good as, if not better than, those of the Army, but of course he knew that he was biased. However, the training team were not. This small but highly trained group of experts, drawn from across the armed forces, had assured him that his unit was not only fit and ready for duty but, in their opinion, they were superior to most, if not all, the Army Commandos. The key question, and the one he had been struggling with, was how could he maintain this level of readiness, this edge, whilst at the same time demonstrate to his superiors at Brigade level and at Combined Operations that the Royal Marine Commandos were ready for action. It was true that Commander Fleming had recently indicated the possibility of operational duties, but to date nothing had materialised. So, he realised it was clearly up to him to get things moving in order to demonstrate their capabilities to the full.

The Colonel turned from the window and re-traced his footsteps across the room to the table on which a large-scale map of the Isle of White had been spread out. What was he looking for? He didn't really know. Something that his men could get their teeth into. Something that would allow them to show that they really were commandos of the highest order. But what? That was the damn problem. Once more, he studied the details of the map. His unit ideally needed a target that they could attack, something to seize and hold. Using the index finger of his right hand, he followed the coastline on the map, pausing here and there, then moving on. A military target of some type would be ideal, he thought. He paused at the fort by the Needles. He had visited it when he had first arrived on the island. The General Officer Commanding had taken him on a welcome tour in his staff car as part of his introduction to island life. The old battery guns had been replaced by more modern and up-to-date weapons that covered and protected the approaches to the Solent and, in particular, Southampton and Portsmouth. The cliffs on which the guns were located were of chalk and were extremely steep. Not, however, a problem to his men should the need arise, but still not ideal for a sea-borne assault. Besides which, a raid by his men would mean that the army gunners and personnel could well be prevented from carrying out their primary task of protecting the Solent. No, that was not an option! His finger moved on, following the coastline on the map. Eventually, having passed Sandown and Shankhill, he ended up where he had begun, back at Ventnor. 'Damn and blast', he said to himself. This was most frustrating. He gazed at the map trying to rack his brains for any sense of an idea.

Then, there it was. Eureka! The possible answer to his problem, had been staring him in the face. Located inland, about two miles from the coast, was a Marconi Radio Station. He studied the map carefully. There were numerous tracks and footpaths in the area, and nearby were the ruins of an old building that went by the name of Cook's Castle. This would be an ideal target. The Colonel realised that he could deploy his commandos in a classic two-pronged attack. He would task his companies to come ashore by landing craft. The first company could land at Luccombe Bay, whilst another company could carry out a beach landing at Monk's Bay.

Both groups could then move inland independently to carry out their main objective which was to seize and hold the radio station. The compound would undoubtedly have a guard, perhaps provided by the Territorials or the Home Guard. But he could strengthen that with a platoon of men from the third company, the remainder of which would provide his reserve. Maybe he could even get them equipped with German uniforms - now that would certainly add a real touch of realism. Time to get things moving, he thought. The Colonel went to the door and called for his adjutant.

(ii)

The officers and SNCOs crowded into the CO's dining room. The air was already blue with cigarette smoke. Chairs, the table and the windowsills had all been utilised as seating; even so, some of the junior ranks had to sit on the floor.

There was a cheerful chatter from those gathered, and an informality between the ranks not unknown in the Marines. At the front of the room stood a blackboard and easel, covered in a grey service blanket. Colonel Picton-Phillipps, accompanied by the second-in-command and the adjutant, entered the room. The RSM ordered the men to sit to attention, standing was just impossible. The Colonel looked around at his men. He was positively beaming.

'Sit easy chaps, carry on smoking,' he said. 'Perhaps someone might open a window or two?' A young second lieutenant willingly obliged. 'Thank you, Ian.'

The Colonel turned to the blackboard and carefully removed the blanket. On the board someone had carefully drawn a map, using coloured chalks. Necks craned and heads moved as people tried to get a better view. Picton-Phillipps let them study the map for a few minutes.

'Right then. Exercise *Marconi*. This night-time operation has been designed to test the fitness and readiness of our commando. Its sole purpose is to convince those in authority that we should be an operational unit. To this end, we are going to undertake a night attack, to seize and hold this radio station, here, *at* Grid Reference 560804. Because there are so many other troops on the island, our area of operation will be here within this boundary, marked by these roads and the railway.'

The colonel produced a walking stick from behind the board and carefully traced the outline on the map. Those watching were frantically scribbling and drawing in their field notebooks.

'This will be a classic two-pronged attack from the sea. We will use landing craft to bring us ashore. Jimmy, your company will embark at 2100 hours at Sandown. You will land here at Luccombe Bay. Oh, and expect a wet landing. You will be in position and ready to assault at 2330 hours at GR 556800. Do you think that gives you enough time to get there?'

James Graham studied the map carefully. 'Yes, sir, that should be fine,' he replied.

'Good man. Now, Dick, your company will embark at Shanklin. Your drop off point will be Monk's Bay. You will proceed to GR 566802, and I want you in position by 2330 hours.'

At this point the Colonel paused and looked at the OC of 'X' Company. 'Simon, I'm sorry but I want you, your officers and SNCOs to leave the briefing at this point. I will talk to you later.' Simon Standwell stood up and looked at his boss quizzically. 'It's all about realism, Simon. We need to make this as real as possible.'

'Aye, aye, sir, understood.' Standwell and his men left the room.

The Colonel continued. 'Now then, back to business. At precisely 0015 hours, I want both companies to assault the radio compound. I shall leave the details up to you. However, I suggest that you use one of your platoons to secure the wire and facilitate entry, another platoon to take the compound and the third to guard the back door, so that you can get back to the beach. Departure time has been scheduled for 0230 hours by landing craft. Now, as you can see from the map, the terrain is quite high, and although it will be difficult in the dark, it should be manageable. Those defending the Radio Station will be 'German'. They will be wearing German uniforms, equipment and will have German weapons. They will also be speaking German, so there should be no problems about identification.

'I want this attack to be completely silent, so no gunfire or noise of any sort, and especially no war cries. There will, of course, be observers with you, but do not let them get in the way. I think that is all. Are there any questions?'

Captain Graham put up his hand.

'Yes, Jimmy?'

'What about civilians or other friendly forces that we might come across. Shall we detain them?'

Picton–Phillipps thought about this for a minute or two. 'No, I think not. If people start to go 'missing' then that might cause ripples of attention that we could do without. So, at all costs, avoid any contact with others, even if that means delaying the start of the attack.'

Captain Richard Whyte had his hand up.

'Yes, Dick?'

'Two things, sir. Firstly communications. I presume we shall have radios?'

'Yes, of course, that goes without saying. Normal call signs for all of us and your companies, but please keep your radio traffic to the minimum.'

'Secondly, sir. Where will you and headquarters be?'

The Colonel looked at his young company commander carefully. What was he suggesting? That the old man wasn't up to this? The seconds ticked past. One or two in the room began to fidget. Embarrassed perhaps? No, decided the Colonel. It was a genuine question.

'I shall be here with the HQ group at GR 564795. I shall also have the remainder of 'X' Company with me, who, in addition to being our reserve, will ensure that our way out is safeguarded. There is just one further thing. The security fence surrounding the compound has eight-foot high iron stakes, with three pronged spearheads, and is topped with barbed wire. Under no circumstances must these be cut. So, do you have any ideas as to how we might gain entry?'

There was silence in the room. Dick Whyte put up his hand. The Colonel nodded at him.

'Well, sir. Just recently, some of my men have been practising how to get over a wall in quick time. I think that was about eight-foot high.'

'Well, come on, lad, give,' said Picton-Phillipps, not unkindly.

'Well, sir, two men hold a rifle waist high and horizontal to the ground, with their sides to the wall. The third man runs up and puts a foot on the rifle, whilst the other two flip him up and over the wall in one fluid movement. It takes a bit of practice, but if we had, say, half a dozen of these teams in place, then we could get a couple of dozen men inside in quick time.'

'Sounds good to me,' said the Colonel. 'I'll leave you and Jimmy to get together over this. Just make sure your men get plenty of practice. If there is nothing else, then I need to brief Captain Standwell about what I want his men to do. Just make sure that everyone gets a hot meal and has some rest. It's going to be a very long night. Thank you everyone.'

The room emptied quickly. Colonel Picton-Phillipps sat down at the end of the table. Major 'Titch' Houghton sat to his left, whilst the Adjutant, Captain Peter Hellings, sat to his right.

'That went well,' said 'Titch' Houghton.

Hellings nodded in agreement.

The Colonel was quiet, calm and unruffled, thinking things through. Yes, things were going well, largely because he had been blessed with some excellent officers, especially his company and platoon commanders, who, although young, were outstanding examples of quality leaders. He flicked open the file in front of him and quickly scanned down each of the enclosed documents:

Captain Simon Standwell MC
Height: 5ft 11" Weight: 12 stone Age:28 years
Born: Greenwich, London. Educated: Dulwich College
Good all-round student, very talented cricketer, played for the MCC.
Attended University College London, Honours degree in Geology.
Employed by Standard Oil Company, spent four years in Texas.
Married to Emily Jane (Irish American citizen), twin girls, Jennifer and Sylvia.
Commissioned 1939. Served on HMS Hood, part of the landing force at Andalsnes, Norway.
Mentioned-in-dispatches and awarded the Military Cross, a courageous and enterprising officer.

Captain James Graham
Height: 6ft 2" Weight: 15 stone Age: 27 years.
Born: Maidstone, Kent. Educated: Maidstone Boys' Grammar School.
Attended King's College Cambridge. Double First in Theology and Philosophy.
A very talented rower and would have been in the next Boat Race.
A teacher at Worksop College, Nottinghamshire.

Commissioned into the Royal Marines in 1939. Served on HMS Sheffield at Narvik, Norway.
A natural, energetic leader.

Captain Richard Paul Whyte
Height: 6ft 4". Weight: 14 stone. Age: 25 years.
Born: Muswell Hill, London. Educated: Highgate School, North London. Keen hockey player.
Excelled in mathematics, turned down a place at Oxford. Joined St Martin's Bank in the City and studied accountancy.
Volunteered as a Hostilities Only (HO) marine in the ranks. Commissioned 1940.
Served on the cruiser HMS Glasgow, Trondheim, Norway.
A dynamic young officer.

Yes, thought the Colonel, he was very fortunate. In conversations that he had had with other commanding officers, he knew that not everyone had been so lucky. He also knew that the rank and file of his commando referred to these young officers as the 'Three Musketeers' after Alexander Dumas heroes, not only because of their bravery, which had become something of a legend, but because of their steadfastness and reliability. Yes, he really had been blessed.

The door to the dining room opened and Simon Standwell entered.
'Ah, Simon, come in dear boy and sit down. Sorry about all the cloak-and-dagger stuff, but needs must you know.
'That's okay, sir, I quite understand. If I may say so, I think it's rather a good idea.'
'Thank you, Simon, thank you. Now I want some of your chaps to play the part of the enemy. You have some German speakers, I understand?'
'Yes, sir. Two in Number Ten Platoon who are fluent, there's Lieutenant Ellis and Marine Dacre. There are also a couple of others that have a smattering.'
'Good, good, just what I wanted to hear.' The colonel looked around at the others. 'So, Ten Platoon will be dressed and fully equipped with German weapons and uniforms. You will instruct them to speak only in

German, at all times. Transport will be available to take your men up to the radio station at 2030 hours. Make sure that everyone has a hot meal before they go. Hay boxes and tea urns will be made available to them. Any questions?'

'I don't think so, sir. It all seems fairly straightforward. What about the rest of my company?'

'They will join me as the reserve unit. We will embark in landing craft at Sandown, along with Jimmy's men, and will land at Luccombe Bay. We will then move independently to GR 564795. I will set up my HQ there. I want your two remaining platoons to form a defensive screen to our rear, between us and the sea. It's not very exciting, I know, but someone has to do it, and it is important that we cover our backs. We are due to withdraw at 0130 hours; the landing crafts have been scheduled to pick us up at 0230 hours. Any more questions?'

'No, sir.'

'Right, then. Let's get on, shall we? There's a lot to do.'

(iii)

Marine Dacre sat facing Pete Wills in the back of a very ancient lorry with the rest of the marines from his troop. They had drawn the short straw and were to be the enemy. The vehicle was making its way slowly up the narrow single track towards the radio station. They seemed to be hitting every pothole that the driver could find. The truck swayed dangerously from side to side, trying to avoid the deep culverts that ran down each side of the lane. Wills was constantly scratching himself, particularly under his arms.

'This German uniform is bloody awful,' he said. 'This poor bugger must have had fleas. And look at this, a fucking bullet hole right by my heart.' He stuck his finger through and waggled it to make the point. 'I mean, just look at us!'

Dacre just grinned at his friend. 'Well, at least you're alive, which is more than we can say for your uniform's previous owner.'

But Wills was right, they did look a strange sight. They had all been issued with German field-grey uniforms, boots, weapons, helmets and equipment. In the half-light they looked very convincing, so much so that the canvas flap of the back of the truck had been rolled down, in case any of the locals saw them and panicked, thinking that the invasion had started.

Pete Wills continued to moan. 'Any way, why us? How come we get to be chosen to be the bloody Germans. I bet it was that Lieutenant Ellis what volunteered us. He's too keen by far, that one. We need to watch him, mark my words.'

Dacre just looked at his friend. He was getting more than a little tired of his constant moaning.

'Just shut the fuck up, Pete, for crying out loud. Enough is enough. Don't you think we all wanted to be in the attacking force. This is what we have trained for and yet here we are playing the part of the Wehrmacht. It may not be what we wanted, but we have a job to do, just like everyone else in the unit. So, we'll do it as well as we can, come hell or high water. Is that clear enough for you?'

Dacre looked around the truck, and, in the gloom, he could just see heads nodding in agreement. Pete Wills sat back in his seat and hung his head. This was the first time that his best mate had ever chastised him.

'And don't sulk,' Dacre added as an afterthought.

Wills looked up, a cheeky smile returning to his face.

'Sorry AJ, you're right. Sorry everyone. I'm really sorry, it won't happen again.'

The friendly silence that followed was interrupted by their arrival at the radio station. As they piled out of the truck, the NCOs began to allocate them to their positions within the wire fenced compound. Although it was a bright moonlit night, the occasional cloud scudded across the sky creating areas of shadow and darkness. All was quiet as the 'German' guards patrolled the eight-foot high security fencing. They had been given very clear instructions. They were to be extra vigilant and were to respond appropriately and with enthusiasm to any entry made by the attacking force. An old ship's bell had been set up in the compound, to be rung when an attack began. For obvious reasons the pre-war floodlights were not being used. All the guards had been issued with blank ammunition, thunderflashes and smoke grenades in order to make the whole exercise more realistic. None of the men guarding the radio station knew what to expect from the attacking force. The CO had deliberately excluded their officers and NCOs from the planning meetings and final briefing. To further add to the sense of realism, Dacre and Lieutenant

Ellis had been instructed to talk and issue all orders in German, since they were the two who could really speak the language

It was 0015 hours. The night, rather surprisingly, was cold - so cold that they could see their breath on the air. It was unbelievably quiet. Dacre and Pete Wills had been patrolling their part of the south side of the perimeter fence since 2300 hours and were not due to be relieved for another hour. Their routine was simple, but effective. One of them started from one end of the fence, and one from the other end. They met in the middle, grunted to each other, turned about and repeated the process. It was a boring and monotonous exercise, and they found it quite difficult to keep focused. The chill of the night seeped into their bones, sapping their energy. What they really needed was a hot drink. As they met again, Wills stopped, his eyes straining to see through the fence into the darkened area beyond.

'What was that?' he whispered.

Dacre turned his head slowly, cocked his head towards the direction that Wills was indicating, opened his mouth and listened intently. He had used this listening skill many times before and it had served him well. However, this was not the first time that Wills had thought that he had heard something.

'I don't know,' he replied shaking his head, 'I can't hear anything.'

Suddenly there was the sound of running feet, faint at first, then becoming louder. Dacre spun around. There, coming out of the darkness were about a dozen attackers, faces blackened and weapons at the ready. Not a word or a war-cry was to be heard.

Dacre broke the silence as he shouted out the alarm. 'Quick, sound the bell, they've got in!'

However, it was too late. Both he and Wills were overwhelmed in a welter of punches and kicks. Wills went down immediately, unable to retaliate, shouting out, 'There's too many of them!'. Dacre managed to stay on his feet for a few more minutes. He wasn't going to make it easy for them. He gritted his teeth as he raised his rifle, trying to defend himself. It was useless. They were on him like dogs tearing at a stag. He narrowly avoided a blow to his chest. The blood was pounding in his veins as the adrenalin kicked in. His muscles were straining, and it was becoming difficult to breath. He was strong, but more men were coming to join the attack. He managed to parry another blow, a real haymaker of a punch, then kneed his attacker in the groin. The man doubled over in pain and, to his credit, did not call out. Someone else grabbed him around his neck and was pulling him backwards. At the same time, his feet were kicked away from under him. He tried to twist sideways but lost his footing. Sweat from under his helmet was stinging his eyes, he could barely make out his adversaries. Then, by sheer weight of numbers, he was forced to the ground. Lying on his back, he stared up at the night sky, he knew then that it was all over. He stopped struggling and went limp, as a sign of surrender. The massive weight of men on top of him eased and, not too unkindly, he was pulled to his feet.

For the first time someone spoke, 'Well done, 'Royal', that was pretty convincing.

One or two of the attackers even patted him on his back or on his helmet. He just
stood there, somewhat dazed. There was blood running down his cheek from a cut on his face. His throat was hoarse from shouting encouragement to the others to stand firm. As the last of the adrenaline faded, so fatigue moved in. The cuts and bruises began to hurt, and his body began to shake. Elsewhere in the compound it was much the same story. The defenders had been completely overwhelmed by this extremely well-planned and executed raid. With the exercise finished the commandos melted away into the darkness, back the way they had come. Those acting as the Germans were given the option of a ride back to Ventnor in the trucks or they could walk if they wished. Dacre, Pete Wills and several others decided to walk. They wanted the exercise and needed to unwind.

(iv)

It was about 0430 hours by the time the little group found themselves walking past the Parish Church and the Post Office, down towards the High Street. They had already passed a sand-bagged gun emplacement, manned by a couple of sleepy territorials, when they came across the local police sergeant talking to several men from the Home Guard who were going off-duty. They casually looked at the 'German' soldiers marching down their street, then carried on with their conversation, totally unperturbed.

'Well I never,' said Wills. 'What do you make of that? You'd think that they would have challenged us at the very least, rather than just ignore us altogether.'

Dacre just nodded and smiled. He took off his helmet and scratched his damp hair.

'People see what they want to see. Despite our uniforms they just don't see Germans. I think life on the island must be too comfortable for them. Despite all the troops here, perhaps the war seems to be a long way away. I don't blame them for that, I suspect it's an easy frame of mind to slip into. However, I'm sure the Colonel will be interested when he gets to hear about it.'

Later that week, the unit heard that Colonel Picton-Phillipps had been delighted with the results of the raid. There was also more good news. Both the Brigadier in charge of the Commando Brigade, and Combined Operations Headquarters, had been given the green light for Royal Marines 'A' Commando to become fully operational. Since Number Ten Platoon had already been tasked with a specific role, it was now just a question of finding something for the rest of the unit to do.

PART FOUR

INCURSION

Foray, infiltration,
inroad, invasion,
penetration,
raid, sally,
sortie, attack.

CHAPTER 21

(i)

Dacre and Pete Wills were sitting in the back of a three-ton truck being bounced about. Sergeant Throttles was up in the front of the cab with the driver. The three of them were on their way from Shanklin to Newport to pick up half a dozen replacement marines and some stores that had been shipped from the mainland to Cowes, and then on by rail.

'I wonder why they couldn't have just sent everything by train,' said Wills. 'You know, send it direct like, straight to us.'

'No idea,' replied Dacre, as he flinched slightly when the truck hit another pothole. Just then the vehicle slowed down and came to a halt in front of a red and white barrier that had been hastily thrown across the road. It was manned by two military policemen.

'That's another thing,' said Wills. 'Have you noticed how many more MPs there seem to be? The bloody Military Police are everywhere.'

Can't say that I've noticed,' replied Dacre AJ, scratching his chin.

'There's something going on, you know, weird like, mark my words, and I bet it will involve us.'

When they arrived at the railway station, they had half an hour to kill.

'Time for a cup of tea and a sticky bun', said Sergeant Throttles.

Having been served, the three marines settled themselves at a corner table in the crowded railway café. They were just tucking into their homemade jam cobs (jam was the only filling available), when the double doors of the café were thrown open and in marched two soldiers wearing kilts. The three marines looked up, as did everyone else. The room went quiet.

'What the hell are Scotsmen doing here?' whispered Wills.

The chatter in the café resumed.

'They're not Scots,' replied Dacre. 'Look at their shoulder flashes. They're Canadians.'

'They have Scottish regiments in Canada?' asked Wills incredulously.

'They certainly do,' said Sergeant Throttles. 'I've heard a rumour that the Canadian Second Division has moved onto the island. Looks like the rumour was right. AJ go and ask them over, perhaps we can find out a bit more.'

Within minutes, the two Canadians were seated at their table on a couple of spare chairs. During the introductions, it turned out that the they were from the Queen's Own Cameron Highlanders.

Munching their way through what looked like a piece of stale fruit cake, one of the Canadians said, 'So then, are you commandos looking forwards to the exercise?'

The three marines nearly choked on their tea, in fact Wills actually spat some out, such was his surprise.

'Exercise? What exercise?' asked Sergeant Throttles, a real look of concern on his face, which in itself was interesting as nothing ever seemed to faze him.

'Why, the one set for next week. I think it's near some place called Bridleport. No, that's not right. Hang on, let me think. Bridport! Or, to be more precise, West Bay near Bridport, which we are told is somewhere in Dorsetshire.' He looked to his mate for confirmation.

'Yes, I'm sure that's right. We had our briefing yesterday afternoon.'

The Canadian looked over his shoulder and lowered his voice to a whisper. 'The exercise is to be called *Yukon*, or something like that.'

'What sort of an exercise is it going to be,' asked Dacre quietly, his curiosity aroused.

'Hey man, it's the full works. Beach landings, cliff climbing and so on, all under battle conditions. Infantry, commandos and even tanks, all in a joint combined operations raid. There's even some Americans and French taking part. You guys haven't heard?'

'Maybe we're not going,' said Wills, not sure if he was disappointed or not.

'Sure, you are. You're from the Royal Marines Commandos aren't you?'

'Yes, we are,' said Sergeant Throttles.

'Well then, you're damn well going!'

The three marines sat in stunned silence. The two Canadians stood up.

'Time for us to be going. It's been real swell talking to you guys. Good luck next week, perhaps we'll meet up.' With that, they were gone.

'Do you think our CO knows about this?' asked Dacre.

'I don't know,' replied the Sergeant, but he will as soon as we get back.'

'Do you think this is anything to do with that training we did for that naval officer in Portsmouth, you know, when we were at Eastney Barracks? Dacre rubbed the back of his neck as he spoke.

'Seems likely. I'm just surprised that we haven't heard anything sooner. If we are going, then you, my little safebreaker, need to get your fingers warmed up.' said the Sergeant to Wills with a crafty smile.

As soon the three returned to Shanklin, they immediately went to see the second-in-command, Major Houghton, to report their conversation with the Canadians. To their surprise the Major and the CO knew all about the forthcoming exercise. In fact, the unit officers had received their briefing that very morning. They had planned to tell the rank and file the next day.

(ii)

The following morning Lieutenant Huntington-Whiteley, the platoon officer, accompanied by Lieutenant Ellis, stood in front of Number Ten Platoon. Ellis had been tasked with delivering the briefing – his first. He was nervous, his palms were sweaty, and he had butterflies in his stomach. In fact, he felt decidedly ill. He had been up half the night preparing his notes, together with the two maps that he had drawn in chalk on a blackboard. He had been very particular about getting the maps right. The platoon officer had moved, to sit at the back of the schoolroom that they were using for the briefing. In this way the men's attention would be just on the younger officer, and it also meant that it would be easier for him to assess the competence of the Lieutenant.

Lieutenant Ellis took a deep breath and began. Although he stumbled over the first
couple of sentences, he soon got into his stride. He even managed to put his notes to one side, as he found that he knew every detail by heart. He

carefully and thoroughly explained how the exercise, code-named *Yukon,* was to be carried out.

'Let me begin by giving you some background information. West Bay is a very small coastal town south of Bridport, with a harbour that is fed by the River Brit. It has steep cliffs on either side. The beach is made up from shingle, and on the western side of the harbour there is a promenade. The people planning the raid have chosen this place because the geography of the area closely resembles where we are going in France.'

There was a sharp intake of breath from everyone in the room when they heard that they were rehearsing for a full-scale raid on the German held French coast.

'I'm afraid I cannot tell you the actual name of our destination just yet for security reasons but, be assured, it is France. Now you might like to know that this whole part of the Dorset coast and surrounding countryside is designated as a training ground. It is also part of the 'stop-line' for any potential invasion force and, as such, is part of the south coast defence system which comprises coastal batteries and inland gun emplacements. Most of the beaches have been mined, and there are also reinforced concrete tank traps.

Now, some more details about West Bay. Since about the 1900s, this has been a busy commercial harbour, and a popular destination for visitors and holidaymakers. However, the harbour is a lot older. Paddle steamers were regular visitors here. Sometimes they would tie up between the two wooden piers, but, more often or not, they simply ran up onto the beach to unload their passengers. To the north west of the town there is a municipal camp site, very popular in the 1930s – mostly tents and a few caravans. It was well used by the Boy Scouts, Army Volunteers, and such like, for their annual camps.

The harbour can be a problem. In rough and stormy conditions, it can be difficult to get into. The wooden piers were built so that, when necessary, boats can be pulled in by hand. At low water, boats wanting to enter must wait offshore until the water is deep enough to get them over a sandbar at the harbour mouth. Equally, boats wanting to leave during 'slack' water time must also wait. Before the war, the sluice gates were periodically opened to flush out the harbour, in order to remove the sandbar. With the harbour having been closed since 1939, this routine has fallen by the wayside.'

Lieutenant Ellis carefully removed the blanket that covered the blackboard. The first map showed the coastline around West Bay and as far inland as Bradpole and the town of Bridport. The marines shuffled around in order to get a better view. The beaches had been designated by colours, with broad arrows showing the direction and destination for each part of the landing force. The young officer had cleverly decided to explain the whole plan of the exercise, before getting down to the detail with which the platoon had been tasked.

'The overall plan is for the raiding force, made up mostly of Canadian troops, to seize and hold the harbour and nearby Bridport, plus a 'fictitious' airfield at Bradpole, which is one and a half miles north east of Bridport. Prior to these landings, the Army commandos will land on the east and west beaches (now called Yellow and Orange), scale the cliffs and secure the headlands.' He pointed to the map. 'Once they have taken their objectives, they will then move inland to these specified positions, dig in and hold.' He pointed to West Cliff Farm and the village of Wych. 'Thirty minutes after the cliff assault, the first wave of the main landing force, supported by their Churchill tanks, will arrive on Red, White, Blue and Green beaches. As you can see from the map, the troops from White Beach will move towards Bridport and secure the left flank. Red Beach will secure West Bay, whilst Blue and Green will also move towards Bridport and the aerodrome. Troops from Green Beach will also secure the right flank at Burton Bradstock. This will be followed almost immediately by a second wave of Canadians. Apart from 'X' Company the remainder of the Royal Marine Commando will be held, offshore with the floating reserve. They will come ashore as part of the third wave if, and when, they are needed.'

One or two of the platoon sniggered at this last part because they were getting into the action, whereas the rest of the commando had to wait. Lieutenant Ellis chose to ignore this minor interruption, but the Platoon Officer knew who they were and had marked their cards.

Having completed the overall plan, Lieutenant Ellis then revealed a more detailed chalk map of the harbour area. He explained that this small harbour had once been busy with fishing boats, coastal motor vessels from as far away as Gothenburg and other Scandinavian countries, as well as private yachts. Although the harbour had been closed since the beginning of the war, boats that brought in coal were still needed by the

Bridport Gas Company. Most of the inhabitants of West Bay had been evacuated elsewhere. The Navy had left a number of boats in the harbour for 'X' company to liberate. Also, several points around the quayside had been made available for the demolition teams. Ellis had several pre-war postcards which he passed around. He explained that Ten Platoon would enter the harbour. They would proceed with all haste to the large building on the quayside, known as Pier Terrace. Built as five separate houses, one of them had been fitted out to represent the German Naval Headquarters. A number of the rooms would contain a safe that had to be opened and the 'secret' documents removed. They were also to look for an Enigma machine. All these items had to be taken as quickly as possible to Commander Fleming, who would be waiting offshore in a destroyer. The whole of the harbour area would be defended by an Infantry Battalion from Southern Command, and by members of the local Home Guard Unit. The Platoon had also been given an emergency RV point, a half mile east of West Bay, near Burton Bradstock. If all else failed, they were to proceed to that point where a Navy boat would be waiting.

At the end of the briefing there were one or two questions which Ellis dealt with effectively. It all sounded so straightforward; how could it possibly go wrong?

The platoon was dismissed. Lieutenant Huntington-Whiteley sat writing up his notes. He was impressed by the younger officer's briefing. He had spoken in a pleasant Home Counties accent, which had reflected his origins from the village of Chesham in Buckinghamshire. His delivery, competence and planning had all been extremely good and authoritative. The fact that he had taken the time to give both background details and an explanation of the overall plan was unusual but had been well received by the men. The two maps were also extremely helpful, although they must have taken some time to draw. Given time and more experience, this young man might well make an excellent senior officer, if he managed to survive the war.

(iii)

Two days later, the entire Royal Marines Commando embarked on boats heading Westwards along the English Channel towards Dorset and West Bay. Dawn was just breaking in the east. The sky was dark grey and overcast, with heavy rain clouds gathering over the Channel. The sea was distinctly choppy, the prevailing wind whipping off the crest of the waves in a fury of white foam. The fast gunboats, on which Dacre and others of Ten Platoon were on board, rose and fell with vicious hammer blows as they hit wave after wave. It was not a pleasant experience for the marines, who were either squatting or sitting on the metal deck. Many of the men had already been seasick. Wild spray from the surf was flying onto the open deck, and everyone was already soaked to the skin. This was a tough challenge, even for those who had survived Achnacarry. Had the marines bothered to look over the gunwale, they would have seen dozens upon dozens of other craft. Out to sea, the flotilla was accompanied by frigates, destroyers and mine sweepers. Altogether, it was a formidable armada of over eighty ships, all heading for the same destination.

After what seemed to be hours of hell, the fleet arrived at their destination. A dense smokescreen was laid down by the Royal Navy from their warships. So thick was the smoke, that much of the harbour, the beaches and the cliffs were almost invisible. The wind increased in velocity to almost gale force, turning the sea into a mass of white-capped waves that stormed ferociously towards the shore. The rain was coming down like stair-rods. The landing craft and gunboats found it almost impossible to maintain course and direction. For the larger ships further out at sea, the sudden change in the weather was less of a problem, although they still experienced considerable discomfort. As dawn appeared over the horizon, the rain eased to a drizzle. On many of the landing craft, the troops found themselves standing ankle deep in a combination of icy sea water and vomit, as it sloshed around the decks. To make matters worse, the very strong offshore current continued to make it virtually impossible to helm the landing craft with any accuracy. Boats were blown off course, consequently missing their landing points. To the west, several boats ended up a fair distance away, one even as far as Seatown, others as far as four miles down the coast. To the east, the situation was no better. Landing craft struggled to put their troops ashore, many of them broaching as they came into the beach. Only a fraction of the two Army commando units were able to climb the cliffs. The frontal assault came to a virtual standstill as the Canadians tried to battle their way ashore to their objectives. The landings on White and Red Beaches were eventually cancelled due to the appalling weather conditions. Other troops landed on the wrong beach, but did not realise it until they were ashore, by which time it was too late. The move inland was extremely slow, where the natural terrain did not help. Some troops from *Green* beach managed to get to Bridport eventually. A small contingent even managed to attack the 'aerodrome', only to find that they could not penetrate the outer line of defence due to insufficient numbers of soldiers.

The boat containing the Assault Unit missed the harbour completely and was swept westwards onto a nearby beach. Somehow or other, the combination of wind, waves and offshore current spun their boat one hundred and eighty degrees. The marines jumped out into water that came way up to their chests. It was a minor miracle that no-one was drowned. It was only down to their superb levels of fitness that all of them survived. However, many of the marines were forced to jettison their equipment and webbing, and some even lost their weapons.

Elsewhere, it was just as bad or, in some cases, worse. The tank landing craft arrived one and a half hours late and failed to deploy its armoured vehicles with any real success. Because the shingle beach was quite steep, chestnut paling fences had to be laid down to act as roadways. Those tanks that managed to land, struggled to move inland. A number of tanks were bogged down and had to be towed out with the aid of tractors and bulldozers.

Added to this, the landing force had been hampered by inadequate communications and poor liaison. In Bridport itself, it was utter chaos. Those that had got ashore found themselves muddled up with the defenders and vice-versa. There was no way to distinguish friend from foe. The umpires tried to intervene but only made matters worse by declaring soldiers wounded or dead, who clearly should have been left alive. Those men who found themselves declared a casualty, spent valuable time arguing the toss with umpires.

In short, the whole of Exercise *Yukon* was an unmitigated disaster. By the end of the day, General Roberts shuddered to think of the outcome had this been the real thing.

(iv)

Several days later, General Montgomery and Rear Admiral Mountbatten met with General Roberts on the Isle of Wight to discuss *Yukon*. The reports received from the observers and umpires had not been encouraging. Setting aside the appalling weather conditions over which nobody had any control, the main criticism focused on the inability of the troops to move off the beaches and inland quickly enough. It was also noted that insufficient attention had been paid to the photographs of the area, provided by aerial reconnaissance from the RAF.

Without any hesitation they all agreed that *Operation Rutter* should be delayed in order to allow further training to take place. *Yukon 2* was scheduled for ten days later, with the proviso that if the landings had not drastically improved by then, the operation would be permanently cancelled.

CHAPTER 22

(i)

The next ten days on the Isle of Wight were spent at a feverish pace as all the troops involved in Exercise *Yukon 2* practised and practised their own part in the re-run. Many felt that they could carry out their tasks in their sleep, if need be, and probably could have, they were so well rehearsed.

The Army commandos climbed every cliff they could find, whilst the Canadians stormed ashore on a variety of beaches, much to the amusement of the locals. Number Ten Platoon once again found themselves back in Portsmouth, only this time they were billeted at the Naval barracks *HMS Victory*. Making use of a powerful and fast motor torpedo boat, the marines became even more proficient at speeding into the harbour, then climbing up and over the harbour walls and dashing hell for leather into the nearby warehouses. Then, under the watchful eye of Lieutenant Ellis and Sergeant Throttles, Dacre and Pete Wills proceeded to break into every safe that they were presented with.

Even the Canadian Tank Regiment found themselves suitable beaches of sand and shingle, which allowed them to practise their beach landings. Day after day, they could be seen and heard grinding their way slowly off their landing crafts, up and down the beach, backwards and forwards.

Meanwhile, the remainder of 'X' Company had to practise the vitally important task of securing the harbour, both to protect Number Ten Platoon and to allow the demolition teams, who would be hard on their heels, to complete their tasks. Timing and speed were of the essence. Mistakes were not allowed, and failure was a word never to be mentioned.

At the final briefing, held the day before the exercise was due to commence, all the attacking force were issued with red arm bands. The defending force, or the enemy, were to wear blue, whilst the umpires would wear white. It was emphasised that the authority of the umpires was never to be questioned. Their decision had to be final, come what may.

Whilst it was still planned that Number Ten Platoon would be extracted the same way that they had gone in, by boat, they were reminded about the emergency RV point at Burton Freshwater. It was emphasised again that this was only to be used as a last resort, but it would ensure that, in the event of something unforeseen happening, the contents of the 'pinched' safes could still be delivered to Commander Fleming, who, as previously stated, would be waiting offshore in a destroyer.

(ii)

At 2300 hours, when the majority of the islanders were safely tucked up in their beds, the troops taking part in Exercise *Yukon 2* were silently boarding their boats and
landing craft for the four-hour trip down the Channel. The landings were scheduled to take place at dawn. The Platoon found themselves boarding another MTB, this time a Vosper, with its three powerful, super-charged Packard marine engines softly growling a welcome.

'This is more like it,' said Pete Wills, settling himself comfortably between a torpedo tube and a depth charge on the aft deck. 'Proper luxury, I call this. So much better than those other boats. That last trip did my back in and no mistake.'

Dacre nodded and smiled a reply. He couldn't have agreed more with his mate. They really were very lucky, and he hoped that this would continue.

The gun metal grey sea was amazingly calm, although there were dark clouds
hovering away in the distance. The armada of ships arrived in good time but had to wait patiently offshore whilst the guns of the accompanying

naval ships laid down a barrage of smoke onto the beaches. Ashore, the defending force ignited smoke pots and smoke grenades in order to add to the realism.

First ashore were the two Army commandos, climbing the East and West cliffs, using ropes fitted with grappling irons fired from their landing crafts by beach mortars. Thirty minutes later, the Canadians stormed ashore onto their designated beaches, each unit with a specific mission and objective. These troops were closely followed by the tanks, some of which trundled up the beach onto the small promenade, directed by the beach master and his team of RM policeman. Others came right into the harbour and up the narrow slipway at the far end. The bridgehead had been established.

The Platoon on their MTB powered into the harbour, only to find that the tide had turned and was now on its way out. There was only just enough water for the skipper to get his boat alongside the quay. The marines found that they had to climb the slippery, seaweed-infested stone steps that were set curved into the harbour wall. To add to their woes, there were only two other ladders available, which meant that they had to queue to get up topside. Up above their heads in the harbour yard, all hell had been let loose. The defending force had occupied nearly every building. Their vehicles had blocked all the roads out of town. Heavy, blank gunfire had been laid down from all quarters, whilst smoke grenades and thunderflashes added to the general sense of realistic mayhem. The umpires were dashing about everywhere, doing their best to determine who had been wounded and who had been killed.

The remainder of 'X' Company, unable to enter the harbour because of the lack of water, had to land on the beach. From there they had to make their way, under very heavy enemy fire, to the harbour yard, and in doing so sustained considerable casualties.

By this time, the Platoon, led by Lieutenant Ellis and Sergeant Thrattles, had managed to cross the harbour yard to the relative safety of Pier Terrace. Then they had to dash around to the far side to gain access. However, casualties had also been heavy, with over half of the thirty-man unit declared wounded or dead. Once inside the building, the sergeant took a squad of men and began the dangerous task of clearing the building of any enemy, room by room. This was a slow and difficult task, and enemy resistance turned out to be tough. However, the marines gradually gained the upper hand until it was safe for Lieutenant Ellis, Dacre and Wills to carry out their task without being shot at.

Each of the rooms had been set up as Kriegsmarine offices; all the notices, documentation and files were in German.

'Someone has been very busy,' said Lieutenant Ellis, flicking through a pile of papers.

'You're right there, sir,' replied Dacre. 'Just look at this lot.' He held up a handful of aerial photographs.

'I suppose, from their point of view, there is no point in doing things by half measures. If we are to be tested then everything must be as it might be, were this the real thing, if you know what I mean'

'I do know what you mean, sir, and I think you are right,' replied Dacre.

'Will you just look at this?' said Wills excitedly. He pointed to the corner of the room. 'This is a real beauty - the Rolls Royce of all safes. Look? See that?' He pointed to the company name over the safe's door which said *Chubb & Sons Lock & Safe Co. Ltd., Wolverhampton, England.* This is real quality, you know. It's made from reinforced steel and is totally unbreakable. It's also protected by a numeric code. If, by chance, the wrong code is entered, it will trigger a siren which will alert the guards.'

'Well, you have nothing to worry about there because there are no guards. Well, not any longer,' replied Dacre.

'There is just one other thing,' said Wills, scratching his head.

'Oh, and what's that,' asked the Lieutenant, coming across the room and staring intently at the safe.

'Well, sir, I forgot to mention that in addition to sounding the alarm, the contents will also be incinerated.'

There was a stunned silence in the room.

'Do you mean the whole lot will go up in smoke if you get the combination wrong?'

'Yes, sir. I'm afraid that is exactly what I mean.'

Dacre interrupted the conversation. 'Well, can you open the bloody thing or not?'

With a twinkle in his eye, Pete Wills replied, 'Open it! Of course I can fucking open it. I can do it with my eyes bloody closed.'

Dacre gave a long sigh. 'Well, what the hell are you blathering on about. Get your bloody finger out and get on with it, we haven't got all sodding day.'

Muttering more to himself than anyone else, Wills put his left ear against the safe
door and gently eased the tumbler - slowly clockwise and then anti-clockwise - until he heard each number drop into place. The other three marines held their breath. After two minutes, the safebreaker was satisfied. He yanked down the handle, and the heavy safe door slowly swung open. Inside was a single shelf, and on it were two bulky brown envelopes. Wills reached in and took them out, then passed the envelopes directly to Lieutenant Ellis. On the front of each envelope, stamped in large black Gothic letters, were the words 'STRENG GEHEIM'.

'What does that mean, sir?' Wills asked.

Dacre, peering over the officer's shoulder, looked at the envelope, then at his friend.

'It means 'Top Secret' my clever little friend,' replied Dacre, with a broad grin on his face.

The officer nodded in agreement, as he carefully opened the first package. Inside was a small booklet. On the front cover the words 'Short Signal Codes' had been written with a red pen. The other envelope was the same. Lieutenant Ellis slid both envelopes into his backpack. At that moment, Sergeant Thrattles and his team reappeared in the doorway.

'There are three more rooms to do, sir, and each one of them has a safe just like this one.'

Lieutenant Ellis looked at Dacre and Wills, who was still kneeling on the floor at the open safe door.

'AJ, you know what to do?'

'Yes, sir,' he replied. With that, he grabbed Wills by his webbing and dragged him to his feet. 'Come on, Pete, my boy, you have more work to do.'

As they left the room the sergeant produced, with a flourish - rather like a conjurer - what he had been hiding behind his back. It was a small portable typewriter. In it was a single sheet of paper on which someone had typed, 'This represents a four-wheeled Enigma machine.'

'Well, I'll be damned,' said the Lieutenant. 'Well done, Sergeant. Where on earth did you find this?'

'It was locked away in a wooden box, sir. I simply used my skills to open it.'

The officer looked confused.

'Your skills, Sergeant? And what might those be, may I ask. I thought we only had one safe-breaker in our unit?'

The sergeant gave a lop-sided grin. 'Oh, I'm not as good as young Wills, that's for sure. So, I simply smashed the lock open with my rifle butt. It seemed as good a way as any. Now that we have the codebooks, do we really need this?' He pointed at the typewriter.

'I don't know, Sergeant. I just don't know. The Short Signal Codes are the really important things, but someone has put that typewriter here for us to find. So, all things being equal, I think we had better take it with us,' replied the Lieutenant. 'Now let's get the others and get the hell out of here, mission accomplished don't you think?'

The sergeant frowned before replying, 'Nearly, sir, nearly. Let's not count our chickens just yet.'

'No, you're quite right I'm sure.'

Just then, Dacre and Wills returned to the room. Dacre handed over three more brown envelopes. These, together with the typewriter, also went into the officer's backpack. The whole group then moved towards the main door. Ellis paused in order to give some last-minute instructions.

'Sergeant, you will lead us out, followed by our escorts. I'll follow on, whilst Dacre and Wills bring up the rear. All of you be on the alert because we do not know what the situation is out there. Head back to the quayside. Hopefully, our boat will be there waiting for us. Good luck everyone.'

With a nod from the officer, Sergeant Throttles threw open the door, and he and the escorts charged out – directly into the face of enemy gunfire. According to the umpire, who was standing outside, all the marines were said to be seriously wounded or killed. The Lieutenant, shaken at the unexpected turn of events and perhaps blaming himself, hesitated for just a fraction too long. He, too, was declared mortally wounded. The umpire looked at Dacre and Wills who were still standing in the doorway. Then he pointed at Dacre.

You're the senior marine now, you're in charge. Do something! Make a decision! You can't stay here! Oh, and by the way, you no longer have a working radio. Now get a fucking move on, in double time!'

Dacre slammed the door shut. He leant back against the wall and closed his eyes. Fuck! What a bloody mess, he thought. What to do? What to do? There was a sense of panic growing deep down within his body. He felt sick to his stomach. Fuck, double fuck! Pete Wills was hopping up and down like a schoolboy who desperately needed a piss.

(iii)

'What are we going to do, AJ, what are we going to do? They're all dead and gone. There are only us left. What are we going to do?' The marine looked at his friend.

'Well, to start with you can bloody well stand still. I need to think and for heaven's sake shut the fuck up.'

'First things first,' he said aloud, more to himself than his mate. 'We need to get the backpack off the Lieutenant. Here's what we'll do. You give me your Tommy gun. I'll open the door, fire off a whole magazine, whilst you crawl out and get the backpack. You okay with that?' Dacre asked.

'You want me to go out there after what has just happened? You must be bloody mad AJ.'

'Okay, okay. You stay here and give me covering fire. I'll go out.'

Wills thought about this for a split second.

'No, I'll go. You're a better shot than I am. Besides, they're going to be shooting at you, not me.'

'Alright then. On the count of three. One, two, three – go! Wills threw open the door and, fighting to control the weapon, fired off an entire magazine. He couldn't have got any lower unless he'd become a snake. He slithered out of the door, grabbed the Lieutenant and heaved the body inside.

'Bloody hell, Pete. I said just get his backpack, not the whole body. Never mind, well done. That must have taken some effort.'

Lieutenant Ellis opened one eye, winked at them, then went back to playing dead. Dacre retrieved the officer's backpack, then, adjusting the straps, slung it onto his back.

'Right then, let's go.' He paused. 'Hang on a minute. Have you got a toggle rope?'

'Yes, AJ.'

'So have I. That means with Ellis's we have three, and at six feet each that gives us a rope of about eighteen feet.'

'Where are we going?' asked an anxious Wills.

'Well, there are no back doors to these houses, so it's either the front door or out through a back window.'

'We can't use the bloody front door, can we?' said Wills. 'Look what happened to the others.'

'So, it's the back window then,' relied Dacre. 'Remember there's a drop of about six or seven feet, so don't go twisting an ankle. If there's a boat in the harbour, we'll try using that. If not, I suggest we head for the beach.'

Moving quickly to the back of the house, Dacre peered out of the window. From what he could see through the billowing smoke, the Canadians and the defending force were still heavily involved in a tremendous firefight. He could just make out several tanks lumbering along the roadway over the sluice gates, on the far side of the harbour. From what he could see, the main roads out of West Bay were all blocked with barricades, made up with anything that had come to hand: domestic furniture from the empty houses, overturned rowing boats, old vehicles, wooden carts and wheelbarrows that would normally have been used to carry gravel from the beach to the railway yard. Although hastily put together, these obstructions had clearly been made by experienced hands. The ground and the buildings rocked again as another explosion, then another, shook the whole area.

'Time to go, Pete, said Dacre as he opened a window. 'Follow me and don't forget to roll when you hit the ground.'

With that, Dacre climbed up onto the windowsills and was gone. Pete Wills hesitated momentarily, then, shutting his eyes tight, launched himself out of the window. Landing safely, they both sprinted across the quayside to the harbour wall. There were boats and landing craft in the harbour aplenty. However, the tide had finally gone out, leaving the craft sitting on the harbour bed.

'Well, that's our way out up the spout,' shouted Dacre. 'Let's try the beach.'

Moving as quickly as they could, they zigzagged their way towards a small group of fishermen's cottages that overlooked the beach. Keeping their heads down and breathing heavily, the two marines paused to take stock of their situation. It was quite clear to Dacre that with the tide now fully out, it was impossible to use the beach also. He took out a small pair of binoculars from inside his jacket and studied the east cliffs with interest.

'I think we may have to climb out,' he said.

'Climb out? What the hell do you mean, climb out?' said Wills in a shocked voice.

'Look, our only chance of getting this stuff out of here is to make for the emergency RV point. The footpath to the top of the hill is blocked and mined – here, see for yourself.' He passed the binoculars to his friend. Wills frantically searched the hillside.

'Yeah, I see what you mean. Can't we go along the beach? It would be easier, and it leads straight to Burton Freshwater doesn't it?'

'Yes, it does, and I agree it would be easier. But look beyond where the commandos landed. What do you see?'

Wills studied the beach intently. His heart sank.

'Well?'

'Barbed wire and more mines,' replied Wills dejectedly.

'So, unless you have any more bright ideas, I suggest we get moving.'

Wills shrugged his shoulders; he knew when he was beaten.

As they stood up to move, an umpire walked around the corner of the cottage. He looked the two marines up and down. Then with something resembling a smile he said, 'I've been watching you two for the past five minutes or so. I'm with you now - where you go, I go.' Dacre nodded his head. It didn't matter to him, as long as the umpire could keep up. He had a plan and wasn't going to stop for anyone.

(iv)

The three of them moved cautiously along the narrow gravel track, hugging the brick wall at the back of the Bridport Arms Hotel, alert and weapons ready for action. Dacre stopped suddenly and crouched down, the others followed likewise as two tanks lumbered off the beach, headed down past the Methodist Chapel towards the harbour and into the raging battle. Dacre signalled to the other two and moved on. They passed a couple more buildings on their left, then stopped again. In front of them was an open expanse of beach with only a couple of fishermen's huts and several old fishing boats pulled up well above the high tide mark. In the near distance they could just make out a row of buildings on the side of the hill.

'They must be the coastguard cottages,' said Dacre to no-one in particular, remembering Lieutenant Ellis's map. 'Right, here we go!'

Keeping their heads down, they sprinted the three hundred yards or so across the shingle without stopping, hoping and praying that no-one would see them. It was a tall order, but fortune often favours the brave. They arrived at the foot of the cliffs, the two marines winded and gasping for air, but elated that they had got away with it. The umpire, however, was in a sorry state. Clearly not as fit as the two marines, he collapsed onto his knees and vomited up the remains of his early morning breakfast. Wills gave him a swig of water from his canteen as the officer slowly recovered both his breath and composure. Meanwhile, Dacre was checking out the rock face, which crumbled away in his hand. What the hell was this type of rock, he wondered? Limestone or sandstone perhaps? He wished he had paid more attention to his geography and geology lessons at school. Too late for that now, he thought. Clearly the rock face was unstable, which meant that free climbing was out of the question. Then he noticed half a dozen long climbing ropes swaying in the breeze. Of course, the Army commandos had used them to scale the cliff face. How convenient he thought. Cautiously, the little group moved along to the foot of the cliff. Selecting a rope Dacre gave it a couple of sharp tugs to make sure that the grapnel was still secure. It held.

'Right Pete', he said. 'Assemble the toggle rope, then tie a bowline around your waist and I'll do the same. I'll lead, you follow.'

'What about the umpire, AJ?'

'He's on his own. We can't carry any passengers.' Dacre looked at the umpire. He was a captain in the Home Guard. 'I'm sorry, sir. It's nothing personal, you understand. We are trained for this sort of thing and you're not. We don't have time to help you. Our responsibility is to complete our mission. Indicating his backpack, 'We have to get this little lot to where it belongs.'

The captain looked up at the cliff face and slowly shook his head in amazement.

'You marines must be bloody mad. Anyway, good luck to you.' With that he turned and walked away.

Dacre gave the rope another good tug. Then, settling his rifle comfortably across his shoulders, he began to climb. Whilst much of the cliff was near vertical, there were small cracks and crevices into which he was able to put the toes of his boots. It wasn't easy, but it was possible. After all, he reasoned, the Army chaps had done it, and anything they could do, the marines could do better. It had been a couple of months since his last climb and his hands had softened. With the rope trailing down the centre of his body and lying between his legs, he began reaching up, hand over hand. Wills was only about twelve feet below him. He appeared to be climbing, and seemed to be enjoying himself, which Dacre thought was strange. Wills hated climbing normally. Dacre's arms and shoulders were beginning to feel the strain. The added weight of the secret plans and the Enigma didn't help, but he shouldn't be this tired. His heart was beating like the clappers, and he found he was gasping for breath. The sweat was pouring off him, and his hands had become slippery. He knew that he had to really concentrate in order to make that final effort. He was only too aware that if he slipped and fell, then his bodyweight would pluck the two of them off the rope in an instance, and they would plunge to their deaths below. He paused and looked down. He estimated that they must be about one hundred feet up. It can't be far now, can it? The adrenaline was coursing through his body. Spurred on, he gritted his teeth with savage determination, and climbed the final fifty feet or so, almost in a rush. At the top he rolled over the cliff edge onto the closely cropped grass. Rabbits, he thought, as he lay there gasping in the pure air. Slowly, his body began to return to normal. As he sat up, Wills rolled over onto the top of the grass. He barely seemed to be out of breath. Dacre looked at his mate in amazement.

'I thought you hated climbing,' he said.

'I do,' Wills replied.

'How come you're not out of breath like me, then?'

Wills lowered his head. He looked decidedly sheepish, even embarrassed. He blushed bright red.

'Well, come on, give. We haven't got all day!'

Wills looked up, a twinkle in his eye, as a sly grin spread across his face. 'Promise you won't be cross if I tell you?

'What? Cross? Why should I be cross with you?'

'Well, I shortened the rope by six feet, so you've virtually pulled me all the way up the cliff.'

Dacre slumped back onto the grass. 'Well, I'll be damned! No wonder I was struggling to make the climb. You little bugger! I'll get you back for that, I promise, sometime, somewhere, just you wait and see. When you are least expecting it!'

'Well, I just knew that I couldn't make it on my own, and I rather hoped you wouldn't mind too much.'

Dacre gave a long heart felt sigh. Then, not too unkindly said, 'You're a toe-rag, Pete Wills, that's what you are, a bloody toe-rag.'

Rolling onto his knees, he looked around. In the distance the sound of gunfire and explosions drifted towards them on the wind. They had a magnificent view of the town and harbour, and of the surrounding countryside. Whilst the battle was still going on, the Canadian troops could be clearly seen advancing inland, a column of tanks and lorries passing the small railway station, as they headed towards Bridport. Of the Army commandos who had scaled the cliffs, there was no sign. Dacre looked up at the sky. Dark clouds were gathering out at sea and were scudding towards them.

'We're in for a storm. Best get moving.'

As he spoke, a streak of lightning flashed across the sea, accompanied by an almighty crash of thunder.

'We can't stay here, we are too exposed. Keep low and follow me.'

With some difficulty, the two marines began crawling through the heather and shrubbery, trying to avoid being skylined. It was a slow and painful process.

Suddenly another almighty clap of thunder crashed out, followed by a flash of lightning that lit up the surrounding countryside. The heavens opened, as the rain pelted down, and the cloudburst soaked the two men to the skin. They staggered to their feet just as another clap of thunder erupted all around them. It was so loud that for a second or two neither could hear anything else. The rain seemed to have a will of its own, such was the intensity. It was so heavy that visibility was reduced to only a yard or so. The two of them splashed through ditch after ditch, the wet banks so slippery that they were constantly slithering and sliding. In some instances, standing up proved to be impossible, so they had to crawl up the banks on their hands and knees. They grasped at tufts of grass or small bushes which often came away in their hands, sending them slithering down into a ditch where rainwater had gathered.

Using all his strength and determination, Dacre dragged his mate along by his equipment. It was the only way they could continue. Left on his own, Wills would have laid down and given up, he was exhausted. Somehow or other, the storm had sapped all the energy from him.

The rain continued to sheet down mercilessly. Every footstep was treacherous.

Several times the pair ended up on their backs, slipping dangerously towards the cliff edge. On one occasion Wills actually overtook Dacre, sliding on the wet grass, completely out of control. Dacre just managed to grab the little marine by his collar as he went past. Fortunately, he had had the presence of mind to brace himself, lest he be pulled of his feet as well. There was nothing to stop the pair from plunging to the bottom of the cliff and certain death. It was thanks only to the Dacre's physical strength that he managed to halt Will's unscheduled descent.

'Fuck my old boots, that was a close one,' Wills said, panting from the exertion. 'Cheers, AJ, you're a life saver.'

Both marines stood breathing hard, trying to control the adrenaline that was coursing through their veins. They had arrived at a wide inlet cut into the cliff face by ancient meltwaters from a bygone age. Dacre realised that this was where they had to descend to the beach. Through the incessant wind and rain, he could just make out a small village in the distance, nestling behind the cliffs on the far side of the inlet.

'That must be Burton Bradstock,' he said to Wills, remembering Lieutenant Ellis's briefing.

'Yeh, I suppose so,' replied Wills, shivering violently. 'What are all those tracks down there on the beach?'

Dacre pulled out his binoculars and scanned the whole area.

'Tank tracks, I think. Look, you can see where some of the barbed wire fences have been pulled away.'

'Isn't this where some of the Canadians were supposed to land?' asked Wills. 'Blue or green or something. I can't remember.'

'Green Beach, I think. You can just make out where they landed. Strange, though, that there is no-one about and no boats or landing craft offshore. Even those concrete blockhouses appear to be empty.

'Do you suppose the beach is mined?' Wills asked nervously.

'I expect it was before the landings. Don't worry. All we have to do is follow the tank tracks – we should be alright.' He hoped he was right. 'Come on, time to get moving.'

Slowly and carefully, they began to make their way down the cliff to the beach below. He could imagine that on a warm, summer day the more adventurous families would, perhaps, climb down with picnics and blankets to what might be considered a secret beach, for an undisturbed day of swimming. Now, each step of the way down was fraught with danger. Dacre needed to use all his mountaineering skills. On several occasions he had to belay Wills down by using the toggle-rope. Thankfully, they reached the shoreline without any further incidents. They struggled past a dilapidated building, all boarded up and looking very sorry for itself. The going was difficult, and the wind and rain howled across the open beach, forcing them to take two steps forward and one back.

'What do you think this was?' asked Wills as he tried to peer through a crack in a board?'

'An inn of some sort. Perhaps used by smugglers in the old days.'

'Smugglers? Here?'

'Sure. This whole coastline has a history of smuggling, and worse.'

'What do you mean, worse?'

'Not now. Ask me later.' He pointed to several large boulders. 'We need to head for those.'

Splashing through the small stream, the two marines carefully followed the tracks in
the sand, across the beach. There, on the far side of the boulders, was a large black rubber dingy that had been pulled up well above the high tide mark. Crouching in the lee of the rocks were two very wet sailors, covered from head to toe in dark naval waterproofs. The rainwater was pouring off them. One of the sailors, the elder of the two, looked up as he heard the sound of boots crunching on the pebbles. He nudged his mate.

'Eh up, Chalky, here come the bloody marines, late as usual. Where the fuck have you been? We've been here for bloody hours waiting for you. Are there only two of you? We were told to expect a lot more.'

Dacre looked the sailor up and down. Probably some old three-badger who had drawn the short straw. He decided not to rise to the bait. Instead, he calmly, and with as much authority in his voice as he could muster, simply said, 'Are you going to sit there on your arse all day complaining or are you going to get us out of here, as per your orders?'

The sailor, somewhat taken aback, got to his feet muttering something about bloody bootnecks. The four men carried the dingy down the beach and across the sandy expanse of low tide to the water's edge. As soon as they were underway, the two marines lent a hand paddling, by using the butts of their rifles. About a hundred yards offshore was a ship's cutter, riding at anchor, waiting for them.

About thirty minutes later, the two marines boarded *HMS Warspite* and were escorted to the wardroom, where they presented their trophies to a delighted Commander Fleming. Fleming knew that, despite the high number of casualties his unit had suffered, he had been proved right. His idea for a special unit devoted to stealing enemy secrets had been exonerated. He felt certain that both Admiral John Godfrey, his boss, and Rear Admiral Mountbatten would now be his greatest supporters.

(v)

A few days later, General Roberts held a full debriefing for his senior officers. Exercise *Yukon 2* had been more of a success than he had dared to hope. Both the harbour and Bridport had been successfully taken, as had the 'aerodrome'. Even the pinch raid organised by Naval Intelligence, of which he had some reservations, had been achieved apparently.

Shortly afterwards, General Montgomery visited the Isle of Wight, and spent time going over the details of the forthcoming Dieppe raid with the General. By and large, he was pleased with the planning and the way things had progressed. *Yukon 2* had definitely shown that the plan was achievable. However, Montgomery had some private reservations about Robert's lack of command experience. He sent a guarded, yet optimistic, report to Winston Churchill in which he referred to the Canadians as 'grand chaps'.

That same evening, the Prime Minister held a meeting at Number Ten with Mountbatten and General Brooke, amongst others. Churchill made it very clear that he wanted to avoid another disaster like Tobruk. In his mind, the raid on Dieppe had to be successful; he couldn't afford another failure. It would have been both impossible and foolish for anyone at the meeting to actually guarantee the success of the raid. Consequently, Churchill was eventually persuaded to take the risk and, somewhat reluctantly, gave the venture his blessing.

CHAPTER 23

On the 2nd of July, the joint force of Canadians and British troops, together with the handful of American and French soldiers, began boarding troopships. For the most part, these were converted cross channel ferries. There were more than two hundred vessels of all shapes and sizes that eventually gathered in and around the Yarmouth Roads. Sealed aboard their ships, the Canadians were, to their great joy, eventually told their real destination. This was now their chance to have a go at the Germans, something for which they had been waiting for over two years.

Security ashore was something of an issue. Rumours about an impending raid on France were flying around everywhere. The island's Chief Constable was asked to look into the rumours, but he was unsure where to start. Both brigades had been loaded in daylight and in full view of anyone who had cared to watch. Added to that, some of the soldiers had girlfriends, many of whom would have known where their men were heading.

After two days of the troops being sealed in their ships, four Luftwaffe fighter planes swept in over the waiting fleet, machine gunning at will. Fortunately, no-one was killed and only four soldiers were wounded. Nevertheless, the Germans knew that something was up, something big, and it was likely to be heading for France.

By this time the weather had rapidly deteriorated. A full-scale westerly storm blowing up the Channel had unleashed itself on the waiting armada of ships. Despite being at anchor, the ships were tossed about without mercy. Below decks, in the enclosed spaces, the atmosphere and language were foul. Reluctantly, the Commander-in-Chief Portsmouth, Admiral James, took the hateful decision to call the whole thing off.

There was total disbelief, and even tears from grown men, when the news reached those below decks. It was devastating news. Eventually the Canadians were disembarked and returned to the mainland. The Army and Marine Commandos remained on the Isle of Wight. Their situation was different.

As a result of the security having been blown, the South Eastern Command recommended to London that the whole operation should be cancelled permanently. Rather surprisingly, General Montgomery was not too disappointed. His concerns about Major General Roberts and his inexperienced troops had thankfully not been put to the test. Besides which, he had other things on his mind. Montgomery had just been appointed to take over command of the Eighth Army in North Africa. He and General Erwin Rommel had an appointment.

CHAPTER 24

(i)

Admiral Mountbatten, Chief of Combined Operations, walked the short distance from Room 39 at the Admiralty Buildings which overlooked Horse Guards Parade and the gardens of Number 10, Downing Street. There was a jaunty step to his walk as he made his way to the underground War Rooms. It was here that the Prime Minister, Winston Churchill, and his war-time coalition cabinet and senior members of the armed forces ran the war. The time was 0930 hours. It was a quiet day. The sky was a grey-blue, and there was not a cloud in sight. The occasional barrage balloon could be seen high up above a war-torn and heavily bombed London. He smiled to himself as he recalled all the activity in Room 39. It was there that the cream of Naval Intelligence worked incessantly in a smoke-filled room, fuelled by an open coal fire, dozens of lit cigarettes and pipes, surrounded by desks, filing cabinets and Bakelite telephones. Those red-eyed, pasty-faced young men and women were intent on giving their all to satisfy the ever-demanding needs of their senior officer, Admiral John Godfrey. Mountbatten's smile broadened as he walked. Godfrey had finally been convinced that the Royal Marines' special platoon should be part of the forthcoming raid. The recent and successful results of *Yukon 2* had finally convinced him.

It had been only a week ago that *Operation Rutter* had been cancelled once and for all by the Commander-in-Chief Portsmouth because of the continuing bad weather. At the post-mortem meeting that followed immediately, the Prime Minister made it quite clear that he still wanted a large-scale operation to take place during the summer, for both military and political reasons. Mountbatten realised that it was far too late in the year to find another suitable target and to get all the planning and organisation of troops in place. Then it came to him. Why not make use of *Rutter*? It could be revised and amended easily enough; all the essential groundwork and training had been done. Even if the Germans had known about the previous plan, as some people seemed to think, perhaps they would assume that the British would never be so stupid as to run the same plan again quite so soon. It was a risk he knew, but was it one worth taking he wondered? He knew that he must think this through very carefully. The right decision could have a major impact on the way that the war was going. If he got it wrong? Well, there was no telling what that might lead to.

The Admiral was in a thoughtful mood as he made his way to the entrance of the War Rooms. He was really looking forward to this morning, and his presentation to the Chiefs of Staff Committee. At long last, here was a chance to prove that he was the right person for the job, despite the whispered criticisms from some that it was his royal connections which had guaranteed his appointment. The Royal Marine sentry on guard duty gave him a smart salute as he entered the bunker and then checked his identity card. The Admiral walked the short distance along a narrow corridor to the briefing room, where he let himself in. The lights were already on. He stood silently studying the large-scale map of Dieppe that had been laid out on the top of a table that had been covered in a grey army blanket. His backroom boys and girls had done an excellent job in getting things ready. There were labelled cards that clearly showed each of the beaches to be used. Small pieces of wood that represented the key naval vessels had been painted white, with their names in black. He picked up a shortened billiard cue that someone had taken the time to paint yellow with a red tip, and prodded one of the ships. He was satisfied that everything was ready. In fifteen minutes he would give the final presentation on the proposed raid to those who had the authority to say either 'Yes' or 'No' to his plan. He already knew that he didn't have to convince Churchill of the plan for the raid to go ahead. However, with the Chiefs of Staff it was a different matter. They were amongst those who resented his appointment. So, in order to overcome their prejudice, his plan had to be not only extremely worthwhile but also foolproof for them to give the final go-ahead. Major General John H Roberts, the Commander of the Canadian Second Infantry Division, would also be present, not that he was going to be a problem. Roberts was only too pleased that he and his men would be given a second chance to see some action. Mountbatten just had time to check through his notes. He liked to be well prepared.

(ii)

At precisely 1000 hours, the door to the briefing room opened and General Ismay ushered in Winston Churchill, who this morning had chosen to wear one of his more comfortable boiler suits. Behind him came all the Chiefs of Staff and General Roberts. They gathered around the table. They were immediately impressed with the all the detail - as they were meant to be. They all sat down, with the exception of Mountbatten. In front of each person had been placed paper, pencil and a small metal ashtray. The Prime Minister took out one of his Corona Corona cigars and lit up. Taking this as a signal, others lit up cigarettes or pipes. Soon the room was full of a thick blue-grey smoke; you could taste the tobacco in the air. The Admiral's eyes began to water. Despite this discomfort he began.

'Good morning, gentlemen. What you see before you is a map of the proposed raid on the Port of Dieppe, now re-named *Operation Jubilee*.'

There was an audible gasp from the members of the Committee. They were, as one man, stunned by the arrogance and stupidity of Mountbatten in suggesting such a plan. The Admiral immediately realised that this was going to be difficult, in fact far more difficult than he had anticipated. He had to convince them of the validity of his plan.

Biting the bullet, he continued, 'This plan has some similarities to that put forward recently by General Montgomery. However, we have made several significant changes. Firstly, we have replaced the use of parachute troops with commandos. Secondly, there will be no heavy shelling of the port by the Royal Navy or bombing by the RAF.'

Despite his previous reservations about this, Mountbatten, always a pragmatist, had
decided to go along with current thinking, despite his own personal view. He recognised that it would be one less hurdle to negotiate.

'We hope to avoid too many civilian casualties and, perhaps, prevent the French from turning against us, their closest allies. There will be some light shelling from our destroyers, as well as some strafing from our planes.'

Several of the Chiefs of Staff nodded in agreement.

Things seem to be going well thought the Admiral, now he must press home his advantage. He continued, 'However, I must make it very clear to you that this raid should not be considered by anyone as the opening of a 'second front', despite what Mr Stalin might have hoped for, or, indeed, our cousins across the water. As you all know, our Russian allies are now under dreadful pressure from the Germans.'

Churchill made a clicking sound with his fountain pen tapping against his teeth. Was that annoyance, wondered Mountbatten? It was annoyance, he realised, but at what? He pushed the interruption to the back of his mind and continued.

'This operation will be the largest cross-channel attack on the enemy so far. The main purpose is for our Anglo-Canadian Force to seize and hold the port for a prolonged period of time. They are to destroy specific targets, take prisoners, and are to break into the Kriegsmarine Headquarters to steal their secrets.

'As you can see from the map in front of you, Dieppe lies in a gap the River Arques
has cut over the millennia through the chalky headland. To either side of the town there are high, and steep, escarpments.' Someone had drawn heavy black lines on the map in order to make these features stand out. 'The enemy have some heavy guns and artillery located here and there.' Mountbatten pointed to the relevant positions with the cue. 'Failure to secure or neutralise both these headlands would certainly mean that our operation might be put at risk. This raid will be an eight-pronged amphibious assault. Our troops will go in on the early morning tide and will attack the German defences along a dozen miles of the French coast. The attack has been planned using six colour codes. Numbers 3 and 4 Army Commandos will land at *Yellow* and *Orange* beaches, here and here at Varengeville and at Berneval respectively. Their task will be to move inland and to take the batteries that both threaten the harbour and our ships out at sea.' He pointed to the two beaches in turn. 'Incidentally, Number 4 Commando will have a group of fifty United States Rangers with them. They have recently completed their training at Achnacarry, and I have asked that they be included in order to give them some battle experience. These two independent but related actions are crucial to the

success of the whole operation. At the same time, the Canadians will land and attack here at Pourville and Puits, on Blue and Green Beaches respectively. These troops will have a small detachment of engineers who are tasked with destroying the Radar Station. With the enemy guns out of action, the Royal Marines will be able to enter the harbour to carry out their primary task, which I will come to in a minute. Thirty minutes later, the main assault by the Canadian Infantry, supported by their tanks will take place here on Red and White Beaches which are along the promenade of the town.' The Admiral used his pointer. 'Meanwhile, in the harbour, members of the Royal Marines Commando, including Number Ten Platoon, aboard *HMS Locust* will enter the harbour. Their task is to raid the German Naval Headquarters. They will steal all documents, secret codebooks, bigram tables and anything else to do with the Enigma encoding device. We are assured by a reliable French agent that these documents, plus at least one of the new machines, are to be found there. Of course, you do not need me to remind you of how vital these codes are for Bletchley Park to continue its work.'

Mountbatten paused for effect. All the Chiefs of Staff looked at him intently. Was that envy he saw on their faces? He couldn't be sure. But he did notice Churchill gave a small triumphant smile behind his hand.

The Admiral continued, 'Other Royal Marines will follow in using fast French patrol boats. With them will be demolition teams. Their task is to destroy the harbour installations. A small group will be tasked with capturing enemy soldiers, preferably of a substantial rank, whilst others will remove any useful German boats, such as landing craft. The remainder of the Royal Marines Commando will be out at sea as part of the floating reserve. If, and when, they go ashore, they will be accompanied by a small group of Fusilier Marins who will act as guides.

'General Roberts, you will be here, on board *HMS Calpe*, located with the offshore fleet. A provisional date has been set for the 20th/21st of June. Are there any questions or observations?'

The room went very quiet. The plan looked good and, in principle, could not fail. The Prime Minister watched his Chiefs of Staff very carefully, searching their faces for any shadow of doubt. He could see none. Churchill desperately needed this operation to go ahead and to be successful. The most recent disaster at Tobruk was still fresh in his mind. He had been in Washington, in conference with President Roosevelt, when the pink telegram had arrived. The loss of over thirty thousand men and their equipment had been a bitter pill to swallow, especially after the fall of Singapore. Britain could not afford to lose Egypt and the Suez Canal. The country needed access to the Persian Gulf and to India, as well as to other countries of the Empire. Churchill had had to fight off several votes of no confidence by Members of Parliament. He had been accused of being too dictatorial. Even some of his American friends were beginning to question his leadership. Indeed, on one occasion he had even threatened to resign his premiership if he lost the support of Roosevelt. Back home, Sir Stafford Cripps, the Lord Privy Seal, had seized the opportunity to question the whole idea of 'empire'. Over this matter he and Churchill disagreed unreservedly. The Prime Minister wanted to maintain the *status quo*; Cripps wanted to move towards Indian self-government. To complicate matters, in Egypt the support for Germany was increasing. What the country and the Prime Minister had needed was a decisive desert victory. What they got instead was the defeat at Tobruk. Of course, Rommel was a brilliant general, Perhaps the appointment of Montgomery could save the day - only time would tell. In the meantime, Mountbatten's plan had to be successful. Churchill doubted he could survive another disaster.

General Roberts put up his hand. What now, wondered the Admiral?

'Yes, General?'

'I just wanted to say how pleased my government will be that we, the Canadians, are being given this second chance to prove ourselves.'

Mountbatten looked around the table at the Chiefs of Staff before replying. One or two were nodding in agreement.

'Thank you for your comment, General. I am sure the Chiefs of Staff will bear that in mind when they make their decision.'

Churchill decided to interrupt. He still wasn't entirely happy about security.

'Keeping this whole thing a secret will be a problem, Dickie. How do you propose to keep it quiet?'

Mountbatten was prepared for this; he had done his homework.

'Firstly, sir, I suggest that nothing be put in writing – no minutes or instructions or orders. Everything must be done verbally by me. Secondly, with General Robert's agreement, there should be no further large-scale exercises or training. Lastly, security on the Isle of Wight should be beefed up, and General Roberts should come down hard on anyone with a 'flappy' mouth.' Roberts looked taken aback by this last comment, but

Mountbatten chose to ignore him. 'It is a well-known fact that prior to *Rutter* the Canadians made no secret of where they were going. It was, I believe, a common lavatory rumour.'

Churchill looked intently at the General. 'Well, General, do you accept these conditions?'

Roberts could see the writing on the wall. 'I accept them, sir, without any reservations.'

Mountbatten let out a long, heartfelt sigh.

'Well, gentlemen, if there are no further questions, I respectfully submit this plan for your consideration and approval.'

Two days later, *Operation Jubilee* was given the green light to proceed.

CHAPTER 25

There was a knock at the door. Alan Turing was leaning back in his chair with his large feet propped up on the desk. He had been leafing through a pile of encryptions.

'Come in,' he called out.

A young WRNS popped her head around the door.

'Commander Fleming is here, and he has an American with him.'

Turing noticed how she blushed when she said the word American. He swung his feet to the floor and sat up straight. A sense of panic surged through him. This was not one of their scheduled meetings. So why was Fleming here? More demands and more pressure, he
supposed. Damn the man, he thought.

'You had better show them in, Julie,' he said, 'and see if you can rustle up some tea, would you?'

Two minutes later the door was thrust open and Fleming strode purposefully in. He was followed by a tall, blonde American, who wore a black patch over his right eye and whose face was badly scarred. The American was wearing a dark green uniform that Turing didn't recognise.

'Sorry to barge in like this, Alan,' said Fleming. 'Mind if I smoke?' He lit up immediately, not waiting for an answer. 'I felt that you needed to meet my new friend, here. This is Colonel Tony Faragher of the USMC.'

Turing frowned and looked puzzled. The American spoke for the first time. His voice had a very distinctive soft, mid-western drawl.

'That's okay, Mr Turing. 'The letters stand for United States Marine Corps. I guess
you Limeys don't know much about us, but we know a hell of lot about you and your work.'

Turing, somewhat startled, looked towards Fleming for confirmation.

'It's alright, Alan. Everything is above board. We are now sharing a lot of information with our cousins from across the water, and that order has come from the very highest authority. Anyway, the reason we are here is that the Colonel wants to share something with you, but I'll leave him to explain.'

Turing had been studying the Colonel's uniform, in particular the badges on his collar. There appeared to be a small globe with a diagonal anchor, surmounted by a small eagle with spread wings. How clever, he thought, and wondered what on earth they meant.

The American began talking, 'Well, sir, I am part of a fact-finding mission sent over by our President Roosevelt to assess the situation, here, in Britain. However, the reason I am here talking to you is that I am the senior Signals Officer for our Marine Corps.'

At the mention of the word 'signals', Turing sat bolt upright. The Colonel had his full and undivided attention.

'Back home, we are developing a system of communication which we consider to be unbreakable.'

Turing leant forward on his desk. Now this is very interesting, he thought.

'You may know that during World War One we used some of our Indians as signallers. They were mostly plains Indians such as Sioux or Cheyenne. It was a crude, but effective system, and it caused the Hun some real problems, I can tell you. Anyway, to cut a long story short, we have taken this a step further. We are now developing a system using Navajos, as our conventional cyphers are being broken at every turn by the Japs.'

Turing wanted to ask a question, in fact several, but the American forestalled him.

'I know what you are thinking – why? It's all quite simple really. These folks, these Indians, are from Arizona, not that that's relevant. What is important is that they don't have a written language and there are very few people - and I mean few - that speak it. We've recruited a small group of Navajo men and trained them to transmit messages using the Navajo language. We call them the Navajo Code Talkers. They have allocated Navajo words for every letter of the English alphablet. They have an A-Z list of words that they use for the spelling out of English words. For instance, *be-la-sana* meaning *apple* and *tse-nill* meaning *axe* are used for the letter A and *na-hash-chid* meaning *badger* is one of the words used for the letter B. They use more than one Navajo word for each letter to make it more difficult for the codebreakers. In addition, they've made the system more efficient by creating shortforms for words that we use a lot. For instance, in the Navajo world the phonetic sound *atsa* means *eagle*, so it's become the word for 'transport plane'; *lotso* equals whale equals battleship. Get it? I can't remember any more – I don't have any Navajo blood in my veins. I can see that you get the idea, though.

Turing was, in fact, impressed. It was very clever, he thought. 'So how can this help us, here at Bletchley Park?' he asked.

'I'm not sure that it can. But I thought that the sharing of every sort of system between our selves may help us solve the problems we face individually. For instance, at a stretch, there might be Germans with Navajo blood working for their home country, Germany. A good number of German Americans did return to the States in 1939 and 1940. But it's a possibility that some stayed behind. It's probably a very remote possibility that they are influencing the current German cypher system. Nevertheless, I thought it important that you have an understanding of this new system we have, and where the boundaries might cross.

Turing sat back in his chair. He closed his eyes and rubbed his temples with both hands. He couldn't see for the life of him how this Navajo system was relevant. However, something about A for A words and B for B words was nudging his mind. Maybe, just maybe there was something here…

And there it was, rather like a light bulb that had just been switched on. How stupid of him not to have thought of it earlier. The one small weakness in the whole of Enigma. It might be small, but it was highly significant. Enigma could not transpose the letter A into a letter A or a B into a B, and so on. It was the one flaw in an otherwise perfect encryption code. So that meant that if the Germans were using Navajo Indians in their cypher system, then they couldn't possibly be using Enigma - although there was no reason why they couldn't be using Morse code. Turing let out a long and heart-felt sigh. So close, yet so far away.

Slowly and carefully, Turing explained briefly to his visitors how Enigma worked. Both Fleming and the Colonel were disappointed that they couldn't contribute to the current problem, each for his own reasons, but they accepted Turing's unarguable explanation without comment. After some further pleasantries, the two visitors made their excuses and left to catch their train back to London. At the doorway, Colonel Faragher paused and turned back.

'Just in case you were wondering, Mr Turing, but were too polite to ask, I picked up these souvenirs in Spain when I was part of the International Brigade.' He pointed to his face. Alan Turing nodded a thank you as the door closed.

He leant back in his chair and put his feet back on the desk. He turned his mind to a new set of problems. He was studying two pamphlets that had been sent to Bletchley Park. One was a Short Signal Book and the other was a Short Weather Cipher. He knew that German submarines made daily weather reports – air temperature, barometric pressure, wind speed and cloud cover. This information was reduced to a dozen or so letters which were then enciphered on Enigma and sent by Morse code to the German Navy's weather stations, so that they, in turn, could compile their own meteorological reports. These were then sent to all German shipping by using the standard three-wheel Enigma, a cipher that the Park had already broken. Could this be the back door into *Shark*? wondered Turing. First you had to read the weather report. Then you put it back into the short weather cipher. What you were left with, by a process of logical deduction, was the original text that had been sent from a submarine using a four-wheeled Enigma. It should have been a perfect crib. Yet Turing and his associates couldn't break it. Every day, possible solutions were being fed into the bombe machines that would clatter away through millions of permutations. And every day there was no answer. How on earth were the weather stations reading the U-boat transmissions? That was the key question they faced. Until they solved this, *Shark* would remain unbreakable.

CHAPTER 26

'On, off, on, off! I wish they would make up their bloody minds.' Marine Baz Phelps was voicing the opinion that many in 'X' Company held and was probably shared by the rest of the Commando. Everyone from the CO down was fed up with the endless training and then the waiting. They all wanted was to get on with the job. From the moment that *Operation Jubilee* had been given the green light, the men of Royal Marines Commando had been keyed up with anticipation. They had an important role to play in this Combined Forces raid and were anxious to get started. So far, there had been nothing but delay after delay. First, it was the weather, then it was the tides. They had embarked on the transport at least twice, only to be told to get off again. Hence Phelps's complaint.

Lieutenant Ellis caught the eye of Sergeant Thrattles, his Platoon NCO. The officer
gave a slight nod of his head towards the complaining marine. The Sergeant stood up and walked down the mess deck on *HMS Locust*, in which they had been living for the last couple of days. Squeezing onto the marine's bunk, Thrattles managed to sit down.

'Now then, young Phelps,' he said in a quiet avuncular voice, 'That will be enough of that, trained soldier. We wouldn't want to give people the wrong idea about our commitment, or go upsetting folk, now would we?' Sometimes others can get the wrong idea when we sound off. We all know that a marine is not really happy unless he has something to complain about, but there comes a time when we need to keep quiet and just endure. This is one of those times. Do I make myself clear?'

Phelps looked around at his mates. There were tears of embarrassment in his eyes when he replied, 'Yes, Sergeant. Sorry, Sergeant. It won't happen again.'

The mess deck was cramped and overcrowded. Space was at a premium. The bunk beds were stacked four high with just enough room for a man to turn over. Most of the marines spent their time lying and reading in the dim light, or smoking, or trying to sleep. There was little space to do anything else. One or two managed to clean and check their weapons, but then only at the inconvenience of his neighbour. The Navy had made them as comfortable as they could, given the limitations, but even they couldn't work miracles. However, the food was good and plentiful, but the queue for the galley always seemed endless, and you had to take your own mess tins, mug and cutlery. On the plus side, despite being embarked troops, they were actually 'victualled in'. This meant that they were entitled to draw a 'tot' - the Royal Navy's rum ration. For the ranks this rum was diluted with water which was carefully measured out. Sailors or anyone else under the age of twenty were not allowed rum. They and anyone of a temperance nature received an extra three pennies per day in their pay. 'Up Spirits' was usually piped between 1100 hours and midday. For the ranks of Petty Officers, sergeants and above, their rum was taken neat as 'grog'. Officers were not entitled to a rum ration and had to be content with whatever was being served in the wardroom.

As luck would have it, it was Burt Kelly's birthday. Whilst it was against Navy Regulations to give your tot away to someone else, there was a tradition, both for sailors and marines that when on board ship they could discreetly offer someone 'sippers'. Usually this meant a group of friends would allow the celebrant to have a very small sip from each person's cup. This was usually done quietly and without too much fuss, lest it drew the attention of the Master-at-Arms or his Regulating Staff. Generally, this was tolerated as long as things did not get out of hand. Kelly had had about half a dozen small 'sippers'. When his mate Steve passed his mug over, he whispered, 'Go on, have 'gulpers'.' Kelly needed no second bidding. He took a large mouthful and swallowed; a huge grin on his face. Five minutes later, he slid slowly to the deck, completely incapable of standing. Dacre shook his head sadly, then organised getting the marine to his bunk and into a position that, should he be sick, he would not choke on his own vomit.

A little later, when Sergeant Thrattles and Lieutenant Ellis carried out their rounds after the midday meal, the NCO encouraged the young officer to look the other way when they came to the marines' mess deck.

'It's a tradition, sir,' he explained. 'Both for us 'Royals' and the matelots.'

However, the smell was so overpowering as to be unbelievable. Someone somewhere had been sick. The stink of rum fuelled vomit was unique. The mess deck was hot and sweaty. Despite this, many of the marines had turned in and slept through the whole charade. Dacre needed some fresh air. He was not averse to drinking rum; indeed, he had enjoyed his tot like everyone else. But there was a limit to what he would put up with, and this mess deck with its appalling smell was his limit. He climbed the two decks, up the steep ladders, and through several hatchways until he found himself on the main deck, starboard side, just below the bridge. It was a bright but cool day. A stiff breeze was blowing off the sea. It smelt and tasted of salt. The sky was clear with hardly a cloud in sight. The day looked promising. Perhaps they might get underway tonight, he thought.

Dacre turned and walked up towards the bow, breathing in the fresh air. In doing so, he passed a small sea-going store. The top half of the door was open. Above it was a small sign that read 'Chief Boatswain's Store'. On instinct, the marine popped his head inside. An elderly Chief Petty Officer was sitting on a stool, smoking an old pipe and reading a newspaper. The smoke from the pipe smelt like old socks. This was a very senior sailor who deserved to be treated with respect. His face was weather-beaten and wrinkled. He had a huge, bushy grey beard, or a 'set' as it was called in the Navy. He was wearing an old white rolled-neck sweater, waterproof trousers and sea boots. On his head was a battered cap which gave the only clue to his rank. The CPO badge was clear for all to see.

'Afternoon, Chief,' Dacre said with a smile on his face. The older man looked up. He broke into a toothy grin.

'Hello, 'Royal'. What can I do for you then?'

'I don't suppose you have a spare hammock that I could borrow?'

'For you, anything, son. You'll want a couple of stretchers as well?'

Dacre nodded. The Chief disappeared into the back of his store and rummaged for a couple of minutes. He returned with a neatly rolled up canvas and two short lengths of wood that had small notches cut into each end. He looked the marine up and down and liked what he saw.

'You with this lot, going ashore then?'

'Yes.'

'Well, I'll not ask any more questions, otherwise you might have to kill me.'

He gave a short laugh at his own dark sense of humour.

'I'll wish you good luck then, and God speed. I suspect you are going to need it, you and those other poor buggers. Just go and get your head down for a few hours.' With that, he re-lit his pipe and picked up his newspaper.

Dacre turned to leave.

'Oh, and you might sling your hook down on deck one, by the ammunition hoist. You won't be disturbed there.'

The marine waved a hand in gratitude as he left.

CHAPTER 27

At precisely 2100 hours, *HMS Locust* slipped her cables and moved gently away from the inner wall of Portsmouth Harbour. The *Locust* was a flat-bottomed gunboat of five hundred tons. The ship had two four-inch guns and a 3.7-inch howitzer. She had been built before the war on Clydeside, for duties in the Far East, particularly in China. The *Locust* had also taken part in the evacuation of British troops from Dunkirk in 1940. Dacre instantly recognised her distinctive silhouette and profile.

Now, in the twilight of the evening, the ship moved silently to her allotted position amongst the vast armada that was heading for France. It was a fine summer evening. The sea was smooth and the sky clear, with just a slight breeze. Despite this, the *Locust* began to pitch and roll, mainly because of her flat-bottomed hull. There were well over two hundred and fifty ships and landing craft from the five ports of Portsmouth, Southampton, Shoreham, Gosport and Newhaven. Not a single light was to be seen anywhere. Apart from the gentle thudding of the engines, there was barely a sound to be heard. Even the seagulls had given up and gone home.

Dacre and the rest of the marines were, by now, sitting or lying on the main deck, just for'ard of the wheelhouse. No-one uttered a word; each marine silent with his own thoughts and, perhaps more importantly, with his own mortality. One or two tried to get some more sleep - that precious commodity that would help them when the going got tough. All the marines were fully booted and spurred: their faces blackened, their weapons and personal equipment by their sides. They were all carrying extra bandoliers of ammunition. Some were also carrying platoon weapons such as the .303 Bren light machine gun, a two-inch mortar or a

PIAT rocket launcher. Others carried an assortment of boxes containing spare magazines, HE bombs or rockets. Each marine also carried a selection of Mills and smoke grenades. Added to this, each man was carrying a fully laden backpack that weighed about fifty pounds, which contained all the essentials that each of them might require. God help us if we end up in the water, thought Dacre. With that amount of kit, a person would go straight to the bottom like a stone, and that would be that.

The ship was barely underway. In the wheelhouse, the helmsman struggled to maintain his course and direction because of the reduced speed. High above the heads of the marines, the lookouts scanned the surrounding sea with powerful binoculars, ever vigilant for approaching surface vessels or submarines - enemy or otherwise. The last thing anyone wanted was a night-time collision with a friendly boat.

Dacre checked his watch, yet again. The luminous hands told him it was 0146 hours. Suddenly a shadow appeared in front of him, the body shape dark against the night sky. It was Sergeant Thrattles. He leant down and whispered into the marine's ear, 'You and Wills follow me.' Together, the little group threaded their way across the rolling deck and around the tangle of bodies and legs, doing their best to avoid treading on anyone. They arrived at a small cabin door half-way down the starboard side of the ship. The sergeant tapped gently twice with the butt of his weapon. Instantly the door was opened outwards and the group entered a darkened space, so pitch black that you couldn't see your hand in front of your face. As soon as the door was closed and secured, several red lights were switched on. The unearthly glow looked unreal, almost demonic.

'It's to protect our night vision,' said the Sergeant, by way of an explanation.

In the small cabin, not much bigger than a cupboard, everyone had to stand; there wasn't room to sit down. As Dacre's eyesight adjusted to the gloom, he could just make out the other occupants. In front of him was the Company Commander, Captain Standwell, beside him was his Platoon Officer, Lieutenant Huntington-Whiteley, and next to him stood the young Lieutenant Ellis. Squeezed into the corner was the unit's second-in-command, Major Houghton. Clearly this was an important meeting, thought Dacre.

Captain Standwell was the first to speak. 'We've just received an urgent communication from Commander Fleming. He has asked us to alter our plans when we raid the Kriegsmarine headquarters, which, as you know, is at the Hotel Moderne on 21 Rue Vaugalain. Dacre, you and Wills are to go directly to their communications centre and are to remove the codebooks and bigram tables as quickly as you can. You are to ignore everything else, including any safes that may or may not contain secret papers. A fast launch will be at your disposal which will take you straight out to a warship waiting offshore. You will hand over the codebooks and bigram tables to the Lieutenant Commander, who will then return to 'Blighty' and see that they get to Bletchley Park as fast as possible. You will gather from all this that there is a real sense of urgency to this mission. You don't need me to remind you how important it is that the boffins at Bletchley get these codes.'

He paused to emphasise the seriousness of the situation. Lieutenant Ellis took over the briefing.

'You will have a section of men who will act as your bodyguards. Their job is to ensure that you get to and from the building in one piece. They will also ensure that any enemy opposition in the building is dealt with. The rest of the platoon will be close behind you. Our task will be to remove anything else which may be of value. The timing will be tight because hard on our heels, and yours, will be the demolition teams - so no slip-ups please. Oh, and one last thing. Mr Fleming has now decided to refer to this operation as a 'pinch' raid. I suppose he is using this instead of the word 'steal'. Why, I am not sure. No doubt he will explain it himself, in due course. So, apart from that, do you have any questions?'

Dacre still had plenty of questions, of course he had, but he realised that now was not the right time to ask them.

CHAPTER 28

(i)

HMS Locust, with its precious cargo of Royal Marine Commandos, continued to move through the darkened night at a snail's pace to the rendezvous point south of the Isle of Wight. From there the armada of ships would head off towards the French coast. So far, the entire fleet had remained undiscovered. The *Locust* continued to roll uncomfortably. More than one bootneck' could be heard vomiting into the scuppers, or over the side into the dark waters below. With a chill wind now blowing, some of the marines were getting cold. Fortunately, the cooks and galley staff had the presence of mind to brew up some thick pusser's hot chocolate together with plenty of doorstop spam sandwiches. The marines were soon warmed and revived.

At 0345 Dacre checked his watch again. It was difficult to estimate how far they were from the French coast. Far away to the starboard side, he could just make out a flashing light on the horizon. Was that the lighthouse at Dieppe he wondered? Strange that it was still operating. He figured that they must be a good ten miles from their objective.

All of a sudden the silent night sky was lit up by a single star shell on their port bow and burst high up above the fleet of ships. This was immediately followed by heavy gunfire and streams of tracer bullets, followed by further star bursts. The flotilla had been spotted. Despite this desperate activity, *HMS Locust* and the other ships steamed slowly on.

Dawn broke. The marines on the foc'sle were able to see the hostile shore for the first time. Strangely, all seemed to be quite normal when viewed from a distance. There was little or no sign of the war. White cliffs, so similar to those between Newhaven and Brighton, sheltered the town. Apart from some distant thuds and booms, all seemed to be quiet.

As the morning light increased, so the embarked troops could see and appreciate the size of the operation. They were surrounded by hundreds of ships and craft of all shapes and sizes. It was a magnificent and awe-inspiring sight, perhaps one that they would never forget.

Suddenly the sky was full of low flying aircraft, both Allied and German. There were hundreds of planes everywhere, diving and wheeling all over the place. The troops on board began firing their weapons enthusiastically at anything that moved, theirs or ours. Eventually the officers and NCOs managed to restore some sense of order, but not before several planes were seen to nosedive into the sea. There was no sign of the pilots.

At 0510 hours, four of the Hunt class destroyers opened fire on the port and the town. At the same time, RAF Hurricanes flew in low over the water, blazing away with machine guns and cannon fire. The bombardment was brief and hardly did any real damage. The landing craft, with the Canadians on board, were less than a mile from the beaches.

(ii)

It was at this time that *HMS Locust* came under heavy and accurate gunfire from both the east and west cliffs. The little ship received numerous direct hits. The marines laid down flat on the deck, hoping for some protection from the onslaught of the enemy guns. They covered their ears as the ship's guns began to return fire. The captain hoisted his battle pennant as they headed for the harbour. They were just about five hundred yards from the mole and the quay. The noise of the returning gunfire was so loud that they couldn't hear themselves think, let alone hear their mates shouting and screaming. At the harbour entrance all hell was let loose. Bullets and shells were coming from every direction, all aimed at the *Locust*. The protective mole was covered in a pall of thick black smoke. Lines of red-hot tracer bullets arched their way across the harbour towards them. The steep escarpments to the left and right that dominated the harbour seemed to be alive with the muzzle flashes of heavy German guns, which poured unceasing and well-aimed gunfire down onto the boat.

The noise was unbelievable and terrifying for everyone, but especially for those who had never been under enemy fire before. Their training at Achnacarry had done nothing to
prepare the marines for this nightmare. Pete Wills was petrified. He had already wet himself, and he wasn't the only one. Dacre gripped his friend's shoulder as hard as he could.

'Are you okay?' he shouted. Wills shook his head. He just wanted to crawl away somewhere - anywhere, to hide. This was all too much for him. However, despite his fears, his training and instinct took over. He gave Dacre something akin to a grin - more of a grimace really. They would survive. They would get ashore. They had a job to do. Then a shell struck the ship, not more than twenty feet from where they were lying.

In the immediate aftermath, there was silence. Then the heart-rending cries and groans of the wounded and dying began. The whole place stank of cordite and something else. Dacre recognised it immediately: blood, guts, shit and body parts. As long as he lived,
he would never forget that disgusting and filthy smell. Slumped against the bulwark was another marine, 'Jock' Redmonton, a red-haired Scotsman who was due to get married shortly. A sick bay attendant was going through his pockets.

'What the fuck are you doing?' shouted Wills.

The sailor looked up.

'He's dead! I'm collecting his personal stuff to send home, and his ID tags.'

Wills and Dacre exchanged horrified glances.

'Our orders are to throw all the dead overboard. We are not to take any bodies home. Here, come on, give me a hand, will you?'

(iii)

Still under a torrent of enemy fire, the skipper of *HMS Locust*, Commander Ryder, quickly realised that it was suicide to continue with this mission. He sent a hurried signal to Major General Roberts informing him of the situation. Roberts ordered him to withdraw, to join the destroyers offshore and to await further orders. Accordingly, Ryder hoisted his negative flag and carried out a fast one hundred and eighty degree turn. The little ship continued to return enemy fire as best it could. Even some of the marines began using their Bren guns, although as the distance from the shore increased they had to cease firing.

Meanwhile offshore, on a Type I Hunt Class destroyer, Commander Fleming sat and waited. He could see very little: for although the day was clear and the sea calm, the accompanying destroyers had laid down so much smoke that the shoreline was completely obliterated. Eventually, he received a message to say that the raid on the harbour, his raid, had been called off. He was beside himself with disappointment, which slowly turned to anger. Didn't Roberts realise how important it was that his marines steal these documents? Fuming to himself and, perhaps not fully in control of his emotions, he sent a hurried and terse radio message to the General to remind him that the pinch raid must still go ahead, one way or another. Fleming knew that he had overstepped the mark with the General but felt certain that in the end both his boss and Admiral Mountbatten would support him.

CHAPTER 29

(i)

Standing on the port wing of *HMS Caple,* another Hunt Class destroyer, Major General Roberts the Ground Force Commander stared intently at the coastline. Even with the aid of powerful binoculars, it was impossible to make out what was happening. The heavy smokescreen laid down by the Royal Navy, in an effort to offer some protection to the vulnerable landing craft, had done its job only too well. Exasperated, Roberts turned to his senior officers who were gathered around him.

'Well, just what the hell is going on?' he demanded.

His frustration at not being able to see what was happening had turned to anger.

'How the goddamn hell am I supposed to conduct this war if I can't see a bloody thing? What about communications? Are there any radio messages?'

Nobody answered him because nobody had an answer. They were all as blind as he was. The General suddenly clutched his stomach and gave a low groan. He had eaten something the night before, maybe the shellfish, which had upset him. He had spent most of the silent hours sitting on the toilet, trying to cope with the waves of diarrhoea. This morning, of all mornings, he was desperately tired and drained of energy.

'I am going to the toilet. When I get back, I want some damn answers. Is that clear?'

He glowered at everyone, then hurriedly left the bridge. His senior officers looked at each other horrified. Nobody had the answers.

Ten minutes later, a very pale and clearly unwell General returned. 'Well?' he growled.

Nobody dared speak, until his ADC decided to take the bull by the horns.

'Firstly, sir, you need to be aware that despite the thirty or more additional radio and navigation systems that we have on board, our actual radio communications with the troops ashore are extremely poor, and in many cases non-existent. Many of the radios have failed to work, others are only passing on half a message, and some of those are so garbled as to make no sense at all. The beach Signals Sections have taken heavy casualties, whilst many of their wireless sets are water damaged and beyond repair.'

The ADC looked to his fellow officers for confirmation. They all nodded in
agreement. He continued. 'It would seem that on the basis of the information that we have received the current situation is as follows. On Yellow Beach, Berneval, only a very few of Number Three Commando have made it ashore. The enemy battery was eventually attacked and put out of operation. Unfortunately, the Commando has taken heavy casualties, both killed, wounded and captured. On Orange Beach, Varengeville, Lord Lovat has successfully led Number Four Commando. They have attacked and taken the guns at the point of bayonet and are now waiting to be evacuated. We do not yet know of their casualties. At Green Beach, the South Saskatchewan Regiment has landed, but it would seem that they are in the wrong place. I am given to understand that they have moved inland in order to find a way across the River Scie. The Queen's Own Highlanders have also landed but are under heavy enemy fire. They have also started to move inland. No casualty figures are yet available. There is no news from Blue Beach, except that we know they have landed and are also under heavy enemy fire. As I said before, we have no radio communications with anyone.

On Red and White Beaches, our troops have also landed. They have experienced stiff resistance but are slowly advancing. Thankfully, they are supported by the tanks of the Fourteenth who are now ashore, so that should help. We understand that the Casino has been taken by our forces and they are now carrying out their assigned tasks.'

'How reliable is this intelligence?' asked the General.

The ADC hesitated before answering, not sure what to say. He decided to cover his own back. 'It's the best we have, sir, at this moment in time, but as for it being reliable and up to date, I can't really say. The battle situation will be changing all the time, and without wireless communications…'

'Yes, thank you. I understand what you're saying,' Roberts replied abruptly.

(ii)

The General stood very quietly, taking in the information. It was true that casualties seemed to be a bit high but, having said that, the raid seemed to have gained momentum, and his boys were obviously giving a good account of themselves. Now he thought was the time to send in his reserves, the Fusiliers Mont-Royal and the Royal Marine Commandos, to help consolidate the situation. He was also mindful of the very sharp message that he had received from that bloody Naval Intelligence fellow Fleming, reminding him that the marines still needed to carry out their raid on the German Naval Headquarters. As if he needed reminding! However, since this man obviously had the support of Mountbatten, he had better try to do something about getting their mission underway. Actually, this all seemed to be working out rather well, he thought. He went through the whole thing again in his mind, just to make sure that he hadn't overlooked anything. Then, completely satisfied, he gave the necessary orders.

The time was 0830 hours.

CHAPTER 30

(i)

On board *HMS Locust*, Lieutenant Colonel Picton-Phillipps hurriedly called a briefing of his officers. He had to explain to them that General Roberts wanted to send them onto White Beach to support the Canadians. Those marines on the *Locust* would have to transfer from the ship onto landing craft for the run in. The remainder of the Commando were already in the French Chasseurs and would follow on. Once ashore, the Commando would split into two groups. Firstly, 'X' Company had been tasked to fight their way across the port, and to ensure that the Ten Platoon got safely to the German Naval Headquarters, as previously planned. The remainder of the unit were to skirt the town to the west and south, and had been tasked with attacking the batteries on the eastern cliff from the south. Having checked a local town map, the Colonel had estimated that the distance that they needed to cover was well over two miles. The two companies carrying out this attack were to use the 'leapfrog' method, so that each group gave covering fire whilst the other moved forward. In this way the Colonel hoped to reduce the casualty rate.

Heavily laden with kit and weapons, the marines began climbing over the side of the
ship and scrambling down the rope netting into the waiting landing craft below. These mechanised craft were flat-bottomed and were designed to land either a couple of lorries or a single tank. They were not ideal as troop carriers. Each craft was about forty feet long with a front ramp that dropped down. Made of steel, they had high sides that would offer some protection for the marines who would be sitting or squatting on the deck.

Ten Platoon found itself in the same boat as Number Eleven Platoon and the Commando Headquarters. Dacre spotted his old room-mate Ken Shakespeare, who was now a full corporal.

'Don't you just love this man's army?' he called out. 'Here we go again, By Sea by bloody Land!'

Shakespeare gave a huge grin and a thumbs-up sign. Now was not the time for a conversation, no matter how hurried.

Dacre, Pete Wills and Mac McKnight found themselves sitting next to Major Houghton, the unit's second-in-command. Next to him was a very pale looking Lieutenant Ellis. At the front of the landing craft sat two more men from the Platoon, Burt Kelly and Steve Whitnell. Both men had exchanged their rifles for Bren guns. They had reasoned that you couldn't have enough firepower. As the landing craft pulled away from the ship's side, everyone huddled low. Many of the marines chose to cover themselves with their water-proof capes in order to give some protection from the spray from the sea.

As the little flotilla got under way, the supporting mine sweepers and destroyers gave what covering fire they could. Despite this, enemy shells and mortar bombs began to fall amongst the landing craft. Thankfully, these vulnerable boats entered into the safety of a thick smokescreen that had been laid down to give them some concealment. It was not to last. Within minutes, they emerged into brilliant sunshine and a clear sky. Dacre took the opportunity to take a quick look over the high metal side. The steep pebble beach was only about a hundred yards away. All he could see was that it was strewn with dozens of damaged and destroyed landing craft and tanks. It also seemed to be covered with the bodies of wounded and dead Canadian soldiers, lying where they had fallen.

The next second, the marines were enveloped in a curtain of shells and bullets. Several boats received direct hits and exploded. Dacre ducked down as a maelstrom of machine gun bullets hit the side where he had just been standing. The sound was like hailstones on a tin roof. No-one expected this amount of German firepower, or this level of accuracy. The marines crouched low, their faces tense and grim. One or two had been sick and several had unashamedly pissed themselves. For many of them this was their initiation into a real war. A sense of fear gripped their vitals. They wanted to be anywhere but here. Then, as if by some minor miracle, the training and discipline took over. They just wanted to get ashore and get on with the task in hand.

The flotilla re-formed then sailed eastwards for several hundred yards before turning towards land and White Beach. Dacre gripped his rifle more tightly. He waited anxiously for the landing craft to hit the beach and for the ramp to go down.

(ii)

Immediately their craft hit the shingle beach, the cry went out, 'Down ramp, out troops.' Major Houghton led the first group of marines ashore at a sprint, they needed no urging. Within seconds they were under heavy and intense machine gun fire, whilst mortar shells exploded all around them. They plunged into several feet of water which slowed them down. Bullets tore into them, scything men down like grass in a hayfield. Dacre was hit in his left forearm by a heavy calibre bullet. Fortunately, it passed neatly between the two bones. He let out a yelp, more of surprise than pain. Blood spurted everywhere. The force of the bullet hitting him, and the weight of his equipment, knocked him over the edge of the ramp and into the sea. As the cold water closed over his face, he could taste the salt in his mouth. He tried desperately not to swallow. He struggled manfully to get to his feet, but it was too much. He was being dragged down by the weight of his equipment. He felt as if his lungs were going to burst. He swallowed a mouthful of water and choked. Strangely, it seemed that everywhere had become quiet and still. So, this was it, he thought. What a bloody silly way to die. Suddenly, a strong pair of hands were under his arms and he felt himself being pulled back up to the surface. Coughing and spluttering, he looked up into the grim face of Lieutenant Ellis.

'Come on, Royal, this is no time to be pissing about!' he said.

Bullets and tracer rounds were plucking at the water all around them, and then kicking up pebbles by their feet. Somehow or other Ellis, helped by Pete Wills, half carried, half dragged Dacre to some cover behind a burnt-out tank. Major Houghton and several other marines had already taken shelter there. Someone produced a field dressing and Dacre's wound was quickly bandaged. Blood immediately seeped through the bandage, turning the white linen a dark red. The Major looked on with concern written all over his face.

'How is he?' he asked.
'He'll live, sir, at least for the present.'
'That's good because I think we are going to need him. He's the only one with a rifle.'

Dacre took the opportunity to look back along the beach. It was clear that within minutes of hitting the beach, the Commando had been reduced to a dazed and shell-shocked body of men just trying to survive. Many of the marines in the other landing craft and boats had not even managed to get ashore. They had been gunned down as soon as the ramps went down. The carnage and absolute horror that Dacre and his colleagues were witnessing was horrific. The stink of blood hit the back of their throats. The bodies of the dead were everywhere. It was like a slaughterhouse.

He wasn't sure how long they had huddled behind the tank. It may have been as long as five minutes; it was difficult to tell. The coldness of the tank's metal pressing against the side of his face was somehow reassuring, he was reluctant to move. He felt safe there.

Further down the beach, the Commanding Officer's landing craft had hit an underwater obstacle. The landing craft had slewed sideways, inviting even heavier enemy gunfire. To add to the disastrous situation, the ramp of their boat had become jammed. Despite the valiant efforts of those on board, it refused to budge. Clearly visible from the shore, the boat's skipper, seeing the problem, ran along the narrow deck to try and release the ramp. He was immediately shot dead and fell into the sea. A company sergeant major could be seen trying to get some Bren guns firing. Several of the gunners were killed as soon as they put their heads above the metal sides. Other marines tried to get ashore by climbing over the sides, only to be forced back by a hail of bullets. Mortified, Dacre and the others watched helplessly as more and more marines were wounded or killed. The men who did manage to return enemy fire, simply became living targets for the German snipers who were unfailingly accurate.

Looking back along the beach, Dacre was able to see even more stranded and wrecked boats. On the beach, the dead and wounded, mostly Canadians, had now been joined by an increasing number of Royal Marines. Amongst them he could just make out a small group of assault engineers who had managed to get ashore without any covering fire at all. Their task had been to breach the three-foot high sea wall, in order to allow the tanks to move off the beach and inland. Most of these engineers had become casualties. The wall had not been breached and the tanks were still on the beach, sitting targets for the German anti-tank guns. Where the sand met the sea, there was yard-wide river of blood, gently lapping up and down with the rhythm of the small waves.

Suddenly a figure appeared, climbing onto the top of the wheelhouse of a nearby beached landing craft. Dacre couldn't believe what he was seeing. It was the Colonel. Horrified, he let out involuntary shout of despair. The rest of the little group turned to see what he was looking at. Major Houghton shouted out a warning, which was lost in the fearsome noise all around them. Appalled, they watched in stunned silence. In full view of the Germans, the Colonel was seen to pull on a pair of white gloves. He then began waving away other boats that were trying to come into the beach. Some did alter their course and veered away, others ignored him and continued to come in towards the beach. Within seconds he was gunned down under a hail of gunfire.

Nobody said anything. There was nothing to say. They had just been privileged to witness a very brave man trying to save his men in a completely unselfish act of courage. Dacre wondered if the CO had realised that the beach hadn't yet been taken by the Canadians. For some unaccountable reason, he thought of a short passage from the Bible: *Greater love hath no man, than he lays down his life for his friends.* Dacre had no real love or belief in religion. It was true that both his grandfather and mother had been of the Roman faith, and he knew that as a baby he had been baptised, whatever that meant. However, his grandfather had lapsed after his mother's death, so he had never followed the faith. Nevertheless, in certain life-threatening circumstances he had prayed, why, he didn't really know. He prayed now.

(iii)

The little group sheltering behind the tank suddenly had their attention drawn back to their own landing craft. A mortar shell struck the stern causing a massive explosion. This was not so surprising because it was carrying most of the explosives for the harbour demolitions. Almost immediately a fire broke out. The group could clearly see marines and naval ratings engulfed in flames. Some of these wretches tried to throw themselves into the sea. Several actually managed to succeed, but the majority were simply shot down. Others could be seen stripping off their equipment but as soon as they tried to climb over the side, they, too, were shot and crashed back down on those below. It was total chaos. The few that did make it into the water then had to decide whether to swim the few yards to the beach or swim out to sea in the hope of being picked up by a friendly ship. Some did one thing, some the other. Those that made it to the beach were immediately gunned down as they staggered, exhausted, from the water.

Further along on White Beach, Dacre could just make out a detachment of Royal Marines Policemen who had landed in the first wave. Like everyone else, they were taking heavy casualties. He nudged the Lieutenant and pointed.

Ellis looked up, leant over and shouted into Dacre's ear, 'They are to police the withdrawal, and to look after any prisoners. I think their Colonel is also acting as the 'Beach -master'.'

Too much information, thought Dacre. There are some things that I don't need to know right now. As they looked on, three more policemen were cut down by the murderous crossfire.

Mortar bombs and shells were continuing to explode all around the little group that were still sheltering behind the tank. The ripping chatter of machine guns and the whine of bullets from German sniper rifles, combined with the explosions, all sounded like some unearthly thunderstorm. Added to this was the screaming of the planes overhead, as they repeatedly dived and released their bombs onto the troops below. All these explosions merged into one horrendous and continuous, deathly roar. The little group of marines felt as if they were going mad.

Major Houghton realised that his group of 'Royals' could not stay where they were for much longer. Several of them had already received slight wounds, and one had been killed outright when he tried to look around the side of the tank, a third eye appearing in the middle of his forehead as if by magic. To the front of them, just a short distance away, was the sea wall. It was about three-foot high and was topped by a double row of barbed wire. Beyond that was the promenade. The wall didn't offer much protection, but it was marginally better than their present position. Somewhat reluctantly, everyone got to their feet, and, in a mad charge, zigzagged after the Major up the steep shingle beach. By some miracle they all arrived virtually unscathed. One or two had some minor nicks, and Dacre had received a slight skin wound where a tracer bullet had scorched his neck.

From this new position, they could clearly see the sand-bagged positions of the Germans in the buildings to the front of them. Most of the enemy fire seemed to be coming from this direction.

Major Houghton leant across and shouted at Dacre, 'Can you keep their heads down?'

The young marine nodded. He hefted his Lee-Enfield .303 into a more comfortable position. He suddenly noticed that there was a piece of wood missing from the rifle butt. It looked like a bullet had gouged out a chunk. But it was sound enough and wouldn't affect him using it. He pulled back the bolt with his right hand and ejected the unused round. Then he licked his forefinger and pushed it into the chamber of the rifle in order to clear out any sand and grit that had accumulated during the beach landing. Satisfied, he replaced the round and pushed the bolt forward, taking the round smoothly back into the breech. He flipped up the back sights and set them to one hundred yards. At this distance, wind and elevation wouldn't be an issue. Finally, he removed the French letter from the top of the barrel. At least the barrel would be clean and dry, he thought. Dacre brought the rifle up and settled the butt into the crook of his shoulder. He felt the coldness of the wooden stock on his left hand as he pressed his cheek against the butt. He then placed the index finger of his right hand alongside the trigger guard. He closed his left eye and raised the rifle barrel slowly until the foresight was in line with the notch on the back sight. I am no hero, he thought. Frightened – no! Fearful – yes! Any man who said he didn't know fear would be deceiving himself. Everyone knew fear at some time or other, or else they weren't human. However, discipline and training helped you overcome fear, and not wanting to let your mates down drove you on. The others in the group could only watch because he was the only one with a rifle. Tommy guns and pistols were useless at this distance. He tried to ease his injured arm. It hurt like hell, but he pushed any thought of pain to the back of his mind. He had work to do, work that he had been trained for.

Lieutenant Ellis rolled over towards the marine, and pulling out his binoculars shouted, 'I'll spot for you.'

Giving Dacre clear and precise directions, the two of them set about their task.

Slowly and methodically, Dacre selected the first target, a German sniper on the second floor of the building to his front. His finger moved onto the trigger, he squeezed gently just as he had been taught. His body was tense and braced, waiting for the recoil from the rifle, his right eye fixed on the German. It wasn't a man he told himself, it was just a target, nothing more. The rifle kicked hard against his shoulder; it jumped several inches. There was a ringing in his ears as a small puff of smoke emerged from the barrel. He watched, fascinated, as the sniper toppled out of the window, spiralling down, his arms flailing onto the ground below. He blinked, forcing back the tears. This was the first time that he had ever killed in cold blood. It wasn't a living breathing man like himself, it was only a target. He realised that he couldn't be doing with these thoughts. He had a job to do. He pulled back the bolt, ejected the spent round, slammed the bolt viciously forward and inserted another live round. He was ready to kill again.

One by one, the German soldiers disappeared or fell from the buildings opposite. Dacre did not hesitate or stop to think what he was doing. He was automatically pressing the trigger, then operating the bolt to feed in another live round in one fluid movement. His training and discipline had automatically taken over. It was rather like shooting targets at a fairground. The others in the group tried to make themselves useful by loading some of his spare magazines – there was little else for them to do. He continued shooting like a machine, a lethal machine. His right cheekbone and shoulder were bruised and ached from the constant recoil and kick-back from the weapon. The barrel and wooden stock were becoming dangerously hot. The palm of his left hand was smarting from the heat, whilst the wound in his arm throbbed with pain.

Everywhere on the beach, small pockets of marines were doing their best to return fire. One group nearby could be seen clearly trying to dig a 'tunnel' in a desperate attempt to find themselves some cover in a shallow trench. Mortar bombs continued to smash down on the few survivors. Those not directly hit were then at the mercy of the murderous crossfire of the German machine guns that continuously swept the beach.

Dacre's success at shooting so many of the enemy - well into double figures - had drawn even more unwelcome attention from the Germans. Heavy machine gun fire was now peppering the top of the sea wall above their heads. Small pieces of shattered concrete tore into their hands and faces. So ferocious and accurate was this gunfire, that Dacre had to stop shooting. Major Houghton did not like the way things were shaping up.

Turning to the Lieutenant he said, 'If we stay here much longer, we are all going to be killed or taken prisoner. I'm going to take a couple of the chaps and try to get through the barbed wire. You, Dacre and Wills stay here. If you get a chance, I suggest you try and swim for it. Now give us some covering fire...' With that, the Major and his men crawled away, as Dacre started firing again.

(iv)

Lieutenant Ellis quickly realised that the Major was right. The three of them didn't have very long before their position would be overrun.

'Get all your equipment off and undo your boots. If, and when, we get a chance, we'll leave our weapons and make a dash down the beach and into the sea. It's every man for himself.'

It all sounded so simple, thought Dacre. If only....!

Then, as if by order, a flight of RAF Mustangs flew in low from over the sea, their machine guns strafing the enemy positions.

'Come on!' shouted the Lieutenant. 'It's now or never. Move your arses.'

As they scrambled to their feet, Dacre just had time to see that the Major and his men were hopelessly entangled in the barbed wire and under heavy machine gun fire. To add insult to injury, the flight of RAF aeroplanes seemed to have shot up the little group, causing further injuries.

Together, the three marines hurled themselves down the steep shingle beach and into the water. Boots were kicked off, as they dived beneath the waves. Sporadic gunfire zipped after them, plucking at the surface around them. Dacre, with his head down, swam as fast as he could, grabbing great handfuls of water. He had always been a good swimmer, never afraid of the water. He had a natural instinct for survival. All around him floated bodies and body parts. The smell was terrible. He ploughed straight on through them, not stopping for anything. He felt the acid trying to rise from his stomach. He kept his jaws firmly clamped together and his lips shut tight, in case he took in a mouthful of the contaminated seawater. At first, he tried to zigzag, so as to be a more difficult target, but he soon gave this up as a bad job and concentrated on speed. Pete Wills was right behind him. He was not as good a swimmer but was doing his best to keep up. Suddenly, shrapnel from an overhead airburst began to splash into the sea around them. Wills was hit on the back of the head by a particularly large piece and sank quietly out of sight. He never called out, and never even knew what had hit him. Dacre swam on, unaware that his friend was gone.

After a couple of hundred yards, he eased up in order to get a sense of his bearings. About a quarter of a mile away, he could just make out another swimmer. He hoped it was Ellis, but at that distance it was difficult to tell. He trod water whilst he attempted to wipe the saltwater from his eyes.

Of Wills, there was no sign. He had disappeared. It was as if the little safe-breaker had never existed. Fuck! he thought. What a bloody mess and what a waste of good men. And for what? It had been mad, and pointless. Saddened and angry by the loss of his friend and all the others, he rolled over and resumed swimming out to sea, only this time more slowly, as he needed to conserve his energy. He didn't know how far he might have to swim, and England was a long way off.

CHAPTER 31

(i)

Dacre wasn't sure how long he had been in the water. His watch had stopped. Possibly a couple of hours, at the least. He was floating on his back, resting as best he could. Although the sun was still out and the sky was a clear blue, he was beginning to get cold. His legs were starting to develop cramps; he couldn't feel his feet and his hands were bitterly cold. His mind was wandering, and his brain did not recognise the fact that this body was shutting down. He didn't realise, either, that in another fifteen or twenty minutes he would lapse into unconsciousness and then drown. Far away he thought he heard a deep throbbing, but for the life of him he couldn't work out what it was - besides which he really didn't care.

The crew of a passing French Chasseur motorboat had spotted the marine. At first, they thought it was just another body - they had passed dozens since they had left Dieppe. The sailor in the bow had seen a movement of the body. At first, he thought it was just the swell of the waves making the arms appear to move. He watched fascinated, then saw the head rise up and look around. He shouted to his crew mates that they had a live one here. The helmsman slowly brought the boat alongside Dacre, where they managed, after a real effort, to haul him on board. By this time, he was shivering and shaking from head to toe. His feet and hands were white and wrinkled, and he couldn't feel a thing. The crew wrapped him in blankets and an old tarpaulin, then fed him sips of Cognac, whilst others massaged his legs and arms to get the circulation going. As luck would have it, another destroyer, *HMS Berkeley,* was lying close by. With the minimum of fuss, the French managed to transfer the marine aboard. He was immediately taken below into the warm, where he was kitted out with some dry clothes and a pair of plimsolls. A sandwich and a hot cup of sweet tea laced with rum helped him regain some of his old self. His arms and legs were slowly returning to normal, although the pain from the pins and needles was excruciating. However, he knew that this would wear off.

There were a couple of dozen or more other rescued men on the mess deck, mostly Canadians, several marines whom he didn't recognise, a couple of army commandos and a sergeant from the American Rangers. All of them looked to be in a state of shell shock. No-one wanted to talk. Each of them was lost in his own thoughts of the horror and carnage they had witnessed. Dacre stretched out his legs on a nearby bunk, closed his eyes and was asleep within seconds.

Suddenly the door of the mess deck opened and in walked a petty officer.

'Do any of you lot know how to operate an Oerlikon gun?' he asked. 'We're a crew member short. Any volunteers?'

Nobody answered. Nobody looked at him. It wasn't that they didn't want to respond, they had nothing left to give. They were totally exhausted.

Dacre sat up in his bunk. 'Show me how it works, and I'll give it a go,' he said.

The American sergeant, Glen Novakovski, also stood up. 'You can count me in. But, like this 'Limey', you'll have to show me how.'

'Right then, you'll do, beggars can't be choosers. Follow me.'

(ii)

On deck, the two men were given a very brief introduction to the gun. It was a twenty-millimetre, high velocity cannon that was belt fed and capable of firing five hundred and twenty rounds a minute. Dacre took the firing seat, whilst Novakovski laid on the ammunition. Both men were clad in steel helmets, flash defenders, goggles and gauntlets. Having introduced themselves, they didn't talk much. They said nothing about their recent experiences. Instead, they focused on the gun and how it operated.

They stared intently at the clear blue sky overhead, looking for the German planes that they, and everyone else on board, knew would come. Within minutes, grey shapes appeared high up in the sky – Stukas and ME110s. The dull drone of their engines soon turned into a banshee wail as they descended in terrifying and ear-splitting dives. At unbelievable speeds, they aimed for the ship, released their bombs and sprayed the decks from stem to stern with machine gun fire. The destroyer began to tremble as the ship's Captain demanded more speed from the engine room. Dark black oily smoke belched forth from its two funnels as they 'made smoke' in a futile effort to hide from the onslaught. Some of the bombs from the German planes bracketed the ship, sending up huge waterspouts that drenched the deck, plus everything and everyone on it. The air filled with noise, and men shouting, and with dust, smoke and flames as the ship's guns opened fire on the low-flying enemy planes. The chatter of machine guns mingled with the clatter-clatter of Lewis guns and the hump-hump of the Bofors and Oerlikons. Dacre and the Ranger gave a good account of themselves during the firefight. It only lasted for about fifteen minutes, by which time they were ankle deep in used shell casings.

The German attack had been thwarted, at least for the time being. The Luftwaffe had paid a heavy price and withdrew to lick their wounds. However, they would be back – everyone knew that. Time, now, for the ship's company to draw breath. They had to put out
the fires, and to attend to the wounded and the dead. It was also time to re-stock with ammunition and, if possible, get something to eat and drink.

Dacre and Novakovski exchanged grim smiles as they kicked the empty shells over the side and into the sea.

'That was a hell of a baptism', said the American in a croaky voice. He could still taste the cordite in the air.

'Agreed,' replied Dacre quietly. 'I don't know about you, but I think I prefer to do my fighting on dry land. Being on a ship, in the middle of the sea, seems to be such a restriction, if you know what I mean. And I speak as someone trained to fight both at sea and on land.'

Novakovski thought about this for a second or two. 'I certainly know what you mean,' he drawled. 'It seems to me you're right. You have nowhere to go, no possibility of escape. You're stuck here, come what may.'

The two of them lapsed into a companionable silence.

Just then the petty Officer who had initially recruited them popped his head over the bulkhead that enclosed their gun platform.

'You two alright, then?' he asked with a broad grin on his face. 'I could hear your gun blazing away. Did you hit anything?'

'I don't think so, PO,' Dacre replied. 'But we sure as hell gave them a headache.'

'Here, share this between the two of you. You've certainly earned it.' He passed over a half bottle of rum. 'Keep up the good work, they'll be back!' With that, he disappeared.

Ten minutes later a sudden cry went up from an anonymous voice, 'Here they come again!'

The ship was hit a further six times on their way back to 'Blighty'. They were under constant air attack almost the entire way home. On one occasion, Dacre and the Novakovski were subjected to a hail of bullets from a low-flying fighter plane. They took shelter behind the steel guard, whilst the bullets tore up the decking and nearby bulkhead.

'That was bloody close,' said Dacre, sticking his head out. Then he noticed the sergeant's hand. 'Bloody hell you've been hit!'

The American hadn't noticed that the middle finger of his right hand had been shot clean away.

'Well, I'll be damned. There goes another ten cents worth of hamburger.'

As each successive attack happened, they blazed away at anything in the sky. Dacre wasn't sure that they actually hit anything, but they certainly gave the Luftwaffe something to think about.

(iii)

They reached Portsmouth Harbour at about 2100 hours. The two unofficial gunners shook hands and wished each other well. From there, the handful of marines were taken to the *HMS Victory* barracks where they were given a large tot of neat rum, some blankets, a new uniform. They then bedded down for the night. The following morning, after a hearty breakfast of eggs and bacon, they were shipped back across the Solent to the Isle of Wight.

Their landladies greeted them with hugs and tears. Mrs Peacock was almost inconsolable over the loss of Pete Wills. Standing on tip toes, she threw her arms around Dacre, buried her head on his chest and cried with genuine tears. 'He was like a son to me,' she wailed.

He held her in his arms, gently patting her back. She smelt of lavender water. Mrs Peacock was not alone in her grief. Throughout the town, other landladies were just as grief stricken.

Dacre took himself up to the bedroom that he and Pete Wills had used. Lying on the bed he felt tears begin to well up. Silently, they rolled down his cheeks and onto the pillow, leaving little damp patches.

What a real fucking mess, he thought. Deal, Scotland, the Isle of Wight and West Bay. For what? Just a waste of good men for some poxy raid that the bloody planners couldn't get right. So-called senior officers. More like bloody wankers who couldn't organise a piss-up in a brewery. Then something he had learnt at school came to mind, Tennyson's, *The Charge of the Light Brigade*

...Someone had blundered.
Theirs not to make reply,
Theirs not to reason why,
Theirs but to do and die.
Into the valley of Death
Rode the six hundred.

That had really been the raid on Dieppe - only this time it had been from the sea. With that, he rolled over, closed his eyes and fell into a deep sleep.

CHAPTER 32

(i)

On the morning of the 20th August, the remains of the Royal Marines Commando paraded at Sandown. It was very clear to Dacre, and to everyone else on parade, that the Commando had suffered grievously, with perhaps as many as twenty per cent killed, missing or captured. The unit had started the raid with three hundred and sixty-nine officers and men. At least sixty-six were killed or captured on the beaches, whilst many others were killed or wounded in the landing crafts. There was no doubt that the casualty rate would have been much greater were it not for the self-sacrifice of their Commanding Officer who waved away other craft from what had clearly been a suicidal mission.

Dacre was both surprised and pleased to see that Lieutenant Ellis was on parade. Later, he learnt that the officer had been picked up by a small boat manned by other Royal Marines. Already overflowing with wounded troops, they managed to limp back to Portsmouth, despite being harassed continuously by the Luftwaffe.

Of Number Ten Platoon, the Troop Officer, Lieutenant Huntley-Whitney, survived and had been rescued. Sergeant Throttles had been badly wounded and then captured by the Germans. Amongst Dacre's own comrades, Marines Mac McKnight, Kelly and Whitnell all survived. Baz Phelps was wounded and then captured, whilst Dave Taylor and Pete Wills were both killed. Major 'Titch' Houghton and his small group of marines were eventually captured, after having become entangled in some wire at the beachhead.

Back on the Isle of Wight, the unit was immediately brought back up to strength with reinforcements. There was no lack of volunteers. The

Commando then carried on with a programme of further training. These fit young Royal Marine Commandos were remarkably resilient. Despite everything, their morale was very high and their sense of humour, typical of marines everywhere, continued to be both dark and funny at the same time. The new recruits, that arrived to take the places of those killed and seriously wounded, found it difficult to believe that these men had just fought a major engagement. They had gone to Dieppe as boys and had returned as battle-hardened men.

In October the commando became officially known as Royal Marines 'A' Commando.
Then a second commando was formed under the title of Royal Marines 'B' Commando. Later that month, the two units became 40 Commando RM and 41 Commando RM respectively.

At about the same time the Green Beret was issued to all Commando Forces. At first it was somewhat unpopular because of the colour. It was considered by some to be a little effeminate. Later it was worn with real pride, an outward sign of being a special force, much as it is today.

It has been said that being a Royal Marines Commando is all about a 'state of mind'. That is just as true today as it was yesterday.

EPILOGUE

The raid on Dieppe was a costly failure, particularly for the allied soldiers who took part. Without a doubt, it had been ten hours of unbelievable hell. For those on the beaches, disaster after disaster struck as the soldiers and marines were massacred by the murderous crossfire from the German artillery and troops. The slaughter was added to by the Luftwaffe, who sent in wave after wave of fighters and bombers to attack, not only those on
the beaches, but those who had been trying to come ashore.

As for the Canadians, their losses were staggering. The South Saskatchewan Regiment that had landed on Green Beach at Pourville lost nineteen officers and four hundred and ninety-eight men. Their Commanding officer won the Victoria Cross for his bravery and valour at the Scie Bridge. In addition, the Canadian Queen's Own Cameron Highlanders lost three hundred and forty-six officers and men from a total of just five
hundred souls.

Meanwhile, on Blue Beach near Puys, the Royal Regiment of Canada had been annihilated. Just sixty out of five hundred and forty-three men managed to get off the beach.

The situation on Red Beach was no better. The Essex Scottish Canadians had suffered over forty percent casualties within the first thirty minutes of landing. Of the 14th Calgary Tank Regiment, only fifteen of their twenty-seven tanks had made it up the beach, only to discover that every exit had been blocked.

On White Beach the Royal Hamilton Light Infantry lost all their officers and all but one hundred men. The Fusiliers Mont-Royal had fared little better. Out of a total of five hundred and eighty-three officers and men, they lost five hundred and twelve individuals.

Casualties for the whole of the Canadian 2nd Division were high. Three thousand, three hundred and sixty-seven had been killed, wounded or taken prisoner.

The British Army Commandos at Yellow Beach 1, No. 3 Commando, lost one hundred and twenty men killed, wounded or taken prisoner. However, at Yellow Beach 2, Major Peter Young attacked the Goebbels Battery near Belleville-sur-Mer for nearly two hours with just seventeen men and two officers, before were forced to withdraw.

At Orange Beach, a two-pronged attack by No.4 Commando, plus fifty U.S. Rangers, led by Lord Lovat and his second-in-command, Major Mills Roberts, was successful. Although they encountered stiff resistance from the Germans, the gun emplacements were eventually taken at the point of a bayonet, and the guns were put out of action. Captain Peter Porteous was awarded the Victoria Cross for his actions on the day, whilst Lord Lovat received the Distinguished Service Order (DSO).

Altogether the Army Commando losses amounted to two hundred and seventy-five men.

The Royal Navy lost one destroyer and thirty-three landing craft, and suffered five hundred and fifty dead and wounded men.

The Royal Air Force lost one hundred and six aircraft. The Germans lost forty-eight.

The German ground force casualties were approximately six hundred men killed or wounded. Only a handful were captured during the raid.

Despite the failure of the raid where none of the key objectives were achieved, Major General Roberts was awarded the DSO. However, in 1943 he was heavily criticized for his tactical weakness during *Operation Spartan*, which was large-scale exercise in preparation for the D-Day landings. Consequently, he received no further operational commands.

Major John 'Titch' Houghton was a prisoner of war until 1945. For the first four hundred and eleven days he was held in chains on the direct order of Adolf Hitler. Houghton and his men were lucky not to have been shot. He was awarded the Military Cross (MC) for his bravery on the beach, and for his stoicism whilst in captivity. After the war, he briefly became the Commanding Officer of 45 Commando RM. Then after attending Staff College, he became the CO of 40 Commando RM which he took to Hong Kong.

Lieutenant Graham Ellis was promoted to the rank of Captain. He became the Officer Commanding 'X' Company of the newly named 40 Commando RM. He survived the war, and over the years became the Commanding Officer of several commando units. As a Brigadier, he took command of the 3rd Commando Brigade RM. Towards the end of his career, he was the Commandant at the Depot RM at Deal in Kent. As such, he became instrumental in *Operation Saint George*, which involved a certain Marine Dacre in a daring rescue.

The Royal Marines Provost landed on White Beach in the first wave. Their task was to maintain good order and discipline, particularly when the troops withdrew. Their officer commanding, Lieutenant Colonel R G Parks Smith, also took on the role of Beach-master. This small unit took very heavy casualties and their Colonel, wounded twice, died the following day back in England. He was posthumously awarded the 'oak leaves' for being mentioned in dispatches.

The raid on Dieppe was seized upon by the Nazi propaganda machine and portrayed as a resounding German victory. The Third Reich went to great lengths to achieve this. They described the raid as a 'military joke', emphasising that the huge losses suffered by the Allies pointed to their incompetence. The propaganda value was greatly enhanced in order to raise the morale of the German people, who were suffering by the growing intensity of the Allied bombing campaign. In addition, the casualty rate on the Eastern Front was steadily increasing, much to the horror of the German population.

The Germans decided to reward Dieppe for not helping the Allies during the raid, and also for not freeing prisoners of war which, at the time, were held in custody on a train in the town's station. Later, Hitler gave Dieppe ten million francs to help them rebuild and repair the damage caused by the raid, and for what he called the residents' 'perfect discipline and calm'.

The failure of *Operation Jubilee* has led some military historians to consider whether or not the Germans had advance knowledge of the operation. For example, had they been warned by French double agents about an impending raid. There is no doubt that security along the Southern English coast prior to the raid was not as good as it could, or should, have been. The preparations were there to be seen by anyone who cared to look. In addition, the BBC had been broadcasting warnings to the French for some time of a 'likely' war and urging them to leave their homes along the coastal districts.

Some accounts, by Allied survivors of the raid, have suggested that the German defences were so well organised that they must have had prior knowledge of the landings. The fact that the Allied landing craft were immediately shelled with the utmost precision, just as the troops were coming ashore, seems to support this idea. Indeed, it was later discovered that the Germans had deployed four additional machine gun battalions because of an impending raid.

However, not everyone agrees. Whilst it was very likely that the Germans were expecting landings somewhere along the French coastline, and had taken the precaution of reinforcing their troops everywhere, it is less likely that they actually knew that it was going to be Dieppe. The fact that some of the town's beach defences were unmanned would seem to support this idea.

It was, therefore, more likely that the German forces may well have been on full alert all along the coast, and not just at Dieppe.

The town and port of Dieppe, and the flanking cliffs, were very well defended. The garrison of fifteen hundred troops were provided by the 302nd German Infantry Division under the command of General Gerd von Rundstedt. The soldiers were mainly from the 570th, 571st and the 572nd Regiments, each consisting of two battalions. Also present were elements of the 302nd Artillery Regiment, Reconnaissance and their Anti-tank troops, plus Engineers and a Signal Battalion.

German Army Engineers had reinforced the cliff bunkers with concrete by using slave labour and prisoners of war. They had also positioned artillery and heavy machine guns on rails, so that they could be easily run out from the camouflaged caves on the cliff face. Gun and rifle pits, that were well hidden, had been prepared at every vantage point for snipers to use. Land mines and barbed wire defences had been installed on the beaches and cliff staircases and steps were either blocked or made un-usable.

Troops were deployed all along the beaches, in the port and town itself, as well as in nearby neighbouring towns. They had covered most of the likely landing places. Defensive positions had not been just limited to buildings. Open areas, the beaches and the cliffs had been all utilised. Elements of the 571st defended the radar station near Pourville, whilst an artillery battery covered the River Scie at Varengeville. To the east, the 570th were deployed at Berneval.

In the air, the Luftwaffe stationed only a few miles away provided one hundred and twenty operational fighter planes, as well as Dornier 217s and other anti-shipping bombers.

As a whole, the German ground forces were well trained. They were fit and tough men. The Allies, in their planning, had clearly underestimated the veracity and preparedness of these troops, and it cost them dearly.

The two German commanding Generals had their own views about the raid. General Konrad Haase, an elderly sixty-year-old recalled to the colours, said, 'It is incomprehensible that a single division was expected to overrun a German regiment that was supported by artillery.' General Field Marshal Rundstedt was more sanguine about the raid. 'Just as the defending force has gathered valuable experience from …….. Dieppe, so, too, has the assaulting force………. He will not do it like this a second time.'

It has been said by some commentators that *Operation Jubilee* was a necessary evil, as the lessons learned from their experiences, albeit largely negative, were invaluable when it came to the planning of future operations, especially the D-Day invasion of the French coast. Indeed, Mountbatten always supported this view. However, as the Chief of Combined Operations, he was, of course, responsible for the success or failure of the raid, so you might expect him to be of that opinion. He later tried to justify the raid, arguing that the lessons learnt at Dieppe were put to good use later in the war. In addition, he claimed that for every soldier, sailor, marine or RAF pilot that died there, countless thousands were saved at Normandy two years later.

On paper the plan seemed to be straightforward. Recently, it has been suggested that those responsible for the Planning of *Operation Jubilee* at Combined Operations Headquarters, were, in the main, from the Royal Navy. As such, perhaps a more thorough military appreciation might have been more prudent. The geography of the beach was something that the planners should have looked at more closely. The Canadians had rehearsed their landings at Lyme Bay in Dorset where the beach was mostly sand and small pebbles, with a gentle gradient. At Dieppe it was very different. Steep banks of heavy shingle were everywhere. Consequently, the Canadian tanks, each weighing about thirty-eight tons, found it very difficult to move. Of the twenty-nine tanks that landed, two were drowned and twelve never even got up the beach.

It is now readily accepted that the pre-operation information was not as good as it should have been. Holiday photographs from the 1930s of the beach and port were poor. Aerial photographs, such as they were, did not identify the caves and tunnels in the cliffs that the Germans had skilfully hidden with camouflage.

The quality of the German 15th Army had, as already stated, been underestimated. It was, without doubt, an efficient and effective fighting force, and had been extremely well trained. On the beach, black and white mortar ranging posts were to be seen still in position from an exercise held just the day before.

Winston Churchill was quoted as saying, 'My impression of Jubilee is that the results fully justified the cost. The Canadian contribution was vital to the final victory.'

Initially the Prime Minister and Lord Mountbatten were held to be responsible for this disastrous, some might say grotesque, waste of lives. However, there were no written records showing approval of the raid in its final form. The Chiefs of Staff were eager to blame Mountbatten. They disliked him and regarded him as an upstart who had been foisted on them by Churchill. They were keen to establish that the raid had been unauthorised, and that Mountbatten should be removed from command. There was, however, little substance to this claim and the whole idea of blame has now been discounted.

Commander Ian Fleming kept a very low profile after Dieppe. He needed to keep in with Combined Operations, especially Mountbatten and the Director of Naval Intelligence, Admiral John Godfrey, if only so that he could develop further his idea of an 'intelligence assault unit'. Later this became better known as the 30th Assault Unit RM. Their main purpose under his leadership was to gather, steal or pinch enemy top secret information. Much of what they liberated went straight to Bletchley Park. The unit was very successful throughout the war, particularly in North Africa, Sicily and Normandy. They were also amongst the first troops to liberate Paris.

Later, Ian Fleming became better known as the creator and author of the fictional secret service agent James Bond, 007. Using much of his wartime experience, he wrote fourteen books, many of which have been turned into highly successful films.

In the North Atlantic the situation continued to be dire. This was one area that Bletchley Park could not influence. Then came a lucky breakthrough. A German submarine had been forced to the surface off the coast of Palestine. The crew had abandoned their boat and left it to sink. Fortunately, but at the cost of their lives, two British sailors managed to locate and save the current codebook and bigram tables used by the Germans. Within weeks the documents were at Bletchley Park. Within days, the codebreakers had cracked the *Shark* code. The relief at the Park was tremendous – they were back in business again. At Whitehall, and elsewhere, the sense of relief was also immense. Britain could now survive in order to carry on the fight against Nazi Germany and its allies.

Alan Turing's contribution to the success of Bletchley Park in deciphering the messages encrypted by the German Enigma machines was unparalleled. It is now widely accepted that his work in cracking the U-boat codes was not only fundamental in enabling Britain to survive 1942, but it shortened the war, possibly by as much as two years.

However, in 1952, Turing was convicted of gross indecency. As his punishment he chose chemical castration over imprisonment. Two years later he committed suicide. He was just forty-one years old.

Campaigners have long called for the government to give him a posthumous pardon. In 2009, the Prime Minister, Gordon Brown, made an apology to Turing and his relatives for his appalling treatment. More recently, a spokesperson for the government said that it would not stand in the way of a proposed Bill that would grant Alan Turing a 'statutory pardon'. On the 23rd December 2013, it was reported that Her Majesty Queen Elizabeth II had been pleased to award Dr Turing a posthumous pardon.

On the 13th December 2013, some sixty years after Fleming's original idea, the 30th Assault Unit lives again. At Stonehouse Barracks in Plymouth, the newly formed 30 Commando Information Exploitation Group RM paraded to receive their new colours: a yellow and blue standard, their motto 'Attain by Surprise'. The name 30th was chosen in recognition of their forebears. 30 Commando IEG RM is now part of the 3rd Commando Brigade RM and, as such, is a key component in the United Kingdom's Rapid Reaction Force.

Royal Marine Dacre was awarded the Military Medal with oak leaves for his performance on the field of battle. His medal was presented to him by King George VI at Buckingham Palace, which, at the time, was most unusual. His citation read: 'This medal is awarded for outstanding bravery under heavy enemy fire on the beaches of Dieppe during Operation Jubilee.' Dacre's only recorded comment was that he was just doing his duty.

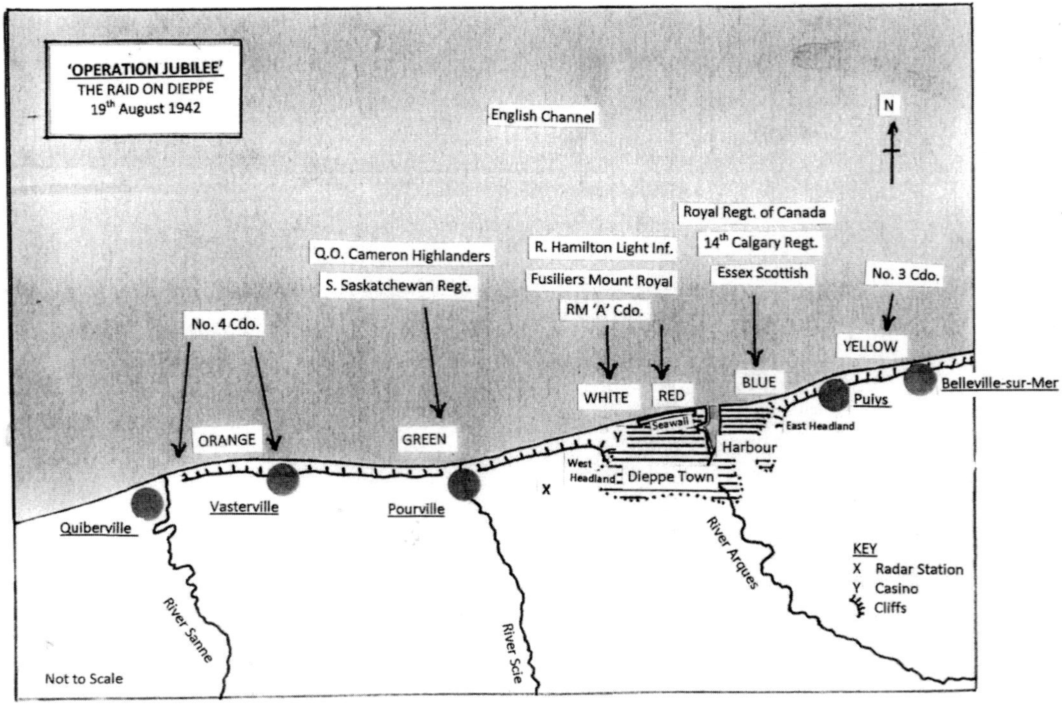
'OPERATION JUBILEE'
THE RAID ON DIEPPE
19th August 1942
English Channel
N
Royal Regt. of Canada
14th Calgary Regt.
Essex Scottish
No. 3 Cdo.
R. Hamilton Light Inf.
Fusiliers Mount Royal
RM 'A' Cdo.
Q.O. Cameron Highlanders
S. Saskatchewan Regt.
No. 4 Cdo.
YELLOW
BLUE
RED
WHITE
GREEN
ORANGE
Belleville-sur-Mer
Puiys
East Headland
Harbour
Seawall
Y
West Headland
Dieppe Town
X
Quiberville
Vasterville
Pourville
River Sanne
River Scie
River Arques
KEY
X Radar Station
Y Casino
Cliffs
Not to Scale

Historical Footnote

The use of the Short Signal Book and the Short Weather Cipher by the Germans to produce daily meteorological reports continued to perplex everyone at Bletchley Park for some time. The key question that they had been struggling with was how were the weather stations, which had the three-wheel Enigmas, reading and deciphering the messages from the U-boats which had the four-wheeled machines. Surely a four-wheeled machine was needed in order to read a four-wheel. Or was it?

Eventually the penny dropped. The U-boats were using a four-wheeled Enigma but as a three-wheel machine. The wireless operators were actually disengaging one wheel in order to send their weather reports.

Once this had been established, Bletchley Park was able to break *Shark*, translate the messages and teleprint the results to the Admiralty in London. Over ninety signals were decrypted, which gave the position and tactics of well over half the German submarines operating in the North Atlantic. Consequently, the loss of merchant shipping - supplies, munitions and men - was cut by over seventy-five per cent. Bletchley Park and the Admiralty knew as much about the disposition of U-boats as did the Germans.

However, sometime later a *Shark* decrypt told the Admiralty that a U-boat tanker was due to meet a submarine somewhere in the mid-Atlantic. Someone at the admiralty had forgotten the rule that all *Shark* Enigma information must never be acted on directly, lest the breaking of the codes be compromised.

Throwing caution to the wind, an attack was planned, approved and made. It failed. Both U-boats managed to escape. But the damage had been done. Admiral Donitz knew immediately that his *Shark* code had been compromised. A short while later, a number of the British listening stations picked up a broadcast, not in cipher or Morse, but a voice, using a single word 'Akelei', repeated over and over again. It was clearly a pre-arranged signal of some sort. Almost instantly the *Shark* intercepts stopped. Bletchley Park and the Admiralty were once again in the dark. At the Park, all leave was cancelled. The eight-hour shifts became twelve hours and then sixteen hours – all to no avail. *Shark* was dead in the water.

With this total blackout came an increase in the number of ships sunk in the North Atlantic. In January it was forty-eight allied ships, by May this number had risen to one hundred and twenty.

Convoys had been leaving New York and other ports all the time. For example, on a Monday forty merchant ships carrying meat, explosives, oil, lead, timber diesel oil, sugar and powdered milk sailed for the Britain. The next day another convoy of twenty- seven ships left, and on the Wednesday a further convoy set sail. In total there were one hundred and seventeen ships carrying about a million tons of cargo. There were nine thousand merchant seaman and about a thousand passengers, mostly troops, American Red Cross and some children. There were, of course, escort vessels such as destroyers, corvettes and frigates. But many of these were old and slow and had only recently been pressed back into service.

The Atlantic Ocean covers thirty-two million square miles, and nobody knew where the German U-boat Wolf packs were. They, on the other hand, knew exactly the positions of the ships of the convoy!

AUTHOR'S FOOTNOTE

Whilst carrying out research for this book, I came across a series of wartime magazines. These were called *The War Illustrated* and were edited by Sir John Hammerton and published by William Berry, the owner of the *Daily Telegraph*. The magazine was issued fortnightly at a cost of three pence, right up until April 1947. It was a pictorial record of the conflict of the nation at war. As such it made considerable use of photographs and illustrations, as well as stories of dramatic events. Often there were personal accounts by War Correspondents, such as Hamilton Fyfe.

Volume 6, Number 137 had on the front page a photograph of two commandos holding a Union Jack. The story was as follows: '*HOME FROM DIEPPE. After a fierce nine-hour raid by British, US and Fighting French troops on August 19, these two Commandos – tired, battle stained, but happy – have just stepped ashore at a British port. They triumphantly display the Union Jack which was planted by one of the first parties of British troops to land in the Dieppe area. The flag acted as a beacon to guide incoming raiders to the landing stage and assisted our men to find their way back to the waiting ships.*' Clearly this was meant for home consumption, the magazine being widely available to the public. The four pages inside devoted to the story (pages 196-199), complete with photographs and a detailed map under the title of: '*HOW BRITAIN'S COMMANDOS ATTACK DIEPPE*' describes the raid as a '*reconnaissance in force*' and that it was '*the biggest and most successful commando raid to date*'.

The story itself, whilst factually true in part, bears almost no resemblance to what really happened. To the casual reader of 1942, the story is clearly designed to accentuate the successful side of the raid whilst minimising the terrible losses. Britain needed a lift at this time, and Churchill was determined to use the news of this raid to raise the morale of the general population. In that part I am sure he was successful. In today's language, it was a good way to bury bad news.

Judging from many of the other magazines in the series published during those war years, their purpose was clearly to inform, but to always put a very positive gloss on what was happening. To this end the truth concerning the raid on Dieppe seems to have been distorted, or just plainly omitted. The dramatizing, and even fabricating, of events that involved the Germans seemed to be acceptable. Clearly Britain's propaganda machine was working well. Somebody in Government had clearly decided that for morale purposes, whilst the general public needed to know how the war was progressing, there were also certain things that they did not need to know at that time.

It is only now, with hindsight, that we appreciate how our parents and grandparents were informed by the press. Some might agree that they needed to be protected from the truth. But was it for the best?

GLOSSARY

BEF	British Expeditionary Force
Bigram	Tables used to write codes
Boatswain	Petty Officer RN responsible for maintaining a ship
Bootneck	Naval slang for a Royal Marine
Bombes	Mechanical device used to help break codes
BP	Bletchley Park
Bulwark	Steel plating around the deck
C in C	Commander in Chief
CIGS	Commander in Chief of the General Staff
CO	Commanding Officer
C of S	Chiefs of Staff
CSM	Company Sergeant Major
Dolphin	German code for surface vessels
Enigma	German machine for encoding messages
FS Knife	Fairburn Sykes double edged fighting knife (also called a commando dagger)
Heads	RN/RM toilets
HO	Hostilities Only troops (conscripts)
JNCO	Junior Non- Commissioned Officer (Corporal & Lance Corporal)
Matelots	Sailors in the Royal Navy
MM	Military Medal (only awarded to men in the ranks, at that time)
MNBD	Mobile Naval Base Defence
NCO	Non-Commissioned Officer
NI	Naval Intelligence
NGS	Naval General Service Medal
Piat	Rocket launcher
Pussers	Anything to do with the Royal Navy
Royal	Naval slang for a Royal Marine
RMB	Royal Marines Barracks
RV	Rendezvous
Scuppers	Drain on ship's deck to remove excess water
Shark	German code for submarines
SIS	Secret Intelligence Service
SS	Steam ship
Stag	Sentry duty
Star shell	A shell containing a flare suspended from a small parachute
WAAFS	Women's Auxiliary Air Force Service
WD	War Department
Wing	Deck area either side of a ship's bridge
Wolf pack	A group of submarines acting together
WRNS	Women's Royal Navy Service

ACKNOWLEDGEMENTS

I am deeply grateful to all those who helped me with my research for this book. In particular I should like to thank former Royal Marine Commandos, those who served with Combined Operations and Naval Intelligence, and members of the Canadian Armed Forces. They are too numerous to mention here, but I really appreciate everyone's contribution, no matter how small. I should also like to thank the staff at the Bridport Museum Trust, the Clan Cameron Museum at Achnacarry, and the residents of West Bay. A special thank you must also go to Bletchley Park's historian, Dr David Kenyon and to the Royal Marines Corps Historian, George Gelder Lt Col RM (Retd), both of whom spent time correcting my errors, thank you! Without all them this book could not have been written.

I must also extend a very particular thank you to Mr Alan John Dacre of Woodbridge, Suffolk. His memory is as sharp and clear as ever and it has been my privilege to listen to his recollections. He is as enthusiastic as ever for the truth to be told.

Finally, no acknowledgement would be complete without thanking my wife for her help and support, and especially for correcting the final draft.

To you, the reader, I must say that this is an extremely complex story that few, if any, of our parents and grandparents, knew about at that time for obvious reasons. I have tried to do justice to these events. I hope I have succeeded. Any mistakes in dates or facts are down to me. However, it is an adventure story and I have, where appropriate, tweaked history just a little to make the book more readable.

J.G. White

BIBLIOGRAPHY

Atkin, Ronald. Dieppe 1942: **The Jubilee Disaster.** Book Club Assoc. 1980
Atterbury, Paul. **West Bay.** Post Card Press 2003
BBC, World War 2 **People's Stories – Dieppe** 44/92665244
Beadle, JC. **The Light Blue Lanyard.** Square One 1992
Churchill, Winston. **The Second World War.** Riverside Press. 1953
Collins English Dictionary. **21st Century Edition.** Ted Smart.
Couture, Claude-Paul. **Dieppe-Dawn of Decision.**
Dunning, James. **A Short History of the Commandos.** The Commando Assoc. 1993
Edwards, Bernard. **Attack and Sink.** New Guild 1995
Gilchrist D. **Castle Commando.** Oliver & Boyd 1960
Harling, Robert. **Ian Fleming- A Personal Memoir.** Robson Press 2015
Harris, Robert. **Enigma.** Arrow Books 2005
Hoyt, Edwin. **U – Boats.** McGaw-Hill 1987
Hughes, John. **Military Intelligence Blunders & Cover-ups.** Robinson 2004
Hunter, Murray. **Canada at Dieppe.** Canadian War Museum 982
Ladd, James. **Royal Marine Commando.** Hamlyn 1982
Leasor, James. **Green Beach.** Stratus 2011
Lee, Christopher. **This Sceptred Isle.** Penguin 1999
Lewin, Ronald. **The War on Land 1939-45.** Vintage 1969
Legg, Rodney. **Dorset at War.** Wincanton Press 1986
Lund, Paul & Ludlam, Harry. **The War of the Landing Craft.** New England 1976
Maguire, Eric. **'Evaluation' Dieppe, August 19th.** Cape 13
McKay, Sinclair. **The Secret Life of Bletchley Park.** Aurum 2011
McMichael, David. **Shadows in a Photograph.** Austin Macauley 2016
Moulton, JL. **The Royal Marines.** Sphere 1973
Neillands, Robin. **By Sea by Land.** Pen & Sword 2004
Parker, John. **Commandos.** Bounty 2005
Ramsey, Winston G. **After the Battle** (No.5) Edited by.
Rankin, Nicholas. **Ian Fleming's Commandos** Faber & Faber 2011
Saunders, Hilary. **The Green Beret 1940-1945.** Joseph 1949
Spaven D & Holland J. **Mapping the Railways.** Times Books 2011
Smith, Michael. **The Secrets of Station X.** Biteback 2011
Stacey, CP. **Operation Jubilee Report.** CMHQ 1942
Thompson, Julian. **The Royal Marines.** Pan 2000
Villa, Brian. **Mountbatten & the Dieppe Raid.** Oxford University Press 1989
White, JG. **Operation Saint George.** Austin Macauley 2013
Whitaker, D&S. **Dieppe: Tragedy to Triumph** Ryerson 1993
Woodward, Guy & Grace. **The Secret of Sherwood Forest.** Oklahoma Press 1973
Young, Peter. **Storm from the Sea.** Kimber 1958

Dear Reader,

Thank you for reading my latest book '*Do or Die Royal*', which is the second in the trilogy. I hope that you enjoyed it as much as I did in carrying out the research and eventually writing this fascinating story.

Now I would like to tempt you with the first two chapters of the third book in the trilogy, featuring Marine Dacre. The title of this one is '*First Ashore Royal!*'. The story is set in 1944. Dacre has been accepted for training as a swimmer canoeist with a special group of volunteers, who later become better known as 'The Cockleshell Heroes'. However, after being injured, he is transferred to the Royal Navy's Beach Clearance Unit.

Meanwhile Britain and its Allies, particularly the United States of America, have begun to prepare for the invasion of Europe. *Operation Overlord* is being planned and rehearsed, prior to the Normandy landings.

As a frogman, Dacre is one of the very first ashore on D-Day. These men were required to carry out the most dangerous work of clearing the beaches of mines and obstacles, prior to the arrival of the first wave of the invasion fleet. After the initial landings and the completion of this work, Dacre joins up with 48 Commando RM that landed on Juno Beach.

It is with this unit that Dacre finds himself promoted to Sergeant. Later, he is awarded a battlefield commission in order to command a Troop, as they battle their way into France. War has a strange way of bringing out the best in some people, and Dacre is no exception.

I am sure you will find this an enjoyable read and will want to read the rest of the story. You will not be disappointed.

JG White
Nottingham 2020

FIRST ASHORE, ROYAL!

PROLOGUE

It is 1942 and Britain has been at war with Hitler's Nazi Germany for three years. The country and the people have suffered much, but under the leadership of their pugnacious Prime Minister, Winston Churchill, they have not given up, even in this the darkest of times.

Withdrawal of the British Expeditionary Force from Dunkirk in 1940, then the disastrous collapse and surrender of France, followed by the Battle for Britain when the Luftwaffe had attempted to gain air superiority, so necessary for Hitler's planned invasion of these islands yet denied him by the magnificence of the fighter pilots of the RAF, had done nothing to diminish the fighting spirit of the country. If that had not been enough, the 'Blitz', the deliberate incessant bombing of our towns, cities and ports then sought to bring Britain to its knees. In this it failed, despite the devastation and the huge loss of lives; it simply made the people even more determined to survive.

Elsewhere in the world it was a similar story. In the Far East the Japanese had rampaged through country after country: Malaya, the Philippines, Borneo, the Dutch East Indies and Indochina had all succumbed to the might of their rapidly expanding empire. To make matters even worse, the pride of the Royal Navy *HMS Prince of Wales* and *HMS Repulse* had been sunk off the coast of eastern Malaya by Japanese bombers. Then, to add insult to injury, the fortress island of Singapore had inexplicably surrendered. Winston Churchill referred to this news as 'the worst disaster in British history'. Those closest to him said that he aged ten years overnight.

Britain's ally Russia had also been suffering badly as Hitler's triumphant invading armies forced the Russians into retreat as *Operation Barbarossa* headed for Moscow. Elsewhere in Europe, country after country was swallowed up as Germany continued to expand. In the Mediterranean and North Africa, German troops aided by Mussolini's Fascist Italian army continued to dominate the region. In North Africa, Field Marshall Erwin Rommel and his Afrika Korps pushed the British Eighth Army back to El Alamein, having captured Tobruk. The one glimmer of hope was that the small plucky island of Malta, alone and in the middle of the Mediterranean Sea, refused to be defeated, despite being heavily bombed over a long period of time.

The Royal Air Force and the Army were still rebuilding their forces, and this would take time. This meant that it was only the ships of the Royal Navy that were capable of challenging the Germans. However, the German battleships *Scharnhorst, Neiman* and *Prinz Eugen* still managed to force their way up the English Channel unharmed, and return to their home ports, much to the embarrassment of the Admiralty.

In the North Atlantic, German U-boats hunted in groups known as 'wolf-packs'. They had managed to sink thousands of tons of shipping, sending essential supplies and men to the bottom of the sea. Despite some limited success by the Admiralty, Naval Intelligence and the codebreakers at Bletchley Park, the Germans still managed to continue sinking convoy after convoy. To make matters worse, many of these submarines had been operating out of German controlled French ports such as Bordeaux and La Rochelle, where newly constructed facilities had been built, mostly by slave labour.

As Hitler swept through Europe, he simply seized the raw materials that he needed to continue with his pursuit of expansionism and world domination. So, iron ore from Scandinavia, food from France, Denmark and Holland and oil from Romania provided much needed supplies. This German strategy of seizure by conquest also allowed them to neatly sidestep any attempts by Britain even to consider imposing a blockade by ships of the Royal Navy. Even those materials not readily available in Europe, such as rubber, tin, tungsten, animal and vegetable oil, and opium for medicines were transported overland via the Trans-Siberian Railway from the Far East.

Japan's success in dominating the Pacific Region led them to make a trade agreement with Germany. Both countries realised that they needed certain war necessities which they could obtain from each other. However, with Britain still controlling the Suez Canal, German crewed ships had to go all the way around Africa and the Cape of Good Hope. This long sea voyage took about three months and meant that ships had to be refuelled and provisioned whilst still at sea. In many cases these ships were heavily armed and fast, and some could even out-run a number of the slower British warships. The prevention of these supply ships from reaching their home port meant that they had to be caught whilst still at sea, which became a priority for the Royal Navy. When these German ships made it successfully to a friendly port, as many did, serious consideration had to be given as to how to prevent them from leaving for another trip. With this in mind, the Royal Navy were tasked with operating a blockade, particularly on the port of Bordeaux which was positioned several miles up the River Gironde. Yet blockade runners still managed to get through, much to the annoyance of the Admiralty. The Royal Air Force were asked to consider bombing the port, but operational problems such as the availability of aeroplanes, bomb loads, distance and enemy ground defence meant that such raids were, at that time, unrealistic. Britain, therefore, had to rely on the Royal Navy to do their best.

With the war not going well for Britain, even though the USA was gearing itself up after having declared war against Japan and then Germany following the attack on Pearl Harbour, Churchill had decided not to sit back and wait for things to improve. He had it in mind to go on the offensive, albeit in a small way. To this end he ordered the creation of two new organisations. Firstly, Combined Operations. They had been tasked with developing a 'reign of terror' along the coasts of occupied Europe, from Norway all the way down to France. Secondly, the Special Operations Executive, whose task was 'to set all Europe ablaze'.

Part of the remit of Combined Operations was to form a new breed of highly trained soldiers, capable of carrying out clandestine attacks. This task had been given to the Army and these soldiers were given the name 'Commandos'. By May 1942, Commandos had carried out over twenty raids on the enemy coastline, small-scale yet stinging attacks from the sea that were designed to annoy and worry the hell out of the Germans. They were amazingly successful. Whilst these raids gained little strategically, they were good for lifting the general morale of the country, and every success was made very public. In March 1942, Rear Admiral Louis Mountbatten had been appointed as the new Chief of Combined Operations. A short while later the Royal Marines were ordered to form a Commando unit of their own and so the Royal Marines Commandos came into being.

Meanwhile, the planners at Combined Operations Headquarters were giving some serious thought to an idea, put forward by Major General B. Montgomery, for a large-scale attack on the French coast, with the idea of seizing and holding the port for several hours. This was to be the first major test of the German-held coastline since Dunkirk back in 1940. It was code named *Operation Jubilee*. The planners were convinced that the attack would provide vital information for a possible invasion and second front in the future. The raid was, however, a total disaster. In nine hours of carnage and horror, over three and a half thousand men were killed, wounded or captured from the five thousand that took part. British Army Commandos and a small group of American Rangers successfully carried out flank attacks on the cliffs, destroying the German guns. However, the task of seizing the port itself and the beaches had been given to the Canadian Second Division. One of the units supporting them in reserve were the Royal Marines Commandos. Within this marine unit a small, specially trained group were tasked with breaking into the German Naval Headquarters. Their job was to steal the vital codebooks that Naval Intelligence had identified as being there. These were vital for Bletchley Park, to help them break the secret encryptions that continued to be used by the German U-boats in the North Atlantic. This well-planned 'pinch raid' died on the beaches of Dieppe along with many of its men.

Meanwhile, in other parts of coastal Britain, certain small groups of independently minded men from the three services were experimenting and developing a new form of warfare, albeit on a very small scale, that of attacking the Germans by using canoes and frogmen. It had been in the summer of 1942 that both Combined Operations and the SOE, independently of each other, had seriously begun to consider using unconventional means and irregular forces to enforce the blockade of German controlled French ports. This change in strategy was brought about by the increase in blockade running. Every cargo that got through strengthened both the Germans and the Japanese. Consequently, there was now a real sense of urgency to meet this increasing threat. Small-scale raiding forces such as the Special Boat Section of the Army Commandos (SBS) and the Royal Marines Boom Patrol (RMBP) suddenly found themselves in the vanguard of providing possible solutions.

CHAPTER 1

A young man, not much more than a boy really, but clearly a soldier judging from his battle-stained and torn uniform, stood silently at the edge of a field full of ripening wheat. The shoulder flashes on his jacket said that he was a Royal Engineer. There was a large hole in the back of his battle dress jacket, the edges of which were stained a dried dark brown. He watched, absolutely fascinated, as a slight breeze blew across the field, causing a wave-like effect on the wheat. The soldier moved slowly into the field, parting the wheat like a swimmer moving through water. His hands lightly brushed the tops of the stalks. They were soft to the touch on his dirty, begrimed hands. The sun overhead was warm on his back, not so surprising for that time of the year. The sky was a brilliant blue; not a cloud to be seen. Nearby, a bird began to vigorously chirp its song. The young man smiled to himself. The war seemed a long way off. He plucked a few grains of wheat and rubbed them in the palm of his hand. They seemed to be ripe and ready for harvesting.

Then he saw them. A small patch of wheat had been trampled to the ground. There, in a neat row, lying side by side were some children. Their eyes were closed, and their hands were neatly folded over their chests. Four girls and two boys, all about the same age, maybe twelve or thirteen years old. There was not a mark on them. It was if they might have been asleep or playing some sort of a game and would suddenly jump up, laughing at their childish joke. But no! The soldier uttered a strangled cry as he sank to his knees, the bile from his stomach rising in an uncontrollable wave. He turned away, heaved and vomited what little he had recently eaten. What the fucking hell had happened here? His mind screamed in anguish and pain.

Marine Dacre awoke in a cold sweat and sat up in his bed, perspiration dripping from his body. It was that damn dream again. Would he ever forget he wondered? He couldn't be doing with this, he thought. He checked his watch. It was precisely 0600 hours. Springing athletically to the floor, he grabbed his towel and headed for the showers. Soaping himself down under the cold water, he wondered why his dreams were always about these children? Why not about the more recent horrors that he had witnessed on the beaches of Dieppe only a few weeks before? There had been some terrible sights. The dead, the dying and the wounded being cut down in their hundreds, as if the grim reaper had scythed through a field of wheat. What a bloody, suicidal raid that had been.

Royal Marine Dacre, Regimental Number CH/X 06821 stood smartly to attention in front of the Officer Commanding 'X' Troop of 40 Commando RM, recently renamed from what had been the RM 'A' Commando. The nameplate on the desk in front of him was new. It was so new that you could still smell the paint. It read: Captain G. Ellis RM MC. The marine stood perfectly still, his eyes unflinching, focusing on a spot on the distant wall. He knew the routine and what was expected of him. His uniform was immaculate, the creases razor sharp, the crossed rifles of his marksman badge freshly whitened. His Green Beret, only recently issued to all Army and Marine commandos, freshly brushed, his Globe and Laurel cap badge polished and gleaming. On his right arm was his King's Badge, awarded for being the best all-round recruit in his training squad back in 1939. His shoulder flashes proudly said 'Royal Marines Commando', with the number '40' underneath. On his chest three medal ribbons – the Légion d'Honneur, the Naval General Service Medal and the newest, the Military Medal with Oak Leaves for having been mentioned in Dispatches.

The officer and the marine were both about the same age, barely twenty years old. Four weeks before, both of them had been unblooded in conflict - boys really. Now, after the Dieppe Raid, they were battle-hardened veterans. The Captain looked up and smiled, then indicated that the marine should sit down. Ellis had then been the new, naïve subaltern, whilst the marine had been through Dunkirk, albeit unauthorised, serving on one of the small boats. Together, they had gone through commando training at Acknacarry in Scotland, then onto the Isle of Wight, and finally to *Operation Jubilee*, the raid on Dieppe. Landing on the beach, the marine had been wounded and had fallen into the sea, only to be rescued by this young officer. Later, when patched up, Dacre had demonstrated his prowess as a sniper and, in his way, had saved the subaltern's life. They had been through a lot together and there was an unspoken bond of trust and respect between them.

'I'm recommending you for promotion to the rank of substantive Corporal with immediate effect and then to Acting Troop Sergeant. As you know, we are short of good senior non-commissioned officers. You have all the qualities necessary. So, what do you say?'

There was a long pause. Dacre looked uncomfortable, even embarrassed; he blushed slightly.

'Thank you, sir, for your confidence in me, but with all due respect I would prefer to remain in the ranks.'

Captain Ellis was not entirely surprised at the reply.

'May I ask why that is? What's the reason?'

'Personal reasons, sir. It's just personal,' Dacre replied quietly.

'Are you sure that's your decision? It's a great opportunity you know. You could go all the way to the top, assuming you can stay alive, that is.' They both laughed. 'I know what you are thinking, the same applies to me.' They laughed again. 'Are you really sure?'

'Yes, sir, quite sure. Thank you.'

'Mm, I don't know why, but I had a suspicion that you might refuse,' replied the Captain. 'Anyway, to change the subject, have you seen this order requesting volunteers for hazardous duties? It was published by the Royal Marines Office at the Admiralty, let me see, back in May, so it's a little bit out of date.'

'No, sir, if you recall we were a bit busy then.'

'Of course, we were. How stupid of me. Anyway, listen to this. The order stipulates that applicants should be eager to engage the enemy, indifferent to personal danger, intelligent, nimble, free from strong family ties, able to swim and of good physique. The name of the unit RMBPD should not be taken to indicate its true function.' Captain Ellis sat back in his chair and scratched his head. 'Have you heard of them?'

'No, sir, but clearly something to do with the Corps.'

'You're right there. It stands for the Royal Marines Boom Patrol Detachment. Any the wiser?'

'No, sir, I can't say that I am.'

'That list of attributes seems to be you right down to the ground, don't you think? Plus, you can already canoe and sail, and on top of that you are fluent in German, French and Italian. How does the job sound to you?'

'Sounds good to me, just up my street, sir, especially if one forgets the old maxim about never volunteering for anything. But surely they must have their fill of volunteers by now and be well into their training?'

'I expect you could be right. However, I somehow thought you might be interested, so I've been in touch with their commanding officer. He has agreed to give you an interview.'

'And how, sir, may I ask, did you manage that?'

'Well, it turns out that he was a friend of my family. My father knew his father. They served together in the First World War in the RAMC. Both had been commissioned from the ranks. Anyway, they were on the troopship *Transylvania* when it was torpedoed and sunk. His father drowned, my father survived.' Captain Ellis paused. The marine's face was one of mixed emotion. 'Oh, come on Dacre, there is nothing wrong with a little bit of nepotism, especially if it works for you.'

The marine shook his head slowly. 'If you say so, sir. It's just that I am not really comfortable with doing something that I haven't personally achieved, if you know what I mean.'

'Okay, okay. I understand what you are saying but this is a chance for you to do something different. Give it a go. If it doesn't work out, then come back here and take the promotion.'

Dacre thought for a moment or two then nodded his head in agreement, a slight smile on the corners of his mouth. He knew when he was beaten.

'Alright I'll give it a try. And thank you, sir, for your faith in me.'

'Good. I'm sure it's the right decision. You are to be at Major Haslar's Headquarters which is at Lumps Fort in Southsea tomorrow at 1500 hours. It's an old Napoleonic defensive stronghold right next to the canoe lake. You can't miss it.'

'Anything else, sir, that you can tell me?' In for a penny in for a pound thought the marine.

'About Haslar or the father?'

'The Major, sir. Just tell me what you know about him.'

'Well, he won a scholarship to Wellington School, but was rejected because his father wasn't a proper officer, having come up through the ranks. Anyway, his mother soon sorted the school out. He made good after a difficult start and finished with outstanding results. He was commissioned into the Corps at eighteen years old and passed out top of his year. By that time, he had mostly dropped his given names of Herbert

George and was simply known as 'Blondie' because of the colour of his hair and his moustache. He is not, I understand, what you might call a conventional sort of an officer. Some have described him as a bit bizarre, even eccentric. He does, however, have a strong sense of what is right and wrong. He also has a habit of testing himself, always trying to do better. He has an iron will and unbreakable determination. There is a lovely story that the wandering guards at Eastney Barracks often stumbled across him sleeping rough outside on the fields. Strangely, he seems to try to avoid violence when he can, preferring to use stealth and cunning instead. Don't get me wrong, he can deliver the necessary when needs must. In 1940 he took part in the Norway Campaign for which he was awarded the DSO. Later he received the Légion d'Honneur for his work with the French Foreign Legion. He's mad about cars, is a gifted amateur artist and plays jazz on the piano and clarinet. He also has a quirky, dry sense of humour which some can't get on with. Yes, now that I think about it you and he should get on well, you're both very similar. One final thing. He has something of a reputation amongst 'Royals' for being very demanding. However, he never asks anyone to do anything that he hasn't already done himself. He's that sort of a person.'

'Thank you, sir, that has been very helpful.'

Captain Ellis stood up. They shook hands as old friends. Dacre formally saluted, turned and left.

CHAPTER 2

The journey across the Solent by ferry from the Isle of Wight to Portsmouth Harbour was uneventful. Dacre arrived at Southsea, the home of the RMBPD, at 1430 hours. Mindful that a good marine is always five minutes early, he took a short stroll down towards the beach. Of course, he knew the barracks quite well. He had been there numerous times, most recently when he and his mates had been training for the pinch raid at Dieppe. Officially it was the home of the Portsmouth Division of Royal Marines who, along with the Plymouth and Chatham Divisions, provided marines for the Royal Navy's sea-going warships.

As he arrived at Lumps Fort, he noticed a group of men on the pebble beach waving and shouting at a group of canoeists who were about fifty yards offshore. Several of the canoes looked to be in difficulties, one had already overturned, the occupants clinging to the sides, whilst another appeared to be filling with water. To make matters worse, a strong offshore current was sweeping the canoes and their crews further east along the coast. Not too good thought Dacre. Perhaps they are new arrivals to the unit and are just beginners. He glanced at his watch. Time for that interview he thought.

He quickly strode the short distance to the entrance of the fort. Inside there were two recently erected, wooden Nissen huts. One was clearly for stores, the other - well it was
difficult to tell its function from the outside. Standing to one side of the open door was a Colour Sergeant, three stripes surmounted by a crown on the sleeves of his uniform. Dacre marched up to him and halted.

'Are you Marine Dacre?' he asked, not unkindly.

'Yes, Colour Sergeant,' reporting as ordered.'

I'm the Company Sergeant Major of this little lot. My name is 'Bungy' King, welcome aboard, lad.'

They exchanged a firm handshake. The marine liked the look of the CSM. A handshake and a welcome like that were rather unusual. This was going to be very interesting, he thought.

'The Major will see you right away.' He indicated the open door.

Major Haslar was sitting behind a table. Dacre marched in, halted and cracked up his best salute - longest way up and the shortest way down. A very quick glance around told him that this was a classroom, complete with a blackboard, desks and a sand tray. The Major returned the salute just as smartly and indicated a nearby chair.

'Sit down, Trained Soldier. Now, what can I do for you?'

'I would like to join your unit, sir, if you have a place available?'

'I see. You do realise that we have been under intensive training for the past four weeks or so?'

'Yes, sir, I appreciate that.'

The Major paused and scanned down the marine's service record that was lying on top of the table in front of him. Despite his initial reluctance to see this man - he was only doing it for an old family friend, let alone take him on - he liked what he saw. Haslar prided himself on being a good judge of character. The marine was smart and well turned out. He liked that. He was carrying three medal ribbons which indicated experience gained the hard way. The King's Badge, not lightly given, suggested a potential leader, and he was also a marksman judging from the crossed rifles on his arm. The Green Beret and the shoulder flashes of 40 Royal Marines Commando, recently renamed from the RM 'A' Commando, shouted out quality, fitness and toughness. Yes, Haslar liked what he saw.

'You were on the Dieppe Raid then?'

'Yes, sir.'

'So?'

'It was bloody chaos, sir. A bit like a naval version of the Charge of the Light Brigade. We didn't stand a chance.'

'So I heard. Enough said then. Your records say that you went to Mill Hill School.'

'Yes, sir.'

'I went to Wellington myself. Any good your place?'

'I enjoyed the sport and the CCF, but not much else. I wasn't very keen on the system, especially the fagging. It didn't seem right to me having the younger boys acting as slaves to the older boys. Some say it was character building, and perhaps it was, but some of the chaps used to abuse the system, if you know what I mean.'

Haslar looked at the marine very carefully, images of his own schooling came flooding back - the bullying, the anguish and the pain.

'Yes, I know exactly what you mean.'

Unknowingly, Dacre had touched a nerve which the Major had thought was long since dead and buried. Haslar pushed the memories to the back of his mind. With a lump in his throat, he continued. 'It says in your records that you speak German, French and Italian fluently. How has that come about?'

'My grandfather was Italian, so we only spoke Italian at home. The other two just came along naturally.'

'Your grandfather brought you up?'

'Yes, sir, my mother died in childbirth and my father was killed in a climbing accident before I was born.

'I see. Well, thank you for being so open about that. Now tell me something about yourself that I will not find in your records.'

Dacre hesitated for a moment or two before replying.

'I built my first canoe when I was about twelve years old. I made it from scraps of timber and some canvas. I was very proud of that. It sank on its maiden voyage, so I built another and then another until I got it right. All my canoeing has been at sea. Firstly, off the Kent coast at a little place near to Whitstable, called Tankerton, then later in Italy off the Amalfi Coast. My grandfather's people come from the little village of Ravello up in the hills. A couple of years ago, just after he died, I spent the winter building a sixteen-foot yacht with a gaff rig. I suppose it was a form of therapy. Anyway, it's still in the garage and has never been to sea.'

'That's very interesting. This place Tankerton, do you know it well?'

'Yes, sir.'

'Only I have two maiden aunts who live there - Aunt Lillian and Aunt Sue. I haven't seen them in years. Lost touch, if you know what I mean. They used to live on the seafront I seem to remember. I don't even know if they are still alive.'

Dacre controlled his surprise at the coincidence. What were the odds of that, he wondered. He wasn't sure whether or not to mention that the two aunts were his next-door neighbours and, yes, they were very much alive and well. He decided to say nothing, in case it complicated the situation.

The Major continued. 'You and I are quite alike you know.'

'Sir?'

'I mean our backgrounds are similar, public school, boat building and canoeing. Do you like music?'

'Sir?'

'Music! Do you like music? Do play an instrument?'

'No, sir, I don't play an instrument. But I quite like jazz.'

'Oh, anyone in particular?

'Glen Miller, Benny Goodman, Louis Armstrong - people like that. I don't know much about jazz, but I know what I like.'

'Good. Do you have a favourite piece?

Dacre hesitated before answering. 'Perhaps Miller's 'Body and Soul.'

Haslar smiled before continuing.

'There is just one other thing. You have been in the Corps now for just over two years. You have Dunkirk and Dieppe under your belt and you also hold the King's Badge. Why aren't you carrying a rank, sergeant maybe, or at least corporal?' The marine felt a warm flush of embarrassment creep up his neck.

'Actually, sir, I have just turned down the rank of Acting Troop Sergeant.'

'Have you, by Jove, now that is interesting. May I enquire as to why?'

'Personal reasons, sir, purely personal.'

The Major quickly realised that this conversation wasn't going anywhere. Why, he wondered, would a young chap like this, obviously well thought of by his superiors and with all the right qualities, not take promotion. Something didn't add up, but he wasn't sure what. Would this lad fit in here? Has he got it wrong? Haslar shrugged his shoulders. No! His gut feelings, which never let him down, told him that his decision was right. Only time would tell. He decided to move on.

'That's enough of me asking you things. Do you have any questions for me?'

'Can you tell me something about the set-up here? What is it all about?'

'Ah, well, to start with we are a very small unit. There are just forty-six of us, all volunteers. You have met our CSM 'Bungy' King. My second-in-command is Lieutenant 'Jock' Stewart. We have a small Headquarters team and two sections. Each section has a second lieutenant in charge, supported by a sergeant, two corporals and ten marines. We also have a maintenance section provided by the Royal Navy. We are not recognised as commandos, so we do not wear the Green Beret. You will have to dump yours. However, I have managed to negotiate commando status and pay. Not much, I know, but it all helps. We are, of course, entitled to live out rather than be in barracks. Number One Section lives at White Heather Guest House on the Worthing Road, whilst Number Two section is at 35 St Rowan's Road here in Southsea.'

'Thank you, sir, that has been all very helpful. But what do you do? What is all the training for?'

'Now that is a very interesting question. Officially the RMBPD's reason for existence is to develop new weapons, craft and materials for amphibious warfare. In reality, we are training canoeists to attack the enemy, particularly their shipping, in a clandestine manner.'

'Small-scale raiding then?'

'Exactly! The idea for this unit came originally from Churchill himself. Then it went to Lord Mountbatten at Combined Operations Headquarters and then to the Royal Marines Office at the Admiralty. Interestingly, I had been pestering their Lordships for an opportunity to do something with canoes. In my own time I had been developing and testing different types and models, so I was quite sure in my own mind that I could make it work. So here we are.'

'What type of canoes are you using?'

'We are using the Cockle Mark II. It's a development of the folboat made by the Folding Folboat Company. Some canoeists like them, some don't and prefer the Mark I version. However, it suits us well enough. They're robust, collapsible and will carry two men and their equipment. Even if it fills with water, it will not sink. They're a good little craft. Have you used one?'

'No, sir.'

'Well, they're about sixteen feet long, and are double-ended canoes. They have a flat bottom with wooden runners to help when you are dragging it over shingle. It has double, nine-foot paddles and two men can actually stretch out and sleep in it. On a good day, with the wind behind them, a fit crew can make about five knots.'

'And the rest of the unit? Are they HO or regulars?'

'They're a mixture, but all drawn from the Plymouth Division rather than the whole Corps, as I originally requested. Few have had any boat experience, one or two couldn't swim, two are married, one even has two children. I know what you are thinking - this wasn't what was asked for in the advertisement - but beggars can't be choosers. Remember, most of the good men had already volunteered for the commandos. Still, they're all good chaps and as keen as mustard. You need to know that my training regime is tough, but I won't ask anybody to do anything that I haven't already done. You shouldn't have any problems, what with your training at Acknacarry. We are quite informal here, especially when out on the water. I find that the crews work better that way. The lads socialise together, usually down at the local pub. However, discipline is important, but the emphasis is on self-discipline, resilience and the ability to think independently.'

'Much like commando training then.'

'Yes, very similar. We are going to be the best of the best, and that includes how we dress and march when in barracks. I still believe that there is a place for close order drill.' Any further questions?'

'No, sir, thank you. When will I hear if I have been selected?'

Major Haslar broke into a real belly laugh.

'Selected? Why I'd decided that within the first five minutes of the interview. You're in! I go on what's in front of me, not what is written down.'

Haslar stood up and offered his hand; they shook. 'Welcome to the RMBPD.' Moving to the open door, he called for the Sergeant Major, who appeared immediately.

'Sir?'

'Marine Dacre is going to be joining us. I think we will put him in Number One Section with Mr Mackinnon. I believe Sergeant Wallace needs a number two. Will you introduce him to lads and get him settled in?'

'Yes, sir, my pleasure.'

Once outside, the CSM spoke quietly to Dacre, 'Well how on earth did you swing that?'

'What do you mean?'

'Oh, come on! I never thought you had a chance. I don't know what you two talked about, but I've never seen the boss in such a good mood.'

'Just lucky I guess.'

'Lucky is it. Well, we shall see about that then, won't we?' replied the Sergeant Major.

Have you read….

OPERATION SAINT GEORGE

by JG White
Published by Austin Macauley

You should! Here is a brief synopsis.

In April 1962, Royal Marine Dacre, with twenty-two years of experience as a commando, is suddenly sent from his unit 43 Commando RM in Plymouth to the Depot RM at Deal in Kent.

Dacre is a most unique marine: a marine's marine. He has seen service all over the world and is the most decorated man in the Corps. Surprisingly he has always turned down the chances of promotion. With his extensive experience of combat, and having served with distinction with the SBS, he is now in the twilight of his career. His task at the Depot is to retrain and revitalise a tired and dispirited handful of marines for a gruelling competition. This requires the group to be super-fit in a way that only commandos can be and which, against all the odds, he manages to achieve.

Meanwhile the Sultan of Brunei flies into the UK on an unofficial visit. He wants urgent talks with the British Government regarding the increasing threat to his country from neighbouring Indonesia. His only son, the Crown Prince, is at that time undergoing intensive training with the Royal Marines.

An audacious plot to kidnap the prince, then kill him and his father, is undertaken by the IRA at the behest of the President of Indonesia. The situation is well beyond the local police and even Special Branch. Can HM Forces help? The only problem is that there are no Special Forces available in the UK at that time and time is the one thing that they do not have.

Failure to rescue the prince and prevent the two murders is not an option that the Government is willing to consider. The political consequences and the resulting instability in the Far East would be such not seen since the fall of Singapore back in 1941.

Have you read….

NEVER SURRENDER

by JG White
Published by Austin Macauley

You should! Here is a brief overview.

It is 1939 – a momentous year in history and the year that Dacre, a young man of seventeen, signs up as a Royal Marine. In J.G. White's novel, fans of historical and military fiction can read Dacre's transition from raw recruit to fully-fledged marine as Hitler's dreams of European domination begin to materialise across the channel.

When the day arrives for the British Expeditionary Force to aid their French and Belgian allies, for some the day has come too soon. But there are other ways to serve their country and, not least amongst them, will be the weeks around the dramatic withdrawal from Dunkirk.

Drawing on thorough research and his own military experience, J.G. White's book is an absorbing read, accurate and faithful to military structures and personnel, and includes the excitement, fear and tragedy of frontline combat.